NEMESIS

John Goldsworthy

First published in 2000 by
Ceres Publishing
PO Box 357
Bolton
BL5 3FS

Paperback ISBN 0 9537991 0 7

It lies not in our power to love nor hate
For will in us is overruled by fate

CHAPTER I

1971

A single drop of perspiration wound its way slowly down the smooth narrow valley between the elegant shoulder blades of the tall computer programmer, pausing only to negotiate the filmy thread of elastic in her sheer nylon panties. She felt the cool drop dissipate itself among the fine hairs at the junction of her buttocks. No other outward sign of her nervousness was apparent to her colleagues on either side of the glass partitioned corridor. Several smiled a smile of acknowledgement, some merely nodded. Others ignored her. Her measured tread belied the aristocratic stance of her body, as if her brain was issuing commands to her legs that were merely a means of motion not intended to disturb the equilibrium of her body's natural beauty.

Everyone had said from the age of twelve that she should have been a model, but her brain demanded more from life than that of a bored cat walk zombie. She could have made it to the top, she knew that, but life demanded more than adulation from a biased, brain washed public. She wanted to be in command. To do what no one else on earth had ever done. To triumph. To succeed in the impossible. That would be reward enough. Her own opinion of herself and her achievements were all that mattered. She had told Peter that, and they had discussed it many times in the years that she had known him. Now this was the moment when the most significant part of that ambition would be put into place.

Her eyes flicked to the left as she approached the large glass windows giving a viewpoint over the centre's heartbeat. The main frame computer and its swarm of memory banks and processors, standing like chess pieces on a giant board beneath her. One of the most powerful computers in England lay on the quarter acre of tiled floor that formed the basement of the National Bank's headquarters complex in northern Cheshire. A small gasp escaped her lips as she took in the enormity of the machine that relentlessly controlled, processed, and deciphered the millions of daily operations that were asked of it. This was her baby.

Although it could work at the speed of light, and complete calculations with the blink of an eye, it needed her. It needed the human ingredient to guide it. To instruct it. To nurture it. To control it. She was that control. The acknowledged head of its insatiable appetite for more and complex directives on which to use its limitless energies.

The double doors at the end of the corridor marked the farthest limit of the vast area below and barred the way to the highly sensitive and temperature controlled room on her left. "Authorised Personnel Only" read the sign. She inserted her plastic card in the security slot and punched in her personal number, at the same time placing her left thumb over the highlighted pad to confirm her identity. The doors clicked open.

Why she felt the surge of adrenalin so strongly, she couldn't explain. She had been into the inner sanctum a thousand times and her visit tonight shouldn't have incited the reaction in her hormones that she was now experiencing. A slight damp feeling around her groin and between her breasts stimulated a heady euphoria that she at once associated with Peter's subtle way of arousing her with gentle touches and meaningful glances over dinner. She stopped. Took three deep gulps of air and her equilibrium returned to normal and she breathed evenly again.

Her descent down the stairs was as measured as her passage down the corridor had been. She forced her brain to think of nothing else but the task ahead. Ten minutes and it would be done. It was so simple she almost laughed out loud. Tomorrow would be Valentine's day. The day. The day when every computer in Great Britain would churn out the biggest production of printouts that the United Kingdom had ever seen. Everyone who had a bank account, from conglomerates to the smallest savings account would be affected by the events of the greatest transformation seen in history of Britain's monetary system. Monday the 15th February 1971 would be a day to remember. Decimalisation day. D day as Peter had called it, but not in the accepted context broadcast by a self congratulatory government, intent in falling in line with Europe and the rest of the world.

No, Peter's D day was Dawn day. The beginning. Upon the next ten minutes or so rested the whole purpose of his life. Retribution. She could not let him down.

The small box nestled in the right hand pocket of her smart blue uniform. Inside the box, no bigger than a scrabble piece, rested the product of three year's research and development. The answer to Peter's quest for justice in the only way he knew how.

The senior programmer made her way to the rear of the computer room, until she was level with number 14 peripheral terminal. Carefully stepping over the floor coving holding the interface cables connecting the myriad of terminals to the main frame computer, she turned her attention to the lock on the cabinet housing her objective. Her presence created no disturbance among the few operatives busy at the far end of the room. They had seen her many times before on her normal duties of inspection and appreciated her interest in the 'mechanical' side of the operation centre. She had always shown great intelligence in following the complicated demonstrations by the technical staff and seemed to grasp immediately the functions of the separate pieces of apparatus which were their pride and joy. She could distinguish the difference between the mere 'function' machinery and the real 'brain' segments that controlled the 'functions.' She knew that in each cabinet rested hundreds of plates full of circuits and transistors, holding millions of instructions that her department had spent months in programming before the bank's computers took on the accounts of its 11,000,000 odd customers' accounts in the early sixties. From that time she had progressed rapidly and gained promotion to the rank where she was deputy chief of programming. Not bad at the age of 29. She hadn't blown it as so many of her contemporaries had. Out on the scrap heap in their early twenties, their brains unable to cope with the heavy pressure and incalculable speed of the change from day to day in computer technology. But she had, and had survived.

The door opened easily to her touch. She had prepared for this in the six weeks previously, by encouraging the head of technical services to explain the 'guts' of each terminal, noticing the various keys which he used to gain access via the rear door. No 14 had been visited in the course of those weeks and on this particular day she had taken care to wear her sheerest overall, washed continually until it was almost transparent. With the light from the glaring overhead florescent tubes, she knew that her body would be opaquely visible as she bent and straightened to follow her obviously animated instructor. The distraction would be enough to break his adherence to his inbuilt grounding on the security of his charge of silicon 'children' as he called them. Smiling sweetly into his hang dog eyes, she had requested that he fetched her handbag which she had inadvertently left on his desk. Not daring to glance down the vee of her bodice, but nevertheless not missing the gentle curve of her perfect breasts with the peripheral vision he had practised over the years, he hurried to accede to her request.

His keys hung in the lock, swinging noiselessly on their ring. It took six seconds to remove the key, impress its design in three dimensional proportions in the special wax pad in her pocket, and replace the bunch before the excited and subservient employee returned.

She gave him one more chance to feast his eyes on her as she paused in front of the open doorway to the stairs, displaying her lithe sweeping curves against the light, as if projecting her image on to a screen for his appreciation. She saw him gulp and nodded her comprehension of his discomfort.

Moving her fingers from the box she located the key to cabinet 14 and clasped it in the folds of her fingers. It felt warm to her touch, its edges carefully milled to match to perfection the original. Inserting it into the socket, it moved smoothly under her pressure to release the door on its silent hinges.

The next operation had been practised so many times before, it had become a way of life, and her hands followed her brain commands with an automation that rivalled the computer around her. Remove twenty seventh plate from the top left hand row. Locate fifth housing of silicon configuration and separate it carefully from its socket. That went into her left hand pocket as she removed the small box from her other. One twist and the lid joined the discarded piece in her left pocket as she reverently removed the small scrabble sized silicon duplicate from its bedding. Her breathing increased infinitesimally as her steady fingers located the empty socket and closed it with the small square chip. Checking to ensure that it was securely home, she painstakingly restored the holding plate to its original setting and closed the door. The lock operated as silently as before and she was walking away before the key had settled beside the two other articles in her left hand pocket.

It was done! Only the final input from her programming keypad to log it into the system and safeguard its presence and no one could ever locate the rogue chip. The bead of perspiration had dried but her skin felt damp against her undies as she retraced her steps along the green carpeted corridor to her office at the head of the line. It was empty. No one had questioned why she had appeared twenty three minutes before her 10pm shift. She was known for her punctuality and belief in 'a flying start' to her duties. Tonight was no exception and she still had time to briefly overlook her in tray to assess the problems that would need to be solved before the big 'switch on' on the night of the fourteenth. That was when every account would be run through the processors to effect the historic change to decimal currency. Twenty four hours to go and just twenty minutes of input from her terminal and it would be done. The greatest fraud ever conceived. She and Peter did not refer to it as 'fraud' just the appropriation of numerical waste that had previously been 'lost.'

Ten pm. She was officially at work. Her fingers moved rapidly over the keyboard as she fed in the series of instructions and directives to complete her 'statement' to the microprocessors that controlled the accounting side of the Bank's memory discs. Certain rigid instructions for movements of accumulated balances and funds in transit were inbuilt and the various designations to where the funds were to be allotted were controlled by 'gates' in the chip. Each chip was capable of holding 50,000 transistors, each one specifically created to 'open' or 'close' a gate to permit an operation or prevent it. The clean white chip resting in number 14 processor was the same in all respects as its predecessor except in it final decision of allotment of certain accumulated figures.

The unique directives from the fingers of the deputy programmer were being incorporated into the system almost before her hands touched the keys. The prompt of words would tell the computer how to interpret the statements already in existence in the original programming. The rogue chip would ensure that those directives were acted upon.

Twenty minutes later the final input was processed. A few additional diversionary commands and the information that had been assimilated over the previous twenty minutes had been wiped from any memory that could produce a printout detailing the unauthorised input. She sat back and breathed slowly in and out, contemplating the complexity of the operation. She, and she alone had lived with the pure logic of this computer for seven years and had advanced with it. It was almost a husband to her. She knew its every move, its every quirk, its idiosyncrasies. She knew its power. A power that was useless without guidance. Her guidance. It was hers now. It had a character deep within its soul, if it possessed one, that was her creation. Unique and unfathomable by anyone else. She stroked the keys lovingly, touching but not depressing, feeling the great giant on the floor below waiting for her caress that could create havoc or genius.

She picked up the grey telephone, dialled and listened for the click. 'It's done,' she said, and replaced the receiver.

The eight hour shift passed quickly as she threw herself into the routine work that had to be completed before 6pm the following day, Valentine's Day, ready for the final processing of the millions of balances for delivery to the branches on 'D Day' when the majority of people in the United Kingdom would eagerly seek the result of the big 'changeover.'

The cold morning was misty and threatened rain. She pointed her umbrella against the wind from the west and was surprised at the effort needed to stand against the force. She smiled as she compared her umbrella to one of her precious command modes. Each section of the taut coloured fabric acted as a gate to collect a portion of the wind as it hit the ferrule and dispersed it in eight separate avenues to wreak havoc with another unsuspecting air flow. Just like her chip. So simple. But then, most brilliant devices are.

The gateman at the high wire entrance vestibule nodded his recognition as he operated the electric security door for her to pass into the compound that held the staff car park. Crunching over the gravel, she was grateful to climb into her chocolate coloured Riley Kestrel and close the door against the unfriendly elements. The 1300 cc engine burst into life and she drove expertly out of the compound and on to the main A559 to Stretton more exhausted than she realised and yearning for the warm bed that Peter would be vacating in a little over an hour. Time enough, she mused, to exhaust her body to the same extent as her mind.

Love with Peter could never be half-hearted. It was all or nothing. The full gambit of emotions that seemed to stem from the very beginning of his suffering. And he had suffered more in his early years than any man could expect in a lifetime. He never spoke of it now. It was behind him. But still part of his being. Part of his fervent lovemaking, his tender caresses, and his triumphant shout of jubilation at achieving an even higher plane of sheer joy in their union. Every experience was precious to him. As if there would be no more. Like living from day to day and not knowing if there would be another. Old habits die hard, and try as she may, she could not break him of his insistence that NOW mattered and every minute god gave should be used. He would not be asleep. He awoke regularly at 5.30am as if by instinct. Then he would cover in his mind the time since his childhood, re-enforcing the driving commitment that occupied that part of his brain that he had only allowed her to see once. That was enough he had said. The pain is mine. Your loyalty will be my balm and your sense of justice my companion. We are, and always will be as one. It was destined from the moment my mother spoke her last words to me in the most hopeless place on earth – "Be avenged my son. Seek the ultimate justice that God demands."

She thought about Peter as she drove along the country lane towards the pretty village of Stretton, set in the green countryside a few miles from Warrington. The church and the hotel were the centre of activity and it suited their purpose well to lose themselves in the anonymity of just residing there without any particular involvement. Their cottage was rented from a local farmer who did not trouble them and they didn't trouble him. Very few mod cons were included in the cottage and they enjoyed the lifestyle as far as they could, of their predecessors in the cottage, with log fires, kettle boiled hot water, and no television. Their one luxury was a stereo record player and radio. Especially the radio which Peter listened to avidly for news in the 'city,' making copious notes of any relevant information that would add to his bulging file. His own bible of philosophy, and the guiding light to his sole purpose in life.

The pious like yew trees in the avenue stippled the light from the awakening dawn onto her dusty windscreen as she pulled into the cobbled track leading to the cottage. The main bedroom light shone through the open window, inducing a warm glow in her stomach as she anticipated the welcome from Peter. A part of the day that belonged to them alone. The hour when both were at their peak; he after his usual deep six hour sleep, and she; when her hyper activity at work had roused her responses to their optimum height. Today would be especially gratifying, with the culmination of the first stage in place of his inexorable search for justice. His warm welcoming arms reached out for her as she slipped between the white cotton sheets. Her long lithe body stretched to encompass itself in the gentle folds, eager to cling to every curve and crevice. And then they were together. As one. Just holding their respective warmth and glorying in the vacuum between them. The vacuum soon became a hotbed as their stomachs sensed an urgency in each other. Her nerve stretching euphoria at the computer centre was eclipsed by the unmatchable fervour of Peter's passion as they celebrated their joint triumph. The moment was lost in time and space as worlds collided and their purpose on earth was reduced to irrelevance. Only the present mattered in their mutual quest for fulfilment. Each giving the other the gratification of their unashamed lovemaking. Their complete dedication. It was as if they were reaching for the goal that would be the final palliative to the task that they, and they alone could accomplish. 'That's the hard part of it done,' he said, as they lay side by side, luxuriating in the virility of their bodies. Satiated but wanting more.

Never wanting this togetherness to end. A love bound by more than the attraction of their minds and character. A love branded deeply within them by their chosen path in life. A substitute for a religion that they had never fully encompassed. It had been found wanting too much for them ever to come to terms with its biblical teachings. It could never translate to the modern world. The modern world where life and lives were held in such scant regard that Solomon could never have contemplated the evilness of men and mankind.

'Are you talking about us or the first step?' she joked lightly. 'You must be feeling your age if it's getting beyond you.' Her laughter rippled around the small beamed room and could be heard by the church gardener as he bent to pull a tuft from the gravel covered drive. He chuckled in tune with the tinkling laughter, not for the first time, and blessed God for moments such as these. When young people were happy. He glanced at the open window of the cottage and moved to the far side of the church out of deference to the couple whom he knew would soon consummate their enjoyment as God intended.

Peter finished his breakfast of toasted oat cereal and coffee, shouting up the bent staircase as he reached for his coat. 'See you at five.' Then he was gone.

Bet he won't do a lot of routine work today, she mused, smoothing the now cool sheet over the contours of her stomach and up over her ribs to the still pouting breasts that hungered for Peter's touch. We are so lucky that sometimes it hurts. Her mind questioned, as it had done so many times in the past, the sanity of a world where so much happiness existed but so little of it was taken up by the ordinary people. So little of it was allowed to percolate through from the decision makers, who themselves lived perpetually in a make-believe state of assumed happiness. Her's and Peter's life was bliss. Perhaps because they had a cause. A cause that could take a lifetime, but the inevitable culmination of that cause would at last put to rest a threat that had grown out of the greatest evil of their lives.

She slept a deep sleep of contentment. Happy in the knowledge that she and Peter were part of history. A history that they both believed would be better for what they were about to undertake.

Peter arrived at the Bank's headquarters at 8.25am after an uneventful drive through the Cheshire countryside to the urban commuter chaos of a large city. Manchester had always intrigued him from the moment he had set foot on London Road railway station seven years ago. A big, thriving, bustling, curmudgeon of a city. The antithesis of London, with its smart set and grandeur to match. This was earthy and basic. Dirty from the honest sweat of the mills and the mines. Real people with real views on life. He loved it from the word go. But he was not here to admire the Victorian architecture. He was here to pursue his purpose. To learn more of the Bank's computer system as it entered its first phase of conversion.

Being part of the Chief Accountant's Department, Peter was responsible for the control of the overall income and expenditure figures obtained from the surrounding branches and merged with the total national figures for daily monitoring in Head Office, London. Budgets and projections littered his desk as he sought ways to curb expenses and maximise profits. New items of commission were always being explored as well as the application of 'cost effective' methods of assessing the work involved in various processes for individual and corporate customers. Gone were the days of 'free' advice and services. The unproductive time spent with customers who wanted nothing more than a confidential and re-assuring chat with their manager. Computers were here and the benefits to the Bank was not just the enormous saving in manpower and thereby salaries, but the opportunity to apply infinitesimal charges to the smallest of operations customer's accounts caused. That brought income. And saved waste. It was the fractions and the smallest decimal part of money that had intrigued Peter from his early days in the Bank. His alert mind had spotted years before that whenever the monetary system had been involved with the decimal system of European countries there was always a 'spare' bit remaining. Twelve pence to the shilling and two hundred and forty pence to the pound did not equate well with currencies based on units of ten.

The 'spare' decimals were always disregarded and the customer either given the benefit of the fraction or more often than not, it was retained and steadily built up until the currencies held by the bank were 'revalued' and the excess taken to profit. Ever since the decision to decimalise Britain's currency in line with Europe, Peter had thought long and hard about the consequences. The more he thought, the more he knew he had found a way to fulfil his mother's last pleading request. Funds with which to fight the evil within the city that no one suspected, or seemed to be able to combat. An evil being nurtured by one man whose power was growing daily and whose ambition was to obtain supreme control over all the media and eventually direct world affairs according to his dictum.

These funds could be syphoned off from the excess decimals that would ensue from conversion of balances. Balances that numbered over 11,000,000. And that crucial day was less than twenty four hours away.

This operation would be a trial run. He could not predict how much if any would be diverted through the myriad channels to their secret destination by the rogue 'chip' quietly waiting its cue to activate its instructions.

Peter and his wife had filled mountains of sheets of paper with their calculations as to the probability of the sum to be realised. Each time different amounts had shown. But that wasn't important. This trial would prove the effectiveness of the programme and its capability in the years to come to generate the size of funds to mount their campaign.

Basically Peter had explained, each balance ended in one of twelve possible figures. 0 pence to 11 pence. As each 'new penny' was equivalent to 2.4 old pence, fractions would arise and be allotted to balances either to round up or round down the converted amount. This would not balance out evenly and a 'spare' fund would arise, either in credit or debit. The bank's computer system had been so programmed to prevent the bank showing a loss on the operation, but no one, not even the programmers themselves could estimate the sum that would be shown as 'profit.' A special account to receive the fractions had been set up and a decision would be taken when the amount was known as to the application of the funds. Peter had his own ideas. The special account would not be the only one receiving the benefit of the surplus fractions. A second, hidden account, not appearing on any printout had been originated by him, bearing a non-compatible eight figure number which the computer would not recognise. If it did not recognise the number then the computer would assume it did not exist. That's the beauty of computer logic, smiled Peter, they always act logically. Of the twelve possibilities the one old pence would disappear, two old pence would be upgraded to one new penny and three old pence would be converted to one new penny. In those three conversions, there would be a surplus of 1.2 old pence; i.e. a full half new penny diverted to bank funds. Multiply this by four for the twelve possibilities and it was evident that two whole new pennies would be available from each twelve balances if they contained the full twelve possible balance endings. Working on an assumption that each twelve balances would show at least six of the possibilities, the profit from each twelve balances would be one new penny for every twelve accounts. From 11,000,000 then the surplus would approximate to just under 1,000,000 new pence – £10,000. An additional factor in the equation was the effect on debit balances. These would be treated in exactly the reverse of the system for credit balances, with debts being rounded up with fractions rather than down.As the bank would be expecting to realise a surplus of its own, half of the expected 'shavings' would be allowed to divert to their special account. Like Peter, no one was certain of the amount, and so no suspicion would be created by its size, large or small. That was his department and he could justify any balance that appeared, especially as the bank was not anxious to create a surplus from customers. They would prefer it if the conversion happened to even out exactly the previous total balances with the new converted decimal balances. As long as the total balances held on all accounts, debit and credit, assimilated as near as possible to the bank's previous figures, the General Managers would be happy. Balancing was the name of the game, but no power on earth could balance a twelve unit system with a ten unit system perfectly. But Peter could get as near as possible to satisfy the dictates of the hierarchy and the eventual audit by the bank's accountants for publication to the city and the world.

The secret account that Peter had created stood waiting its first pickings. It already held an instruction to immediately transfer any balance held to a designated account at the Regency Building Society some ten miles from the city centre. Since the surplus funds did not form any part of the bank's balances, their disposal and subsequent remittance out of the bank's books would be compatible with the certification of the daily balance.

The building society account was only the first of many. Small amounts would cause no concern, but in the months and years ahead, any significant sums might bring enquiries from keen managers for their better investment than a mere share account in the suburbs. Peter had other ideas for future funds. Funds that even now were raising the adrenalin levels in his blood as he thought of the ultimate challenge which he had set himself.

The morning passed in a state of expectancy as he viewed figures and budgets and the likely outcome of the exercise. The bank was more involved with the mechanics of the conversion and the satisfaction of the changeover than any surplus or deficit. The crucial time for the activation of the transference from the old money to the new decimal system was approaching. Months had been spent on teaching various members of each branch of the effect on balances, on customers, and on the staff themselves. Exercises and mock counter tuition had been carried out for dealing with the dual currencies that were to run in tandem for some time before the gradual withdrawal of specific categories of coins. The cost of this extra workload would probably outweigh any profit the bank would be fortunate enough to make, but the savings in the years to come would be incalculable. Peter ran his eyes down a column of figures and idly counted the different endings of the balances to try to assess the probability of 'inaccurate' conversion amounts that appeared. He was pleased to see from his sample that more than he had anticipated bore pence endings other than the straight 'nil', amount. Before he could reflect any further, he was dealing with numerous enquiries from various branches who had last minute panic attacks for when they opened their doors on decimalisation day. All banks had been closed for two days to assist with the operation, but no amount of preparation would be enough for some and they all viewed the approaching day 15th February with trepidation. All except Peter. He knew exactly what he was doing and exactly how the enormous task would be finalised. He had studied, probably more than anyone else, the effects of the decimalisation. Not always for the benefit of the bank, he smiled to himself. But his work on their behalf would not be found wanting as he knew he had instigated a very professional and competent training programme for his branches in the north. As far as the mechanical side of the transfer was concerned, no one need have any concern. The odd exceptions and queries that would undoubtedly arise could be dealt with by his assistants who were also extremely conversant with the programme. Peter drove home from the centre of Manchester, glad to be out of the confining atmosphere of the enclosed office which was his domain. The city was strangely quiet, as if it was aware that tomorrow would see the beginning of a decision that would alter forever Great Britain's historic monetary system. Peter had no opinion on whether it would be of benefit for the country, only that it gave him the opportunity for which he had been waiting. The emptiness of the streets disturbed him. Although it was a Sunday and normally quiet, today appeared especially significant. He had spent the last three Sundays working at the changeover and had not known it so quiet as today. His car engine was muted. People, what few there were, walked silently. No horns sounded, no one shouted. No children cried. His eyes saw only grey pitiful figures, dragging one slow leg behind the other. Gaunt, staring faces, looking nowhere. Going nowhere. One turned toward him, raised its hand, and disappeared into the misty greyness that clouded his eyes. He was crying silently, like the people. The vision cleared and he was in Piccadilly and driving past the shuttered windows of Woolworths and the Doll's hospital on London Road before he had time to remonstrate with himself for losing control. It would not happen again.

He saw a flower seller on the corner of London Road Railway Station and stopped to buy some freesias to go with the Valentine's card he lovingly felt in his pocket. It would be a very special day for them both. A day that they would always treasure. How apt that today of all days, their dreams would be answered and tomorrow mark the beginning of the rest of their lives. That had been his philosophy for as long as he could remember. Tomorrow is the start of the rest of your life. There was no other way to accept life after experiencing the deprivation of any concept of what a tomorrow would be, if it existed. Now there were innumerable tomorrows, all arrayed before him like pages in a book. Blank and waiting to be filled in. One day at a time, until the day of reckoning happened on one of those tomorrows.

Peter pulled into the cobbled driveway as the church bell called its parishioners to worship at evensong. Chaffinches and robins were already celebrating with their own chorus, desperately trying to urge Spring to come and warm their bodies. Peter and his wife did not need the Spring. They had the warmth of their bed and the comfort of their mutual love and purpose to sustain them through the cold winters. Their marriage vows were as significant to each other as the vows that they had unspokenly taken when Peter had told her of his promise. An oath that would override all other considerations as he sought to justify his deliverance for the sole purpose putting right a terrible wrong. And that wrong was now being compounded daily as it seeped inexorably into the financial system of the world.

Monday the 15th February dawned as the world awoke to a new language of pounds and new pence. Most struggled with the complications of converting the new currency back into the old to assess the price of common articles. The elderly were lost. They would never understand. Only pay the excesses that would inevitably occur over the coming months and years as the currency was debased and previous units completely obliterated from use. Where before, consumer goods were graduated in old halfpennies, now they were priced at 1.2 old pennies. Soon the graduations would be greater. Whole pence or even greater. There was no stopping the flow of 'higher' grades of pricing which would occur, hidden by the seemingly innocent 'new pence.'

Peter approached his terminal to carry out his usual enquiries for the overall position of the district's total funds on deposit and on loan, together with all the ancillary balances that made up the total balance sheet of the bank in the North West. At the end of his stint of concentrated effort he carefully fed in the non computerised number which would show the special account and the entries which would be applied in the overnight update of balances. He waited, not daring to breathe or to guess at the amount, if any, he suddenly thought, that would appear. The number appeared on the screen with the name of the account – 'Niemand' – nobody.

The date imprinted itself and then the first entry showed, glowing on the blue black screen like a beacon focusing on him alone. £13,487.89. It sat there, staring at him with all the starkness of coal in snow. None of his estimates had come anywhere near the amount displayed. But that didn't matter. The system worked! It was infallible. He had already checked the total balances held on customers' accounts before and after the conversion exercise and the total tallied. He rapidly applied the enquiry to the 'slush' account into which the intended fractions from the 11,000,000 accounts had been programmed to appear. 'Surplus Differences from Decimalisation Account' read the screen. The official account documented the usual information that it was an 'Impersonal' account and as such did not appear in the current account totals. Again Peter held his breath. There had to be some balance to prove that the intended fractions had gone somewhere. Even the tiniest fractions of the old pennies must convert to a fair proportion of the total balances converted. Had the proportion built in to the chip been correctly assessed so that an amount to satisfy the auditors would appear? The balance flashed onto the screen. £8,905.53. Perfect! The bank would be well pleased that an exercise involving millions of accounts had been conducted so precisely that the relatively small surplus shown proved that no individual had lost or gained more than one new pence. If any did complain, then the balance could be used as a contingency fund to satisfy anyone who queried why he had not been given the benefit of the fraction over and above his whole pence balance. There would not be many of them and the effort would not be worth their while. Peter was extremely happy. But as well as the happiness he felt the first stirring of a determination re-born within him. The years of waiting were over. He now had the tool to accomplish the task he had set himself. The amount he now had under his control was paltry to the amount he required. But, what could work on a 'one off' basis could be applied methodically in the coming years to various operations within the banking system. Not only fractions, but whole pence could be creamed off the staggering funds being shifted daily throughout the banking world.

He hurried home to their small cottage on through the outskirts of Warrington, joyously joining in the clattering chorus of starlings wheeling and swirling in the darkening sky as they sought their roosts for the night in the confines of the yawning yews and the church precincts.

She met him at the door with an expectant question in her dark velvet blue eyes. 'It worked,' was all Peter said as he took her in his arms and held her closely. They both felt the excitement of the moment. An exquisite pain which ran through their bodies and salved all the doubts that had hidden there. It was like all their birthdays and Christmases rolled into one. The first birthday when they had been able to comprehend the meaning of the candles and the relatives gathered to celebrate. The gifts and the joy and the kissing and the photographs. The thoughts filled their minds and dispelled the chilling aftermath of those early birthdays from their immediate memory. They moved up the narrow twisting staircase, unbroken in their hold on one another. They undressed quickly and with purpose, savouring every moment of their intimacy as each admired the loving curves and sweeps of their bodies, soon to be joined in a rapturous union of such intensity that nothing mattered any more. Only that moment and the two of them joined in love and a purpose which now took second place to their ecstatic carousel, whirling them to greater and greater heights of delight. It was as if the gift of perfect intimacy had been granted to them. So perfect that they could not stop until sheer exhaustion of their bodies dictated that their minds and emotions sleep. The room closed in on the still figures, its warm black blanket protecting them from the nightmares that threatened to invade their euphoric dreams. Tonight was for lovers. There would be other times to remember the past. Times that would give them the incentive and resolve to reach the nemesis which was their sworn duty.

They awoke together, hands clasped, staring at the light through the open window. Not yet morning, with night reluctant to let go of its hold on the still landscape. One beam from the still hidden sunrise broke the eastern sky and patched a framework of the lattice window on the ceiling. A grid of squares emblazoned their image on Peter's gaze, searing his retinas and matching perfectly the checkerboard symmetry of a place long ago. So square and so colourless. Like a grille dropped onto the sand and removed to leave an instant indentation of ruts between raised rectangular shapes. He knew the pattern so well. It was part of him. His life. His being. Why he was here. His purpose.

He turned to look at the beautiful face that reminded him of so much that had been good. A smile formed around his mouth. Not a smile of joy or happiness, or even one of sadness bravely forced on to those affected. It was a cold smile of utter belief and conviction. A smile of satisfaction that the woman by his side would have sheered away from in terror if she had not known of the purpose behind it.

Peter's head moved to face the gridiron on the ceiling. His hand tightened its grip, almost forcing the blood from her fingers. The light faded and the pattern dissolved into the grey ceiling, leaving nothing but a blank canvas.

'And now it begins,' he said.

CHAPTER II

1941

No one spoke. No one moved. It was virtually impossible to turn or adjust the body against the crammed human occupancy of the dim rough wooden carriage trundling under their feet. The forty nine men women and children clung to each other with gaunt faces and fear gripping their stomachs. Eyes asked questions that no one could answer. Little Lazar Kawalek clung to his mother in sheer terror. Bodies stifled him. He could not see the sky. He was enveloped in the stench of human bodies too long together. His own toiletry requirements had not been seen to and he was ashamed. For two days the train had jolted and jarred their bones, never stopping for more than a few moments to replenish the guards' rations and allow them to stretch their legs. Not the occupants of car number 43. The only relief from the cloistered and putrid interior was a few small cracks in the wagon sides through which the fortunate ones could describe what they saw. Now no one bothered any more. The scene was always the same. Vast wasteland with few towns to break the monotony. 'I am hungry mummy,' Lazar said. He looked upwards at the unfamiliar face of his mother, embedded with an indelible fear and dread of the journey they were making. There was no smile now, no comforting cuddle and a brush of his long silky hair from his forehead. They were all strangers. Even neighbours of longstanding no longer spoke. There was no point. Their destiny no longer remained in their hands. There were no law makers, no advisers, no acquaintances with whom to swap opinions. Every independent thought had been driven from their minds. They were as subservient as the cattle that usually occupied the space on which they were standing. Ignorant and submissively submitting to the grossest treatment that was usually reserved for livestock about to be taken to the abattoir. The thought was expelled from their minds. If you didn't think about it, it might not be true. Each mind formed a barrier to the outside world which had so devastatingly changed their lives in one inhuman and remorseless stroke of evil.

Lazar's mother reached out for her children beneath her. She sensed their need and could feel the warm faces against her stomach. Lazar's sister Taghi clutched at her mother's skirt with tight little fists, terrified to let go. The two children's faces were smudged with the tears that had long ago ceased to flow. She could not even bend to kiss them, and oh how she longed to smother them with her warm lips, to comfort them and reassure them that they need not be afraid. To tell them that God would look after them and that they would all be together one day in their pretty holiday house in Bad Durkheim. Their father would see to it as he had always done in the past. She looked at her husband with pity and compassion. He was a broken man. His ability to protect the persons he loved most in this life had been taken away from him and he was no more. Poor Werner, she thought. The love of my life, destroyed and betrayed by his own unselfishness. She loved him for that. The children did too. The children! Panic tried to enforce its grip on her body and mind but she could not allow that to transmit itself to those around her. God knows that there is no hope. All she could do was to comfort those who needed it and to wait for whatever was to become of them.

The 49 persons rocked with the wagon and stood rigidly on the urine soaked floor with legs that had grown stiff with immobility. That alone and the proximity of the mass of bodies around them prevented collapse. Two or three had succumbed to the stifling air and lack of food and had been dragged out by the guards and thrown roughly to one side. That had made a little more room for the remainder, but no one voiced their relief at the improvement from being crushed to being compressed.

Suddenly the doors were flung open with a crash and shouts and commands in a cruel vicious vernacular filled the air around them. 'Aus! Aus!' The carriage had stopped without them realising and the unfortunate few at the open sliding door were being dragged and flung to one side by men in uniform as if the exercise was a giant game to see who could empty the wagons first. Lazar and his family moved as swiftly as they could to tumble under their own weight on to the harsh ground beneath to protect themselves from the butts of the guards' rifles. 478 living beings stood forlornly grouped in a straggling line at the side of the train. Guards harangued them constantly into some form of order. SS men strutted their familiar and almost comical theatrical swagger as they enforced the orders of their minions with 'Schlange stehan!' But the miserable wretches could not stand in line, their legs and sensibilities could no longer obey what their brains were hearing. Many felt the butts of the rifles and fell, to be cruelly kicked upright again into some sort of order. Lazar and his family stood at the head of the line, his mother staring defiantly at the guard assigned to their section.

'Where are we going mummy?' Taghi asked. The first words that she had spoken since being bundled onto the train on the outskirts of Berlin. 'Sssh, my darling. We are nearly there.' As she spoke, Taghi's mother felt a lump in her throat that betrayed the assurance of her voice. Yes we are nearly there, she thought. At the end of the road. No where else to go. God help us.

They were moving now, orders had been snapped out with assistance from the cold steel of the rifles to those who failed to understand. The line shuffled aimlessly after the leaders, not knowing where, or how far, they were going. All around was grey. Grey earth, grey sky, grey faces and grey uniforms. No one knew if it was morning or afternoon. With no food it didn't matter any more. It helped not to remember meal times and bedtimes. It helped not to remember at all.

The line stopped. Then moved grudgingly forward, one step at a time, as those at the front were asked 'Wie alt?' – how old? and 'Gesundheit?' – health? The line was split into two, some going left, some right. It was soon obvious that the younger and fitter people were being diverted left with the remainder to the right.

Lazar's mother nudged her husband to straighten him up and told her children to hold their heads high. 'Behave as if this were a Sunday afternoon children. Walk proudly as a family.' The dread in her heart almost broke her resolution, but the grip of the two tiny hands in each of hers reminded her that she must not fail her family. Her husband was walking better now as she constantly talked to him about pride and self respect. The sanctity of their marriage and the love that no force on earth could destroy. The officer's eyes bored into hers. The questions rapped out from his cruel mouth in the monotony of a job repeated endlessly and uninterestedly. 'Twenty eight years old,' she indicated,' holding her family to her. 'Healthy and fit,' she added proudly.

The eyes shifted to Werner. He noted the drawn grey empty gaze and the slumped shoulders. 'Recht,' the officer barked and the guard enforced the order with a blow from his rifle.

Little Taghi ran after her father as her mother screamed in anguish, and fought with the guard in desperation to reach her husband. She was thrown forcefully back to where Lazar stood, stunned at the destruction of his family by one word from this callous, impersonal monster before him. He threw himself at the sneering face intent on scratching the derision from the hateful face of those whom he now knew as evil. The officer beat him easily to the ground and muttered to his guard that 'this one and his mother had spirit. They would last quite a while before the Reich was finished with them. Or them with the Reich', he added with another another self-satisfied jeer of a laugh.

Lazar and his mother moved brokenly to the left, their last sight of a husband and father and his daughter denied them as the guards closed around them and herded them onto lorries waiting like sombre sentinels in the gathering gloom.

The transport was no better than the rough carriages. Most were too weak to hold on to the stanchions that supported the canvas covers. Those that could stand, did. Those that couldn't sat wherever the crush was least resistant. Lazar and his mother were at the rear, able to see the scene before them as they left the railway yards, still awash with milling humanity, slowly but surely being divided into two like a surgeon splitting a tendon. At last she cried. She cried for everyone out there. For her husband, Werner. For her daughter Taghi. For her son, who clung to her arm as if it were a lifeline. But there was no lifeline. All hope of life had gone. The reassurances from her friends before they were arrested, that the camps were for work in the war effort, were of no substance. The reality was here. They were in a death camp. At least Werner and little Taghi were. Her own fate had yet to be decided. 'Juwellen, armband?' The guard at the rear of the truck demanded to know if any on board possessed jewellery or wristwatches. 'They will not be needed where you are going,' Lazar interpreted and looked at his mother in terror as she removed her wristwatch with the others. She felt the tiny gold single ring ear clips under her mass of golden hair and hoped that they did not show. A present from Werner on their last anniversary just two months ago. Or was it longer? She could not assess time any more. It was a bygone age. Another life. Two other people. She felt her head wrenched back and the precious ear-rings ripped from her lobes as the guard went among the others for their valuables.

The lorry jerked to halt. 'Monowitz-Buna.' The name echoed over the loudspeaker system and they knew that they had arrived. It was one of the camps in Auschwitz, next to the dreaded Birkenau. 'Wieviel stuck?' The guard saluted and confirmed the number of 'pieces' as 39 from his lorry. He reluctantly handed over some of his hoard of valuables to the officer in charge as was the routine.

Lazar helped his mother down from the truck as best as he could. They were jostled to a large wooden building and pushed inside where a team of 'Kapos'; trustees of the camp waited to take their clothes and shave the hair from their bodies. It was all so impersonal that resistance was useless. Throngs of naked people stood around like pink pigs awaiting slaughter. The shaving was rough and swiftly done. The trustees had had many groups to practise on and were expert at removing every last vestige of hair. Some even enjoyed embarrassing the females and delighted in comparing their prize with their next door trustee. Lazar held his mother's hand and copied her detachment as far as he could. No one was going to see him or his mother cringe at the touch of the trustees.

As soon as the shavers had finished, they were forced through a door and drenched with icy cold water from overhead showers and thrown rough sacks on which to dry themselves.

Their clothes were returned for the time being and then they were lined up again like so many Cistercian monks, devolved of their last remnants of individuality. The blood once again began to ooze out from the coarse blade scrapes on their scalps. Lazar and his mother and several other females and children were taken to the far end of the camp to block 27 where they were met by suspicious stares from the incumbents. Seeing that they had no other possessions than they, the interest lapsed and everyone sank on to the few remaining rough wooden bunks at the far end. Where there were not enough, families shared one bunk and Lazar and his mother forcefully commandeered the end bunk and cuddled together with their backs against the wall. They did not sleep. Their bodies and minds were weary beyond sleep. They just stared until the thoughts of their plight made them shut their eyes to prevent the tears that threatened but could not flow.

'Name?' 'Susan Mallory. I am English.' Lazar's mother replied directly to the piercing eyes of her interrogator.

'You are a Czechoslovakian slut. What is your real name?' the SS officer screamed.

'I am Susan Mallory and I was born in England, in Dorset and – '

Susan's head snapped sideways under the force of the officers slap. She staggered and resumed her position.

'Your papers say you are Mrs. Anna Weisz, wife of a Jewish capitalist Carl Weisz. Where is your husband?' Again the interrogator screamed in her face, half rising until his eyes were level with hers. Susan composed herself and said in an even a tone as she could muster, 'I am Susan Mallory and you have taken my husband and daughter away. What have you done with them?' This time it was Susan demanding an answer in defiance of this man attempting to intimidate her.

Again she reeled from the blow from his left hand. An ugly weal began to appear on her right cheek. She wiped the filth of his hand from her and repeated her assertions that she was English and that her husband was not a jew, but a simple book dealer.

Her diatribe was cut short as the SS officer snapped an order to his assistant. Before Lazar could move his trousers were ripped from his bottom and his penis produced to the Lieutenant. 'Circumcised! I knew it!' he shouted triumphantly. 'You are filthy jews. Take them away to Birkenau, block 25 and place them with the rest of their breed of scum.'

Susan protested vehemently that the circumcision was because of problems when Lazar was young, but to no avail.

Birkenau was even more forbidding than Monowitz-Buna. An enormous camp of 200 'blocks' set in neat regular lines of 17 for 9 rows with a further set of blocks at right angles between what Susan was later to discover were the gas chambers and crematoria. These were on the north side of the camp, four in number and continually employed. Block 25, to which Susan and Lazar had been assigned were on the west side, divided from the remainder by a fence. The inhabitants of block 25 had no illusions about their fate. A short walk one morning to gas chamber no 2 and they would be no more. Susan clutched Lazar to her in desperation. He must live. He must live to exact retribution on the evil that had put her family here. She thought of Werner and Taghi. Dear little Taghi who was too young to appreciate what was happening. Her mind had frozen in shock at the outrage of the SS when they had come to arrest them. Susan knew there was no hope for them. They may already be dead. She put it out of her mind and concentrated on her son. She needed to assess the position in the morning and act quickly for she did not know how long remained. She asked around her for details of the camp and the comings and goings of new prisoners. Who brought them? How were they brought? When did they arrive? She gleaned a little information but not enough to satisfy her as the inmates had no chance to observe much outside of the block.

The Blockfuhrer, that was the answer. She went to the door, surprisingly it opened. Who could go anywhere? she asked herself. No sane person would want to risk a beating or be shot for trying to escape. She searched for a guard or a trustee. There must be someone close at hand, especially around the Death Block.

'Halt!' The guttural command shattered her calm and she spun round to see a grey uniformed guard – a 'scharfuhrer' as she found out later, an under sergeant. Susan thought quickly. 'I am looking for my husband, which block is he in? I have to tell him that my son is ill.' It wasn't difficult to fake her anguish and apparent loss of sanity. That occurred to almost everyone at some time or other.

She was ordered back into the block helped by a blow from the guard's rifle butt. 'Perhaps he will arrive tomorrow,' she burbled, 'how many are coming tomorrow?' Susan grabbed at the guard's coat, screaming at him to answer, taking most of the blows that were rained on her with her arms, until a vicious kick took her legs from under her and she collapsed grovelling to the ground.

'Get back into your block, you Jewish slime. Tomorrow you will be making room for five lorry loads of your filthy brethren. Perhaps your husband will have your bed after you have gone.' He laughed uproariously at his own joke as he continued to kick at Susan's buttocks as she scuttled on all fours into her block.

Five lorry loads tomorrow! That meant that lorries arriving would be departing, going out of the camp to fetch another contingent from the endless cattle trucks sucking the Jewish nation out of Europe. She looked at Lazar, pitifully asleep on the wooden bunk. Two filthy sacks covered his body, but his cherubic face still shone through to wrench her heart in two as she thought of tomorrow. How to get him out of this death trap. Their numbers would be counted at Stehappell – stand up roll call – he must be there at that. Then would begin the terrible journey to the north side of the camp where . . . , she dared not even breath the name. He must be at stehappell, but he must be hidden by then. How could she fool the Rapportfuhrer? The block contained 194 persons of all ages. Children as young as two were continually crying and retching for lack of food. The majority were elderly. The next block was similar, a women's block not yet ordained for the gas chambers. There were children there, many the same age as Lazar. That was it! It flashed through her mind that she could somehow find a substitute for Lazar from the next block, or any block within reach. Her heart sank as swiftly as it had risen. That would entail someone else's child being taken for extermination before his time. She could not even consider that any mother would make that supreme sacrifice. The children were all that were left of their lives. An anchor to hold on to, to remember when they were born and when life was normal before this malevolent insanity seeped its incessant maniacal message into the lifeblood of the fascist believers. There was no one to stop it. Like a plague it infested the souls of the Nazis and gathered strength with every success, with every annihilation of another batch of Jews and enemies of the Reich.

Death. That was the answer. Where the system demanded that the final solution was obliteration, then they could be given the bodies they required to balance the records. Children in arms and children stumbling alongside their mothers made no difference to the inhuman guards. Bodies were bodies. Naked and defenceless, they all died and were disposed of by the horde of bunker clearers who dragged the bodies on carts to the incinerators.

Susan prayed. She prayed that a tiny soul would leave this world before the time determined by the camp commandant. A death that would be more desirable than the choking terror that awaited them all. She balked at her own selfishness. But if Lazar was placed in the same position, she would allow his body to be utilised to deceive this evil canker eating away at the very fabric of human existence. She had already seen corpses dragged from the blocks and left to fester in piles until conscripts loaded them onto carts to tip them into a communal pit on the outskirts of the camp. It was a daily job and was carried out with all the oblivion of automatons. Survival was paramount in all, except the Musselmen, beings who had given up the will to live. While they were useful, their chances of life were better than even.

Susan again went to the door and peeped out. There was no moon. What little light there was came from the stars and a few windows from the main guardhouse separating their quarters from the vast camp on the other side of the high wire fence. It took her three quarters of an hour of desperate searching the 25 huts, crawling on her hands and knees and dropping to the ground as soon as she heard the slightest sound. She smelt the putrid stench of death before she came across the door to hut 16. Three bodies lying where they had been flung by the Blockfuhrers. Incongruous in death and starkly reminiscent of skeletons in the desert. Knees crooked up and arms spread as if appealing for one more chance of life. Susan's stomach spewed bile onto the dirt, her body unable to perform the normal function of retching through lack of food.

Cold sweat broke out onto her forehead as she pulled the corpses apart to assess them for size. One was smaller than the others. A girl so emaciated that she could be taken for a child. Here was the answer. Lazar's body was approximately the same proportions, but which guard would notice the difference? She removed the ragged trousers from the first man, almost ripping them apart over the stiff legs rigid from the two days he had lain there. The girl was more pliable and the trousers were transferred and tied under her armpits with part of a ripped shirt from the third body. Susan took a deep breath and heaved the thin body over her shoulder, amazed at how easily the spindly limbed girl hung, pendulum like on her back. She half ran, half stumbled, in a frantic race to return to her hut. She couldn't be discovered now. Not when she had the means to defy death. Her heart pounded and her breath seemed loud enough to waken the dead. She couldn't even find any amusement in her own thoughts and continued to run and stop and start again as she closed on hut 25. The Blockfuhrer was there again!

Please God let him not enter the hut. Let it not be another stehappell before the final count tomorrow. The guard raised his hand and took a long draw from his cigarette. The glow lit up his brutish face for a moment before he crunched the stub under his booted foot. A cruel grin crossed his lips as if he were thinking of tomorrow and another batch that would be crushed under the boot of the Third Reich.

The departing figure of the Blockfuhrer gave Susan the strength to heave herself and her burden from the crouched position and dash for the door and comparative safety. No one questioned her movements. She made her way to the far end where Lazar awoke at her touch. He puzzled at the figure of his mother holding another and rose to speak. Susan deftly placed her finger to her mouth and Lazar obeyed instantly.

Over the next three hours Susan whispered to her son of the plans that she had for his escape. As she spoke, she realised how futile they must seem to an eight year old. He must be made to believe that he had the chance. The alternative was death. For an eight year old to be faced with this ultimatum was beyond belief, but Susan knew her son. He had the resolution and the determination to succeed where most of his friends would have given up long ago.

'You must hide when the guards come for us. I will carry this poor girl in your place. No one will notice, if I tell them you are too ill to walk. Fortunately she has not been long dead,' she cringed at her matter of fact tone, 'so I shall be able to fashion her into some sort of cradle position to look as if she is clinging to me.' Susan could not believe that she was talking of a corpse as if it were a puppet to be manipulated and moulded for her benefit. But her resolve was as strong as Lazar's and she noted with satisfaction his acceptance of the situation.

'Once we have gone,' Susan tried desperately to sound dispassionate but her voice betrayed her and she had to repeat her words. 'Afterwards, I want you to watch for the lorries that will be arriving at the Main Guardhouse. You can see it from the front window on your left. There is a small wooden storeshed opposite hut 12 which is adjacent to where the lorries stopped when we arrived. If you hide in there, you will have a chance of getting into the toolbox of one of the lorries. Do you remember where the box is situated?'

Lazar nodded. 'Under the tail gate. I fell against it when we jumped down.'

'Good boy. You may need a tool to force it open, but more than likely it will be held with a hasp and nail.' Susan heard herself giving the instructions as if it were part of a game and not a life and death struggle for survival. She continued to reassure Lazar that it could be done and that it was his only chance. 'You must not fail my son. We are relying on you. Your father and your sister and I will always be with you. Nothing can separate us from you. We are one and we shall be with you forever.'

They said a short prayer together and Lazar tried to sleep. Susan was busy with the corpse, bending her legs and raising her arms in a loop to fit over her shoulders. The task was completed none too soon as rigor mortis was already creeping into the stick like bones of the young girl. Susan suddenly panicked. They would all be naked when they marched to the bunker. How would she explain the white pallor of her 'child?' She thought of the others in the hut and their waxlike skin clinging to their bones. Everyone had the pallor of death anyway. A paler shade would not be noticed.

She removed her left shoe, thankfully rescued from the heap after the shower. On her little toe shone a gold band, her wedding ring. She had secreted it there before the lorry guard had chance to steal it with the other valuables. Held underneath her tongue, she had transferred it between her foot and her mouth to avoid detection. Now she gently eased it over Lazar's middle finger of his right hand. Loose but it would hold. A small bandage from her dress wound over the fingers would prevent it being seen by outsiders. Her faith was such that she could believe that Lazar would be among the outsiders soon. 'Sleep my son,' she crooned. 'Tomorrow is the beginning of the rest of your life.'

The targesraum was full to overflowing. The Quartermaster surveyed the mass of naked humanity before him through practised resigned eyes. Regular selection of those to be disposed of was a routine with which he was all too familiar. Each of the persons standing before him had been handed a card showing number, name, age, profession, and nationality, which they all clutched at with unreal zeal. This sole piece of history of their being was all that stood between them and the gas chamber. Age could be the factor that swayed the SS subaltern, or it could be the profession. Certainly anyone with a jewish connection was immediately selected. At a given signal the door to the targesraum opened and each inmate handed their card to the Blockaltester and ran or stumbled the short distance to their hut on the far side of the road. The SS subaltern observed the fitness or otherwise of the owner of the card and with hardly a glance at the details handed it to an assistant on his left or his right. Schlechte Seite, the bad side was the dreaded death sentence. Whether it was left or right no one knew. Susan glanced back at her card as she stumbled into hut 25. Lazar was close behind. She had tried to look as fit as possible and was convinced that she was far healthier than her unfortunate counterparts. Lazar was a boy and easily able to work. With dismay she thought she saw that her card had landed on the left side. The bad side. Her heart sank. If hers had been chosen, for whatever reason, probably the jewish annotation on her card, then surely her son's would have been also. She raced to the end of her hut and dragged out the body hidden under the last bunk. She quickly dressed it and herself and told Lazar to hide in the place where a few minutes ago the corpse lay. He put on his clothes and held the small bag made from the remnants of the girl's dress. In it were two slices of bread saved by his mother from her ration with a little margarine.

'Stay there until you hear the guards calling out our numbers,' she cautioned him. 'Once we are clear of the hut, slip out of the back window and hide. Get to the storeshed as quickly as possible and stay there until the lorries arrive.'

'They may not call our numbers mummy,' he cried. Afraid now that the time had come. 'If they don't then we shall have to prepare again for the next selection.' Susan tried to appear calm for the sake of Lazar but her heart was reaching out for him. The emptiness in her stomach was not through lack of food but the certainty that it would never see food again. 175. 177. 178... the numbers echoed over the speaker system bringing an immediate response from the holders of the numbers. Some just rose and stripped off their clothes again. Others sat and refused to move. Guards entered, examined the numbers on their tags and kicked them outside. 235. 347... Susan held her breath and squeezed her eyes against the inevitable. 379. 380. Hers and Lazar's numbers shot through her body like an electric shock. They had not escaped. Already the remaining few were walking like zombies to the door. Ten seconds and Susan was stripped, and standing upright with the girl clutched in her arms. Her right arm encircled the legs of the girl to pull the outer thigh over her other thigh to hide the gender. The girl's arms looped over her head in an embrace with her head cuddled underneath Susan's chin to disguise the features. Lazar lay as still as the girl had under the bunk.

246 breathing, unthinking, de-humanised naked people began the slow march to the gas chamber. The roll call had been made and the number found to be correct. Lazar's tag around the girl's arm had been examined perfunctorily, Susan letting everyone know within earshot that 'he' had become ill in the night with some mysterious ailment. The trustees did not want to risk too close a contact and were satisfied with the numbered tag of 380 to check off on their list.

The escorts barked their orders and the cortege moved as one in a straggling line of white shapeless nonentities to meet their maker.

Lazar watched with eyes that did not move. A film of heinous magnitude played itself out in the spectacle before him. Forever etched in the innocent cells of his brain, yet to come to grips with the atrocities of war. A mind so innocent that the scars would burn as violently as the furnaces being prepared for his mother. He did not cry. He could not cry any more. His mother's trust had instilled in him the determination to free himself from this hell and seek out the cause of this blatant betrayal that had robbed him of his family. His little mind could not quite grasp the significance of the events that led to this nightmare, but he would find out. He owed that to his mother, to his father and to his sister. He owed it to all the lost souls who had and would perish in this unspeakable human processing plant.

Slipping out of the window and dropping immediately on to the ground he covered himself with debris from the foundations of the hut. It was almost dark, and the lights of the main guardhouse shone dully on the ground and on the wire fence, causing an intermittent flashing of silver as the wires moved in the wind. Underneath the fence Lazar could see the storeshed. Just 45 yards to safety. 45 yards of clearing to cross before the lorries arrived. If they arrived. What would he do if they didn't? He had no time to consider the alternative before a detachment of workers entered the gate among shouts and blows from their guards to 'get a move on you idle bastards.' Lazar took his chance. As the crowd passed he ran into their midst and mingled in and out of the throng, working his way to the far side as it passed the fence. The guards were too busy kicking the stragglers to see the small figure dart outwards and throw himself under the fence supports.

The party moved on. One more day done. More strength expended. Less with which to impress their Rapportfuhrer when the next selection process was held.

Lazar lay for what seemed an hour, unable to move or daring to risk showing any flash of light from his face. He scraped in the dry dust and moistened it the best he could to smear a covering over his face and hands. Slowly he began to crawl the 20 yards or so to the hut. Would it be open? No reason why it should be locked. It had long been disused as a storage place, holding only a few spades. Lazar shuddered at the thought of the spades and their use. Five yards more and he would be safe. For a while. Suddenly the sound of labouring engines and exhausts broke the night's cloak and shouts and orders barked through the air. The main guardhouse sprang to life and the 12 foot barbed wire gates swung open on their axis to allow the convoy of jolting lorries to enter the compound. Lazar moved under the cover of the commotion to the side of the hut and frantically searched for the hasp. It was free. He slipped the lever and slid inside pulling the door silently behind him. He hung on to the latch not daring to breath. Had he been seen? Would anyone inspect the shed? How long would the lorries remain on the compound in front of the guardhouse?

'Sie alle!' 'Leer!'

Lazar distinguished the words over and above the general hubbub. He knew that the lorries were clear of all prisoners. Now he must make his move. The lorries would have been searched for malingerers and the numbers checked with the lists. No further searches would be necessary and if he could get aboard he would have achieved the next step to freedom. His excitement rose despite the position he was in. Many times he had played with his friends in hide and seek and the thrill remained the same. But this time he was playing for higher stakes – his life!

The lorry nearest to his shed stood unattended and blocking out the roofs of the huts beyond. That meant it was comparatively near. No more than a dozen yards. A dozen yards to freedom. A dozen steps from his short legs and he would be able to slip into the toolbox slung underneath. It would have to be all or nothing. He could not afford to creep. A straight dash was his best chance. Less chance of being seen in the gloom. Less chance of being caught in the open if a guard decided to walk around the lorry.

He slipped out of the shed, took one breath and sped like an arrow for the rear of the truck. The backboard was down barring his way in to the toolbox! With a heave he lifted the heavy tailgate, fumbled for the box flap, wrenched it open and slid inside. Two and a half feet long and twelve inches deep, it barely held his puny body. Luckily the tools were virtually non-existent, their use long ago forsaken. If a lorry broke down, the inhabitants were crammed on the next. The lorry could be rescued later and repaired if anyone bothered to take the trouble.

Laughing voices broke the silence within the toolbox as the drivers returned and banged the tailgates into position, fastening them with the hasps in a noisy demonstration of their satisfaction to be on their way again. Much as they enjoyed their work they did not enjoy the time spent in the camp. While they were there, they were as much a prisoner as those they transported to the death camp.

The first lorry's engine burst into life and each of the following five lorries followed suit in a cacophony of joyful revving of accelerators which threatened to blast the valves from their sockets. Slowly the convoy moved off, turning in a tight circle to navigate the narrow gate by the guardhouse. Each driver acknowledged the gatekeeper with a raised hand or two fingers dependent on his mood of the moment.

He was out! Lazar could sense it. The air smelt fresher even within the confined space of the box. The perpendicular lid continually bounced open to give him a view of the moving track like a khaki conveyor belt moving backwards to Birkenau.

I must think ahead he reasoned with himself. Where are the lorries likely to he heading? The railway sidings where we were unceremoniously bundled off he calculated. Where my father and sister were separated from us. He dare not dwell on them or his mother. He must concentrate on the task in hand.

He tried to remember all that his mother had told him. The place where the lorries would probably go to. The railway junction where trains arrived daily. That was the place to head for.

If the lorries stopped at the rail junction, then they would be expecting another train load of 'workers.' If the train arrived then it must return. If it returned, it would return empty. His mother's logic ran through his fertile mind. That's my chance he thought. I must get aboard the empty train and hope that it will not be searched again until it arrives at its destination. Wherever that is.

Lazar dismissed any further conjecture from his mind and waited for his opportunity to scramble from the box and hide. He felt a jolt and cursed the few tools that bit into his back. The lorry had stopped. Gingerly he peeped out of the side of the box. The driver would be getting down from the left hand side of the lorry, so gently he eased himself down and hid on the right side until he could find his bearings. The transport of lorries had stationed themselves on waste ground some way from the maze of railway lines that ended in the scrub of the bleak landscape. A journey to nowhere an observer would have assumed. No terminal. No friendly railway station to greet the travellers. It was what it signified. A journey to hell.

Taking his chance, Lazar ran for the cover of some rubbish to the side of the lorry park. A further lorry was parked nearer the lines than the rest. Its tyres were flat and the whole of its outer surface was covered in dust. Abandoned. That was his hiding place. The drivers had disappeared to drink the vodka stolen from the last Russian contingent and their laughing could be heard crackling in the distance. Lazar crept aboard the lorry and settled himself just below the level of the side window, to keep an eye on anyone who approached. The tension of the previous few hours seeped out of his little body as exhaustion took over and within three minutes he was asleep.

His mother was calling to him from the open window of their cottage in Bad Durkheim. The frothy white bedcovers hung over the sills like foam on a waterfall. He skipped around the garden so carefully tended by his father and pretended he was The Lone Ranger tracking the bankrobbers over the prairies.

His gun hung low on his hip, strapped to his thigh like the real cowboys. A small stetson and mask completed the outfit. Susan laughed out loud at his antics as he caught the 'robbers' and fought with them in his imagination, finally ending in a gunfight in which he was 'wounded' before killing the leader. Lazar sat under the apple tree still preoccupied with his game. He checked his gun and adjusted his stetson before setting out once again on the trail of more 'baddies.'

A loud bang on the side of the truck woke him instantly and paralysed him with fear. 'This will be a good place to store it.' The voice spoke in German and Lazar overheard sufficient to warn him that any minute now his hiding place would be discovered. The men, two of them as far as he could gather, were speaking from the rear of the lorry, testing the covers and tailgate. The sound of one jumping up on to the boards and walking to the front and a further crump on the floor sent Lazar into a cold sweat as he squeezed as much of himself under the passenger seat as he could.

The steps receded and he breathed again. He risked a quick glance out of the window on the driver's side and saw the two men disappearing towards the two huts on the far side of the terminus. Crawling through the connecting window into the back, he saw three suitcases stacked in the corner. He remembered their own suitcases which had been taken from them as they were herded into the rail trucks. No one ever saw their belongings again. They were the property of the Reich or of anyone who could divert them for his own use.

He opened the first case. Clothes and soap and a few mementos were all it contained. The second was the same, but provided some food in the shape of hard boiled sweets which Lazar sucked greedily. The third produced some clothes which drowned his body but with some scissors found at the bottom of the suitcase he fashioned the trousers and sleeves to fit his puny arms and legs. The clean shirt, far too big for him, felt like silk to his skin. He used the comb to straighten out his matted hair. Washing would have to wait. He pocketed the soap and scissors and tucked the comb into his top pocket, hanging near his waistline. A further search revealed a packet of hard biscuits, some cheese, and cooked beef. The smallest suitcase was manageable and Lazar carefully selected items from the three cases to fill it. The remaining two were replaced where he had found them. He could not remain here. The men may return. Keeping the lorry between him and the two huts he ran as fast as his short legs would carry him to where a junction box protruded above the skyline, some two hundred yards from where the trains came to a halt. He would be hidden there from prying eyes down the line. As he was not 'missing' from any list then there was very little likelihood of anyone bothering to search for him. He sat and waited.

He heard the monotonous rumble in the distance and felt the vibrations in the shiny line of metal not three yards from his eyes. A train was coming. Slowly with effort it was pulling its ten or so carriages joltingly over the purpose built rails to where the grim line of lorries stood. Far too many for the lorries to carry. Some would have to walk, delaying the inevitable shock of the entrance to their final destination. Auschwitz and all its attendant camps.

"Arbeit Macht Frei." The sign over the gate would greet all those who entered, but no one believed the sardonic message that 'work sets you free.' Perhaps it was meant to convey that as long as you were capable of work you would not be eliminated. A few clung to the flimsy hope that it would save them, but most did not believe it.

The great belching engine coughed its last bellyful of smoke into the darkening grey sky. The bogey wheels ground to a halt, screeching in pain at the contact between the two metals. The last carriage had passed Lazar and stood some forty yards from where he hid. He waited.

Grey uniformed guards arrived and at a given signal the wagon doors crashed open. Streams of living humanity spewed forth and were beaten and shoved and shouted at to move to the head of the train. Soon every wagon stood immobile and empty. Shorn of its cargo of crying, pleading, praying people. The impersonal wooden cladding took the chance to breathe the air of the vast open plains before it undertook the next cramming of Hitler's final solution into its stark interior.

'The train arrives, so it must depart.' His mother's words came back to him. 'Get back on the train that brought us. It will return to another destination for more Germans, French, Russians or Chechs. Wherever it goes, stay with it until you are as far away as possible. You are small. Hide in a corner and get out as soon as the train reaches its destination.'

Winter was already grabbing at every face and finger it could find. Lazar wondered if he dare risk returning to the lorry to snatch another jumper to fashion gloves and a balaclava for himself. He would surely need it as the temperature dropped ominously in the biting wind.

Without the cover he would surely perish. Three minutes later he was back aboard the lorry, turfing out a suitable jumper from which he cut the sleeves. One sleeve was fashioned into a hood with a gap for his eyes, the other into two 'mittens' with the ends folded under his grasp. He felt warmer already. Now for the train. Which wagon should he use? Not the last. Too obvious a place for a guard to glance in. Three from the end he decided. The oldest looking wagon with stark gaps in the boarding. That would enable him to see out of both sides and to watch for approaching danger. Most of the gaps had been made by previous occupants. Tiny windows on the world that would be their last sight of freedom.

Lazar ran around the opposite side of the train from where the SS and guards were gathered near to the engine. Tracks and sidings and junctions were everywhere. The engine would have to be detached and shunted on to the other end of the train for the return journey. Lazar panicked. What if the train did not move tonight? What if it never moved? It would he convinced himself. It had to.

He scrambled aboard the carriage carrying his precious parcel of goods and settled himself in the far corner away from the open doors. He dare not close them for fear of them being noticed. Some sacks had been piled in the opposite corner, bedding for the fortunate few who had been lucky enough to inherit this wagon. After eating a little meat, cheese, and bread he settled as flat as he could under the sacking, keeping a wary eye on the doors from a fold in the rough hemp across his face. It grew dark as suddenly as the noise of the crowd from the far end of the train disappeared. Only the engine drivers remained. Refreshing themselves in the small hut before the long journey back. Lazar's fragile limbs ached and his body was cold. His mind was numb at the events that had happened in the last twenty four hours. He could no longer think what day it was. When he had seen his mother last. His father and sister. Was it yesterday? Or a week ago? Time fused into a black hole in his head. He could only think of now. Of when the train would move. Of when he would be away from this place of misery. Of all the places in the world this was the most miserable that he could remember. He wanted it out of his mind, out of his body. He wanted to return to the lovely days with his family. The beautiful days. The days of wonder and discovery. Would they ever return? His mind refused to think any more and succumbed to his frail body's demands as he fell into an exhausted sleep.

The loudest crash that he had ever heard accompanied the jarring shock administered to the wagon by a giant cudgel two feet from his ear. This train driver was not too particular about his shunting expertise and the shock waves reverberated through each carriage like a pack of falling dominoes. Lazar was awake immediately. He cowered beneath the sacking, clutching his bag in the comfort of his curled up knees. His elbows completed the circle with his tiny fists clenched against his chin. The train began to move. So slowly it barely moved the sacking from his face. But it was moving! The first junction jolted him from his cowering position as he watched the countryside moving gradually away from him. He rose and strained with all his puny strength at the sliding door until it reluctantly gave and, aided by the movement of the train, slid protestingly into it socket. The opposite door moved easier and once closed the temperature improved dramatically. He had not felt the effect of the cold until the comparative warmth of the wagon enabled him to shed some of the ridiculous clothes he had made for himself. His balaclava was no longer necessary but he stowed it in his 'bag' together with his mittens. He estimated that it must be early morning as the light was dim but gaining strength. Snow was beginning to appear on the landscape adding its reflection to the white sky and slatting the carriage floor with beams through the cracks. It must be nearly Christmas. He remembered that his mother had been preparing for the celebration the week before the soldiers came... A large fir tree in the corner with pretty decorations and crackers and baubles and tinsel. Presents under the low branches, wrapped in beautiful shiny paper and ribbons. None of those were his of course. Santa would bring them next week. He still pretended to believe as the thrill was still there. Next week... It was next week and there had been no Santa. No presents. Nothing except this vast emptiness around him and the emptiness in his body.

He must plan ahead. He had spent two days on the trains to reach Auschwitz and in all probability would spend two days on the return journey. IF it was returning to the same place. He divided his meagre rations into two and carefully re-wrapped them. Sufficient to keep him from starving but he had no liquid. The whiteness through the gaps in the boarding prompted him to slide open the door a foot to view the snow covered land rolling under his gaze. Some of the snow had formed a ridge on the outer bottom board at the end of the door runners and he scooped a handful, greedily sucking its cold moistness into his mouth. If only he had a container. The hard boiled sweets! They were in a greaseproof bag. Emptied out into his pocket, he filled the small bag with snow and watched it melt into the bottom. Further handfuls were added to nearly fill the bag with liquid. Propped between his discarded balaclava and mittens, it would be available for some time before the liquid seeped through the seams. He slept and dozed, never fully awake or asleep. Villages and towns passed. The train never seemed to stop. Or if it did, he was not aware of it. 'Lazar, come and see what I have made for you.' His mother's voice from the front room sent him running to her side. She proudly showed him a little overcoat, just like his father's. Six buttons, double breasted with a top pocket and black velvet collar. She had fashioned it out of a new army blanket that she had been able to purchase on the market. It was a lovely shade of light blue. Like her eyes, Lazar thought. And soft like her body when she cuddled him to sleep at night. It smelled like his mother. Like everything that was good and lovely. New; specially made for him. His very own 'grown up' overcoat. I will always have good clothes he promised himself. He had seen how everyone admired the smartly dressed gentlemen, especially his father. Tall and refined. His dark hair slicked back to emphasise his honest brow and kindly eyes. He had a way of suddenly smiling that lifted the hearts of anyone receiving his graciousness. 'Now there is a coat fit for a prince,' he joked as he turned Lazar and made him parade up and down the apartment. 'Keep your head up high,' he commanded. 'Yes, that's it. No one will ever look at your shoes if you hold your head up.' He repeated his grandmother's axiom as he had so many times before.

'This is my very favourite coat. I shall wear it always,' pronounced Lazar in his determined way.

'You will keep it for best. It is not for playing in and certainly not for wandering in the forest. I've seen enough of your escapades to last me a lifetime. That coat is to be put away until we have a special occasion.' Lazar was glad really. He would be proud to show it off at the right time. He couldn't remember ever wearing it again. The soldiers came and he was taken away without it. He desperately tried to reach the wardrobe before they shunted him out of the door after his family and down the staircase. He shouted for his coat, but they would not listen...

Lazar awoke with the dream still vivid in his mind. He looked wildly for the wardrobe. For his coat. He saw only the stark empty wagon and his pile of rags on the floor.

"SOSNOWIEC." The sign on the station wall flashed by his peephole as the train clanked over the rails. People stood around, disinterested in the empty train. Were they waiting for a train to take them the other way? Or were they the permanent population of stations that always seemed to be waiting for a train to somewhere? Lazar wondered where they all went. Meeting for one brief moment in time to nod to one another and then to part never to meet again. He saw the SS officers and the grey suited army personnel mingled in the crowd. Was there nowhere to escape their presence?

The town passed and soon the train began to slow as if to stop. "KATOVICE," said the sign. He remembered the name being shouted on his outward journey. "An important place," he had heard the mutterings from above his head. More information from his mother returned to his head. "If you reach a main station, change trains. You will be safer. Look for another train that is heading out of Poland, westwards. That is where Germany is. Try and reach Berlin. Your auntie Anna will help you. You must find her. Remember where she lives?' Lazar automatically nodded as he recalled his mother's earnest entreaties. '43, Weinstrasse. If anyone asks you, that is where you live.' Her eyes bored into his, as if trying to impart all her knowledge in a secret telepathic effort to fill his mind with all that she knew he would need for his survival. She had choked back the tears and the anguish. She had to be strong. He must not see weakness in her.

The train jerked as the wheels screeched their resistance to the brakes. Lazar's carriage was clear of the station. It appeared as if the train had taken refuge in a siding awaiting its next load for Auschwitz. Where to hide? He dare not be on his own, he would soon be noticed. In a crowd. Jumping down from the wagon he stealthily crept behind the cover of trucks and railway stock to the end of the station platform. Several groups of people stood, sat or slept on the benches. He dusted himself down and replaced the balaclava and mittens. It gave him a sort of immunity from the outside world. If they couldn't see his face, he would be safe he consoled himself.

He noticed a family of three adults and four children of differing ages gathered at the end where he had crept. The children were playing ball. The parents or those in charge sat on the bench talking in low tones with secretive glances along the platform to where the administration block was. Lazar placed his bundle on the ground and leaned against the wall near the children. Soon the ball came his way and he joined in the game, laughing with the others as if he knew them. They spoke a language he did not understand. He shouted with them and fetched the ball when it rolled towards their parents, smiling at the old faces looking at him quizzically. 'Mama? Papa?' they said. Lazar shook his head. Dare he risk confiding in them? 'Mama? Papa?' they repeated. Their eyes were kindly and worried. They bore no suspicion or condemnation. Lazar decided to risk confiding in them. "Search for people who are like us. Put your trust in families." His mother's counselling rang in his head as he uttered the word that he knew would tell him if he could trust them.

'Auschwitz,' he said. 'Mutter und Vater, Auschwitz.'

The gasp from the younger woman told him that he had not been wrong to trust them. She took him into her arms and held him to her as in fear of her own children's lives. The father looked up and down the platform and encouraged his children, who had stopped to watch, to continue to play.

Slowly in broken German, the lady understood what had happened. Lazar's German was only a smattering of phrases, but it was sufficient to tell them of his escape and that his mother, father and sister were dead.

Tears came into her eyes and deep controlled sobs were contained within her chest as she appealed to her husband for help. 'He wants to get to Berlin, he has relatives there.'

'That is impossible,' replied Staszek her husband. 'He cannot travel alone over 800 kilometres. He is but a child.'

'Exactly.' Halina's face took on a determined look. She saw her own children, happy for the moment and thought how different it would be if they had not been able to persuade the authorities that they were 'essential' to the country. She was proud of her husband's achievements in the field of fuel refinement, but never guessed that it would be their saviour from the labour camps. Prague was the home of V K S Chemicals, his employers since his first class degree in Petro-chemistry at the university Plzen. That had been twenty years ago. Twenty years of happiness and comparative fortune.

'Exactly,' she repeated. 'And we have four children. What difference will one more make?' The simple statement was directed at Staszek as if he had no further discussion in the matter and that it was settled. 'Watch the children my husband.' She took Lazar by the hand and lifting a suitcase in the other made for the Ladies Room a few steps to the right.

Staszek was nervous. He had never felt entirely at ease in his forced employment for the German scientists who had descended on V K S Chemicals earlier that year. All heads of departments had to report to imported overseers and all research became the property of the German Reich. Fuel seemed to be their preoccupation. His department. He realised the importance of his work but also realised that it would be used for other purposes than for which it was intended. He therefore had deliberately slowed down the progress to just a sufficient pace to meet with the grudging acceptance of those in command. He must not produce the fuel they desired, whatever happened.

Halina returned with the boy who was unrecognisable from the urchin who had appeared within their midst. He was washed and now possessed an appropriate jacket and trousers from the suitcase. 'One of Teofil's,' she said quite calmly. The children clapped and swarmed around Lazar until their father told them to behave and continue playing ball.

'We are going to take him with us to Prague?' queried Staszek. 'What about his papers?'

'Our papers will be sufficient. We can altar the number of children from four to five easily. In fact, I've already done it.' Her smile of satisfaction cut short her husband's further protests as she kissed him lightly on the lips and gripped his hand through the woollen gloves she had knitted him for Christmas. That wouldn't be for another two days but the weather had demanded an early present.

'You will come with us to Prague,' Halina told Lazar in the best way she could. She had discovered that he spoke English and utilised her own prep school English to convey her message. That he understood was confirmed when he held her closely and kissed her cheek with the softness that she would not have thought possible from his roughened face.

It began to snow. Slowly at first and then in waves of white soap flakes as big as Lazar's fist. The train drew majestically into the station and declared its arrival with an ear splitting blast from its smoke funnel and the platform was filled with dissipated steam, threatening to melt the clinging snow. The family climbed aboard. They squeezed into a compartment with two other families until four of the children had to be held on knees to prevent them being squashed. Papers were examined but there was no way that the horde of children could be assigned to any family with certainty and a quick count to match the number on their papers was considered sufficient.

Eleven hours and innumerable stops later the great shiny leviathan pulled into Prague central station. A hive of activity and bustle and black smoked glass with large clock faces and trolleys everywhere. Taxis were still evident and Staszek managed to commandeer one to take them to their home in the suburbs. The eagle stamp of the Third Reich on his permit worked wonders with all drivers, porters, and staff whenever he was forced to employ its use.

Lazar looked eagerly out of the window of the cab as it sped through the near deserted streets. Such a big city. Beautiful buildings. His father had taught him to appreciate the architecture of numerous cities on his travels. Travels that had enthralled him from the age of four. The first to Berlin when he had fetched he and his mother to live with him there. He remembered how his mother had hesitated, torn between wanting to be with her husband and the safety of her home in England. But Werner had persuaded her that all would be well. He was an important book dealer and as such had the confidence of the new regime, whose publications he regularly sold. Mostly propaganda, but he was allowed to continue to promote the sale of vital textbooks on technology and science. The whole world was interested in that. The only restriction was the advances being made by the Third Reich's own scientific team. That never reached the public. Publication of their experiments were limited to a few copies for the elite of the party. Staszek and Halina's house was set in a residential part of Prague where trees and avenues abounded and rooftops peeped through the elms and poplars to denote an affluent population.

Their house was smaller but quite comfortable with ample room for the children. Lazar was assigned to sleep with the younger boy Teofil, about the same age. Geonek and Georg had their own rooms as did Lisa the youngest. He was home. His mother would have been very proud. And very grateful to this family that had adopted him without question. He said his prayers at the foot of the bed in the little room at the end of the landing. 'Please look after mummy and daddy and Taghi. Tell them I will always remember them. God bless my new mummy and daddy and their children.' The little eight year old opened his eyes and looked upwards as if trying to see God himself. 'And tell mummy that I will find that man and that one day he shall pay for all the hurt that he has done to our family.' His eyes burned with the fierceness of an adult as he repeated the promise that his mother had instilled in him.

'Be avenged my son. Seek the ultimate justice that God demands.'

Halina watched and listened from the doorway. Shocked but subdued by the intensity of the child's hate and the utter commitment in his voice and stare. Without a word she quietly closed the door and left Lazar to his dreams of retribution for a wrong that she only dare guess at.

CHAPTER III

1975

The undercurrent of conversation barely rose above the muted sound of the continuous traffic on the road four floors below. Grey sombre suited men talked, read, or pondered on the outcome of the 22nd Annual General Meeting of the Global Publishing Company. It was the first meeting conducted by the new chairman and chief executive. Everyone was eager to assess this larger than life epitome of the 'godfather' to ailing businesses. Maximillian Holst was a byword in the publishing business. No one knew precisely where he had emerged from or where his origins were. He had simply appeared one day as the saviour of Comprehensive Publishing which had filed for liquidation in 1948. Like a tornado tearing its way through the scrub, his method of 'resurrecting' the company was swift and ruthless. Staff were discarded like confetti to the wind. Out of date machinery and systems were scrapped and eager creditors, who smelt the whiff of a larger payout than the pittance of the administrators, lent, leased, or sold at advantageous terms the necessary plant to continue. Not a penny was paid for these services, and no creditors were paid within the scheduled time. Only the bankers were kept sweet and every due loan repayment was met in full promptly. Within eighteen months the fortunes of the company had been turned and to all intents and purposes was trading profitably. Mysterious contracts with clients abroad were promulgated in all the media at regular intervals, forcing the share price to reach record levels. The investors made fortunes in the five years that the company flourished. Maximillian Holst made the most. He carefully unloaded chunks of shares secretly over a period of two months at the height of the share bonanza and finally resigned as Managing Director and Chairman in the summer of 1953 when the focus of the media was on the coronation of Elizabeth II. His passing was a nine line item on page two of the Financial Times.

Several companies and astute investments since 1953 had brought his name to the notice of the Fleet Street moguls as his notoriety spread throughout their ranks. Small publishing businesses and educational book agents all seemed to have a link with the all powerful network of vital components on which the industry depended. His method of ignoring the unions and demanding that his conditions be met, enabled him to undercut any competitor and streamline the businesses into economical units without the interference of 'the trade practices.'

A hush descended on the gathered throng as whispers floated from the back of the hall that a party was approaching the magnificent double regency style doors, placed exactly in the centre of the room to lead on to the red Arabian carpet running the whole length to the gigantic desk provided for the chairman.

Harrods had spared no expense in the decor of the room. A regular convention centre of the publishing magnate. His style was matched exactly by the ambience of the surroundings. Big. Brash. Opulent. Challenging. Undeniably expensive. Everything about the atmosphere spoke money. And power. Maximillian was all of these things. And he had obtained it all through his own efforts and guile from nothing.

He smiled the benign smile he reserved for his underlings when he was about to fire them. No one argued. His immense bulk and overpowering dominance reduced most men to subservience and acquiescence, even when their livelihood was being cast to the wind. His entourage in the luxurious lift smiled with him and Maximillian chuckled secretly at the obvious sympathetic affiliation to his mood. He did not like men who stood on their own two feet. He did not brook any contradiction of his edicts. These were men who would do his bidding. He was the head of his empire. What he said was law.

His Rolls Royce Camargue sat smugly on the two yellow lines outside the main door of Harrods, chauffeur in waiting. No traffic warden or policeman would interfere. MACH 1 was a registration that struck terror into mere mortals. It transcended all laws to which ordinary people had to adhere. Deep blue like his eyes. His own special colour, commissioned and approved with the factory in Crewe and matched perfectly by Rolls Royce's chief colour consultant.

Maximillian Alexander Carl Holst. A name conjured up from his gigantic ego to project himself on the gullible public of the television age. Only Carl had been retained from his correct name and even that had been usurped in his early days when whole families had been 're-named' by the Russian invaders. Maximillian because it typified his aura – 'all encompassing' like the original namesake who had a similar philosophy to his own. Contacts can gain more prestige and fortunes than honest hard graft. Hadn't this Maximillian acquired the Low Countries through his marriage to Mary of Burgundy in 1477 and married his son Philip to the heiress to the Spanish throne? He didn't have the advantage of the city of London and its vast financial opportunities, but he saw the way that power could be usurped.

Alexander, the greatest commander of them all. King of Macedonia and conqueror of the Persian Empire. Where was it now? Greece, Egypt and on to the Punjab. If he had lived he would have established the greatest empire known to man. Greater even than that of the British Empire, which had slowly crumbled under its Colonial burden. Not that Maximillian would have lived in the 4th century BC, he could only deal with the world at large, where the advantage of private jets and all the trappings of seemingly unlimited affluence opened gates to the highest conquerors in any country. That was what he regarded them as. Conquerors, like he was. Masters of the ruling classes. Not quite god, but god inspired. His assistant pushed open the heavily embossed golden decorated door to the chamber and with a dramatic change of the air circulating throughout the room, Maximillian strode, emperor like to the far end where his desk awaited him. The hush was almost reverential as all eyes followed his progress, none daring to catch his gaze for more than a second. His exquisitely tailored double breasted suit was cunningly designed to disguise his paunch body. To the onlookers he appeared like a mammoth gliding softly over the figured carpet as if his weight was suspended from above.

'Good afternoon gentlemen.' The voice spoke quietly in the dulcet tones of a predator. His forward stare took in every important member of the group. His deliberate seating plan enabled him to identify the front two rows of important or impertinent components of his audience.

'Let us begin shall we?' His disarming politeness infiltrated the taut expectancy hanging over the assembly and the visible relaxation was noted by the speaker with self congratulatory satisfaction. His opening statement of the fortunes and success of the company also comprised cleverly cloaked compliments on his own participation in the dynamic progress now evident from the reams of figures liberally scattered to the reporters at the far end of the room.

Accountant's report and several minor Head's of Divisions comments completed the formal business and as was the rule, the forum was thrown open to question. Several prominent financiers put questions specifically designed to bring out the fortunes of the company. His men had been briefed well, Maximillian nodded his pleasure.

'Can the Chairmen assure the people gathered here, and more importantly the rank and file shareholders, that his statement that the company will achieve a turnover of three to five billion pounds with comparative earnings per share to match in 4 years?'

The meeting was stunned. Several of the investors gathered recognised the significance of the question. A ninefold expansion of the present business in five years. No company could, or would, promulgate such a provocative statement without good grounds and figures with which to back it up.

Maximillian's face did not change. He waited for his lawyer, always at his side, to give him the cue. The small bespectacled man whispered for a few moments under cover of his hand and Maximillian's face broke into a condescending smile of apology. 'Unfortunately the Company Law forbids me from expanding on that question. We wouldn't want to breach the law would we?'

The questioner sat. He failed to see the problem of giving a verbal answer to his question when the promise was clearly printed in the glossy manifest held by every member present.

The auditors Alexander Cruickshank and Laing's notes had absolved them from commenting on the rash prophecy, sticking to the figures produced by Maximillian's accountants. They did not mention the highly inflated profit figure obtained by several inter company sales and fees for licences, not yet paid over. These companies, well known in the city were in one way or another owned by Maximillian or his nominees by means of several trusts set up in Liechtenstein where the exact influence in their conduct could not be established.

Another respectable figure rose from the ranks. 'I think the meeting has to be satisfied as to the authenticity of what we have been presented with today.' Maximillian again went into a huddle with his lawyer fearing another challenge to his integrity. 'It has been mentioned in the past that the present Chairman, who now sits before us, has not conducted himself in accordance with city laws and recognised practices. And for that misdemeanour he should not be seen fit to be in charge of a public company again.' The huge man's frame withdrew slightly and his eyes narrowed to black slits as he waited for the condemnation from this prominent financier bent on destroying all that he had built. 'Some may agree.' The man paused feeling all eyes centred on him as he calmly looked straight ahead at the bulky frame sitting behind the enormous desk like a black warlock controlling his minions. 'Most would not.' Maximillian breathed again. A slow imperceptible draught of air like a tyre deflating through its valve.

'Those of us who have followed Mr. Holst's career from the beginning will know instinctively that here is a man who will carry out his promises. Will achieve what he sets out to achieve. No matter that the city doesn't like it. They do not carry the overall responsibility or have the expertise to turn failure into profitability. Something that Mr. Holst has done again and again. No one should be in any doubt that this company will continue to grow. It has as its head the most versatile entrepreneur of them all. He cannot fail. If those of you managing pension funds and investment companies have not the faith in Mr. Holst that the majority have then they should themselves be considered not fit to run those enterprises.'

Maximillian Holst stood to acknowledge the polite applause and himself applauded the speaker as he resumed his seat three rows from the back of the chamber. 'Get me that man's name,' he said to his lawyer.

'I want to know where he gets his good sense from.' He was fully confident that he could have extricated himself from the situation but to have his credentials certified by someone other than a 'plant' was manna to his ears.

The Annual General Meeting concluded to enthusiastic applause and a euphoric aura of the fortunes of the company in the coming years. The price of its shares rose 45 pence to 368 pence, the highest point since floatation. No one in the city wrote of the doubtful points raised at the meeting.

'Get me all the financial information and background of West End Publishing Co. I also want the usual CVs on all its directors and the unofficial dossier on their extra marital activities and penchants. Names of union leaders and shop stewards and their weaknesses.' Maximillian rapped out his orders on his car phone as rapidly as a machine gun. He also expected answers just as swiftly. He was moving again to another prey. A company ripe for takeover and 'massage' in his own unique way to add to his growing conglomeration of 'successful' business enterprises.

He lit a cigar and leaned back into the sumptuous luxury of his Rolls, enjoying the sharp burning of the brandy recently dispensed from the mini bar in front of him. The cigar glowed in the shade of the dull blue interior, lighting the face of its owner from below. The full force of the evil therein was highlighted by the effect. The same effect most people perceived when they looked up at him from beneath his six feet four inch height. Not bad for a peasant, he mused. I am almost there. Not quite the foremost owner of the greatest communication network in the world, but soon. He puzzled why it had taken so long to achieve the impossible as many reporters put it. With his expertise and special way of persuasion, the goal should have been his before this. But try as he may he could not quite put his finger on why a great many of his 'deals' were thwarted at the last minute or stories leaked to his opponents causing the breakdown of negotiations. A whole army of confidantes were working for him to untangle the mysterious leaks to the press and temporary loss of respectability through some trumped up story. Completely untrue he lied to himself.

The cigar glowed again illuminating his thick bushy black eyebrows. The eyes beneath took on a fixed stare as the traffic on the Cromwell Road faded into a montage of foreign cars and surroundings. A side road appeared through the windscreen of his Mercedes, one of the few operating in war time Berlin. A present from one of his grateful 'customers.'

There was a fortune to be made on the black market as supplies dried up and essentials became non-existent. But more important matters were at hand. The Nazis were getting curious about his origins. Jealousy of his activities and the opulent lifestyle that he portrayed had focused their attention on this brash dealer in anything purchasable. Jews were being rounded up daily and disappearing to camps somewhere as far away as Poland. He must obtain a new identity before they discovered the truth. Werner Kawalek; he was the answer. The Rolls stopped at the usual traffic jam at the end of Cromwell Road. Drivers craned to see the occupant of car number MACH 1. Most knew of the flamboyant owner but had not seen him in the flesh. His mind was elsewhere, otherwise he would have acknowledged the envious stares.

Where were they now? he wondered. Werner and his family. He experienced no remorse or feelings of regret. If an opportunity presented itself, then you took it. If others suffered then they should have protected themselves better. It was fate. His freedom was threatened and so he had taken the only course open to him. Someone else had to lose their freedom. A cruel twist pulled his lips from the cigar and his tongue dampened the smooth exterior of his mouth to further savour the excellent taste of the green Havana. Just as he had done when he conceived his plan for escape from the Nazi witch hunt.

'Come in Carl. It is good to see you again.' Werner's greeting was always the same. He was always genuinely pleased to welcome guests to his comfortable house in Kronenberg Strasse, ten kilometres south from the city centre. 'Will you stay and have dinner with us?' Again the open invitation to all and sundry. You should pick your friends more carefully, Carl thought to himself.

'I should be delighted to sit with you and your family at your table.

There is always a delicious meal provided by your good wife. But I have not come specifically to gratify my appetite, demanding as it is. I have come to ask you a favour.' He paused for a moment, seeing no resistance only a query flit across the kindly eyes of his host. 'But the favour can wait. I smell a sumptuous meal being prepared. It is as if you were expecting me.' He laughed and clapped his friend on the back in his over exuberant manner and held out his arms to the two children who came running at the sound of his raucous outburst.

'Uncle Carl,' they shouted. 'You have come to see us again. What have you brought us this time?'

'Do not be so rude,' their father chastised them. 'You must not connect every visit with a gift. It is not seemly behaviour.'

'Nonsense,' roared Carl, 'if you cannot take advantage of every situation then you will not obtain your just rewards out of life.' His hands reached into his voluminous fur edged coat and produced two parcels. The children ran off shrieking with delight and excitement.

'Come Carl, I will pour you a drink. Schnapps?'

'Fine.' He settled himself on the enormous settee, an heirloom from Werner's grandmother and capable of holding more than Carl's tall frame. 'Have you had any visit from the party?' he asked casually as Werner handed him his drink.

'No, why should I?'

'Nothing, it's just that I understand that every household is to be visited.'

'Surely not. They are not after the likes of us; honest, true German citizens.'

Carl looked directly into Werner's slightly worried eyes tinged with a frown. 'But you are not are you?'

'What do you mean?' Werner suddenly felt himself under interrogation.

'Your wife for instance. She is not German. And you. Your origins are not Arian.'

'That does not mean that we do not support the German administration, wrong as it is at the moment. I may not agree with it, but there is very little that can be done by a mere publisher of textbooks.'

'Ah but there is. You have the power to speak to the people. To the Jews. To warn them to leave Germany before it is too late. Many of them still believe that the work camps are just that. Camps where people, mostly Jews, are sent to work for the glorious Third Reich.' Carl's voice rose in an imitation of one of Hitler's forceful diatribes at the enormous rallies that were now becoming a permanent fixture of the news.

Werner was taken aback by the force of Carl's seemingly tyrannical outburst. Was that maniacal menace in his eyes real or was he just making fun of the Fuhrer? The glass of brandy in his hand was shaking, but Carl's wasn't. Werner replenished both tumblers to cover his nervousness. 'What will you do?'

'Me?' Carl smiled and lit a cigar taken from his breast pocket. 'Why should I worry?'

'But you . . . you are a Jew.'

'Strictly speaking – yes. But I have not practised the faith for many years. In any case, I have good connections with the ruling forces in the government.' He waved his cigar to demonstrate. 'They need me more than they need to get rid of me. I am their contact with the Jewish nation in Berlin. They trust me.'

For the first time Werner felt a sense of apprehension in the presence of this man in front of him. Susan had warned him many times that he was not to be trusted or encouraged to come to the house. There was something inherently evil about him, she said. Charm and courtesy and all the attributes of a gentleman were there, but like a well camouflaged scorpion's lair, the sting was always beneath the surface.

'By the way, are your papers in order?'

Werner jumped again. Like he was part of an inquisition. 'Of course they are,' he said too abruptly.

Susan came into the room, and Carl rose immediately to kiss her hand in greeting. He knew she would never offer her cheek. 'What brings you here Carl?' she said evenly, never betraying with her eyes the contempt she felt for this man.

'Just a courtesy visit to my old friends,' he smiled looking down at her from his great height. 'And to ensure that they remain safe from this ever increasing threat to non desirables.'

'Non desirables? You sound as if you agree with what is going on.' Susan tried not to sound angry as she stood her ground and refused to shift her gaze from his piercing deep blue eyes. 'Just who are these "non desirables" as you call them?'

Carl resumed his seat and waved his cigar in an open gesture of resignation. A movement that would have immediately condemned him as a member of the Jewish race. 'I am for one; probably,' he said, again shrugging his acceptance of the position. 'Although I have lived in Germany for many years, my origins are in the Russian borderland before it was annexed and given to Czechoslovakia. We were never part of that country, as you know. Our race was declared a separate nationality, but we were deprived of our rights to live in equality with others.' Carl paused as if waiting for acquiescence from the others. 'But my papers are fine. I have ensured that no mention of my birth is recorded. As far as Germany is concerned I was born here and so were my parents.' He laughed out loud and proffered his glass for a refill.

'The bottle is empty. I will see if we have another,' Susan made her way to the cool cellar where cheeses and meat were stored in a vast underground pantry.

'Let me see your papers.'

'Why?'

'Because I wish to ensure that the authorities will find nothing wrong.' Carl's voice was urgent. Something of the urgency transposed itself into Werner as he opened his bureau and searched for the precious documents. 'I can see nothing that would arouse any suspicion. They are perfectly in order.' Werner's mind was not as composed as his voice as he showed the official papers to Carl.

The measured nod from his friend as he examined the small print dispelled the doubt that had begun to niggle his subconsciousness. 'There is one thing though,' Carl said.

The doubt returned. 'What?'

'Your wife.' He smiled at the confusion on Werner's face. 'She is English.'

'So?'

'Germany is at war with England. I take it she has never registered as a citizen of Germany?' Carl knew very well that Susan had retained her British nationality and still held a valid passport.

'No she hasn't. Does that make a difference?' Werner was more confused and beginning to panic. 'She has lived here nine years, long before the war started.'

'Yes, yes,' Carl consoled him. 'I am sure everything will be in order. It just needs to be confirmed that's all.'

'What do you mean, confirmed?'

'All papers need to have the official stamp of the local party to signify that they have approved the validity of the holders. That way they will not bother you when the house searches begin.'

Again Werner's heart missed a beat. He was not sure of his ground. 'How do we go about getting this stamp or whatever it is?'

'It is simple really. My friend at the Verwaitung will certify the papers, that is all the administration necessary.'

Werner thought for a moment. Before this man appeared this evening, everything was in order. Now there was grave doubt that his family was in danger. But why? The authorities knew of his English wife. And always had done. What had changed? He must protect them. 'Can you do this for us? How soon? What will it cost?'

'Cost?' Carl's laugh echoed down the cellar steps as Susan found the last bottle of Remy Martin from their French trip two summers ago. 'For you nothing. You are my friend. And what are friends for?'

Despite the bonhomie, Werner could not join in the mood of his companion. 'What will we have to do?'

'I will take your papers and have them stamped for you. I will have them back tomorrow. Do not worry. I have done it before for many of my Jewish compatriots.' He continued to examine the contents of the papers and the blue British passport bearing the young photograph of Susan.

'You said you had a favour to ask of me.' Werner glanced nervously at the tall dark man occupying most of the sofa, unsure if the favour to be asked would be within his power.

‘Oh yes. Just in case they, and you know who I mean by “they” start to investigate my background; no reason why they should you understand; my false papers in the name of Boris Vukadovic have been good enough to fool them so far. Just in case they do question their authenticity, I need a back up from a respected citizen, such as yourself to vouch for me. Would you do that?’ His innocent blue eyes bore all the appeal of a dog asking for a bone. Werner did not see the icy calculation beneath, only someone who was in trouble, or may be, someone who had just offered to help him out.

‘Of course. What would you want me to do?’

‘Oh nothing much. Just say that you have known me since schooldays and that I am who I say I am.’

‘Boris Vukadovic?’

‘Exactly. Sorry I haven’t told you about that before, but it doesn’t do to broadcast one’s aliases does it?’ The words rolled as smoothly off his tongue as the brandy had down his throat. The papers disappeared into the inside pocket of his expensive double breasted suit together with Susan’s passport.

‘By the way, don’t mention this to Susan, she may only get upset. I’ll have it all settled by tomorrow.’

Susan returned with the brandy and the remainder of the evening was spent in swapping old stories of life in the good years. Before this dread had entered their lives. Carl left just before midnight with a re-assuring nod to Werner that all would be well.

Maximillian’s Rolls Royce picked up speed as it entered the dual carriageway of the A3 to Portsmouth. He was now heading for the Surrey stockbroker belt as it was known. Where else could I possibly live? he asked himself. Unmarried, he had no use for women, only as a means of obtaining his ultimate goal, the power which would give him control of the world’s media. And then? Then he – . . . but that was in the future. He was enjoying the past.

He could hear again the splinter of the woodwork and the sound of breaking glass as the soldiers smashed the ornate front door of Werner and Susan Kawalek's home. The door literally jumped off its hinges as they burst in scattering precious ornaments and mirrors from the beautiful hallway. Susan's scream rang out to her children, asleep upstairs on the first floor. They were instantly awake. Werner Kawalek shouted his protests but they were ignored as he was roughly flung to one side to make way for the tall man bringing up the rear.

'Car… Boris! Thank goodness you are here. Tell them that they have the wrong house.' His pleas were ignored. Only the unemotional eyes of Carl Weiss fixed themselves on him with the ice cold impersonality of a cheetah stalking its prey.

'Papers!" The officer in charge bellowed his order at Werner. 'Where are your papers?'

'They… they.. er.. are…' Werner turned to Carl for help but he knew in that moment that if was futile. 'They will be in here.' Carl's forthright statement seemed incongruous in the charged atmosphere of the room as he turned to the bureau near the rear window. He didn't even ask for a key, was all Werner could think of, as the lid gave under the pressure of a borrowed bayonet. His antique desk was no longer antique. His grandmother's heirloom from her grandmother. Irreplaceable. The dark teak lid was ripped from its hinges as Carl frantically searched for the evidence. 'Here! Here they are! What did I tell you?' His crazed triumphant declaration was accompanied by a fistful of papers waved in the officer's face.

'But –' Werner's shout was cut short by a blow from the butt of a soldier's rifle and he crumpled at the feet of his wife. Susan was distraught. What was it all about? Why was Carl acting this way? Why had Werner called him Boris? She couldn't answer any of the questions, only hold Werner to her and pray that the children would try to hide.

The officer's face gleamed with supercilious satisfaction as he read the names denoted on the papers. 'Carl Weiss and Anna Weiss. You were right Boris. Right under our very noses. Take the Jewish scum away.' The last order was issued to the soldiers milling around the hallway, eager to cram the lorry waiting outside with another load of the hated race.

Susan's eyes spat venom as she glared at Carl or Boris or whatever his name was. She knew instinctively that it was useless to argue. His sardonic grin told her that it would be shouted down. He had used them. Like he had used so many before. The little bits of information that he had let slip in their meetings. They all made sense now. He had no allegiance to anyone. Only to himself.

'There's two more brats upstairs.' Susan's resolve broke. She begged him to save her children. They were innocent, as innocent as they were. Let them go to their grandparents, anywhere, but do not take them.

Carl Weiss kicked her hard in the stomach as she knelt beside her Werner. 'Upstairs. First floor. A boy and a girl.'

It was all over in less than ten minutes. One suitcase was allowed and the Werner's family were bundled into a dark green lorry whose engine was still running. It was as if time itself was hurrying their departure from their haven to a destination they could only guess at. Susan's anger was white icy cold. As cold as Carl's eyes had been. She took her son into her breast and told him of the evil of this man. This man who had betrayed them. Who had probably betrayed many more Jews. He'd 'helped' them hadn't he boasted? Now she knew his real intent. His real purpose. His own survival by whatever means he could employ. That is the man, she told her son, as the lorry jumped and lurched, who must never be allowed to forget his treachery. 'He is a Judas, he must be punished as God would punish all traitors to their own kind.' Why was he condemning his own race? His own people? Did he have no regard for his birth? The lorry sped away into the black night, into a void that would swallow up thousands more before the purge was finalised. The ultimate solution.

No shadow of regret or remorse passed across Maximillian's face as he pushed the button to operate the car window. Guildford's sentinel of a church rose from the hill and towered over the moving traffic below that paid no heed to the majesty of the edifice's dominance over the surrounding countryside. That should be me, he frowned, dominating all around. The press, the public, their thoughts, their allegiances, their absolute subservience to me. But it has not happened yet. Sixty one years old and his ambitions had not yet been realised. Why was he not accepted in the city? In the world of the media? Everything he had done had been as if Midas were at his side, until... three years ago. Three years in which he had seen his attempts to gain control of at least seven major companies thwarted by various means over which he thought he had control. But someone or some organisation was one step ahead at each stage of his delicate operations. He had dismissed it at first as just sheer bad luck, but lately the bad luck could not be put down to chance. There was a movement against him. Deliberately undermining his pronouncements of unrivalled success. Confidence in the city could only be sustained if the results backed up his proud boasts. They always did, he saw to that, or his accountants did, but always there appeared odd little doubts thrown into the smooth pool to ripple the surface. Like today. The query about his forecast for the growth in Global Publishing Co had been satisfactorily dealt with, but he knew that the item would appear somewhere in the financial press to mar an otherwise triumphant meeting. Scratching at him. Peeling an inch at a time. Needling him. Never letting him get to the next step in his quest for power. Who was behind it? No one from his past. He was unknown. No one knew his real name or his beginnings. Or did they?

He would start with the shareholders. It had to be someone with a vested interest in the success or the downfall of the company. He picked up his telephone and rapped out a stream of rapid orders to his secretary in Maximillian House, Sloane Square. A full list of every shareholder with their addresses and date of purchase and holdings. Recent sellers and recent purchasers. 'When do you require this information for sir?'

'Now!' He slammed the telephone down on its rest and noticed for the first time in his life that his hand was shaking. Not with rage, but an inner feeling that his secure life and dreams of an empire were beginning to crumble.

Peter Mallory caught the 10.43pm train out of Kings Cross station with ten minutes to spare. On the towering wall at the junction end of the station the great clock hand jumped to the seventeen minutes to eleven dot on its circumference and the carriage moved smoothly away from platform three. He would not be in Warrington until early morning, but he consoled himself with the thought that he would be sleeping contentedly for the next three hours. Maximillian Alexander Carl Holst would not.

CHAPTER IV

1976

A thin line of dribble oozed its way down the ample chin of the large man sitting motionless at his desk in the corner. The black coffee found its way on to his bulging waistcoat to join the clotted ash from his recent cigarette still smouldering in the ashtray. A present from his staff on his fifty third birthday. His initials were in bright blue on the aluminium plate. G.R.P. George Reginald Parker. The Reginald had been inserted by his mother as an afterthought to avoid being confused with a doctor. Now his minions had twisted the intitials into "grope." He would have preferred the doctor bit.

His full Stalin like mustache gave him the air of a comedian, although most of his witticisms were lost to all but those on his wavelength. It twitched now, like it did whenever he felt the slight tingle of something that he could not quite grasp but knew was there to be grasped. Or groped, he muttered with a wry grin.

'Not going home George?'

He turned to see his first assistant swinging his jacket expertly in an arc to catch the hole of the left hand sleeve and secure the button about his midriff in one easy movement.

'I'll not be long. You go.'

'I am. On a bit of a promise.' George looked up with his usual frown of disapproval specially reserved for the younger generation. 'Well, you know how it is. I can only keep them at bay for so long and then I have to give in.'

George watched as the young man scuttled for the door, chortling at his audacity to his boss. The ash on the waistcoat was dissipated on to George's trousers as he joined in the merriment and shook his head in admiration. Then he turned his attention to the sheet in front of him.

Something was wrong. Or rather, something was too right. All the figures and calculations that he had been working on for nine months all added up to the same conclusion. It was all too perfect. Like when a gambler throws a dice nineteen times and scores every time. It just did not happen. But it was happening.

'I'm missing something,' he breathed into his coffee as more found its way to join the permanent stains on his waistcoat. He rose and strolled to the window to look out over the vast array of slated rooftops stretching as far as the Thames and beyond to the gentle slopes of the Oxfordshire countryside in the distance.

Two hours later he was disturbed by the cleaner clanging her bucket against the metal desks as she swabbed the tiled floor. Blasted modern metal, swore George. Wouldn't have happened in the days of wooden desks. Great teak edifices that gave solidarity to his profession. A sign of permanence and security. That was all going along with the old doctrines and practices.

'You still here sir?' said the cleaner in an obvious statement of fact. 'Aint you got no 'ome to go to?' The same observations, delivered in the same dry caustic fashion over the past six years or so, had become so much a part of his working life that he had developed a set reply. 'Yes. And no.'

'Shame. Shouldn't 'appen to a saint.'

George laughed and the cleaner laughed with him. It was true that he had no 'home' as such to go to. Only a rented flat, or half house in Haslemere Surrey. It suited his purpose. Plenty of room for his books and his vast collection of newspaper cuttings, articles, and leading comments from all the classier publications.

He lit another cigarette and contemplated the printouts scattered over his large desk. Quarterly summaries of the past five years charges and interest applied to the accounts of the National Bank's customers. He was used to printouts. They told him a great deal about people's accounts, bank profits, and the huge sums shifting like sand from one source to another. Not like the old days. He could examine one customer's account and tell you his life story. How often he ate out. How often he bought a present for his wife. Or his lover. His bookie. His personal habits. His integrity. His honesty. Anything you needed to know about someone was discernable from the amounts and payees on his current account statement. Now the statements were all numerical. No names, No give aways. It took longer to ascertain the spending habits and irregularities that did not belong to a 'routine' statement.

George liked his job. Chief Fraud Officer. It payed sufficient to cover his liking for good food and fine wine. Very little else needed the ample salary he earned. And he did earn it. No set times for the union to argue over. He worked as long or as short as he felt necessary. The bank appreciated what he did and there was no one better in the city to trace small or large frauds or sheer incompetence.

'Goodnight sir.'

'Goodnight. Sleep tight.' George waved his farewell to the cleaner as she packed away her materials and brush before catching the 8pm tube to Golders Green. George would be a while yet. Nice man, she thought. Always has been. A sort of quiet charm that endears you to him despite his untidy habits and his smoking. Bit like my Arnold really.

The outer door banged and the quiet settled over the lone man studying the items in front of him. His thoughts once again mulled over the irritating facts that stared him in the face. There was nothing missing from the bank's figures. No one had reported a loss of income or a sudden explosion of expenses. So why was he so involved and so certain that something was amiss? A hunch. They had more often than not proved reliable in the past. The bank had the evidence in the form of numerous files on the inside and outside frauds and deceptions that he had successfully pursued to the bitter, and more often disquieting end.

There was only one way to approach this, he concluded. With factual figures. It would be a painstaking task for one of his assistants, but somebody had to do it didn't they? That's what they were paid for. The graft bit.

George Parker left his empty tower of a Fraud Office and made his way to the ground floor via the stairs. He abhorred lifts but with fourteen flights to climb he had no alternative but to allow the lift to transport his sixteen stone bulk up to his office, whenever he visited it, but he needed the exercise of walking down the stone stairs.

Time for something to eat. The best part of the day. The time when he could really do his thinking. Tucked away in the corner of his favourite French restaurant just off Regent Street, he ordered a well done sirloin steak with onion rings, and fries, with a mushroom sauce. He knew that Bertand would cook it to perfection and that he would be left to enjoy it in complete isolation. A bottle of 1970 Chateau Haut Batailley raised the steak to its succulent best. The wine was not at its peak but he drew the line at the 1961, a superb vintage, but far too expensive for this particular meal. He hadn't anything to celebrate yet, but when he had . . .

With the last glass of the excellent fifth growth Bordeaux sitting on his palate, he wiped his mouth, called for a pot of coffee and pondered his problem. Or the bank's problem. That there was a problem he had no doubt. Just as he had prophesied many times in the past, when overlings had cast doubts on his judgement of seemingly innocent and upright employees. He could smell deception. The little signs shouted out to him. The attitudes. The glib phrases. He did not like it but it was his job. Besides the persons involved were cheats and he disliked cheats even more than exposing them.

'More coffee Mr. Parker?'

'Er, no thank you Bertand. Keep me awake.' He laughed as the restaurateur deftly wiped the table cloth and replaced the full ashtray with a gleaming clean glass wedge.

Could be pure crystal, like the one in the manager's office seven years ago. He could see him now in his perfectly cut suit and hand tailored shirt, proudly pushing the cut glass ashtray in his direction as ash started to fall from his cigarette. It was only a routine inspection, or so the manager thought. For all intents and purposes, a normal inspection would be carried out, but George would dig a lot farther than the 'tickers' and the overseers of correct system application. George had smelled something fishy, or out of 'cinque' from a review of the achievement figures for the various areas throughout the country. Anything out of the ordinary made George suspicious. People do act out of character occasionally, but not consistently. Suddenly a branch in the North West Area had risen up the league table in Personal Loans. Both in numbers and total lent. The town itself did not aspire to any great increase in wealth or spending power or commercial activity, so why should the branch's customer's suddenly desire to spend beyond their means?

'How long have you been here David?' George used the manager's christian name. It always made them feel secure.

'Two years. Yes almost two years.'

'You've done rather well haven't you? George's smile accompanied the compliment.

'I suppose I have yes. It hasn't been easy, but with the right approach to my customers, I am achieving my targets in most categories. The results speak for themselves.'

'Especially the Personal Loans.'

'They've done rather well haven't they.' A slight movement in the manager's mouth spoiled the smile that should have confirmed his words.

'Tell me David. Do you gamble?'

'No.'

'Drink?'

'In moderation.' His hand shook slightly as he slid them beneath the desk that separated him from George.

The big man sat back in his chair, lowered his eyes to David's and said quietly, 'then it must be a woman.'

There was no argument. The veneer of confidence disappeared as quickly as the smooth surface of a pond in a rainfall. 'How did you know?'

'The pattern of the accounts. Every one of the Personal Loans that you have opened in fictitious names, some of them may be real I grant you, have been perfectly conducted. There isn't an office in the country where there wouldn't be one slip up in the monthly repayments. Each Personal Loan is backed up by a current account whose only income is a similar amount to that required to service the loan each month. People are not like that. They forget. They pay in late.'

'It was too perfect?'

'Yes. Your management of the accounts was too well done.' You should have acted like a customer and not a bank manager.'

George produced the seventeen rogue Personal Loan accounts and confirmed them all to be the invention of the manager. Each one funded by the opening of a further account, then another and so on. 'There would have to be a time when it would be impossible to sustain the ever increasing borrowing wouldn't there?'

'I suppose so. I just got involved and then it couldn't stop.'

'One other thing,' said George in his best advisory manner. 'When you book a hotel for the night, don't use your cheque book. Use cash.' He produced the manager's cheques payable to the Adelphi Hotel Liverpool over the past six months. George stubbed his final cigarette out in the already full ashtray, nodded his goodnight and made his way to the station for the tedious journey to Haslemere.

Glad I'm not involved with women, he puffed as his legs strained to propel his bulk over the gantry to platform three. They are always at the root of trouble, as if that were their purpose in life. His round, full of life, overcaring mother had warned him many times to be on his guard. 'They'll take all your independence away if you don't watch them. If you must have a woman, start as you mean to go on. As master of the household. Your dad did, and I was never happier. All this nonsense about women's rights. Has it made them happy? Has it heck as like.'

He smiled as he recalled the Wigan vernacular punching through her forthright views. She was right of course. He'd never seen his dad chastise his mother. Or his mother, his dad. Only in fun. Each knew where to draw the line. A trait that many of his fraudsters could adopt. They always went too far and that was when he caught them.

Peter Mallory noticed the letter from Inspection Department on the Administration Manager's desk as he popped in to collect the circulation file. The usual courtesy of advising the Manchester Office of the arrival of a team of inspectors at the Bank's main computer centre in Cheshire had been dutifully carried out.

Nothing out of the ordinary in that, he thought. But it will take more than a team of untrained personnel in computer technology to make any sense of the complex operations at Kidthorpe.

'Hello. Can I speak to Mrs. Mallory please?'

'What extension is she on?'

'Three one two, I think.' Peter could never remember the number and usually spoke to someone else in the section before reaching his wife.

'Wendy Mallory speaking. How can I help you?'

'No need for the official jargon Wendy, it's Peter. Just thought I'd let you know that the inspectors are on their way to you, probably downstairs now.'

'Yes, we've heard. Everyone's running around like scared rabbits. Never seen such a fuss. Suddenly tidiness is the in thing. The office doesn't look real or worked in.' She laughed and blew a kiss before embarrassing him with bed talk before she rang off.

The gentle sweep of her dark silky hair brushed her shoulders with the same effect as a breeze disturbing the trailing fronds of a willow to let in the sun in a streak of metallic light. Her smooth neck and partly bare shoulders were not lost on George Parker as he walked along the green carpeted corridor towards the office of the Director of Computer Services, an old friend.

'Good to see you again George. Coffee's ready.'

George acknowledged the handshake and the welcome cup of coffee and raised his eyebrows in an unspoken request to smoke. Charles Lofthouse opened the box on his desk and indicated that George should join him.

'Anything I should know about George?' The Director's query was friendly but a certain defensiveness showed through. If George was part of the inspection team, then it was no routine inspection. He had learnt that over the years and had been glad to co-operate to ensnare some miscreant through his system. Usually their confidential exchanges were conducted by telephone or letter. Very rarely did George uproot himself from his southern surroundings to travel north to his domain.

'Must be fairly big to bring you out of hibernation in the smoke.'

George blew a great draught of blue smoke toward the window overlooking the green sweeping fields of Cheshire, admiring the different hues in full colour. 'I don't know. I've never met one like this before. If there is one.' He looked at Charles and adjusted his seat to face him squarely across the desk. 'Deep down I know there is something amiss. Some quirk in the system that is being used by a clever operator, or an incompetent programmer who has set up a waste disposal unknowingly.'

'I don't really follow you George. Are any funds missing?'

'No. That's the clever part of it. If that had been the case then I would have been on to it like a shot. There would have been a trail to follow; you know the routine; and someone would have been identified. To tell you the truth Charlie, I'm stumped.' He paused reflecting on his thought processes. 'For the moment.'

'What do you want me to do.' Charles knew better than to argue with George about his hunches. He was dog persistent in his methods and no one would escape examination. Many departures from the bank's strict code of practices had been unearthed in the pursuit of another's follies. Illegal betting. Liaisons with married staff. Part time jobs and all manner of small indiscretions.

'I want a full list of all personnel whom you would consider capable of beating the system. The sophisticated system that is. The real computer whiz kids, as they call them. I shouldn't think that there will be too many of them would you?'

'Shall I include myself?'

'No. You're too old.'

Peter and Wendy poured themselves another drink from the litre bottle of Frascati as they meticulously listed the balances from the array of Building Society pass books in front of them. Further lists of share holdings in Nominee Company names were piled to one side. The seventeen books of Building Society investments totalled £223,476.98. The value of the stockholding in various companies was more difficult to calculate. 'Taking the middle price in the Financial Times this morning, I consider that our total investment portfolio is worth £23.4 million.'

Wendy let out a slow gasp of astonishment. 'But that is impossible. We didn't pay anything like that for the shares.'

'It is nearly six years since the operation started and the growth has been phenomenal. The companies in which we have invested have shown the type of expansion that only gamblers could contrive. Or crooks.' Peter smiled grimly at Wendy. And we know which of those is responsible don't we.'

Peter went on to show Wendy how the differing and improving methods which the bank used to calculate interest and commission had all added to the regular 'creaming off' of the surplus. All interest calculations, both debit and credit were now being rounded off to the nearest 5p. While commission was rounded off to the nearest 25p. A vast expansion on the original margins on decimalisation. Now the fraction that was 'lost' in the millions of pounds of interest and commission was being applied to Peter's secret account quarterly with the main charges and daily as the bigger and more lucrative accounts were charged for miscellaneous services. In addition the foreign and arbitrage departments were showing vast profits on currency deals and the large swings in the exchange rate were providing sums beyond even the estimates that Peter had hoped for.

'Take the change in your pocket. If you have say – thirty three coins and I remove one, you wouldn't know would you?'

'I would if I had counted them.'

'But you haven't counted them have you? The bank does not know the extent of its interest and commission earnings in advance. Only estimates in their forward budgets. If it expects seventy five million pounds in interest and only gets seventy three million, the margin of expectancy is within the forecast perimeters.'

'How much are we making each year?'

'Difficult to tell. Just as the bank could not tell until after the event. But last year I calculate that our total income from bank sources was something in the order of 5.6 million pounds.'

Wendy gasped again. She had been used to seeing the movement of sums beyond her wildest imagination during her spells on the investment section of the computer complex, but this was unbelievable. 'And no one can trace this?'

'No. All funds are held in Nominee company names, registered in Liechtenstein. I have taken a leaf out of our adversary's book. It has worked superbly well for him. But that will end won't it?' Peter looked hard into the dark pools of Wendy's admiring eyes. 'Soon we shall begin his humiliation and destruction. But not until he has the ultimate prize almost within his grasp. I want him as high as possible, within a fingertip of the summit. Then I will smash him down to the level where he belongs. And I will be there to see it happen. For my father. For my mother. For my sister. And for all those innocents who were betrayed by this inhuman monster.'

Wendy held him closely as the tears squeezed out of the corners of his unblinking eyes. She knew that he was incapable of killing another human being, but the destruction that he had planned for Maximillian Holst would be unequalled, even in the death camps of Auschwitz.

'Goodbye George. See you in three years time.'

'You'll see me before then, I can promise you that.' George Parker shook his old friend's hand warmly as if to convey his loyalty despite the underlying threat that something was amiss at the centre. 'Thanks for the list and the profiles of your staff. They will remain confidential between us. No one, not even my lot, will have access to them until, or if, I have reason to proceed further.'

'Knowing you George, I would rather bank on the "until" than the "if."'

George laughed. He would have tended to agree with his friend at the outset of his investigation, but after months of seeking answers to vague questions, questions that had no substance; there was nothing missing; he still had no concrete evidence to put before the Board of Directors. That he had to present his case sooner or later, he had no doubt. He could not justify his time by unsubstantiated hunches or theories. He needed one lead. Just one and he could convince them that it was worth following up. At the moment he had nothing.

The fresh air after the close confines of the humidified atmosphere of the centre alerted his mind to the subject of food. But before then he had one check to make on the adjacent car park.

The gatekeeper touched his peaked cap at the sight of George's identification card and allowed him through into the general car park. Twenty minutes later he touched his cap again as the large man returned. 'Find what you were looking for sir?'

'No. Not really. All look alike to me,' he said, a half grin on his face covering the disappointment of his search.

'Bloody narks. Want to mind their own business,' muttered the gatekeeper under his breath as he watched George Parker amble to the executive car park to pick up his Triumph 2000, a car he had refused to swap for a bank vehicle. "Not big enough or comfortable enough," he had told them. "Not big enough for his ash tray," the bank's vehicle department had concluded.

Nice part of the world, mused George, as he drove at his customary 35 miles an hour through the leafy country lanes to Knutsford for lunch. I'll return here one day, he realised, when I retire. When I solve this damn puzzle. If I can't find the method, I'll start looking for the person. Or persons. Something of this magnitude must take more than one mustn't it? Collusion. That's what usually brought them down. One can keep his calm and his nerve. Two and the chances were halved of getting away with it. What did his old Inspector used to say to him thirty years ago? "If a man can't handle one account, he damn well can't handle two". This was his answer to managers who insisted on opening a number two account for customers whose original account had got into trouble. Very soon, both accounts were in a mess.

The rack of lamb and Beaujolais Villages did nothing to improve his frustration at the outcome of his morning's work. The car park had revealed nothing unusual or expensive, the first sign of affluence beyond the normal income of employees of the bank. Searches of the employees accounts had also revealed nothing out of the ordinary. Only the usual array of loans and mortgages, hard up youngsters, and struggling family members. Some could do with further investigation for minor transgressions of the rules, but that was the job of his minions still working on the routine inspection process.

His friend Charles had been the most help. His own assessment of his staff would prove invaluable to his further research. Seventeen "whiz kids" – some no older than 21, others approaching their thirties. None apparently living a life style over and above that of their income. Nine married, eight single. Twelve male, five female. George wasn't chauvinistic, but why was that he thought? Females are always better at the technological side, so why was there a preponderance of males in the top echelon of the programmers?

Of the married staff, Charles hadn't noted any marital problems. There were far more problems with the single employees. The high performers who seemed to want to excel at all things. Charles' had almost made George blush with some of the stories. But that wasn't against the law. Or the bank's rules and regulations. Good luck to them, chuckled George, with no jealousy or envy. He thought he detected a slight begrudging tone in Charles attitude. Perhaps he was just old fashioned. Or just old, he told him again.

George ran through the names again. Paul Alcott, 24, brilliant innovator of new ideas. Possibility. No political leanings. No aspirations to high office as yet. No sexual entanglement – one night stands were the order of the day to match his effusive energy and not detract from his polarised concentration on his current project, whatever that may entail at the centre.

Brian Coleman, 25. Quiet, studious, and a book lover. No girlfriends, and no girlfriends chasing him.

Daphne Tullit, 22. Vivacious and knew it. A flower that most young virile males would want to disbud, but no one knew if anyone had. George suspected they had not. She was inherently innocent under her guise of the femme fatale.

Several others bore no outward signs of discontent. An attribute that could usually be associated with defrauding the bank. But that occurred mostly in the lower earners, or the comparatively lower scale of income depending on their commitments.

His cigarette had burned its last ash in his fingers as George rifled through the cards again. The stub joined the others in the ashtray as he idly separated his prime suspects – although he had nothing whatsoever to judge them on – from the ones that he felt were not in the running.

Four main contenders for the fraud of the century. Three single, one married. Two male, two female. That's fair, he thought. Won't be accused of being a sexist when I finally come to present my case to the Board. His laugh caught the attention of several of the guests, drowning their large appetites with after dinner brandies. It's an afternoon of hard graft sorting through the information and files, George muttered. Compiling graphs and trends and relationships of figures. Somewhere in the maze of data and backgrounds of the people involved was the answer. That was supposing that he had the people involved, and that wasn't certain.

A room had been set aside for him in the North West Regional Office where there was ample space to view his documents. The lift to the fifth floor was busy with traffic. The fourth floor was the financial division, a place that he would visit in due course.

'Cup of coffee sir?'

George looked up from beneath his bunched eyebrows. His mustache spread along his lip to enhance his smile. 'That would be very nice. Thank you.'

The young slip of a girl, grinned at him and skipped cheekily out of the office to fetch him his beverage. 'No respect for the elderly any more,' crossed his mind. 'But I'm not elderly and she did show respect.' Deference. Yes that was a better word. No deference for his position. But it didn't annoy him as it would others. She was cheerful and probably didn't know him from Adam. She returned with a steaming cup of coffee in a larger cup, almost like a soup bowl.

'Thought you'd like a big one,' she said. 'Nothing in those silly little cups is there?' George had to agree and nodded his thanks to her departing rear.

'Just a minute, young lady.'

The sixteen year old came back to stand before his desk. Eyes agape.

'If you had more money than you could imagine, what would you do with it?'

'How would I get that sort of money?'

'Supposing you could. What would you do?'

'Go on a world cruise, I suppose.' She started to mentally spend this unexpected windfall.

'Over and above that sort of thing. You know, money way beyond your dreams. Where could you spend it?'

'Oh you couldn't spend it sir. You'd have to give it away. Or do something useful with it. Charities and that sort of thing.' Her face took on the concentrated thought of dispensing all her wealth to all the organisations she could think of. The cheeky grin reappeared, 'Have you won the pools or something sir?'

'No young lady. But someone has. Thanks for your comments ... and the coffee.'

'Out of the mouth of babes,' George breathed. The girl had concurred with his own thoughts on the subject, but which had not formed the main part of his conjecture. He was too involved in the centre of it. He hadn't viewed it from an outsider's point of view. Until now.

Funds of the size that he suspected were involved would have to be put somewhere. But where? Charities, as the girl had suggested. He would check. Savings? National figures for various institutions would give him an indication of larger movements than normal for the times of the year. Investment. Yes, that was it. Money on this scale would have to find its way into financial markets. Bonds, shares, Government securities. Abroad? No returns were always made if substantial amounts left these shores, and vice versa. A word with the bank's stockbroking arm would not go amiss.

George's afternoon was filled with routes to pursue and various routine investigations along the lines of exit of funds from the National Bank. Who, how, and where?

Going down in the lift to the ground floor, George noticed a tall, lean, dark haired individual, talking to his companion. Definitely not English, he surmised. The dark complexion and brooding eyes were out of the silent movies. Another of George's passions. Talkies spoilt it all. No one listened to the words anyway. Expression was what it was all about. Conveying a thousand thoughts with a movement of the mouth or a flicker of the eyelids.

'Goodnight Mr. Mallory.' The lift emptied at the ground floor and each went their separate ways. George's mind clicked instantly on the name shouted over the shoulder of the departing employee to the dark man at his side.

Mallory. Wendy Mallory. The name on one of his 17 cards. Husband and wife. Nothing unusual in that. But a financial and computer 'marriage.' That could be a very dangerous combination. For the bank.

Entering the lift again he pressed the button for the third floor. Personnel Department. Showing his pass card, he made for the files of the Financial Division. Mallory. Peter Mallory. Husband of Wendy Mallory and Assistant Chief Accountant.

'Where is the photostat machine please?' His request brought a response from the nearest clerk who pointed out the location as she left for the door.

Peter Mallory's full background, educational qualifications, and normal data were copied and stuffed untidily in George's bag. The contents of the file would form the basis of George's first research into Mr. Peter Mallory. His undercover 'gossip' gathering would supply him with the extra dressing with which to garnish the basic facts.

Three days later, George Parker was fairly certain that he had the perpetrators of whatever was going on. All he had to do now was to find out why? How; only interested his analytical mind. The purpose behind the big frauds were always more fascinating than the methods.

'Clive?'

'Yes.'

'It's George. George Parker. I wonder if you and I could get together some time? I've rather a good one this time and I believe that you could be of some assistance.'

Clive Farnworth of the Metropolitan Fraud Squad smiled at the invitation. He liked nothing better than swapping stories with his counterpart at the National Bank. 'Where shall we meet?'

'Is it your treat or mine?'

'Mine I think. Does that mean, you choose the venue and I pay?'

'You've got it in one. No wonder they made you Chief of Staff.' George's chuckle echoed in the police chief's ear as he replaced the receiver and ran his finger down the list of his favourite restaurants in London. Chequers. That was the one. A favourite haunt of the elite of the city. Where the talk of 'big money' was as commonplace as sitting in on a game of Monopoly.

George booked the table for two. The Maitre D' recognised his voice and confirmed the table in the corner where they usually sat. Gaston reviewed his booking list for the evening. He was fastidious in his arrangement of the seating of guests to his establishment so as to preserve the air of privacy and individuality. No, he smiled in satisfaction, that wouldn't interfere with the party of ten at the next table scheduled for half an hour later. George and his companion from Scotland Yard would have no objection to sitting at the next table to Maximillian Holst, or he to them.

CHAPTER V

1945

'Germany has surrendered to the Allies!' Halina's excited shout echoed throughout the tall rooms and was repeated by everyone in earshot as they took up the chant. She looked out of the neatly curtained window of her lounge and saw the May blossom and the beech trees and birds and people glow with the euphoria of being alive on this day of all days. The day that no one thought would ever come. The day to remember how it used to be. Would it ever be the same again? Halina prayed and thanked God that her children and her husband were all safe. She remembered also the many whose children and husbands were no longer here. Whole families lost in the wilderness of the nazi extermination camps. She thought of Lazar, a fine young man of eleven, and as loving a son as her own. He would also celebrate with them, but it would be a muted celebration. He would remember his father and mother and his little sister Taghi. 'Is it really all over mama?' Lazar's small voice spoke from beside her.

'Yes. It is all over. This is going to be the finest Spring ever. Even the buds on the chestnut trees are bigger and more beautiful. The apple blossom shines like it has never shone before. The whole world is celebrating.'

'Then I must go to Berlin.'

Halina did not hear Lazar's determined statement at first, her heart and her breath were too busy catching up with reality. Everything was twenty centimetres above the ground. Her feet jumped and stomped as if she were treading a red hot coal path. Three of her children joined her at the window, kissing and whooping. They had spent so many years when enjoyment had been stifled that they shouted until Halina thought they would never stop.

'Ssshhh my children. We have the rest of our lives to be a family again. We shall have parties and dinners. Trips to the parks. Holidays by the lake.' It was too much. Too much to consume in one moment. They all cried in happiness and hope. Lazar watched from the perimeter of the group, happy for them and happy that the war was over. Now he could return to his quest. He would wait until the evening to tell Halina that he was going to Berlin. To find his aunt Anna. To find a base. To find the man whose face was emblazoned in his memory like a hot poker etching on wood.

He did not get to Berlin. No trains were available. The city was in ruins and no person in their right mind was going to Berlin. It streamed refugees, bombed out of their homes, nothing left of their streets, nothing left of their memories. Empty, like the whole area of rubble, infested with rabbit warrens where the remains of what once was Berlin's population, now lived and died.

'You must stay with us until we can contact someone in Berlin who can tell us what has happened to your house, to your auntie. To anyone who you can remember from your life there.' Halina did not sound too hopeful but in her heart she knew that Lazar would not be put off. She had seen the resolve in his eyes. Eyes that had only love for her but a hate that lurked in the retina for the man responsible for the death of his family. No love on earth could assuage that emotion, try as she had. Perhaps it is better that way, she had concluded. The child cannot grieve until he has fulfilled his promise to his mother. God help the recipient when that time comes, she muttered as she dutifully crossed herself.

The next morning Lazar's bed was empty. A small suitcase and his clothes were gone also. Staszek did all he could to trace him. The railway station, the bus terminus, neighbours, the postman. No one had seen a small boy with a suitcase. The police could not, or would not, look for him. Thousands of refugees and lost souls were wandering throughout Prague. What chance had they of locating one boy among so many?

One month later Halina received a letter from Bad Durkheim. It was from Lazar. All was well and he was living with the neighbours of his family's holiday home on the outskirts of the spa town. It had not been affected by the war. It had no significance in the political sphere so had escaped relatively untouched. With the exception of regular collections for the war effort, its people lived quietly and unobtrusively apart from the rest. Big shows of solidarity for the Third Reich were made if the military visited, the mayor having devised a plan to sustain the villagers and all agreed that to comply on the surface was the best ploy and in all their interests. Most did not want the war. Did not know what it was about. Most had lost their fine sons. All that remained were the elderly parents and grandparents and the small children. The children must be protected from this evil. They had a future. What future, no one dare guess.

Lazar and his family had always been welcome before the war. Now they had the only remaining son who had returned to them, alone and needing their help. They gave it unreservedly.

Halina cried in gratification that her 'son' was safe. She had never had any doubt, but her mother's instinct made her fret for the cherubic faced individual who had so influenced their lives. Lazar's neat handwriting apologised for the way that he had left them. 'I know you would never have let me leave on my own,' he explained. 'And papa could not have spared the time to take me where I wanted to be.' The tears smudged the copperplate letters into a blur of blue, as she dabbed at the corner of her eyes in happiness and wanting.

"I shall always love you and papa. You are my family now. I promise I shall return one day, give my love to Geonek and Georg and Teofil and Lisa. I shall miss them very much. God bless you all." Lisa cried most of all. He was her favourite. He didn't tease her like her brothers. He was kind and gentle.

'A gentle man,' she said. 'That is what the word means. And my Lazar is a gentleman.'

Halina and Staszek laughed and hugged her. She was so mature and matter of fact. Lazar had taught her that. He had spent long hours talking to her of his own sister and their happy times before the war. He was her hero. He had escaped from the nasty Germans hadn't he? 'Will he come back one day mama?'

'If he says he will, then he will darling.' And Lisa slept contentedly for the first time since Lazar had left them.

The hills to the west were in the full flush of summer. Greens and blues and browns and every shade between. It was as if they were rejoicing in the peace that had settled on the village. A mantle of freedom and smiles and openness blossomed with nature. Three sons returned. One was a cause for thanksgiving. Three out of forty two was more than they had dared hope for. They remembered the thirty nine still missing. Life smiled a little brighter in the hamlet of Bad Durkheim.

Lazar fused into the community rapidly. He excelled with the local harvesting, matching the colour of autumn leaves before they released their last grip on life and gave way to the wind that shuffled them into pockets of shelter under the hedges. His face shone and his muscles hardened faster than the tiny saplings beneath the sycamore trees.

'Where is Lausitz auntie?' Lazar's question took Anna by surprise. He very rarely asked questions. He preferred to find out for himself. He must have a reason.

'I have no idea. Southern Germany I think. Nearer to us than Berlin probably.' Anna had an intuitive feeling that the conversation was leading to something more significant that the whereabouts of a town in Germany. She had learnt to gauge Lazar's motives over the past few months since she had joined him at the holiday home. Where else should she go when Berlin was crumbling all around her. She had been lucky. She had escaped just before the final onslaught. Goodness knows what the Russians would have done to her. She had heard terrible stories of atrocities and carnage. Bad Durkheim was a godsend. Memories of sharing the house with Werner and Susan during the long hot summers were all that she could hold on to. Now they were no more. They only lived on through their son Lazar, fast growing into a replica of his father. Tall and slim. Dark and handsome. His flashing, almost black eyes, turning from tenderness to steel in the blink of a swallow's dive.

'I am going there.'

Again that calm statement of fact issuing from the mouth of a baby. But the determination behind it was matured in the days of 1941 – something that accentuated the growing process a hundredfold and aged children through a generation before their time.

It was no use disagreeing with Lazar. Anna could only hope to persuade him to wait. For whatever his purpose in going was. 'Why do you want to go to Lausitz? How will you get there? Will you come back?'

'Lausitz is where my father stored his books. We have a warehouse there. I saw the name on many of his papers. He took me there once. It was the biggest bookshop I have ever seen. I have to go.'

'Do you think it will still be there? Surely the . . . ' Anna wanted to say Germans or Nazis, but felt embarrassment at the distinction – they were all one weren't they? 'Surely the authorities would have commandeered it – like they did everything else.'

'I have to see. Now that the war is over, someone should go and claim the property. There was a notice in the newspaper in the village that a special commission has been set up to establish ownership . . . and title, . . . I own it now don't I?'

'Yes, you do.' Her heart went out to him. This man in boy's clothing. This small being who had put aside childish things. Too soon, she moaned.

'Will you come with me Anna?'

Anna blanched at the idea of returning to that other world. Where death and disappearance was commonplace. Where neighbour didn't speak to neighbour. The nightmare of thousands living in isolation. 'When do you propose to go?'

Anna was desperately seeking time to dissuade him. To put it off until . . . when?

'As soon as possible. It is now five months since the war ended. The Russians occupy Berlin. If Lausitz is in their hands, I shall never be able to recover our property.'

'Let us see just how far it is first. Then we shall have to make enquiries at the station. Only a few trains are running you know, and only locally.' Anna went to find the leather bound road atlas that had accompanied them on many a trip to the south. To Heidelberg on the river Neckar with its 13th century castle to Rothenberg in Bavaria, the most beautiful walled city in Germany. Would those days ever come back? she pondered, as she searched for Lausitz on the index. 'It is about a hundred kilometres south of Berlin,' she told Lazar. 'More than four hundred kilometres from here.' She looked at his earnest face. 'A long way.'

'So was Auschwitz.' The hard look of resolution crossed his countenance and Anna had no argument.

'I will enquire at the station for trains to Frankfurt. From there the direction will be via Leipzig, and then... well we shall have to see.' Anna shrugged her shoulders in resignation.

'You do not have to come Aunt Anna, but I think the authorities as you call them will prefer to listen to you rather than to me.' Lazar smiled like his father used to do when he was delivering one of his finely barbed comments.

'I will come. Who else have you got to look after you?' A silly statement when Anna considered it. Lazar was quite able to look after himself. It was she who felt his comforting presence. Just like when she went out with her brother Werner. He was always the protector. A little of his looks still lingered in her eyes and chin. The remainder of the resemblance had gone with the ravages of the war and the basic rations they had been forced to live on. She thought of Werner and shuddered at his last moments. Lazar had told her very little of his experience in the death camp, only that they had been separated and that he had last seen his mother walking nakedly in a pitiful file of de-humanised beings to the menacing mouth of the gas chamber ahead of them. Even now, Germans around her were refusing to believe it, but the stories were growing stronger every day as those who had been freed, daily bore witness to the atrocities. I am ashamed of my people, of my country, Anna cried in her sleep. Nothing in this world can ever atone for this genocide. I will help Lazar all I can – I know that something deep inside the boy has to be purged. He had told her nothing of how his family were taken to Auschwitz, but she had guessed that he bore a deep hate for someone, deeper even than for the system that punished them.

Perhaps she could learn to hate. Would that ease her torment? Her feeling that she should be thrashed to expunge the guilt that she felt for her nation? Lazar appeared to cope with it better than most. He was dispassionate and composed in a way that many elders envied. They put it down to his innocence. Anna knew better. He had his mother's resolve and his father's equanimity and ingenuity. Inheritances that would form the basis of a deadly combination against anyone who crossed his path. But was he deliberately planning that path? Tiny snippets of his intentions surfaced now and again, as if he were waiting for signals that would set him on course. "Now the war is over in Europe, can anyone go to Berlin?" "Where will all the people be who lived there before?" and "Who will run Berlin, now that it is in the hands of the Allies?" Interminable questions. Always about his former home. And the people who lived there. When asked about his curious, persistent interest, he merely replied "No particular reason."

Anna knew better. This visit to Lausitz might tell her the answer.

The town was in utter chaos. After a nightmare journey by train and bus, Anna and Lazar were horrified at the devastation all around them. Not by the allied bombers so much, as the wanton destruction of anything combustible, eatable, usable, in every street and alley of the once pretty and peaceful community. Houses were now overflowing with hordes of refugees, deserters, Russian military, and all the accompanying service vehicles necessary for an occupation.

Lazar looked at the spot where his father's warehouse had stood. Or roughly where he believed it should have been standing. The whole street was a line of rubble stretching as far as the eye could see.

'It is no good Lazar. There is nothing here any more.' Anna took his arm gently and led him between the mounds of smashed stones and walls, some higher than his head.

'They cannot take my father's business away by flattening it. He had books and magazines. Textbooks that people could learn from. Everything about the world that people wanted to know. I must find out what has happened to them.'

Anna followed dutifully as Lazar wound his way to more clearly defined roadways that led to a part of the town where some buildings showed an essence of their former glory.

'Lagerhaus? Welche Lagerhaus?' The Russian non-commissioned officer stumbled his limited knowledge of German to Anna as she insisted that he give her information about the warehouse in

Koenigstrasse. 'Surely you have records of the title to these properties,' she implored him. 'We were told that this is now the "Standesamt" for deeds of title. You must have the property registered under our name. Kawalek. Werner Kawalek.'

With a bored look of contempt for the woman, the soldier beckoned to a clerk at the rear of the large untidy room. 'Nachste,' he barked to the queue, as Anna and Lazar made their way to another desk and the soldier dreamt of his liaison with the pretty fraulein who liked his Vodka so much she would do anything. And did, he smirked to himself.

'Koenigstrasse, let me see. We have several factories and stores down that road. Or did,' he ruefully apologised. A resident German who had an inkling of the world of property and quickly conscripted to aid the Russian's ignorant comprehension of the capitalist system of actually owning buildings. 'Ah yes,' he adjusted his pince-nez quizzically and poured over a large volume of painstakingly itemised lists. 'Yes, it is here.'

Anna and Lazar waited expectantly for his proclamation. 'Well?' she demanded.

'Are you a relative of the owner?'

'Yes, I am his sister. And this is his son.'

'Then you should not be surprised to learn that Mr. Werner Kawalek has already registered his interest and has removed the contents of the building. Most of it, I believe, from the cellar. There is very little left of the remainder.'

Anna was flabbergasted. 'When? When did this take place?'

'Let me see,... ah yes. Two months ago. The gentleman signed for the contents and also signed over the title to the property to a Boris Vukadovic. Do you know him?'

Lazar's face contorted and his eyes fixed themselves like a gimlet to the scrawny, pinched face of the clerk, nervously twitching his pen. 'What did he look like?'

'I've no idea. I didn't deal with it. Now if you'll excuse me I have other matters to deal with.' He humped the large tome on to his chest and scurried to the seat from where he had come.

'You know that name, don't you Lazar?'

'Yes.' Lazar's eyes bored into hers. 'I heard it on the day we were taken away. It belonged to a jew, Carl Weisz. He used it to cover his true identity from the nazis. He took our name and papers and denounced us as Jews. He is the one responsible for the death of my family.' Lazar's cold words were not spat out with venom, or anger, or any emotion that would have been expected of a twelve year old in the face of such infamy. They were the words of a cold, dispassionate, practised prosecutor stating the facts. Only beneath the glassy stare, did Anna catch a glimpse of the full force of Lazar's hatred for this man and all that he stood for. Why must innocent minds be tainted with the evil of mankind? she wondered. Is it a price we have to pay for growing up? To be warped into the ways of others who themselves were innocent once? How does a child distinguish from right and wrong where there is no guidance from those around him? Werner and Susan were supreme in their belief of goodness and that had been passed on to their children. Now only the sole survivor held on to that belief, but it was severely seared with an evil beyond his capability of accepting. She took him in her arms. 'I will help you Lazar.' His gaze softened. 'If you will let me.'

'I don't know how, but one day I will find that man, and denounce him for what he is, and then destroy him.' Lazar looked at Anna. 'I don't mean kill him. That is too easy. He took everything away from me and he must be made to feel the same. To experience the horror and the hopelessness. Only someone who loves something beyond all else can feel the pain of its destruction. I want him to feel a pain so intensely that his being screams for release.' He was silent for a moment. 'Only then will Papa, Mama, and Taghi be at peace.'

'What about your pain Lazar? I have not seen you cry. You should you know, it will help.'

'Do you cry Anna? For all those lost souls who are no longer here? For everyone whose only crime is that they were born Jews? I would cry if I could see my mother again. My little sister Taghi. My father. I will cry with joy when they are avenged.'

Anna thought of practical things first. 'If we are to stay in Lausitz, then we shall need somewhere to sleep. I have some money, enough for a night or two.'

'First we have to visit the Standesant again. I want the address of Boris Vukadovic. They must have it.'

The same little wizened man with the pince nez spectacles perched precariously on his nose, looked up with suspicion at Anna and Lazar's entrance. He buried the same nose in a pile of papers pretending not to notice.

'Entschuldigen!' Anna shouted, but politely. 'Can we have a word with you?'

Reluctantly the clerk rose from his desk and bustled to the counter. 'What is it?' he said irritably. He had enough on his work schedule to keep him busy without repeating previous information.

'The man you mentioned. Boris Vukadovic. Did he leave an address?'

'What man are you talking about? I have a hundred queries a day, I cannot be expected to remember every single case.' He polished his spectacles nervously.

'The warehouse in Koenigstrasse. Werner Kawalek. You said it had been transferred to a Mr. Boris Vukadovic.' Anna waited expectantly.

'Yes, yes, of course we have an address. How do you think we can register a new owner without a residence?' Stupid people these days, he grumbled under his breath, they have no idea of the correctness and efficiency of German records. Hitler would have taught the world given the chance.

'May we have it please?' Anna saw the hesitation in the clerk's eyes and hurried to supply a reason. 'This is Werner Kawalek's son, whom he hasn't seen since the beginning of the war. We thought Mr. Vukadovic might be able to guide us to the boy's father.'

'Very irregular, very irregular,' he muttered as he turned the pages of the large tome again. 'You understand that this is very unprocedural. Information such as this cannot be given out on a whim.'

Lazar spoke. '175 Eichenstrasse, is that the address?'

'Why yes.' The clerk stopped, cross with himself for confirming the details before he had made these people sweat a little. 'Why come to me if you knew all along?'

'I didn't. I read it upside down from your ledger.'

The officious clerk jumped as if he had been shot and clasped his precious book to his chest in an effort to retain all its secrets. Anna and Lazar smiled at him, thanked him politely, and left.

'Where to now Lazar? Give me three guesses.'

Lazar nodded slowly. Where else could Carl Weisz head for after seizing control of his father's business. His own house which he could legitimately occupy as Werner Kawalek. He had the necessary papers. 'Will you come with me?'

'I've come this far. There doesn't seem anywhere else I can go. Of course I'll come with you. You need looking after.' Anna laughed out loud. Lazar enjoyed that. Laughter was beginning to return to the people. They had been without it too long.

They found a small house on the outskirts of the town with a broken down 'accommodation' sign hanging dangerously from one hook. 'I haven't had any visitors for over eight months, but I have a room that I could prepare for you.' The proprietor, a thin gawky woman with shortsighted glasses, croaked her thankfulness that a little extra money might come her way. She held out her spindly fingers to clasp the notes that Anna gave her and led them to the first floor front room.

Very soon, clean sheets and pillow cases were brought, with towels and some substitute for soap. 'You are welcome to share my meal. It is not much but it will line your stomachs.'

Anna thanked the old lady and turned to Lazar. 'How are we going to get to Berlin? How are we going to get into Berlin? There will be check points and you have no papers.'

'Most people will be trying to get out of Berlin. Those that are left. What purpose could anyone have to visit an empty city?' In answer to her last point, Lazar smiled his confident smile. 'You will have to be my mother. My papers have been destroyed in an air-raid. They will believe you.'

After a breakfast of rough stale bread and a concoction of lard to soften its brittleness, Anna and Lazar set out for the northern perimeter of

Lausitz in an effort to find the main road. If it existed. It did and Anna breathed a sigh of relief. Why she didn't know. In her heart of hearts she feared for Lazar. How much easier it would be to return to Bad Durkheim and welcome the winter in comparative peace. Winters where, before the war, she had luxuriated in the snowy slopes, tobogganing with her sweetheart and flirting outrageously with any male in sight to make her Hans jealous. Three short months of a dream that was not to be. He was one of the first to be taken by the conscription lorries. One of the first to be killed at the Russian front. It was all beyond her. The reason for the desecration of lives and loves. There was no purpose. Not for the ordinary communities. They had not been under threat, so why threaten others? 'There is a jeep coming.'

Lazar's urgent pulling of her sleeve broke her out of her daydream. 'So?'

'Thumb for a lift.'

'I daren't. It wouldn't be right.'

'The war's over now. The Americans are on our side.'

'He won't know which side we're on. To him we are Germans. We're all alike.' Again she reflected on the non-participants caught in the turmoil of war. Whose side were they on?

The jeep pulled over and a young Lieutenant leant out of the open box seat. 'Where are you going?'

'To Berlin,' replied Anna, still unsure of accepting a lift from a serviceman. She'd heard all manner of things about them, especially the Yanks.

'What in tarnation do you want to go there for?' His Americanised English was beyond Anna's limited knowledge and Lazar spoke in the perfect BBC vernacular taught to him by his mother. 'To find my house. I haven't been back there since 1941.'

Lazar's clipped English surprised the Lieutenant, who still had not taken his eyes from Anna. 'Are you his mom?'

'Er. . no. His aunt. My name is Anna and this is Peter.' She used Lazar's second name, given to him by Susan after his grandfather. If she was going to tell everyone that he was English then Peter would be a better name than Lazar.

'Peter eh. I got an uncle called Peter back in the States. Peter what?'

'Mallory,' Lazar said without hesitation, catching on to Anna's intention. 'My mother was English.'

'Hey look at me sitting here and you standing. Come on, climb aboard. I'll be glad to give you a lift. Against regulations, but hell, who cares?' His smile lit up his face and revealed a full mouth of white teeth that seemed to spread from ear to ear.

The uncomfortable jeep moved off and jumped and lurched along the rutted road with the Lieutenant probing for more information about the odd couple. Between them, Anna and Lazar related their story briefly of the war years and the loss of Lazar's parents in the concentration camp. They did not mention Carl Weisz or Boris Vukadovic.

'Gee I'm awfully sorry about your mom and dad. And your sister. I ain't heard much about them camps but what I have heard ain't fit for decent people to listen to.' He lapsed into his own thoughts of home.

After about an hour he told them that they would soon be seeing the first checkpoint on the approach to the city. The sun was already dropping to tint the tips of the ruins in front of them, where no familiar roofs were left standing.

'The house we want is to the south of the city, Eichennstrasse, do you know it?' Lazar's cultivated English still impressed the Lieutenant, always in awe at the exposition of his mother tongue.

'Yeah, not far from here. To the left I think.'

'We can probably get to it before we come to the check point.' Lazar was worried about Anna and wanted to avoid any confrontation with the armed forces. They might not be as lenient as this Lieutenant.

'Sure thing. Just give me a nudge when to turn off, if there's any turning to turn off in,' he joked. 'Sorry about that, but we have to find our way about like ants on an anthill. Ain't no proper roads any more, the nearer you get to the centre.'

'How long have you been here?' Anna managed one of her rare English sentences, remembered from her schooldays.

'From the beginning, ma'am. Landed in Normandy 6th June 1944 and been pushing east ever since. You know the rest.'

Anna marvelled at his simplification of mass destruction and bitter fighting between old enemies. She wanted to ask him about it. To learn how it had been for them. She felt allied to the Americans, the English, and the French more than to her own people. Who were her own people she wondered? Instead she only commented that it must have been terrible and that he must be glad it was all over.

Despite his apparent nonchalance, the officer was fully aware of the ravages of war. He had seen too much suffering by the civilians to be immune to it. These were the real casualties. He was paid to fight. It was his duty. Who asked the populations if they wanted the conflict? These two passengers were not even statistics in the army's view. Whether the thousands of refugees lived or died had no bearing on their decisions. He had seen it. He had witnessed the impartial annihilation of villages and towns together with their inhabitants. If it served the overall cause, then it must be right. Who was he to argue or puzzle it out?

'There is the checkpoint, ahead. We can turn off here and work our way westwards. Do you recognise any of the terrain young 'un?'

'I don't know. It all looks so different.'

'It all looks the same to me, and I've been here for five months.'

'Over there! That's the Kirche at the bottom of Eichenstrasse. My father used to take me there.' Lazar's exclamation did not betray any sorrow or yearning and it was chilling to Anna to see his detachment from the devastation around him. She felt a cold hand on her back as she witnessed his lack of emotion at the familiar surroundings. Surroundings where he had played so many childhood games with his neighbours. With his sister… She felt the Lieutenant noticed it too and acknowledged his concern for the boy.

The jeep jerked to a halt four buildings down from Lazar's home. 'Stop here please. I do not want anyone to see me.'

The Lieutenant turned to Anna for an explanation of Lazar's curious behaviour. She could not translate her reply with her broken English and merely said, 'He has not seen it for nearly four years.'

They watched the small figure of the man in a boy's frame approach the front gate, pause, and enter.

'He sure is a cool cookie,' the Lieutenant said with a puzzled shake of his head.

'I do not understand.'

'Oh sorry. I meant that he is very grown up.' His grey eyes appraised Anna closely. He saw the youthfulness that had been scarred by the war. The elegant line of her chin and the full lips that hid behind the permanently taut set of her mouth. Only the eyes, large and compassionate, remained of the beautiful young girl he guessed she had been. They blinked now under his gaze, uncertain whether to smile or to rebuff this almost rude intrusion in to her inner thoughts.

'He is a man.'

'Pardon?'

'I said he is a man now. His childhood has gone forever.'

Still the Lieutenant stared into the large pools of dark amber. She had a way of switching her glance from in front of her to meet his curious inspection, lifting her eyelids as if challenging him to take his scrutiny further or back down. His gaze dropped in an apology of his rudeness. He could not cope with this hidden beauty. This underlying gentleness covered with an impervious shell to protect whatever emotions lay deep within. 'I'm sorry if I stared. You are the first handsome woman I have seen since I left home. Back there we revere handsome women. The real ladies. Those who have beauty in their souls, in their movements ... in their eyes.'

He was staring again and Anna did not challenge him this time. A smile tweaked at the corners of her mouth as she doggedly interpreted the gist of his quiet words. His face said it all and there was no need for a literal translation.

'You have been away too long from your country.' She wanted to say "from your own kind, from those gorgeous film star images that adorned the magazines before the war." But she could not put it into English.

Lazar returned and beckoned them to follow him.

The house was empty. The doors and windows closed and unkempt. The garden overgrown and roses running wild. It had died with the war.

Not a slate had dislodged or a brick been loosened, but it had died nevertheless. It had no life in it. Its life had been taken away.

'Come with me.' Lazar led them to the rear of the house where he had uncovered a heavy trap-door. Usually bolted from the inside it had given no resistance under pressure from a lever as the rusted hasp broke under the strain.

'The house is empty, I have checked.' Lazar dropped down the familiar chute into the cellar where his father made so many of his toys, the garden furniture, baskets for his mother's flowers, cots for his sister. The remains of loving labour were all around him and he wept inside. Anna and the Lieutenant followed him up the cellar steps into the large hall and into the rear kitchen.

'I don't suppose there will be any food, but at least we have drink.' Lazar produced a dusty bottle from under his arm, a trophy plucked from the rack occupying the inner wall of his beloved cellar.

'Now that's what I call enterprise. Where's your opener?'

He searched in each drawer and came up with the corkscrew as pleased as a squirrel with a nut. 'Glasses?'

Anna opened an overhead cupboard and set three fine wine glasses on the bare scrubbed oak table.

'To peace,' the Lieutenant said resuming his inquisitive stare at Anna.

'To peace. And to happiness,' said Anna returning his look.

'Amen,' said Lazar, but both of the others knew that he had not finalised his peace or happiness. That was well into the future – wherever that future lay.

'Food. You're gonna need food. I can get you some.'

'We have very little money. It will not buy much.' Anna offered the contents of her purse, but he pushed it away, feeling the heat in her hands as he deliberately touched her fingers with his. 'Thank you,' she said and blinked her eyes to allay the guilt of her gratitude, or was it admiration for the man standing before her?

'I'll be back in two hours. Wait here.'

'Where else can we go?' Anna smiled at his confusion. 'Yeah... well... ' and he was gone.

A thorough search of the cupboards revealed several tins of meat and vegetables, jars of preserves and pickles, and numerous packets of herbs, powders, and spices. Approximately thirty bottles of wine lay in the racks with several bottles of spirits. Water no longer ran from the taps, and Lazar ran to investigate the well at the bottom of the garden. It was useless.

The tasteful furniture lay untouched and dust covered. Items stood on the tables and the bureau gaped open as a proclamation and condemnation of the ferocity of its despoiler. Anna carefully replaced the hinged lid to hide the ravages of its contents and set about clearing the hall of the litter and debris from the onslaught of that terrible day.

Lazar was sorting through a pile of papers from his father's bookcase. Business files, neatly stored and marked with Werner's gothic script. Files that contained the business records of his publishing company and contacts with his customers from all over Europe, some as far afield as Russia.

'What are you looking for Lazar?' Anna noted his intense concentration.

'I am trying to put together a list of my father's customers.'

'Why? He has had no contact with them for years. Who wants books in the war? Only the nazis to broadcast their propaganda.' She left him to it as she explored the upper floor bedrooms.

Lieutenant Domanski returned within the two hours promised. Anna had never seen such food as he produced from the kitbag slung casually over his shoulder. Milk and sugar. Meat and cheese. Peanut butter and bread. Biscuits, or 'cookies' as he called them as he placed his Aladdin's hoard on the kitchen table. 'There,' he said proudly. 'I think I deserve a drink.'

'Thank you. We,.. we thank you ... do you know? We have not been introduced. I do not know your name.' She laughed as if for all the world it was a cocktail party and she was flirting again.

'Joe. Joe Domanski,' and he laughed with her and shook hands formally.

'The meal will be cold I am afraid. No cooker. You will stay for supper

Joe?' Anna's broken English issued from the kitchen as Joe replied that he would be honoured to stay.

'That's OK with you Peter?'

Lazar did not raise his head from the papers he was studying. Anna entered the room. 'Lazar, Joe is speaking to you.'

'Lazar? What's this Lazar?' Joe looked at Anna.

'That is my real name. Peter is my second name. Anna thought it would be better that I use it in Berlin. My mother's name was Mallory. So that is who I am now. Peter Mallory.'

'My second name is Joe. My first is William. Everybody used to call me Billy Joe. I hated it. So I dropped the William. Now I'm just plain Joe. Names don't mean that much. Who'd have a name like Domanski?' He lifted his eyes to Anna and for the first time all three laughed and there was a comfortable feeling of trust between them.

Over the most delicious dinner that Anna and Lazar had tasted for years, they talked of the war and the aftermath. Anna could see no future in Germany. Joe made them jealous with his tales of America and the almost unimaginable wealth of the most affluent parts . . . 'there are some real poverty areas too you know, poorer than here even.'

When they had finished the bottle of wine started in the kitchen, Joe lit up a cigarette and relaxed in the dusted armchair that Anna prepared for him. 'You gonna stay here awhile?'

'I suppose so. We have nowhere else to go.' Anna looked at Lazar for his confirmation. He nodded.

'What do you do Joe?' Lazar looked up from his seat at the table.

'Most things I guess. At the moment I am employed in trying to re-settle the population, such as it is. Encourage the setting up of shops, businesses and trades again. You know, whatever makes a city tick.' He shrugged his broad shoulders. 'Berlin, and Germany will survive you know. You can destroy a country but you can never destroy its people. You will have your country again I promise you. One day.'

'So you will have information on most people in Berlin. Some sort of centre where the public can come for help?'

Joe looked quizzically at Lazar. 'If you're thinking of going there, don't bother. They have enough on their hands with the homeless and the scavengers, the looters and the get rich quick merchants.'

'Will you ask for us at this place for a man named Carl Weisz or Boris Vukadovic?' Lazar wrote down the names for Joe. 'And also Werner Kawalek,' he said in a voice that softened as he spoke his father's name.

'Who are these guys?'

Lazar breathed deeply and looked to Anna for help. 'Tell him Lazar. We cannot do it on our own.'

Slowly over the next hour, Lazar related the story of his family's betrayal and imprisonment in Auschwitz and his parent's and sister's death at the hands of the nazis. His subsequent escape and journey across Poland and Czechoslovakia and on to Bad Durkheim, where he made contact with his aunt Anna. There was no bitterness, no hatred, no tremor in his voice as the stark facts fell on the ears of the two immobile listeners. Like a recording, the full horror of the death camps came to life, and the inconceivable breadth of the atrocities scorched the brain with the indelible pictures that Lazar's words evoked. Pictures that would live in the memories of all who had been victims of the nazi extermination programme.

No one spoke when Lazar had finished. They paid their respects to those who they did not know, but mourned for. At last Joe let out a long heavy sigh, like his lungs were trying to dissipate all the sorrow that he felt. 'I've heard tales of these camps and the horrific treatment of the Jews, but it doesn't really hit home until you hear it first hand. I'm sorry about your parents and your sister, Peter. I'm sorry this whole damn war had to be. It doesn't help I know, but…' Joe's apology faltered as he thought of the villages and towns that his unit had bombarded mercilessly. Because that was what the commander had to do. Innocents in this war were the real sufferers. As Peter and his family had been. He was paid to fight. The civilians were only in the way for a reason that escaped them. There was no reason, no excuse. It just was.

'Thank you Joe. And thank you again for the food and the… well you know.' Anna shyly held her hands on her lap, remembering the looks and the warm feeling of companionship.

'You're welcome ma'am,' Joe said lightening the gloom, 'and I'll get that information for you Peter, you can rely on me.'

Anna knew that from the first moment they had stepped into his jeep and he had smiled at them.

'I'll be back in the next day or so. Don't fret if I don't make it back by then though, you never know what this godamned army wants you to do next.' He laughed as Anna opened the front door heavy with snow. 'Whaddya know, Christmas is coming!' Anna reached out and pulled his smiling face to hers and kissed him hungrily, clinging to his tall frame like a child to her father. He pushed her gently away and stroked her lips with his forefinger into a soft rosebud and held her chin as he kissed her tenderly and was gone.

During the next two days Anna fretted despite Joe's warning. Thanks to him they were well stocked with food and Lazar managed to get some water from a neighbour whose well was still intact. No one asked who they were or what they were doing in the empty house. They had long ago lost any sense of community as they saw their peaceful locality reduced to a patchwork of skeletal stone edifices. A few houses remained, but most had been flattened or rendered useless by the bombing or the shelling as the allies approached Berlin from all sides.

On the third day Joe reappeared with his customary grin and another kitbag full of provisions. 'Can't see you people going hungry now.'

Anna was delighted. She had feared that he had gone for good and he saw the pleasure in her eyes as he unloaded the food. 'Brought a little extra this time. A primus stove. Now you can cook me that meal just like my momma used to do.'

Hot food! Anna was over the moon and set about preparing the steaks and potatoes and cabbage that she found in the numerous parcels laid out on the kitchen table. One tiny stove, but this meal would be special.

No one spoke until the three plates were wiped clean of the sauce Anna had found in the cupboard, still peppery and strong and in good condition.

'Now that beats all the meals in the PX since I got here,' he said contentedly, swinging an appreciative eye at Anna.

'Not only a lady, but a cook too. We got women in the States who ain't got the slightest idea of how to cook a meal. Come to think of it there ain't many who are ladies either.'

Joe's sense of humour warmed the room and for one moment the war was far away, it had never happened, they were a family. Anna's fantasy dissolved as Joe spoke to Lazar.

'I've found what you were looking for Peter. Back in the city centre, or what's left of it, there is an organisation in the British sector called PRISC. That stands for Public Relations and Information Services Control. It's there to encourage the re-opening of German industry. To get people back to work. They have mountains of index cards on everyone and every business that ever existed in Berlin and the surrounding country. A lot of records were lost in the final days of the war and this department retrieved as much as it could and filled in the rest with the information given to them by the remaining inhabitants.'

'Then you have traced the names I gave you?' Lazar interjected.

'Yes. Or I should say partly. A friend of mine in the bureau came up with the name of Boris Vukadovic. He has been operating in the area, generally smuggling and black market items. They've been after him for a long time but could never trace him. Then I gave them the second name, Werner Kawalek, and I told them it was the same guy.' He threw his arms up in imitation of his friend's reaction. "Je-hesus. I met that guy last week! He was granted an exit visa to visit France on business. Showed me his papers and his business credentials from before the war. Naturally the department wanted to help him set it up again." Joe's voice lowered to a normal level. 'So we've traced him, but I'm afraid he has flown the coop.'

'It is what I expected. There would be very little here for him after he confiscated my father's books and licences. He must have smuggled them out of Berlin somehow, or hidden them somewhere else.' Lazar fetched his file that he had compiled from the binders behind him. 'We had a customer in Paris, on the Rue de Tivoli. That is where he will be heading.'

'And you're going to follow him.' Joe caught the inflection in Lazar's voice and the intent was obvious.

'Yes. As soon as we can. That is if you are coming with me.' His question was addressed to Anna who had been trying desperately to follow Joe's drawl with her inadequate knowledge of English.

'Where? Paris? When? How?' Her confusion increased as she thought about the enormous difficulties for them in a strange country, aliens to the inhabitants. 'We can't go there.'

'She's right you know,' Joe nodded his agreement. 'Apart from the distance, how would you survive if you ever got there?'

Lazar smiled. He went to a small cupboard by the fireplace. Removing three books he pressed a tiny lever under the top shelf; the rear of the cupboard swung open and revealed a safe door. Spinning the dial he operated the smooth wheels and pulled open the steel cover.

'English pounds, French francs and German Reichmarks. Father kept them there for us if anything ever happened to him. Enough to live on for a few months.' He fell silent as the significance of his father's foresight made its impact on the room.

'When will you go?' Joe almost whispered the words. He was confused at the feeling of losing something that he had just found and couldn't understand the emptiness in his stomach.

He could see that Anna was fearful too and tried to explain to Lazar that it would be in their interests to wait a while. There was too much chaos and disorder throughout Germany and that their chances of reaching Paris were practically nil.

'At least wait until I have seen what I can do. We have regular connections with our forces all the way back to Normandy. Maybe I can swing something for you. It's worth a try.'

Lazar saw the sense in what was being said and it was agreed that Anna and he should wait until Joe had completed his enquiries.

'Of course there is one other way that you could get automatic passage to Western Europe.' Joe's face split into a huge grin as he turned to Anna. Anna's face registered complete mystification. 'That is if you were the wife of a serving member of Uncle Sam's armed forces.'

The implication did not hit Anna for some seconds as she struggled to come to terms with his American drawl. Then it dawned on her and she turned a bright red and stifled a gasp of embarrassment with her hand. 'You mean … you and … me? Get married?'

'Don't get me wrong,' Joe said holding up his strong hands. 'I was not suggesting that we really got married, … well not in the normal sense. It was just a suggestion that's all. Married on paper,' he stressed. 'In name only,' he repeated slowly and deliberately to assure Anna that his intention was to find a way to help them.

'I am very flattered that you would consent to marry me,' Anna said in her halting English. 'But marriage is something that I have not thought about since … since … well for some time. I thank you for your offer, but no. It would not be fair. We owe you too much already.' Her eyes did not agree with the words that came from her mouth. The light of being wanted shone as brightly as the admiration in Joe's contemplation of this woman who moved so gracefully and shyly. Whose gentle charm outshone her outward war worn image. A woman in her full vitality was trying to shed the ageing cloak of misery and suffering. He wanted to know more, but didn't care if he never knew. He was only aware of the deep gut feeling that would not leave him. An itching that was constantly with him. A feeling of responsibility for these two people who, for no reason other than he had been there at the time, had entered his life. 'You owe me nothing. Forget what I said about marriage. I understand. But in war conditions you don't always have time for the courting bit. Perhaps we can catch up on that before you go.' Again he smiled that broad smile and Anna's heart missed a beat. She nodded and excused herself to go onto the kitchen.

'Did you really mean what you said to my aunt?'

Joe hesitated, questioning his own motives. 'I guess so. I don't know why, but it seemed the natural thing to do. I've seen it done before, but only because the guys got into a mess … you know … they had to get married. I'm sorry Peter if you thought it was not a genuine offer.'

'No. I see the sense in it, but I do not think Anna is ready for marriage or anything like that at the moment.' Lazar turned to the map in front of him. 'When will you know if there is a chance of transport out of

Berlin?'

Lazar's calm deliberation again disturbed Joe. There was compassion inside him, he could sense it, but his fixation, born in the vilest place on earth, would dictate his rationale until his mission was complete.

'As soon as I can. It will take a few days to see if there is a possibility. Meanwhile, rest. You're both gonna need it.' Joe placed his hand on Lazar's shoulder. 'I envy you son. You have somewhere to go in this whole mess. Me, I'm in no man's land. In limbo. Thanks for the stability you two have given me. I was beginning to lose mine.' Anna heard Joe coming through the hall to the kitchen. She heard his deliberate steps on the parquet floor and turned to meet his relaxed, familiar shape. They were the same height and came together naturally, her arms encircling his neck in an embrace that matched his own around her slim waist. A shock wave ran through her body as his mouth sealed her parted lips and all her doubts were dispelled by the force of passion fighting her misgivings. He was gentle and forceful. She never wanted the strong arms to release her into this crazy world. She was safe there. A haven from all the outside terror. Like a child seeking cover in her mother's skirts she strove to cling ever closer to the source of pleasure.

Both Joe and Anna gasped for breath as they broke their embrace and pledged their love with unspoken words. She led him to the door, stroked his unruly black hair from his forehead and whispered her kisses in his ear. 'Hurry back.'

Across the flattened square of rubble and half houses, a black limousine with the Russian insignia on its rear panel, shone in the winter light. Inside two men watched intently as the American Lieutenant waved and climbed into his jeep. The second man's interest was focused on the woman standing at the door smiling her goodbye. Carl Weisz did not recognise the female occupying his property, but he would deal with it as he had done with its previous occupants. The red end of his cigar glowed briefly in the dim interior and then was extinguished as it bloodied the crisp white snow beneath the open window.

CHAPTER VI

1945

Someone told Susan that it was the 27th January. How anyone could be as precise as that was beyond her. The days all merged into one. Monotonous and grey. Like the people around her. Grey faces, grey clothing, grey huts, and grey skies. Like the camp guards' uniforms. It was a grey world with nothing but greyness ahead of them. Rumours had been circulating that the allies were coming. Those rumours had been broadcast for the past six months. There was certainly an air of nervousness among the Blockfuhrers. Their arrogant, overbearing attitude no longer spread its fear among the inmates of Monowitz-Buna. Perhaps the rumours were true.

She made her way to the machine shop where she had worked for the past 14 months. Before that, years in the laundry washing the garments and vestments of the army of guards allotted to the camp. No such luxuries for the prisoners. They could wash their own as best as they could. If they could find enough water. Usually when it rained, which was not often enough. Today was no different. Snow everywhere, slushed into unmanageable bogs, not even passable by the heavily tracked lorries that brought the meagre rations and supplies. And cold. Bitterly cold. But no-one felt it. They had become immune. You survived or you died. It was as simple as that. At least the furnaces had been quiet for some time. No smoke. No trails of human fodder for its ovens. Perhaps that had been one of the signals that registered in the minds of those who accepted the daily ritual as part of their life. And death. The routines had changed. First a desperate attempt to liquidate as many as possible and then a lull as if uncertain of the orders.

The great German efficiency machine was breaking down. Just as it had on that day long ago when she had said goodbye to Lazar. The day that took all of her emotions from her. Her soul had already prepared itself for its journey when there was a hitch. Her empty eyes refused to accept that the hundred or so souls standing beneath the infamous gas jets were not going to die. Not just yet. The system had broken down. In any other place it would have been farcical to see the 'experts' running like lemmings to every control panel in an effort to discover the fault. Orders barked, and insults hurled at the 'inefficient, stupid, artificers who knew no better than the ignorant Jews they were supposed to gas.

Susan did not even feel relieved to be spared for one more day. 'Give me a gas cylinder and I will do it myself,' said a woman at her side. 'Permanent death is better than a living death. There is nothing to live for anyway.'

The words filtered through Susan's stupefied reasoning. Nothing to live for. Is that what everyone here considered to be their purpose? Why did everyone accept the inevitable in such a subservient manner? Why did they walk to their deaths with no fight? With no protests? Were they afraid of being hurt? How hurt could you be before death? Her mind whirled as it fought to resurrect itself to the clear thinking organ it once had been. Was it only a few days ago that she had seen her dear Werner and Taghi dragged from them? Didn't she owe them every last gasp in her body to survive and tell the world of this barbaric place? Where monstrosities the like of which mankind had never witnessed or imagined took place as routinely as children called into class? Deep down in her unforgotten reserves of determination, Susan took the stay of execution as a sign. She would not die. She should not die. She was not a Jew. She was English. Someone had to be convinced of her innocence. A hopeless revulsion racked her body as she realised what she was saying. "She should be spared because she was not a Jew!"

Had she joined the ranks of the anti-semitics? The feeling of guilt would not leave her as they marched back to the hut. The body of the poor emaciated girl dragged to one side to be disposed of later with two others who had succumbed through not wanting to live. Some welcomed their quarters as if it were a sanctuary. Others lay and waited for the next call. Susan went in search of the Rapportfuhrer.

'Why do you keep insisting that you are English. We hate those pig-dogs more than you pitiful Jewish swine.' The Rapportfuhrer sneered at her assertions as she tried to convince him that her very appearance did not equate to the jewish image. 'Look at me. Do I look like a Jew? Does my nose fit? Look at my complexion. It does not conform does it?' Susan turned her head back and forth to reveal the round contours of a true English rose. Surely no one could mistake her for a Jew.

'So what if you are English. What is it to me? Do you think you are the only one destined for the gas chamber who is not Jewish?'

Susan was desperate. 'You do not regard the English in the same way as Jews. We are your contemporaries, we even had sovereigns from German stock. It was a Jew who betrayed my family by pretending to be my husband.'

For some reason the Rapportfuhrer began to listen. He was fascinated by this attractive woman, not yet ravaged by the camp conditions. Her story was plausible, even if he did not believe it. That she was not a Jew he was certain. He had seen thousands upon thousands of Jews. She did not slot into any of the known variations. He had seen pictures of English maidens when he was in his teens and her clear complexion and open round face, framed by a stubble of brown hair matching her eyes, intrigued him. He could not guess her age; late twenties? Still firm and fit. It would be a pity if such a beauty was allowed to degenerate into the nonentity of the animal like scullions occupying the older huts. Indistinguishable from their male counterparts, they were pieces of work units. If they worked, they lived. If they didn't they were got rid of.

It was forbidden for any guard to fraternise on a sexual level, not that any true German would dream of touching a Jew, but this one was different. He knew that the higher ranks regularly took the best of the non-Jewish inmates while they were fresh. The constant intake of humanity guaranteed a steady supply of diversions for them. Perhaps he could have his own diversion . . . ?

The shifting of the Rapportfuhrer's eyes over her body and face gave Susan her opportunity. She had lived long enough to recognise men's lascivious thoughts before they knew them themselves. She had often joked with Werner about his friends' subtle innuendos. He also knew them for what they were. 'You are so beautiful my darling that it is a compliment that you are so wanted. But no one wants you as I do.' And their lovemaking would be all the more fulfilling because of the envy of something as precious as their love.

'I am sure that you could find a use for me on the camp. I can sew, wash, type, keep books, translate. I can speak German, English, a little Czechoslovakian and Russian. I could be very useful.'

The Rapportfuhrer considered. How useful could she be to him? Life was boring on the camp. It secretly sickened him at times, but he had been so ingrained with the philosophy of the 'final solution' that he found himself caught in the euphoria of the super race. Only the constant reinforcement of his outwardly brutal behaviour stopped him from withdrawing altogether from the facade of a typical guard. His own indoctrination sessions never completely convinced him that he was one of the master race. Only a pawn in some vast game that would discard him as easily as it discarded those he was taught to hate.

'You will have to move from the hut you are in. They will die tomorrow. Your number will have to be entered on to the list of those who did not return this morning. What is it?'

'379,' Susan replied.

'I will check. If 378 is in the punishment cylinder, you can take that number. It will be easy to altar the figures.'

That is how life is determined in this place, reflected Susan. The alteration of a figure can mean life or death. No wonder the guards have so little guilt about the enormity of what they were doing. Life of the inmates did not exist in their eyes. A sickness bred by their evil masters. A sickness that had no antidote. No solution. She watched as the Rapportfuhrer strode away to instigate one minor deficiency in the Teutonic master plan. The German hierarchy may dictate the masses which had to die, but in the end it was left to a lowly subaltern to decide an individual's fate.

Susan had no idea of the extent to which her protestations would lead. The Rapportfuhrer explained that to arrange the 'swap' it would be necessary to put her under punishment in the cylinder. Her heart sank. She had seen the abhorrent and inhuman torture chamber. An upright tube of corrugated iron with a small entrance at the foot. Inside, three, sometimes four people were forced to stand, crushed together, without food or water for one, two or three days. The only relief for those inside was when one of them died and the constriction became bearable. That is if anyone noticed, or bothered to move the body.

She braced herself for the terror that she knew would grip her. Think of Werner, of Lazar, of Taghi. Keep them in your mind at all times and you will survive! She forced herself to concentrate on nothing else. Whatever her mind and body felt, it was not real. Only the love of my family is real. Her eyes blazed with determination as she crawled into the cramped aperture. Two other women were clinging to each other for support, their behinds forced against the wall in an effort to relieve their legs. Evidence of the their two days' incarceration infested the muddy floor and Susan immediately retched and vomited to add to the mess. Oh god, she prayed. Deliver us from evil. The only response to the new inmate was moans and curses and feeble struggles to re-adjust their positions. Susan clung to them. She had no option. She closed her eyes and began her fantasy.

She was a little girl playing in the lovely fields at the back of her home in Weymouth. The gentle slopes disappeared into the honey coloured stroke of an autumn sunset. Valleys and dells where romance and adventure were on the tip of every hedgerow, danger and excitement on the branches of the valiant oaks. Mystery and reverence about the stature of the heavy beech trees laden with blossom. The colours filled her mind. The days merged into one great lifetime. Her friends and playmates, the boy who had shyly taken her hand and shared his crab apples and pop with her. She remembered his clean, fresh face, beaming with pride when he had climbed the tallest elm to triumphantly shout his joy at finding the Jackdaw's nest.

Summers lasted all year long. Glorious blue skies and sparkling water. Thousands of holiday makers thronging the beaches, burning and complaining and coming back for more. Her childhood passed like a moving train, never wanting to reach the end of its journey. Puffing slowly through the green meadows, like her mother moving the green fabric under the sewing machine. A new dress for her birthday. She was fourteen! Unbelievable to be so grown up. She knew she was growing up because she no longer felt as she used to when a boy teased her. She sensed some inner excitement that had not been there before. She taunted them back and they enjoyed it. The ones who hoped she would respond to their latent messages.

She had been strong then. In limb and mind. She would need all of that now. How many hours had she been in this compartment of hell? One of the women had died in the night. She still clung to her supports. Soon she would be stiff enough to support the others. A loud banging on the outer shell hurt Susan's eardrums as she vaguely made out the words 'Aus, aus!' She slithered by relaxing the stiff muscles and falling downwards, scrabbling at the festering bodies beside her. She was pulled out feet first by the Rapportfuhrer and directed to the last hut in the line. Her ordeal was over.

Susan was duly moved to hut 22 where most of the women were workers. Scrawny but still strong and able to deal with anything from body removal – they were regularly seen carting a dozen or so to the burial ground or the incinerator, to grave digging and construction work. She was allocated to the laundry. Washing and sewing the pyjama like habits that all were forced to wear. She waited for the call to repay her benefactor, for she knew he would come.

He never appeared around her block again. Transferred? Assigned to another camp? She dare not ask, but prayed that he had completed the exchange of numbers on the official registers. Her own tag had been neatly altered to 378 with congealed blood and the point of her sewing needle.

She was spared! For the moment. As long as she was necessary then there was a possibility of survival. She had to survive now. To find Lazar. If he lived. Three months passed. And then she saw him. Carl Weisz. As large as life and larger than she remembered him. He had always been tall, 6 feet 4 inches, but now his bulk matched his overall size. A giant of a man, who strutted as the Germans strutted. Happy in their company and obviously under no threat. What name did he use now? she wondered. It was at the end of a long shift in the washroom and she was on her way to collect the meagre handouts for her hut. A few toiletries which were now filtering through from the Red Cross, combs and scissors and substitute soap. Luxuries that had almost been forgotten. He appeared walking towards the Office of the Oberhaupt of the Lebbensmittel, the overseer of the camp supplies and victuals. He and the Chief were sharing some secret joke and Carl's raucous laughter infected all the cronies around them. If only they knew, Susan swore under her breath. It was almost worth denouncing him there and then, but she would never be believed. She watched them disappear into the administration block and turned away. Hate burned in her eyes and a bile rose beneath her ribs, threatening to push them further against the emaciated skin. The once youthful contours of her body had long gone. She was now just a shape on which her skin clung to like wet clothes on a frame.

From his dress and manner, he had prospered in the war. There was always a market for goods that were in short supply. Carl had the means and the cunning to supply those goods. No matter who demanded them. And there was a ready supply from the camp Susan heard. Gold teeth, hair, prized possessions cruelly wrenched from the new arrivals. No one saw them again, except perhaps the Oberhaupt and Carl Weisz.

Susan saw him several times over the next two years, looking larger and more prosperous on each visit. It is good, she said to herself. His image was fixed in her mind for all time. An image that would one day be obliterated from this earth forever. The force of her commitment to that end re-invigorated her body with a strength that no food could ever induce. She would survive the camp. She would survive the war. It was written in her destiny as indelibly as the hate ingrained in her soul for this loathsome reminder of her loving family.

The sound of engines in the distance shimmered in the January air. Not the sound of another convoy of 'Juden Wagen' but a deeper, more vibrantly shattering resonance, that permeated the ears of even the most stupefied of the inmates.

Tanks! Great belching dragons, crunching all before them. Tearing a path through mud and snow. Heading straight for the gate that was miraculously being opened by German guards! The few that remained were as pitiful as those whom they had abused over the years. Cringing apologies for human beings. No longer able to strut their superiority, their spirits broken, they were delivering themselves to the mercy of the Russians. Some had shaved their heads and donned the 'pyjama' uniform, pretending to be prisoners. Those were killed first by the strongest of the Jews, still able to wield a piece of wood or stone. They did not die quickly. And the Russians watched. The others were rounded up and taken away. No one cared what happened to them. Susan wondered if the Rapportfuhrer was among them.

It was three weeks before the compilation of the records was complete. All names of those who could remember were noted and their country of origin. Susan proved most useful during this exercise, using her Russian and German to assist the Soviets in their task. She was promised repatriation to Germany as soon as peace in Europe had been achieved. Firstly all inmates had to undergo medical checks and a course of dietary nourishment to adjust their stomachs to normal food.

'You are British you say. And your husband was German?' The Russian captain cast a quizzical eye at Susan as she helped the last interviewee to the door. Most are still not fit to take their place in the world, even if there is a world out there for them, thought Susan. Their spirit has been destroyed. The whole of Europe was under siege. She didn't even know if there was any place the war had not touched. Where would everyone go? The survivors. The few who were fortunate enough to escape the holocaust.

'Yes my husband is... was a publisher, a book-dealer. His parents came from Eastern Germany, near the Polish Czech border. He dealt with the Soviet Union before the war, we had friends there... '

'I am sorry that your husband and daughter were not able to be saved. But I can assure you that the Soviet Army will seek retribution of the highest order for these unspeakable crimes.' The captain's jaw tightened to emphasise his repugnance for the atrocities that had met him at the camp. 'But you will not get the one that matters most to me.' Susan's challenge brought a glint of a smile to the captain's thin lips. He had heard her story and did not doubt for one minute that she was capable of killing this stranger who had so destroyed her life.

'I wish you luck. If ever I can be of assistance . . . '

'Thank you. I shall remember that Commissar Brovnik.'

The soldier looked at the young woman, already beginning to blossom into her former self with the benefit of good, substantial food, and nodded his approval of her attitude. She would never be subdued. Never be dominated. Her spirit was evident in every flash of her tawny eyes, every movement of her determined body. Not like the underlings of the Soviet regime, where women were treated no better than they had been in this hell hole. The system didn't allow it. Male dominance was a prerequisite to communism and he had been sucked into it. He had no choice. It was conform or be thrown to the wolves of mediocrity. So he had joined the revered Soviet army. That way your natural abilities could be recognised and rewarded. You had a uniform and insignia to show your prowess. It was displayed for all of those unfortunates to see. Success in a measure that most men could never hope to achieve. But he had done it. And done it by his ability. His drive. Like this woman's. Something deep inside that told him that he must succeed. The same compulsion that drove her and had made her cling to life when no hope remained.

'Do you know Mrs. Mallory, you are a very lovely woman.' He used her assumed name deliberately as a compliment to her Englishness. 'There is a beauty inside of you that reminds me of the old days. When there were such words as freedom and innocence. And honesty. I think that very few are honest today. Everyone wants something more than they are entitled to. But then, who am I to judge what is their entitlement? That judgement is better left to others. To those who know. To those whose duty is directed to the ordination of justice.' He paused to watch a batch of gaunt, hobbling but free Germans being helped onto a lorry. Their only possession was a small bag of essentials. All they had left in life. He opened the window, despite the cold, and breathed in the chilled air as if to cleanse the spectre of this inhumanity from him. 'You are one of those people,' he said, turning to Susan. 'You have been spared for a purpose. I believe that. But do not let it eat at you until there is nothing left of the beauty within. Promise me that.'

Susan had been watching this commanding figure in the blue grey roughly cut uniform. The gold epaulettes sat proudly on his broad shoulders, pulled back by his arms clasped tightly behind him. The edges of his dark hair were tinged with a whiteness that had come too early. The lines in his face were etched deeper than his youthfulness deserved. But he was handsome. Susan was surprised that she retained the power to assess men as she used to. Perhaps what he said was right. She must not devote her whole life to a hatred. There must be room for love again. For her fellow man. For Lazar!

'There is one thing you could do for me if it is possible. My son. Lazar Kawalek. I told you he escaped, at least I think he escaped. He would head for Berlin where his aunt lived. Would there be any way of tracing if he ever reached there?'

'It is a tall order. The city will shortly be under siege, as our forces advance from the east. The British and Americans will arrive after us from the west, so first Berlin will be in Soviet hands. God knows what they will do to the city. There are many types of Russians. It is a vast country. They are in no mood to liberate the Germans. It would be better if your son had reached another destination. From what you have told me, I am afraid that I cannot discount the fact that he would have been discovered long before he entered Germany.' The officer was thinking aloud, a habit he had developed to let his co-officers follow his reasoning. 'But I will do all that I can. There will have to be a detailed roster of all inhabitants. If he is there, then he will be found. Once we have taken Berlin.' The conviction in his tone eased the tension in Susan's mind as she thought about Lazar's almost impossible task. He will be there, I know it. He must be there. Her impassioned assertion to herself relayed its message through the intensity of her stare and the Commissar matched the intensity, but for a different reason.

A few weeks after the liberation, most of the captives were moved to hostels or hospitals, dependent upon their capability of caring for themselves. There they would await transportation to their own countries as soon as hostilities were over. Susan nominated Germany and particularly Berlin as her place of residence. The captain had promised to see to it personally that she had priority clearance, if it was in his power. 'You are not as strong as you make out. Four years suffering under those conditions cannot be wiped away with a few weeks convalescence. There is nothing you can do about the war. Leave that to us. It will be over in a few weeks and then normality will return.' What is normality? he shrugged. Will there ever be normality again? When will it be normal for a Soviet captain to fall in love with a British-German mother who has lost everything? In any other circumstances he could have made his feelings known. Here in this substitute for normality and the facade of a 'free' life, he found it impossible to impose such a burden on her. She may consider that her ordeal was over, but her mind would never be free while it was in the grip of the two most powerful emotions on earth. Love and hate. The first for her son Lazar, the second for this man Carl Weisz. He could not compete with them. No man could. He would help her all he could and hope that some day... if she ever found what she was looking for... she would remember him.

The day victory in Europe was declared, the captain was far away from the hostel. His services had been needed elsewhere more urgently. He was a fighting man and his unit had been among the first to enter Berlin, or what was left of it. Susan continued to press the authorities with as much fervour as she could muster, to let her travel to the city. But no arrangements for repatriation were to be allowed. Berlin was a closed city. Where no one entered or left without the express permission of the Soviet occupying forces. The British and Americans had joined them. And the small French contingent. It was controlled by the four powers and sank in a mire of international bureaucracy. For weeks Captain Brovnik searched the voluminous records of all four command posts, but no Lazar Kawalek or Carl Weisz was located. They were names among so many. There were very few with the name Carl Weisz in the city's records. Most by that name had suffered the ultimate fate of having been born a Jew. Only five had been registered in that part of the city and they had been taken away. The handsome captain sent word by letter to Susan of his lack of success and wished her well. "… remember I shall be here in Berlin, if you decide to come… yours affectionately, Sergei."

There was a longing in his words that she oddly yearned to return. Starved of any kind of relationship for years, Susan had difficulty in accepting the fact that she was still desired. Her own sensations of attraction to men were stupefied, as if a sedative had been administered daily to block any expression of love or regard for those around her. She would have to learn all over again the delights of a glance, a touch, a soft word. Perhaps one day…

The day came when at last the train was commissioned to take those who wanted to travel west to Wroclaw, Glogow, crossing the German border at Forst and on to Leipzig. The line had been checked and re-opened and trains were running spasmodically again. From Leipzig alternative transport would have to be found to other cities and towns but Berlin would not be available for some time, even to former residents.

Susan considered the alternatives. Go on the train and trust that she could worm her way into Berlin, or stay in Poland for the time being, where there was plenty of work for carers and helpers in the enormous task of looking after the infirm and tracing, where possible, any living relatives.

She could go to Bad Durkheim, but the memories of the glorious summers there and the ecstatic holidays with Werner and Taghi and Lazar could not be faced so soon after… no her duty at the moment was to stay with those whom she could help. There were upwards of 200 in the hostel. Only half would be able to make the journey and then what? The others would have to be cared for until they were fit and well. If that were possible. Those who couldn't make the transition to normal life would see out their days in the hostel, never knowing for sure that they were free. They had only swapped one incarceration for another. They were still prisoners in their minds and always would be.

Susan decided to stay. She wrote a short note to Sergei care of the occupying forces of Berlin and hoped that it would find him. She needed the comfort of someone knowing where she was. No one else did. Or cared, except Sergei.

She considered her feelings for him. She missed him when he left with his regiment to push on to Berlin and the final conquest. He had come to her in her office and told her. There were no secrets any more. The German nation knew they were defeated. Only the fanatic rulers of the Third Reich thought there was any hope. The people had given up. The army had given up. They no longer wanted to fight. They didn't want to die. But they did in their thousands, uselessly and without cause. The Russians spared no one.

'I have to leave tomorrow,' he said, his eyes full of sorrow. 'We have to push on and complete the annexation of Berlin before the allies. Why I don't know. But this is not the end of the war. There will be no more hostilities, I grant you, but the Party,' he paused, considering his position within the communist regime, 'will take all it can get its hands on.' Once he would have backed the Party to "liberate" the uninformed and enrol them in the great Soviet Union. Now he was not so sure. He had seen the results of annexation on smaller states within the Republic and the benefits that the 'free' world could offer. Just like Susan. Even if she were shackled to this hostel, she was 'free.' Free to do as she pleased with her life. Free to pursue her happiness. Or her hatred. He was bound by restrictions that ate at a man's soul and imprisoned his spirit.

'How long do you think the war will last now?' Susan did not want to show any sign of sadness at his going, but she knew she would miss him terribly. 'Will you come back to Poland?'

'Who knows? I may not even have the chance to come back. There are still some units arrayed around Berlin who think it is honourable to die for the Fatherland. There are far more important things to die for than the maniacal dreams of a dictator. One should only be prepared to die for the things you love. Not because of those you hate.' He looked at Susan and recognised the hint of guilt that swept across her eyes.

'One day you will understand Sergei.' The sound of his name embarrassed her when she spoke it. She had refrained from using it over the weeks together, even though he addressed her by her christian name whenever they were alone. But she knew it would please him, although he had never hinted at using it. 'My love for my family is all that I have left. Even though they are gone, my love will never be replaced by hate. That is in a separate compartment. It has to be purged. Until the object of that hate is destroyed, my love cannot fill my mind, my body, my being. Love has to be unshackled. Free and unfettered and complete. Mine is not complete. I have only two purposes in life now. To find my son, if he still lives. And to find Carl Weisz.'

Without thinking Sergei took her in his arms and gently stroked the emerging curls framing her face. He held her as a father holds his daughter. With love and tenderness and understanding. Protectively and possessively. 'I cannot hold you as a man holds a woman Susan. I have no right. But I feel more deeply about you than I have felt with anyone. Love, if it is love, can exist without the physical emotions. I know that because in my family we were not encouraged to make physical contact with our parents, our brothers and sisters. It was frowned upon. I learnt another way of loving. Through the eyes and through the ears. Through the smell and the taste in the air of my sister's fresh girlish perspiration. My brothers' individual scents. My mother's homely smell of polish, and cooking, and milk when she was feeding the youngest. My father was all tobacco and hair grease and boot polish. That is how I learnt to love them. I could not hold them to pass on my feelings. But I can hold you and I know you will understand. I respect you and honour you for being the one person to whom I can open my heart.'

Susan cried for the first time in years. The dryness inside her was beginning to lose its grip and her natural tendency to love beautiful things was being born again. Just as her body was being born again. It had gradually regained the youthful curves and firm muscles and the tone that had once made her skin sparkle with vitality. Her short re-grown hair gave her an angelic appearance and belied her thirty two years. Pride had returned with the provision of basic makeup and hair brushes and combs. That had been Sergei's idea. "If you look good, you feel good." And he had clapped with joy at her first amateurish attempts to remember how to apply lipstick and mascara.

'Thank you Sergei. You have meant a great deal to me. I hope we can remain friends. Good friends. I think I am incapable of love in any other sense. But I can share your emotions. We both yearn for something dear to us. Something in this world that we can cling to as real. I have not felt the warmth of a man's body since my husband's. I have no shame in saying that your body gives me a comfort that I thought I would never experience again.' Susan clung to the man whose tenderness reached out for her, through his strong frame and through the process that he had learnt as a boy. 'I will stay with you tonight, if you want me to… I cannot make love in the normal sense… I don't even know if I am capable any more, I just want to lay with you and talk, and feel, and hope.'

Sergei kissed her forehead and savoured the sweet smell of her. The woman somewhere deep within that would one day emerge to enjoy life to the full again. Snatching at love now, in these circumstances, where death and destruction and misery lay all around was only superficial. A passing experience that substituted for a good meal or a favourite cigar. In this woman was something more precious and permanent. If it could ever be coaxed out of its deep seated isolation. 'I leave at 5am. We have a lifetime before us.'

Susan knew that an hour, a day, a week could mean just that. A lifetime to reflect on the vagaries of life. The unscripted avenues that each were forced to take, or chose to take. The permanence of life just lived. The last second, the last year; once experienced were there forever. The joys, the heartaches, the hopes, the tragedies. Each should be weighed and remembered. 'I remember sleeping with a boy once. It was one hot June evening and a storm had been brewing all day. My parents were away at the time and he had missed the last bus to his home town 12 miles away. Of course I invited him to stay overnight in my brother's bed. I never intended that he should sleep with me, youngsters just didn't do that sort of thing. It was the thunder and the terrible heavy atmosphere that built a fear in me being alone in the big double bedroom where my parents slept. Each flash of lightning reached in through the window and caught my breath; each clap of thunder beat at my eardrums. I was terribly frightened so I went to him and asked him to be with me, just to comfort me, to protect me from the noise and the light. We lay there, side by side, holding on to one another. Frightened by the overhead storm and frightened by the power inside of us. We wanted to make love, but our sense of duty to whatever our parents had told us was stronger. Instead we just lay together – naked – and cried softly together. I shall always remember that boy. I think I loved him more for not making love to me, than if we had had a wild affair for the sake of it. Can you understand that?'

'Yes; some things are stronger than the physical act of love. There is an empathy between people who are in love that transcends other passions – I think it is the thought of being loved unreservedly.' Sergei smiled down at Susan and saw the light in her eyes of gratefulness. No hate showed now, only the love of someone wanting to be loved for her sake alone.

The hut was dark and warm. The single bed snug and cup like, throwing them together in a single hollow, safe from the outside world. There was no storm, no thunder or lightning. A bright starlit night looked down on them through the latticed windows. Their warm naked bodies fused into one beneath the hot rough blanketed covers. No erotic fancies coursed their bodies. Only for one moment had Sergei's responses been automatic. When Susan had shed her simple cotton cloth dress and had turned to the window in her shyness as she slipped clumsily out of her pants. The sight of her silhouette against the pale light of the window took him by surprise. He had reacted immediately from the pit of his stomach and hastily climbed into bed to hide his own embarrassment. She joined him and clasped him to her in an embrace so close that it prevented any movement on his part that his body begged him to initiate. She talked of her home life, his home life, of summers and autumn, of childhood and puberty. Everything that had nothing to do with the war. They escaped the trappings of conflict. They wandered into a world that existed once and existed now in that space that was their own. As she talked softly in his ear his fervour dissipated and he felt at ease with this woman, so strong against his masculine weakness. She had shown him a love that bore no barriers, no set pattern of behaviour. A true simple love of one being for another. And they slept in the innocence of each other's arms.

In the morning when she woke, he was gone. A simple note of farewell was on his pillow: "Your innocent love, Sergei".

When she saw the train that had been arranged, Susan was glad that she had decided to stay. The wagons were no better than the ones used for Auschwitz. Probably the same ones, she reflected, but cleaned out and benches arranged. The journey would be just as gruelling with no guarantee of what was at the other end. But people had hope. Somewhere at the end of the line there would be a patch of land that was theirs. Or a house that was still standing that belonged to them. Susan thought of her home. The lovely garden and the well. The elegant rooms and the lofty landing where Lazar and Taghi shouted their joy at Christmas as they raided the pillow cases set the night before. Where Werner and she had lived and loved. So wonderfully that she was often frightened that it would all end... she snapped herself out of her reminiscences and returned to the hostel to attend to the morning's chores.

Susan was pleased to see a new arrival on the first floor of the gaunt hostel. A young woman who was more bone than substance. A pitiful shadow of her former self, she had been rescued from Birkinau just before the final batch of prisoners were to be disposed of. The Russians had entered unexpectedly and stopped the frantic efforts of the camp Rapportfuhrers to cover their mistreatment of the inmates by getting rid of the evidence of the starvation levels they had been subjected to. In the last weeks before their final release, food was practically non-existent, even for the guards. The camp was running out of control and discipline had broken down. The last orders from the Fuhrer was to "cleanse our work camps of all sick, disabled, and useless workers." Rosa had stood with the last group in the biting wind, holding her baby daughter to her breast. The freezing temperature did not pierce the warmth between mother and daughter. The warmth between them that meant love, something the nazis could never destroy. The loud bangs and the sound of exploding canons scattered the gathered throng. Guards ran first to their huts leaving the mass of naked numbed victims to fend for themselves. It was all over in seconds with the triumphant Russians carving a swathe through the wire fences and flattening everything in their path. Rosa and her daughter were taken to a hut and given clothes and food and clean sheets and blankets. Luxuries that had long been lost in the distant past of their minds. First she fed little Katrina with milk supplied from the ample supplies of the Soviet battalion. Too rich for her tender stomach, starved of nutrients and vitamins for so long, but gradually with care a diluted feed was taken and life began to appear in the tiny girl's eyes. Pray god she will never remember any of this, her mother pleaded.

'Hello. My name is Susan.' She offered her hand but Rosa could not release her grip on the minute bundle in her arms. Susan held out both hands and nodded in reassurance. The frail woman slowly acknowledged that Susan was a friend, someone who would help her. She could be trusted. The war for her and her daughter was over. People would be kind again. Susan talked to her quietly as she had to Sergei only a few days ago, telling her that she was safe. The nazis had gone. Everything was going to be all right.

Susan took the small baby in her arms and sang it a lullaby as the mother's eyes filled with tears and the taut lines, a permanent fixture of everyone in the camp, smoothed out over the angular contours of her once beautiful face.

'What is her name?'

'Katrina. Katrina Wenig Rosenberg. I am Rosa. Her mother.'

Susan did not ask about the father. If Rosa wanted to tell her she would. 'How old is Katrina?'

'She will be two next month. 8th May.'

'She is very beautiful,' said Susan, stroking the fine hairs from the little crunched up forehead. 'We shall soon make her very strong and happy again.'

Rosa smiled. How like her mother this lady was. Confident and knowledgeable, always happy and loving, with the same spontaneous laugh ready to soften the hard edges of any anxiety. 'Are you in charge here?'

'Goodness me no. I work here. I have done ever since we were brought here from ... from the camp. We have nowhere else to go at the moment.' Susan saw the forelorn look return to the girl's face. 'But this place is as good as home. You will have friends here. We are all in the same boat. Perhaps you will recognise someone you know.' Try as she could the sadness would not leave the gaunt face. Susan dare not ask about her family. Very few of those in the hostel talked about their loved ones who were no more. It was as if a guilt hung over them for surviving where their families had perished. Most thought it would have been better to go together. Their lives had been taken from them even though their emaciated bodies still breathed.

'Promise me something Susan.' The words came defiantly from the feeble lips hardly moving over the jutting square bone of her jaw. 'You will look after my baby when ... when the time comes ... I have no one else... no one to turn to. I know you are good... you are like my mother... used to be.' Susan felt the baby in her arms stir and strain to cry. But she didn't. She had stopped crying when it was no longer possible through lack of nourishment. But she was crying, Susan could tell that. She gently placed her back beside her mother on the small bed beside the window. They lay cuddled together as she and Sergei had cuddled. Obtaining the need that each wanted. Food and warmth were no longer a necessity. Only the nearness of a loved one. But for how long? Susan wondered. Rosa had obviously starved herself to save her baby. She could see that it would need a miracle to save her. Like a fire that struggles to retain its heat, but lacks the energy to burn what little embers there are, her life was slowly ebbing away. Susan went to fetch the doctor.

He shook his head sadly. 'There is nothing I can do,' he whispered. 'There is nothing left to revive.'

Susan was Rosa's constant companion. Every minute of her spare time was spent stroking her arm and sharing her stories of her family. Rosa also had had a family. Her mother, father, sister and brother had all perished at the camp. She had been pregnant with Katrina so had been 'spared' for experimentation. She did not go into the unspeakable details of her ordeal. Miraculously Katrina had been born and they had lost interest. Why she never knew. Only that they were alive – just. 'It was a living death; sometimes I think I would have preferred death, but for my baby. She deserves to live. To see those that brought about this insanity are punished. They do not deserve mercy, whatever god may preach. They are beyond that. Especially those of our own race who betrayed us. Selling our souls to save their own traitors' skins.' Susan was amazed at the vitriolic outburst from so frail a form. Something niggled at her mind as she listened to the account of how the family were snatched from their home in Berlin and taken away. They had given up all Jewish practices and customs and had assumed the mantle of gentiles. As far as anyone knew, they were not Jews. But one man knew.

'Tell me about the man who you think gave you away.' Susan coaxed as Rosa grew weak from her exertions.

'He was tall – very tall, with dark hair and bushy eyebrows. I shall never forget his eyes – blue, almost black… and evil.' She cried as the memory became too painful for her.

Carl Weisz! She remembered his boast as if it were yesterday. "Don't worry, I have done it before for many of my Jewish compatriots." Werner had believed him. He was helping them escape from the nazis' net. Poor Werner. His spirit was destroyed long before they put him in the gas chamber.

Susan renewed her vow to Rosa. She also renewed her vow to herself that above all else, Carl Weisz would suffer as those he had denounced had suffered. And she would watch him die.

Two days later Rosa died. Every time Susan visited her, she made her repeat her promise to look after Katrina. On their last meeting Susan took the little bundle into her arms and held her close. She promised to treat her like the daughter she had lost; as if she were her own. Rosa smiled a weak smile of contentment and her hand slipped out of Susan's for the last time. Susan wept.

On the 8th May Germany surrendered to the allies. Hitler and Goebbels had committed suicide the month before. It was all over. Susan rejoiced for the peace in Europe. And for the future peace in the world that would surely come. Her muscles felt light and useless. She was drunk on the euphoria of celebration. Even those who had lost all hope managed the semblance of a smile. Probably because everyone else was smiling. Little Katrina gurgled in happiness as she fed hungrily on the fine food that was regularly provided. A banquet for her second birthday. She seemed to know that today was extra special.

The letters from Sergei were infrequent, but at least he wrote. He had been there at the end. With the detachment that finally stormed the last fanatic stronghold. All were killed; they would never have surrendered, he wrote. It is quite pitiful. We have been killing youths and boys, dressed like men. Brainwashed into thinking that it was glorious to die for the fatherland. I am sick of this war. Sick of men who seek to dominate others. To impose their will on ordinary people who have no choice. I miss you so … Sergei.

The months passed and Susan waited for the latest news from Berlin. How soon would it be possible to go there? Would they let the former inhabitants back? She had no way of knowing. The officials at the hostel could tell her no more than she could guess. She waited eagerly for a letter from Sergei. No matter how infrequent or morbid his letters were, the very act of seeing his handwriting on the envelope gave her a thrill. 'Sergei has written to me,' she would croon to Katrina, toddling around her quarters like a young puppy with legs that worked out of step with its brain. 'Mama,' she would shout as Susan deftly swept her up into her arms and cuddled her in delight. 'We are going home my little jewel. Home to where I can look after you properly and where you will grow up into the most beautiful girl in all the world.' Katrina cooed her agreement and clapped her delicate hands together just as Taghi used to do.

It was not until January of 1946 that Sergei finally sent word that entry to Berlin and the surrounding areas was being allowed. But he cautioned, the Soviets are already making plans to annex the whole of East Germany and put it under communist rule. He anticipated that it would not be long before Berlin became a closed city. 'Come quickly my

English rose, there may not be another chance for us to be together. You must establish your rights in Berlin and then leave as soon as possible, for afterwards you will have no rights.'

His words frightened her. What was happening? Was her house safe? Were Werner's business assets still in place? Had all they had ever worked for been destroyed with everything else? She read on. 'I enclose a special pass for you to get through the check points. I can be contacted through the administration office of the Politburo in the Soviet sector of the city. It is opposite the Zentrale, what is left of it.' Susan recalled the station very well. The hordes of prisoners being bustled and beaten, trampled on and literally flung onto the cattle trucks lined up on the once proud platforms that were used to seeing the pride of German engineering. She was glad it had been destroyed. Perhaps the new station, when it was built, would signal a new regime. A new beginning. An honourable government elected by honourable people. She shook her head. What had gone wrong?

There was a PS at the foot of the letter. 'I have good news for you, if I can call it that. I have traced Carl Weisz.'

CHAPTER VII

1978

'Remember the last time we were here Clive?'

'Yes, ... two year ago wasn't it?' George Parker chuckled and spilt his coffee.

'You have a very good memory Clive my son. Still what should you expect from the Chief Investigating Officer of the Fraud Squad? Congratulations by the way on your promotion. I appreciate it is not generally broadcast but we in the business,' he touched his nose knowingly, 'have ways of finding out these things.'

'Thank you George. Don't spread it around.'

George poured himself a third cup of coffee and ordered a second Reme Martin from Patrice who just happened to be passing. 'Excellent meal Patrice. Always is. Wine was superb.'

Patrice nodded his thanks and fussed his way down the aisle stopping at every table to dispense his wisdom.

'If you remember when we were last here, then perhaps you can also tell me who was sitting at the next table?' George indicated the large table to Clive's right.

'Certainly I can. Do you want a full list or will a general summary of the personnel do?' Clive loved to tease George and show off his flawless memory for details that anyone else would have forgotten almost immediately.

'Just the main protagonists will do. Especially the one who was hosting the table.'

'Oh him. Maximillian Holst. He was entertaining several Fleet Street publishers, two executives from TV companies – do you want the companies?' – he raised his ginger eyebrows to reveal bland badger like eyes challenging George to say yes. George remained silent. 'And three chappies from the new fangled cable computer consortium.'

'Got it in one. I've nothing but admiration for you Clive. If ever you want me to vouch for the efficiency of the Fraud Squad, call on me.'

George's cigarette was lit by the passing Patrice before he could struggle with the lighter in his waistcoat pocket. George nodded his thanks to the Maitre D' and inhaled a great gust of smoke into his craving lungs.

Clive finished his coffee, sat back in his chair, and contemplated the round untidy figure opposite him. He had known George Parker for nigh on ten years and recognised the preliminary banter as a prelude to picking his knowledge about something or someone. 'Who is it George this time?'

George scrabbled at the ash dropping onto his waistcoat and cast his eyes skywards in mock surprise. 'Who is who?' he replied.

'The man on whom you would like further information. That is if you have any information to date.' He stopped George's mock protest and continued. 'I think I am correct in assuming that you would like all of the data we hold on Maximillian Holst.'

'Got it in one again Clive! Must have been that excellent Puligny Montrachet we had with the smoked salmon. Either that or the fish. They say that fish is good for the brain.' George smiled at his old pal and heaved his bulk nearer to the table. 'Tell me about him.'

'How long have you got? If we dined every week for another two years I doubt if I could cover the barest essentials of what we have on him. None of it makes very good reading at that.' Clive sighed and beckoned the waiter for another pot of coffee. George looked at his Seiko wristwatch, a present from his mother. 'I have another couple of hours to spare if you're happy.'

'Before I begin, I would like you to explain to me why I am to give you a resume on someone whom I think is the biggest crook in London. And elsewhere probably.'

'You remember the dinner two years ago. Of course you do. Well you will also remember that I told you about a fraud in the bank that I know was being perpetrated but that I had no idea who, how, or why.' George paused to collect his thoughts. 'Well I think I know who. I am hoping that what you will tell me tonight will give me a lead on to the "how" and the "why".'

'Refresh my memory of what you told me last time. It bore little connection with anything I was working on at the time so I had dismissed it from my mind.' His excuse was taken by George as a request to repeat the details so that both could be fully conversant with the problem. They had practised this in the past and it had worked exceedingly well.

As he was bid George went over his theory about the 'lost' funds swimming about in the computer system, the 'margins' and the 'fractions'. The surpluses that no one heeded. Why should they? They had always been there and until the sophistication of computer technology, no one could accurately assess them. Even then it was an unknown quantity and quite impossible as yet to account for to the n'th degree.

Clive nodded his agreement as George expounded his hypothesis. 'Suppose someone, some persons, could harness all the surpluses and margins and channel them into a precise 'route' programmed into the computer.'

'Is that possible?'

'Theoretically yes,' continued George, a little annoyed to be asked an obvious question. 'But it would need a genius to figure out the configurations and complexities of establishing a system within the existing safeguards. I doubt if it could be done, but . . . '

'But you are convinced that it has been done.' Clive took the words out of George's mouth in his customary manner.

'Do you know Clive, that's why I enjoy having dinner with you so much. We are on a similar wavelength. I suppose it's being in the same business for so long.' The brandy slipped easily down George's throat. Without thinking he popped a morsel of cheddar cheese into his mouth, and sucked on the luscious flavour before expanding further. 'Nothing is impossible, we both know that. Let us suppose that it has been done. And that it has been in operation for some time . . . approximately seven years I'd say.'

'Why seven years?'

'Two things. Since 1971 the figures that I have produced to support my theory all agree in the margin of expectation of the Bank's income since that year. In addition, that is when decimalisation took place – remember that? – when everyone's account was converted from pounds, shillings, and pence, to decimal currency. I simply put myself in the shoes of someone wanting to beat the system and that was an obvious beginning. The figures tied in so . . .'

'So you have proved your theory. But you have no proof. No funds apparently missing. No definite suspect. No motive. At best you have a very arguable co-incidence of so called 'margins' and a vague idea of whom might be behind it. If you came to me as a detective with that information I'd show you the door.'

George smiled. 'How many years have we known each other Clive?'

'Is this another trick question to test my memory?'

'No. But you have known me long enough to take my assessment of a situation seriously. And this is one of them. I know it. I feel it in my bones. And I have a gut feeling that it is bigger than anything that you or I have ever come across.' He raised his eyes and clasped his meaty hands on the table before him. 'And I also believe that it is in some way connected with your man. Maximillian Holst. You tell me everything you know or suspect about this man and I will tell you about my man.'

Over the next hour and a half Clive related the background of Maximillian Holst from the earliest known details of his origins in the German Czechoslovakian border with Russia at the foot of the Carpathian mountains. In the little village of Slahusky he had been one of eleven children of a peasant father and mother who lived the nomadic life of the gypsies, buying and selling horses and anything of use to someone else. Real name was Carl Weisz, Clive told George. But other names had been unearthed over the years and it was uncertain even if the Carl Weisz was an assumed name or one given to him by the annexation of his district by the Russians who insisted on re-naming all families with 'label' names. Weisz or Weiss was 'white' – probably because his parents were paler than the normal gypsy types living in the settlement. Full name was Maximillian Alexander Carl Holst. All taken for their historic significance. 'Thinks he can conquer the world, I suppose,' Clive mused absentmindedly. George knew better. Clive did not make absentminded remarks without some good reason.

'We managed to trace his movements from Slahusky to Berlin, where he settled for a while. Dealing in all manner of goods. The German authorities were very helpful – I gather they too had reason to mistrust any dealings that this man offered. There was talk of illegal black market transactions in food to be supplied to the concentration camps during the war. God knows there was a paucity of it without this Carl Weisz getting his dirty fingers on it. He also played one sector of the occupying forces against another after the war, being able to supply materials that no one else could. He cheated them, not only on the prices paid, but on a special exchange rate for Deutschmarks that netted him his first million dollars. Clive watched as George noted odd details on his napkin. he would apologise to Patrice later – he always did – and leave sufficient to replace the item.

'Paris was his next stop. He set himself up as a book publisher. Mainly textbooks and reference books for colleges and schools. He seemed to have the connections to pick up where prior publishers had lost contact. Another name that cropped up here was Karl Prosser – a publisher back in Berlin before the war. Had a decent business and was well respected. His reputation didn't last long in Paris – the printers and associated trades did not like his ethics and sharp practices. He left suddenly, leaving debts and a defunct company, which never had any capital anyway. He then went to Paris and arrived in England, or precisely London some time in 1948.'

'Just in time for the Olympic games?'

'Yes George. Carl, or Maximillian could always be counted on to get his timing right. Must have made a packet out of the publicity material alone, without the unique licence that gave him a percentage of all printed matter, programmes, leaflets, books, magazines, etc. No one knew how he had pulled that one off, but it was rumoured that he had influence in the Jewish hierarchy that held the major shares in the companies involved.' Clive's eyebrows knitted together uncharacteristically. 'That seemed to go against everything that he had ever professed. That he was not a Jew and hated being linked with them.'

'Anti semitic was he? Is that how he survived the purge before and during the war?'

'I don't know,' pondered Clive, 'but there have been several instances of him being linked to quasi communist movements in the city. That's one of the reasons that he has never been accepted by the "inner circle".'

George took a small diary out of his breast pocket. 'You will be surprised to learn Clive that I too have been delving into the background of a certain person and it bears a striking similarity to the travels of your intrepid entrepreneur. I cannot speak for the period before the war, but from 1945 onwards, my "subject" shall we say, followed near enough the same route as your man. And at about or shortly after the dates you mention. What would you make of that in your meticulous investigations into the devious co-incidence of modern criminals?'

'There are no such things as co-incidence. Events happen as they happen. If they co-incide, that is in the order of things. There is no magic formula. Each instance has to be viewed both on its own and in conjunction with connected matters.' Clive brought all of his public school manner to bear in expounding one of his favourite put downs. George had heard it before and nodded knowingly in mock acquiescence.

'But you will admit that the fact that two Germans, emanating from Berlin, followed similar patterns of travel at about the same time over three or four years.' George stopped to observe the slightly scornful countenance of Clive, ready to destroy his presumption with a masterly comparison of thousands of others who had made the journey proving nothing.

'Given that the co-incidence – sorry – similar happenings occurred you would want other corroborative evidence to link the two wouldn't you?' George waited for a slow nod from Clive. 'Take a look at these investments over the past seven years. I have labelled them A and B. Do you not detect a certain similarity in their execution? An outsider might even be tempted to say that one line of investments was following the other. As if the second were acting on the advice of the former. Good investments too you will note. Mostly to do with the media, newspapers, publishers, television, satellite, advertising . . . '

'Where did you get this information?'

'I have my connections, as you do. It wasn't too difficult to pick the brains of the Investment Houses and ask for significant purchases and sales – they log them all the time. They have to, to keep ahead of the market. Only in most of the cases listed, it appears that the investors were one step ahead of the dealers.'

'You have been very busy George. I commend your persistence. You know of course, that the first line of figures relates to Maximillian Holst's major dealings – there are very few men in the city that can match his capacity for huge gambling in the market; Rudolph Murdock, Charles Hanson and a few others, but not many.' Clive looked up into the self satisfied expression decorating George's face. 'Who is the other person?'

George deliberately replaced his diary in his pocket, folded the napkin carefully into a square and tucked it into his trousers. 'That second list of securities bought and sold over the seven years was executed by a Nominee Company in the name of Niemand. And the principal member of the trustees managing the company is one Peter Mallory; believed to be a German by birth.'

As soon as George mentioned the name Mallory, Clive started and his keen eyes narrowed in surprise. It was almost possible to see the cogs turning in his brain as he knitted the evidence together and tried to form a pattern and a conclusion. He let out a slow inaudible whistle that wafted the surface of George's cigarette ash in the ashtray and spattered the white table cloth with grey dust.

'As you say George, I think that you may very well have the inklings of a subject that I would be very interested in pursuing.' Clive was never one to jump in at the deep end and commit himself absolutely until all the facts screamed for him to act.

'Before we discuss the implications further Clive, I would like your confirmation that the idea I have in mind would be in accordance with your normal practices.' Clive swept his ginger locks to one side and indicated that he was willing to hear George out.

'I have told you that I didn't know how or why haven't I?' Clive nodded. George sat back satisfied that he had Clive's full attention. 'Well, I think I know how, or can have a jolly good guess; now I have to find out the reason why. The only way I can do that is to get close to my man. But that would give the game away before I am ready to move.'

'Get him on your team.'

George was stopped in his tracks. The answer was so simple that he cursed for not seeing it himself. It was perfect. Peter Mallory was ripe for a move to Inspection Department. Why not attach him to the Fraud Office? But it would have to be done carefully. An immediate transfer might arouse suspicion – too obvious. His wife. That was the answer. Her usefulness at the Computer Centre was deserving of a promotion – a higher ranking position in the headquarters of the bank overseeing all computer systems and their eventual expansion. A greater expansion in the funds being extracted? He laughed ironically as he reminded himself of his purpose to stop the fraud not to enable it to develop further.

Clive promised to obtain greater details of the various movements in Maximillian Holst's assets and the complex arrangement of his multi companies, including the ones registered in Liechtenstein. George would meet him again, over dinner of course, to compare the final elements relating to the two Germans. 'I have a connection at the Immigration Office who can work miracles in tracing backgrounds – he's already done it in the case of Holst. Let's see what he can dig up on your man Mallory.' Clive's parting words were music in George's ear as he watched his compatriot place his bowler firmly on his rust coloured head and disappear with the evening crowd.

Wendy Mallory was slightly perturbed by the summons to the Personnel Office on the following Monday. She knew the Personnel Manager very well and no mention had been made of any problem during the usual monthly get-togethers with the remainder of the senior staff. There had been no indication of staff transfers, training, incompetence, or as far as she knew, anything at all that required her presence at the Manager's desk.

'Come in Wendy.' Shirley Johnson indicated the fawn leather seat in front of her desk. She came round the gleaming mahogany surface and sat with Wendy in the adjacent chair.

'Is this a formal meeting?' Wendy's question was posed as she crossed her legs and looked Shirley straight in the eye.

'No, not exactly Wendy. Not in the way that you take it to be. More in the way of informal discussion on where you are going from here.' Shirley smiled and glanced down at her personnel file of Wendy's records.

'Where would I want to go from here?' Wendy was even more puzzled by the phrase.

'How long have you worked at the Computer Centre now Wendy? Ten years? Quite a long time for a programmer. Too long wouldn't you say?' Shirley raised her gaze beneath her blonde perfectly arched eyebrows to note Wendy's reaction. She was not altogether sure why someone in Head Office in London had directed her to move this most valuable asset to a supervisory job in London that would waste the talents needed more than ever in the technology to come.

'Too long? Does that mean that my work is not appreciated?' Wendy knew only too well that her usefulness was of the highest merit and her annual report reflected that. What was Shirley getting at? Did anyone suspect? For the first time there was a doubt in her mind as to the efficacy of Peter's precautions and her own meticulous safeguards. She dismissed the doubt as soon as it arose. Seven years and not a scrap of evidence to suppose that the bank were aware of any discrepancy. There was none was there? So how could they?

'No Wendy. Your work is of the highest standard. That is why you are being promoted to Senior Computer System Supervisor with special responsibilities to the Chief General Manager for our computer enhancement over the next five years. Congratulations, you deserve it.' There was just the twinkling of envy in Shirley's expression which was not lost on Wendy.

'Thank you.' Wendy preened herself inwardly at Shirley's unguarded moment. The position in London would put her ahead of Shirley – that would not go down well with the Personnel Manager's own self importance and aspirations to reach the top. Tough, decided Wendy. This was obviously someone else's decision and there was nothing she could do about it.

She left the Personnel Office clutching her appointment in her hands. She had been assured that her husband would be found a suitable position in London as soon as possible, although not necessarily a promotion. Wendy knew that he would not be bothered over her seniority to him. It intrigued him he said, to make love to one of the 'hierarchy' and be told to do what she wanted him to do. She smiled broadly at the memory of their little games. She had come a long way in her thirty five years. A tribute to her single minded studies and determination that she would educate herself beyond what most people would expect her capabilities to be. Her parents had seen to that. A devotion that outstripped most fathers' and mothers' pride in their children. But then, they had sacrificed so much for her that she could never repay the debt. Never wipe out the misery of those early years after the war. How different it was now – her mother would have been very proud of her, and of Peter. And what they were doing.

She must tell Peter of the intending transfer. They must plan together the last stage of their mission – Peter was almost ready to move against their adversary. To finally reach the nemesis that his life, and hers, had been devoted to. Now the bank were putting in place the last components necessary for the 'final solution.' Innocently assisting them to be where Peter had always intended that they should be. Near the heart of the action. Within reach of the monstrosity that was again about to threaten the lives of people whom she loved. She hurried to the fourth floor where Peter worked and strode along the beige carpeted corridor to his office at the far end. Observing her from the entrance hall to the corridor was George Parker. His mustache twitched pleasantly. His scrutiny never left her lithe figure as it made its way to her husband's door. Could he be wrong? Could he have misread all the signs about this vibrant woman and her comparatively quiet husband? His natural instincts told him yes, but a most reliable indicator overrode his feelings of reservation – his predisposition to follow his hunch. The little something that took into account every minute detail of his investigations and added a little of his intuition to the bare 'paper facts,' which in themselves were only circumstantial. What it was he didn't know. Only that it was there – somewhere deep in the inner recesses of his grey matter and that it surfaced whenever it was needed. It surfaced now to steady his hesitancy as he saw them together, smiling and whispering like young lovers, through the office door. His size nine shoes made no sound as he continued on his way to the fifth floor to collect his bulky files, ready for the journey back to London.

Peter's request for a transfer to London to set up home with his wife was treated with sympathy by the head of his department. 'I'll have a word with a few people in Head Office to see what I can do,' he promised. Two weeks later he called Peter to tell him that he found just the position for him. It would not mean a promotion but it would be a very good chance for him to expand on his knowledge of the bank's accountancy and put it to a completely different use. Inspection Department were wanting someone of his ability to assist with possible fraud opportunities. He would be commissioned to draw up new sets of instructions and checking procedures for branches to follow as the computer system evolved. Having won two awards for suggestions of improving the present system, he was obviously 'ideal for the job.' He joined Wendy at the Kensington Hotel, Knightsbridge, one month later to hunt for a house. The following Monday he met George Parker. A non-committal nod accompanied the meeting as he was shown round the department and introduced to the various sections. Most of his work would entail being 'in house' as opposed to out in the field and that suited Peter. He was at home with complicated equations and accountancy problems. People interfered with his thought processes and he had enough to concentrate on without getting involved with minor fiddles that were the lifeblood of the regular inspectors. George was different. He sensed that he was employed to catch bigger game. A different kettle of fish. One to be respected. As the others did. He would enjoy talking to him to test the extent of his knowledge. It was just what George hoped he would do.

Strangely enough Peter did not show any propensity for the good life. His living was modest and the house he had found with his wife Wendy was no more than an early 'Surrey type' home with half walled outer tiles and neat cottage gardens front and rear. Not the residence of someone who has ample funds to better themselves. George was more than ever convinced that whatever fraud was being perpetrated was not for the benefit of Mr. and Mrs. Mallory.

'Where did you go to school Peter?' George asked idly as they shared a coffee break.

'Weymouth Grammar, why?'

'No reason, it's just that I find the educational background of most of my staff is an indication of their view on people.'

'In what way?' Peter noticed the coffee drops oozing their way onto George's shirt via his second chin.

'Oh, the public school pupils are more tunnel visioned if you like. Never quite viewing a situation from all angles. Too much in a hurry to make an objective assessment. Know what I mean?'

Peter was not sure what George meant but he nodded as he assumed that this large round man, wheezing on his perpetual cigarette was about to tell him. He was not mistaken.

'What one person sees as a common or ordinary daily occurrence, another will interpret it differently. Take the case of a man making a telephone call. From a telephone box. At lunchtime.' George's sentences were separated by pauses that threw up the picture of such a man. As if the talker were thinking slowly of the next picture to present to the listener. 'Nothing unusual in that you would suppose. But then to the casual observer there is nothing unusual. Until you examine the who and the why.' George's expression gave nothing away of the thought processes that were unfolding in his mind.

'Suppose one of those observers knew the man in the telephone box. And he knew that the man had access to a telephone where he worked. Then the picture takes on a different hue doesn't it? Why make the call from a box when it would be perfectly natural to make it from his desk? The logical answer would be that he had something to hide wouldn't it?

What the call was about and to whom the call was being made.' George slurped the last dregs of coffee from his cup and refilled it from the percolator. 'So you see Peter, that is how we in the inspection department work. The analogy could be taken to its ultimate conclusion, but the point is, never take anything at face value in this job. Doesn't matter if you're wrong. Follow each lead and eliminate each one. Eventually you will get there. Especially being a Grammar school boy.' He laughed as he heaved his body out of the too low chairs that he had cursed the day they were brought in to replace the old fashioned arm chairs that he loved.

Peter had never moved a muscle during his little lecture and George admired his ability to hide any facial disclosure of what he was thinking. Must never play poker with him, George silently intoned to himself.

Over the past week, George had discreetly followed Peter during his lunch break and had been a witness to the exact circumstances of his little tale. Now he was certain that he had the right man. Anyone innocently listening to his diatribe would have shown some sort of reaction or laughed at the similarity to his own behaviour. Peter didn't. He had something to hide that was none of the bank's business. Fair enough if it was entirely personal. George would find out.

Right at this moment however, George thought, I have to try to prepare a case for presenting to the Board at the next quarterly review of the Fraud Office's successes or otherwise. 'How is your new job shaping up Peter?' Wendy placed the full English breakfast of bacon, eggs, tomatoes, sausage, and mushrooms before her husband and noted with pleasure the instant appreciation of his nasal senses. His love of good food went back to his childhood in Germany when his mother always insisted "a substantial breakfast looks after the inner man." Peter took a finger of buttered bread and dipped it in the egg, rolling the thick yellow yolk into a golden lollipop before savouring it at his leisure. 'Pretty good. The work is interesting and quite different from the routine figurework at Manchester. Boss is quite a character.'

'Do I know him?'

'Wouldn't think so. He doesn't have much to do with the regular inspections – more of a background counter espionage type. He looks after the big frauds.' Peter laughed at Wendy's apprehension. 'Don't worry. He is not after us.'

'How do you know?'

'We've been through this a thousand times. There is no one, and you said this yourself, no one who could trace the leakage of funds. Why should they? There is nothing missing. No one looks for something that isn't lost. That's the beauty of it.' Another gleaming mouthful of yolk made a mess of his lips and he licked the delicious film carefully into his mouth.

'Have you spoken to him?' Wendy still didn't sound convinced.

'Of course I have. We have regular conversations about all manner of things. To do with the job that is.'

'What is he like?'

'You are asking a lot of questions this morning. Aren't you going to join me?'

Wendy's breakfast was not as appetising as she had expected. Something bugged her and it had to do with George Parker. 'What does he look like?'

Peter realised that Wendy was not going to let it go. His empty plate, clean as a whistle, was placed in the sink before he sat with Wendy to reassure her. 'Big, round, jovial at times, very quick eyes, stained waistcoat, dark wavy hair and a walrus mustache you can spot a mile away.'

'Does he walk with a sailor's gait?'

'Yes, I suppose he does. Why?'

'I've seen him.' She nodded slowly recalling the visit to the computer centre in Cheshire. 'He was at the centre recently. He had a long chat with the Director of Computer Services.'

'Nothing unusual about that is there?'

Wendy pursed her lips as she tried to remember the events that followed George's visit. Several of the senior staff and one or two 'high fliers' had been called in to discuss their present positions with Charles Lofthouse. Routine surely, after an inspector's visit. Or was it? 'I think he was after something. George Parker I mean. Something more than an interest in our future. I saw the files on Charles's desk; more than a dozen – sixteen I'd say. Sixteen of the top brains at the centre. They were copied later, probably for Mr. Parker, I remember Julie complaining that she had to re-charge the duplicator ink and getting it all over her dress.' The picture became clearer as Wendy followed her train of thoughts. 'Why would George Parker want to see the files of the select band working at the computer centre?'

'How do you know the files were for his use?'

'Because when he left, he was carrying two briefcases, not the single one that he arrived with.'

Peter frowned and went over the conversations he had had with George. Were the supposedly innocent examples of people's behaviour subtle hints that he was under suspicion? Or were they mere coincidence? No. He shook his head. They proved nothing. Probably did it to all newcomers to the department to ensure that they were warned not to act in a way that could cause the office any embarrassment. 'Don't worry. If no one has suspected anything in seven years, they are not likely to now are they?' Peter's confident tone comforted Wendy's disquiet and the smile returned to her eyes. 'And now we have to get down to some work. The market is in a bullish mood. Let's see if we can upset the trend and cause a little anxiety for Mr. Holst.'

Over the next two hours Peter and Wendy studied the holdings that their nominee companies held in Maximillian's group of companies. Each holding matched near enough, the private holding of Maximillian Holst, but Peter had concealed the extent of the holdings to the registrars by purchasing blocks in different nominee names. These nominees were hidden pseudonyms for the parent nominee company – Niemand Nominees based in Liechtenstein. The pupil had learnt from the master and was playing him at his own game.

At the end of their deliberations, Peter had a list of the stocks which he would sell immediately the stock exchange opened for business on Monday. The sales, big enough to be noticed, would throw a doubt into the substance of Maximillian's boasts that his immense corporation of communication business was as sound as he professed. A few well placed hints to the financial editors of the leading newspapers would add weight to the notion that the empire was due for a revisal of its fortunes.

The grim smile that adorned Peter's face as he saw again the latticed ceiling in his cottage in Stretton, appeared momentarily before he slept soundly in the arms of his ally, Wendy. On his lips were Churchill's famous words. "This is not the beginning of the end, but the end of the beginning."

Clive Farnworth had some very vital information for George Parker. In return he wanted the full extent of George's suppositions on the activities of one Peter Mallory.

'Lunch today George?'

'Why not. My treat, you choose.'

Clive thought a moment. Tuesday was not a good day for lunch anywhere. Most restaurants were closed on Mondays and hadn't really got into their stride by Tuesday mid-day but – a lunch with George was never dull. In any case the information could not wait. 'There's a nice little eatery over Harrods. How about that? Good selection and some unusual dishes.'

'I know it. I go there every now and again to view the clientele. Never know who might turn up. Even us!' George chuckled as his friend confirmed that he would book a table for 12.30.

There were very few in the sun lounge built on to the side of Harrods when Clive and George sat down. A long church windowed corridor of glass and small tables stretching the length of the main dining hall on the 4th floor. 'What is this piece of good news Clive? Or is it good?'

Clive finished the crayfish gratinee with a relish and wiped the corners of his mouth. 'Good. Very good. You should have chosen this George.'

'I am talking about Peter Mallory. You said you had some news that would please me. What is it?' George was getting impatient with his colleague and his colleague knew it.

'Patience is a virtue George. Don't spoil my lunch. Or yours. Finish your salmon – it's looks equally delicious.'

Throughout the afternoon, sustained by glasses of Sauvignon Blanc the two men sat in huddled conversation exchanging notes on their respective subjects. Clive had done a very thorough job, as usual pointed out George, on the origins of one Peter Mallory. The name had rung a bell somewhere in the recesses of Clive's mind when George had mentioned it. A common enough name but for one thing. It was linked to the name Kawalek, a name which was also used by Maximillian Holst in his early days. 'That couldn't be coincidence could it George?' Clive teased knowingly. George listened intently as Clive related how his contacts in Germany had traced the operations of one Carl Weisz through his aliases of Boris Vukadovic, Werner Kawalek, Karl Prosser, and several other 'temporary identities' before becoming the all powerful conglomerate head of World Communication Network, Maximillian Alexander Carl Holst.

'But where does my man come in?' George could not see the connection.

Clive took George through the complexities of immigration into Great Britain and the formalities which had to be followed for intending residents from foreign countries. The immigration authorities had been very diligent in their search of the names that Clive had given them. Kawalek and Mallory. An unlikely combination, but finally 'bingo' as Clive put it. "I never play the game myself" – there on the printout was a match. Katrina Kawalek and Wendy Mallory. Same date of birth; "you'd be surprised how many we catch on dates of birth" – same country of origin – East Germany, same general features and build. 'Conclusion,' Clive pronounced. 'One and the same person.'

George was stunned. Wendy Mallory an East German? With the same name as one of Holst's? Could they be related? A daughter? Before he could take his premise any further Clive interrupted.

'Fascinating isn't it. The number of permutations as to the connection. Gives the idea of Maximillian Holst's fortunes a rather sinister twist doesn't it? Are you thinking what I am thinking George?'

'That they are working together – she funding him in his fanatical search for power? A possibility, but what of her husband Peter? Why has he taken her name?'

'But he hasn't.'

Again George was puzzled. Clive warmed to his task of scoring over his pal – he was long overdue for a special brandy – the prize for a particular 'coup de grace' between them. 'You will be surprised to learn that our investigations into Peter Mallory's background again threw up the name of Kawalek. His mother married a German national in Dorset in 1932. Weymouth to be precise.'

'But that means that both were called Kawalek. Are they related? That means then, that . . . '

'No. Wendy's real mother was not a Kawalek. She died in a concentration camp shortly after the war ended. Susan Kawalek brought her up and she took her name. The change is registered at Somerset House. Katrina Wenig Rosenberg, known as Kawalek; to Wendy Katrina Mallory.'

CHAPTER VIII

1946

There was change in the air. He could feel it in his bones. It was not anything to do with the sleeting snow that fell incessantly on the grey sombre paving stones below, it was an intuition that now the war in Europe was over, something more sinister was taking its place. Even now relations with the West were deteriorating. Squabbles and misunderstanding of intentions continually arose until there was a stand off. Neither side acknowledging the other unless it was necessary.

General Leonid Chukov looked down through the grey sleet at the Moscow citizens hurrying to catch the last bus to some stone brick apartment in the middle of nowhere to live out their dreary lives. Dreary people, in a dreary city, with dreary expectations. How they had been fooled with the 'great revolution.' Cocooned in a world where outsiders were not welcome and ruled with a fist of iron. Laws and rules were not flexible. There were no grey areas in the diktats issued from the Politbureau. Either obey every creed issued or disappear forever. Regimentation would be taken to the 'nth degree. Uniformity would be the order of the day. Greyness everywhere – like the snow. Even that could not maintain its pristine whiteness for long in this pitiful city.

The tall black haired man turned from the window and smoothed his obligatory Stalin mustache. His wife admired it. But then she would. She was a fervid supporter of all that Stalin and the Communist manifesto proclaimed. Stupid woman, swore Leonid, under his breath, if Stalin advocated bald heads for women, she would comply. He dismissed her from his mind as soon as he reached his littered desk. There was work to be done. To survive in the Soviet hierarchy you had to outsmart the others. Outer appearances and confidential opinions of your contemporaries were always a guiding factor to the heads of the political police force – his so-called masters, the MGB.

Section 13 of the First Main Directorate MGB, formerly half of the NKGB looked after the interests of the Soviet's future foreign infiltration into desired territories. A practice that had been in force for as long as Leonid could remember. Individuals and families specially commissioned to occupy foreign parts and grow up as a native, but commit their allegiance to the Soviet cause. "For communism to proliferate, it must occupy every part of the globe." Leonid recalled part of a missive circulated towards the end of the war to all senior NKGB personnel down to the rank of General.

There had been a series of secret meetings after the conference at Yalta. Stalin, Roosevelt and Churchill had completed plans for the defeat of Germany and proposed the setting up of the United Nations. The summer palace at Livadia had provided the stunning setting for what everyone believed was the beginning of peace. Stalin had other ideas. Clandestine infiltration by agents of the Soviet Union would systematically wreck the West's supremacy and enable the creeping ideals of communism to 'save' the struggling capitalistic countries. Leonid's mind wandered over the dogmatic propaganda expounded at the numerous meetings without ever being fully convinced of its efficacy. Surprisingly he had been charged with putting into operation the sublimation of Great Britain – the supreme symbol to the world of democracy. The Soviet wanted control of the people. Parliament could continue in its ineffective way – the people would dictate eventually the true government of the country. The general had thought about the problem through many sleepless nights. Even moving to the spare room to avoid the attentions of his 'dear' Tasha. Another obligatory duty that he found more and more repulsive as she relentlessly developed the mannish characteristics of many of his staff.

Gradually the germ of an idea came to him as he explored various methods of influencing the populace – something the Soviet Union had been doing since the demise of Nicholas II. What influences people most? he pondered. Contact.

How is that contact put into practice? Communication.

What forms of communication are there? Through the ears. Through the eyes. How? Word of mouth. Radio. Newspapers. Books. Television.

Leonid Chukov had his answer. He must control the communications system. All communication systems. How?

The various forms of communication in the west were capital controlled. Run by moguls who normally held the majority of the shareholdings. Now if such a man or men could aspire to positions where they controlled the distribution of material by way of newspapers, radio, television ... Chukov pursed his lips. A tremendous undertaking, but if he could pull it off, the Kremlin would etch his name in diamonds on his dacha.

Where to find such a man? Or men. He had to be fluent in languages; economically aware; a master at organising others. A dealer. A trader. Completely ruthless.

Chukov pushed an ornate button on his desk to summon his assistant. 'I want the names of all available, known operators, both here and in Western Europe who could fit all the attributes I have detailed on this list. No one must be missed off. Known agents, military men, government officials, acquaintances of the Soviet, Russian or otherwise, however remote, or anyone who has had any dealings with, or has shown any allegiance to, the party.' He fixed his assistant with the ramrod stare reserved for his underlings. 'And I want it yesterday.'

'Yes comrade. I'll see to it right away.' The seedy, careworn clerk scurried away to consort with the vast department beneath, where an army of Politbureau staff beavered away creating files and records on every known subject and person that the powerful MGB might ever deem necessary to justify its existence. Just fifteen more years to retirement. If they would let him complete them. Then he could disappear forever into the country to live out his life as he wanted. Reading, walking, studying nature, dreaming of his youth. Leonid Chukov had been a good servant to the NKGB. Producing results and using his agile brain both for the bureau and for himself. He had walked a tightrope for many years now, balancing the needs of the NKGB with the needs of his own conscience. With maturity he had seen the folly of the system which had spread like a cancer throughout the Soviet Union. Depression of the people into no more than obedient cattle. The privileged few, living capitalistic lives and professing their devotion to the cause. Caring not for the common man, he was dispensable in the irrational pursuit of the 'perfect' society. It did not exist. Leonid had discovered that quite early in his career. From then on, he was determined to play the Marxists at their own game. Always complying with instructions but taking care that somewhere in an operation, faults would occur, the results would not be achieved, or it would be abandoned because of someone's inefficiency. Never Leonid Chukov's inefficiency. He took great care to apportion the blame for his engineered failings to various members of his department, who had been deliberately chosen to execute the fatal mistake that would lead to failure. Chukov had no conscience about that. Each of the supposed culprits was fully worthy of dismissal or worse from the NKGB and the bureau would be better for it. In Chukov's view.

He cast his eyes at the enormous file that his erstwhile clerk placed on his desk. 'Is that all?' he said sardonically.

'We are still working on the latest files from our occupation of Eastern Germany. There could be many more leads there from the contacts that our agents have made both during and after the hostilities.' The clerk twitched his hands nervously. He knew that if Comrade Chukov did not find what he was looking for, then the whole department would suffer and he most of all. He had a wife and four children to feed. He must come up with the answer.

'I want the remaining information on my desk by 6am tomorrow. I shall not be going home tonight. Telephone my wife and tell her the circumstances. You had better telephone yours too.' Chukov dismissed him with a wave of his half moon spectacles and lowered his head to study the first page.

Three hours later he had compiled a provisional list of three persons who may or may not fit the bill. But he was not satisfied with his selection. He knew that the names had been separated from the remainder by the process of elimination of those who did not measure up to the standard that he had set. Each would pass any interview for such an assignment, but there was a vital ingredient missing from each. Flair. None had a record of that unique characteristic that set a man above the rest. Panache; flamboyance; ostentation; verve; a sense of theatre; a sense of style. A man whom all others would look up to. Revere. Admire, for his achievements, no matter how those achievements were gained.

He placed a long distance call to his equivalent number in the Freidrichsfeld district of Berlin. The ugly four storey building was now the MVD headquarters operating from what once had been an apartment block, hastily renovated to accommodate the control point for subversive Soviet activities. Primarily to undermine the unification of the four powers over the question of the division of Germany, and of Berlin.

'How are you Leonid?' The gravel voice of his contact echoed hollowly over the very bad line from Berlin. 'We have not shared a vodka together for far too long. But it is not vodka that you are ringing me about at midnight. You need my help.'

Leonid could feel the self satisfaction seeping through the telephone wires and the glib smirk of Stanislav Dzerzhinsky appeared like an apparition on the unlit wall opposite. He swallowed his first inclination to reply in similar sarcastic mode and merely agreed that he was seeking cooperation in a particular programme that he was working on. Nothing exciting, or earth moving, just routine.

Stanislav smirked even more. 'You should get out of that gloomy office of yours and see the real world in action. It would surprise you.' Leonid winced as he had to endure a further ten minutes of lurid description of the so called libertine ways of the occupying forces. Stanislav excepted of course. But his manner betrayed his enjoyment of the best of both worlds.

'What can I do for you?'

'No doubt with your network in and around Berlin, you will have made many contacts with, let us say, the undesirable elements of post war non-combatants. Emigres, exiles, fugitives, black marketeers or pseudo honest traders who have survived by their ingenuity. The manipulators who really control the market there.'

'Why do you need people like that?' Stanislav's curiosity was aroused.

There were plenty of candidates to fit a description like that in the Soviet Union. Why chase after someone here?

'I don't. A particular friend of mine has a private score to settle and he would prefer that an unknown be used and then disposed of.' Leonid's bland explanation appealed to Stanislav's sense of humour.

'Is there a woman involved?' He laughed lasciviously and poked fun at the staid operative on the other end of the line. 'Wouldn't be one of your women would it?' Again the dirty laugh rattled in Leonid's earpiece.

'Let us just say that the circumstances have made it imperative that I, that this friend, has someone available to assist in degrading and disposing of a certain party who is causing embarrassment.'

'I get the picture Leonid. Leave it to me. I will have a list in the next courier box. But if you wanted I could arrange the removal at this end. Nothing simpler in this city. People die all the time. It's natural.'

Leonid balked at the garrulous self congratulation oozing out of the boastful tones of the Head of Operations – Berlin. Living with the capitalists rubs off on you, murmured Leonid under his breath. I wonder if it would affect us all in the same way?

The files produced by the flagging clerk did not throw up any further candidates and Leonid waited eagerly for the special despatch from Berlin. He knew what he was looking for and would recognise him in an instant. That was his great advantage over others in his occupation. His intuition was invariably right. The large dossier arrived on schedule the following day and he left immediately for home saying that 'he would not return until he had completed his research.' If he was to succeed then the subject chosen, if there was one, would have to be carefully handled and initiated into the ways of the MGB, trained and instructed into their way of thinking. Indoctrinated with rigid guidelines to adhere to the ultimate aim for which he was being prepared. *But*... and Leonid pursed his lips in anticipation of the greatest ploy that he had ever engineered ... the man would have to have that fatal flaw that would ensure that the ultimate success was never achieved. That he was bigger than the MGB, the Soviet Union, the British hierarchy. His ego would have to be monumental without it interfering with the purpose at hand. First he would have to achieve the impossible – then he could exercise all the ego that his megalomaniac mind sought. Did such a man exist? A long night of exploration was in front of Leonid Chukov as he drove through the snow spattered streets to his anonymous concrete apartment on the north west of the anonymous city suburbs.

Stanislav Dzerzhinsky had carried out his research in his usual competent manner. Fourteen pages of possible candidates with the particulars of their background before the war. Details of their activities, tendencies, political leanings, idiosyncrasies, and all relevant information that made up an MVD dossier. A physical description and any peculiarities as well as photographs accompanied each report on each individual.

When Leonid had read through each once, he felt that he had been introduced to every man in the comprehensive dossier. He didn't know some of his relatives as well as he knew these paper individuals. Some of his relatives he didn't want to know, but these encyclopedic sketches made his senses tingle and itch over the possibilities for which these men could be utilised. That was his job. To use his intuition for the highest principles of the Soviet aims. It wasn't intuition really; his sense of judgement had been built up over many years of observation and careful examination of an individual's characteristics, education, content of his speech, his writing, his way of thinking. What one man said, another could repeat but with a completely different inflection to reverse the meaning. Leonid's dexterity and flair for picking up on the slightest hint of deeper meanings had put him in the forefront of those being considered for the head of MGB. The old NKGB had been split after the war into an MVD Section and an MGB Section with each head of the service having special responsibilities to the Kremlin and the covert operational council under Stalin's personal guidance.

His old adversary Stanislav Dzerzhinsky had vied with him to attain one of the posts, gloating when he had been given the MVD position. That entailed more brutal and practical methods of achieving the spread of communism, and the subversion of all those who stood in its way. He gloried in the power and his importance to the cause. Leonid shrugged.

When the Directorate was finished with Stanislav they would eliminate him without the slightest hesitation. They had a thousand standing by to take his place. Operatives were expendable, no matter how high a rank they held. The real intellectuals and communist 'thinkers' were a valuable asset and would be used as long as they produced results. Leonid always did.

He started the process of weeding out the obvious candidates who could be discarded immediately. Any deficiency in the attributes that Leonid was looking for condemned the file to the shredder. He was amazed at such a variety of crooks, criminals, racketeers, rogues, swindlers, and villains could exist in post war Germany, let alone during the hostilities. But exist they did, and from what he read, prospered out of any trade that they put their hand to. But very few had the characteristic he was looking for. That certain something that raised a man head and shoulders above the rest. Cunning and adaptability. And a ruthless quality to undermine any other of the same disposition.

The clock struck 5 am. Leonid breathed a sigh of satisfaction tempered with relief that his exhausted body could allow his brain to relax and mull over the two files that were all that remained of the original pile. Two files on two men that would occupy his further research in the coming weeks. Already he had an idea of the one he would prefer. But; and here Leonid concentrated his whole remaining energies on the question of how to engineer the selection of the correct person for the task, without actually choosing him himself. First he had to observe the two. To speak to them if necessary. To gauge their operation 'in the field' as it were. He smiled to himself. This is where all my training and experience will serve me well. The supreme stratagem with which to seal his future with the Supreme Soviet. He had no illusions about the communist doctrine. It was doomed to failure sooner or later and with any luck the candidate he would choose would be instrumental in bringing about the most gigantic reversal of thinking the world had ever known. Not in his lifetime, but before the millennium. And he was confident that the man he selected for the mission would rise to the challenge through his own particular talents and the Soviet's support.

But 'paper' curriculum vitae were not the ideal source of a person's inner qualities. Those were only observations by others of what a person purported to be. A newspaper's account of a happening from the outside. He had to get into the thoughts and ambitions of the person selected. To ensure that his instincts were in accord with the type of job that Leonid was preparing him for. Leonid's intuitive brain cells raced over the information buzzing in his head. Apportioning vital traits in his two choices to differing departments in his head, cataloguing the favourable points and assessing their value, re-examining the doubtful factors from all angles to see if they could be of an advantage. Physical make-up, age, commitments, attachments, particular idiosyncrasies; all found a niche in Leonid's computer brain which slowly made up his own personal file on each candidate.

He had to go to Berlin. To see the men. To observe them in their normal surroundings. Like a fox on the trail of his prey. He would know the terrain and the outside influences that affected their behaviour. Not until he was satisfied that each could do the job would they be brought into the fold of the MGB. Leonid snapped shut his briefcase, finished the vodka that had remained untouched for the last two hours and grunted in satisfaction at his efforts. He was quite looking forward to his trip and the meeting with Stanislav Dzerzhinsky.

'You have put on a little weight since last we met comrade.' Stanislav's chiding remark was all the more irritating because Leonid could see that the smartly dressed man opposite was as slim as ever. His uniform sat on his small frame like a comfortable bedcover. His small gimlet eyes were never still. They took in every detail of Leonid's appearance as if he was being interviewed for an executive position in the world's foremost commercial enterprise. Or so Leonid thought. Outer appearances and haute couture had no place in the Soviet system. Basic and practical. Able to do the job. You could look like a bear's backside and still be selected. If you were considered able. Stanislav was both able and surprisingly attractive. Dark and sleek, with the smile of a fawning butler, hiding the cruel and vicious temperament that only surfaced when appropriate to his job. His thin black eyebrows rose in anticipation of Leonid's rejoinder.

'I suppose it is due to a contented way of life. It is good for a man to acquire a little extra fat in Russia to combat the bitter winters. Of course you, here in Berlin, have life somewhat easier than we poor servants entombed in Moscow.'

Leonid noticed Stanislav's reaction to the 'easier' comment and knew that he had scored heavily against his adversary. He had always suspected that conditions here in Berlin were far more unrestricted than in Moscow and his taunt had struck home.

'We do have certain privileges, but the work here is far more complicated and intense. I have very little time for relaxation. There is so much to be done. Like conducting an exercise for an old contemporary for instance. The task you set me was not that simple. We do not have the enormous resources of your bureau back in Moscow to assist in computing all the information of individuals in Berlin. You were lucky that I have a competent staff network to dig up the dirt, as it were, for your benefit.'

'Thank you for your trouble. It will prove to be of invaluable assistance to my friend. I am sure that the person selected will bear out all the attributes you have accorded to him.' Leonid smiled benignly and nodded to Stanislav for a refill of his glass. Even in Moscow the vodka was not of the quality of this bottle and he was enjoying it immensely. Just as he was enjoying the game with this man perched precisely on his chair opposite.

'So you have decided to choose one of my 'candidates.' I told you we had the men for the job here. You will not be disappointed.' Stanislav leaned forward and licked his thin lips cunningly. 'But you have not been honest with me Leonid,' he used the christian name in exactly the same way he would with a prisoner being interrogated. 'You do not come all this way to see a man who has been suggested to you for a minor employment. There is something in the wind. I know it. And you know that I know it.' His piercing eyes held Leonid's for a second. 'So tell me. What is the real purpose of your visit?'

Leonid sighed as if Stanislav had wormed some great secret out of him. He would appreciate that and congratulate himself on his astuteness. Let him think that he is running things. That is just how I want it. Leonid glowed inside. This is turning out to be almost better than his chess tournaments with his brother, only with a more deadly objective at 'check mate.'

'The matter is highly confidential, I do not have to emphasise that. It is in its infancy as yet, but I can tell you that the directive comes from the highest source. It will be vital to the Soviet Union's status in the world as Germany is divided and the world turns against us. We shall of course continue to carry on with our subversive activities throughout Europe and the United States, but this is more subtle, more profound. It will be refined to perfection. That is why we must choose the correct person.' Leonid emphasised the " we" and was pleased to see that Stanislav did not miss the compliment. He would never miss a chance to further enhance his own importance to the heads of the MGB, and indeed the select band of Stalin's inner cabinet.

'What exactly is this man, when he has been chosen, expected to do?' Stanislav's throat betrayed his eagerness to be involved in this project, especially if it meant that he could eventually be credited with its inception and success. Everyone else was expendable. Even Leonid.

'I think the first step is to see these men, to observe them, to get to know them personally. Only then will it be possible to assess the viability of the operation. If they are not suitable, then there will be no need to take the matter further at this stage.' Leonid left Stanislav frustrated that he was not privy to every detail, and that was just how Leonid wanted it. He wanted to string him along until the time for the choice to be made. The choice had to be Stanislav's and would be recorded as such. But the choice would already have been determined by Leonid. How to engineer that choice was the challenge that Leonid looked forward to.

The shiny bulbous black limousine sat glistening in the afternoon sun like coal on a white tablecloth. The snow was a perfect depth to cover every house and tree, road and hedgerow with a powder like canopy of pure whiteness. The car looked ominous in such company. White spectred ruins and dilapidated buildings thrust their mournful edifices through the flat landscape. The southern tip of Berlin had suffered almost as badly as the city in the final bombardment. Leonid and his companion observed the scene across the square of cleared rubble. The large bulky man with dark blue almost jet black eyes lounged at his side. The narrowed pupils never left the couple on the doorstep of 175 Eichenstrasse. They were oblivious of the intrusion into their private goodbye as they shyly touched hands still flushed with the excitement of their kiss and their proximity to one another.

'Who are those people?' Leonid spoke quietly in the interior of the car.

'I don't know but I will find out. They are in my property. The American soldier will be easy to identify. The woman is not familiar to me. They may be squatters, or just passers by. I do not use the property at the moment. It has been in my family for many years and I intended to return to it eventually.' Carl Weisz waved his cigar nonchalantly in the confined space of the saloon as if the event had no more significance than an annoying inconvenience. But Leonid saw the clenched heavy eyebrows and the hate festering in his glare. He does not like people to take anything from him. To have his possessions. To have the effrontery to claim something that is his. Leonid's opinion of his choice of candidate was hardening daily. He was almost perfect. Developing into exactly what the project required. How would he deal with this? he wondered. The jeep departed and the woman turned and closed the door. 'Come with me.' It was a command not a request.

Leonid rose without a word and followed the figure ducking through the rear door. He did not mess with niceties or rank. They meant nothing to him. The world was his to command or manipulate, whichever suited his purpose.

He strode purposefully across the pristine snow, leaving a trail of large footprints indicative of his height. His thick mop of black hair waved over his squarish head to end at the nape of his muscular neck supported by heavy shoulders. Leonid noted that the mouth was expressionless beneath the slightly hooked nose running into broad flaring nostrils. The hairs protruding from the orifices were a perfect match for the intensity of his mane. Rather like a thoroughbred cossack horse thought Leonid. Carl produced a key from his waistcoat pocket and strode through the door into the large open lounge. Anna looked up in fear as the black coated, black haired demon bore down on her. 'What are you doing in my house?'

Anna could hardly decipher the words as she jumped for protection behind the teak table. 'Pardon?' was all that she could stammer.

'I asked you a question. What are you doing in my house? Who are you?'

'This is not your house. It belongs to my brother Werner Kawalek and his wife. They were... they were killed in the concentration camps...'

'I am Werner Kawalek and I have no wife. You are a trespasser on my property. Get out and return to wherever you came from.' Carl's barked orders echoed throughout every room in the high ceilinged house.

Suddenly it dawned on Anna that this was the evil Carl Weisz of whom Lazar had spoken. The description fitted and she panicked momentarily as she listened for her nephew upstairs in the attic. She could no longer try to bluster her way out of it. This man and his companion would not listen to reason.

'I must have made a mistake. I must have the wrong house. I am sorry. I only wanted to shelter for a few days before travelling on to Bad Durkheim. I will leave today.'

Carl's smile twisted his mouth into a grin of satisfaction. She was grovelling. She accepted his domination although she knew perfectly well that he was not her brother. How fickle people are when they have no strength to force their opinions on others. 'That is perfectly understandable, Miss er... Kawalek shall we say?' he laughed out loud at his joke. 'Come with me, I will give you a lift to the edge of the city. You can probably get some sort of transport from there. You seem capable of that,' he said as he glanced at her slim figure and fair wavy hair. 'It is surprising what you can get if you offer the right price.' Again he laughed and beckoned Anna to follow him.

Leonid watched fascinated from the doorway. There had been no bluster, no pretence. What Carl said, he actually believed in. Truth was an alien language only used by fools. His truths were universal. The truths of leaders who convinced others with reasoned arguments based on what they believed, or what the public would perceive as the truth.

Anna cringed on the sofa car seat between the two men. The second had not spoken. His impassive face revealed nothing of his feelings. Carl's attitude was almost magnanimous as his charm oozed out of his flabby countenance and his hands made gestures as if he were conducting an orchestra.

'Stop here.' Again the barked order to the driver.

The door opened and Carl and Anna emerged. This time he held her in a vice like grip above her elbow. Walking and propelled by the force of his motion, the couple made for an empty roofless house and a stairway hanging perilously from the remaining rafters. They disappeared inside.

Seven minutes later Carl reappeared lighting one of his favourite Russian cigars. He replaced the silver case in the inside pocket of his overcoat and savoured the first fresh intake through the newly pared end. He was smiling broadly to himself. Leonid shivered slightly. There was no soul in the man. No compassion. No love of anything. Except himself. Leonid knew now that his choice was perfect.

'The American Lieutenant will be dealt with in due course.' Carl's calm pronouncement was not meant for anyone in particular, more a reassurance to himself that the matter would be settled to his satisfaction.

Again Leonid wondered about this impassive individual who had disclosed information about his war time exploits that meant nothing more to his conscience than the woman whom he had just obliterated from his life. She was no longer a threat. No longer a person who could harm him. She was there when it was inconvenient so she had to be removed. Carl Weisz had owned up to many crimes during the thirties and forties, crimes which he knew his Russian companion would not, and did not want to, make public to any other authority. There was no German authority left to take recompense for any wrongdoing. There was no German law as such to prosecute anyone.

Leonid had a full dossier on the assumed names of Carl Weisz. Intricate and exhausting research into the real Werner Kawalek and his family had finally divulged that they had indeed perished in Auschwitz and that Carl had somehow been responsible. Several other families had also given evidence against the man "big and brash. A friend to Nazis, a friend to anyone who could enhance his prosperity and power. A betrayer of Jews, a betrayer of his contemporaries." His own story of Werner Kawalek was that it was he who had betrayed him to the Nazis as a Jew. Fortunately he had been able to convince the local Gruppenfuhrer that he was not the Carl Weisz being spoken of but Boris Vukadovic. Because of his prior dealings with many of the Gestapo leaders in supplying goods not easily available through the normal channels; drugs, tobacco, and a procession of prostitutes and young girls; suspicion had fallen on Werner Kawalek whose family background was connected with a Jewish settlement near the German border. Hadn't they found all the identity papers that proved his name? Carl's bland assertion that his version was the truth had Leonid convinced that in his twisted mind Carl actually believed his account to be the truth.

'I believe you have control of a publishing business that had good connections before and during the war?' Leonid addressed the question to the large man comfortably ensconced on the leather sofa in the room provided for his interviews.

'I have that privilege. Although the contacts have been allowed to lapse and my colleagues have probably moved on or have been killed. Some were in Paris, I recently obtained an exit visa to go there, but have delayed my visit to re-establish my business, until I have heard your interesting proposal.' Carl's thin lipped smile creased the jowls of his cheeks into a buddha like countenance. Not unattractive if the viewer was unaware of the evil behind it. He's like the devil dressed as a genial gentleman. The thought gripped Leonid and sent a shudder of cold fear down to the depths of his stomach. What sort of creature was he going to let loose on the unsuspecting British? Never before had he doubted his own motives to further the cause of his own brand of socialism. Until now.

He quickly dismissed the doubt from his mind and spent the next two hours explaining to Carl Weisz exactly what he had in mind and more to the point, exactly how it would benefit this megalomaniac man, both in wealth and power. Each could gain an advantage from the arrangement. He would be free to pursue his own ends in the search to control every communication system in the UK. Funds would be no object but he would have to prove that it could be done by his own devious methods, or honest methods if he so wished. Leonid knew that if given a choice Carl would automatically take the quickest and more than likely unlawful option. He enjoyed the thrill of ignoring the rules and regulations and proving that money and might could outwit financiers, authorities, governments even. There were always gullible ministers and eager young cabinet members willing to accept as gospel, his own brand of the truth.

'How will your department, or whatever power employs you gain a benefit from this expedition?' That's how he regards it, Leonid realised. A conquest of another brand of people. An adventure where he is the hero and the all conqueror, sent there to relieve the population of their imprisonment by the governing body. He was a Hitler, a Stalin. A Genghis Khan. Attila the Hun. These were such men, who by their sheer magnetism dominated whole nations.

'The Soviet Union has very long term plans for the expansion of its ideals. It has seen the folly of outright war and prefers to conquer other political systems by persuasion and undermining their present democracies. People do not want democracy. There is no such thing anyway. The few who have the power to persuade others really control the populace. So we are back to our system really where the ultimate direction of policies is decided by a very few privileged men in the Politburo. You can influence that power on our behalf. You will be the most powerful man in Europe. Who knows; given the correct circumstances, you may even spread your wings further.'

Leonid Chukov and Stanislav Dzerzhinsky sat in the comparative luxury of the MVD head's apartment overlooking the once tree lined Unter den Linden in the Russian sector of Berlin. 'Pity about this avenue isn't it? Like all of Berlin it has been reduced to a grey rubble. Like its dictators and strutting generals. Grey nothingness. I am going to enjoy seeing them hung – I have been accorded that privilege.' Stanislav turned to Leonid as if to receive his congratulations. Leonid shrugged and drank his vodka.

'We have more important matters to attend to than the disposal of criminals. That is in the past. The Soviet looks to the future. It requires us to safeguard our place in the world. We can learn a great deal from the mistakes of the German nation. Our task is to conquer from within. A stomach that is infected soon takes over the whole body and makes it weak in its resistance to outside forces. That is our aim. We must increase the influence we have in all European countries and the U.S.A.; we already have a strong presence there; but especially we must strengthen our representation in the mother of all democracies, the United Kingdom.'

'So that is the purpose of this exercise. To find more agents for our cause.' Stanislav scoffed. 'But why must we employ amateurs to do a job that the Soviet Union has perfected over half a century? With our sophisticated training methods we could turn out any number of candidates with far better credentials. We already have a network of personnel recruited from Cambridge who are serving us very well indeed. The number will grow, I will see to that,' Stanislav boasted.

Leonid sighed. He had known that his idea would not sit very easily on the shoulders of a died in the wool communist like his contemporary. New and more subtle methods were not the tools used by Stanislav or his band of tunnel visioned underlings. To convince Stanislav would be like persuading hot butter to stay on a knife. It would need patience and guile. He would not accept it unless at some stage it could be shown that he himself would have thought of it, or had mentally contemplated a similar ploy. Leonid refilled his glass and beckoned for the impatient Stanislav to sit on the opposite sofa.

'How did Stalin himself gain the power he has? A rather insignificant individual who was born Joseph Visarionovich Djugashvili in 1879. He was a member of the October Revolution committee of 1917. But he had been working from within, influencing as many of that committee during the following years on his “socialism in one country” propaganda, completely against the ideas of Trotsky who denied that it could work without a revolution in Western Europe. Stalin won that argument. By 1927 he had been the general secretary of the communist party for five years. Long enough to infiltrate any opposing factions. Since then a series of 5 year plans have placated the people and all enemies of the state eliminated in the purge of 1936 to 1938. Stalin did it in 21 years. Our plan may take a little longer but times have changed. We are not dealing with millions of peasants, kept ignorant of matters of state, but a liberalised western culture that demands to know everything its government does. Fools – that only causes delays and confusion.' Leonid saw the surprise in Stanislav's eyes as he calmly talked about the Soviet leader in such dispassionate terms. A small indiscretion that Leonid was sure Stanislav would record for his own personal use, to be produced as and when appropriate. Probably tapes all conversations in any case, conceded Leonid.

'How many of my candidates will you want for this... this implausible proposition?'

'Just the one.'

Stanislav gasped. Had this adversary taken leave of his senses? 'Just the one? It will take an army, perhaps more to shake the foundation of the British constitution.'

'Stalin was only one in the beginning. But he had all the correct credentials to succeed. He built his own army around him as he progressed. Our man could possibly do the same. All known agents of ours, or suspected agents would not get the freedom of a true “capitalist entrepreneur” as our man would be. The British pride themselves on following a success story. He will be so anti-communist that the people will support him without reservation.'

Stanislav paused. The breadth of the idea suddenly burst into his doubting mind like a river bursting its banks. It could actually work. It could be a brilliant success. Whoever carried it through would be feted by the Politburo and the Kremlin itself. Reputations were to be made from the victory of war in Europe and Stanislav Dzerzhinsky aimed to be one with the highest recommendation for promotion.

'Tell me, Comrade Leonid, just what do you expect this "messiah" to achieve, and more importantly, how will he achieve it?' Stanislav's gimlet eyes were rivetted on Leonid's bulky folder that lay on the desk before them. He had to tread warily. Leonid had intimated that the instructions had emanated from the office of the supreme head of state – Stalin. The Kremlin's official seal of highest confidentiality adorned the pale brown cover – overstamping Leonid Chukov's name as the personal trustee of its contents. No one could have access without the permission of the trustee. If only he could peruse the contents, but even he dared not contravene the strict code of authority of specialist files.

Leonid's discourse on the framework of his idea to create a head of a communications conglomerate from the ranks of a Soviet indoctrinee occupied the whole of the morning and another bottles of vodka. At the end of a rather lengthy inquisition into the pros and cons of the plan, Stanislav admitted that the scheme had potential. Secretly he thought it was superb but he wasn't about to divulge that to his erstwhile colleague. 'Who have we as candidates for the position?'

Leonid demurred as he opened the file and perused the closely typed pages at the foot of the pile. He shook his head slowly as if disappointed that a certain choice would not prove adequate for the post. Finally he removed two files from the folder and tossed them to Stanislav to inspect. 'Which of those two would you recommend?'

'Only two?'

'The others have all been eliminated by default on one quality or another. The remaining two, you know. They are from your research here in Berlin. Both linguists, both criminally minded. Both committed to the communist cause.'

Leonid did not blink an eye as he uttered the last phrase. He knew full well that Carl Weisz or Boris Vukadovic or any of his other aliases owed no allegiance to any cause except himself. Stanislav had been fooled but Leonid hadn't.

'Do you want me to make a selection when I have had the chance to study the files?'

'Exactly. If it corresponds with mine then we can honestly say that it was a joint selection and that we have construed to appoint the most appropriate aspirant on behalf of the Soviet Union's further evolution. One who cannot fail to succeed.'

Stanislav was aware that Leonid would not have ventured this far down the road of an audacious stratagem without researching the outcome thoroughly. He had been too long in the game to take chances that were not 100% foolproof. But the right man must be chosen. And that choice would have to be Stanislav's alone. He had to ensure that when the plaudits were handed out, Stanislav Dzerzhinsky was at the top of the roster.

Leonid left him with the problem to return when Stanislav contacted him. He knew the one he wanted. He had to outwit Stanislav to make the same choice. On his own.

Lazar gazed out of the high attic window on to the desolate landscape caked with snow. The black limousine containing his aunt Anna had driven away with hardly a sound to break the silence of the cold, bright, almost funereal neighbourhood. At her side had been the object of his whole existence. He'd known his voice the minute his aunt had signalled him by raising hers. There was no mistaking the smooth, mellifluous tones of Carl Weisz. Once again exercising his brutal authority in Werner Kawalek's house. The small face at the window was expressionless as the exhaust fumes disappeared into the misty distance. The scene returned to one of tranquillity, as if the event had never happened. Lazar shook himself and hurried down the stairs to dress quickly in his warm coat, slip out of the back door and skirt the house to find the tracks of the limousine in the snow. He set off at a slow lope to follow the trail to wherever it led.

Three kilometres from the house the tracks became deeper and less distinct, as if a car had stopped. Two sets of footprints led from the driver's side to the only remaining house within the vicinity. A single set returned. Lazar knew without doubt that Carl and Anna had entered the house and only Carl had emerged. His breath shortened and he gasped for air as he hurled himself towards the crazy building. The front door was non-existent. Litter covered the floor of the hall and the far passage which presumably led to the kitchen. Lazar called desperately for Anna. He had never felt so lonely and alone. He knew in his heart of hearts that the scene he would eventually be faced with would test his resolve to the limit. Carl could not let Anna live to betray him. She had saved her nephew by the only way she knew how. By leading this abhorrent gargantuan away from him. She had paid for her bravery with her life. Lazar prepared himself for the confirmation of his fears.

It was not until he came to the door at the far end of the passage that he felt certain that she would be there. The rubble inside the door had been pushed back by the force of the doors orbit. The room was comparatively untouched. One of the few remaining with a roof, the furniture was in place and serviceable. Anna lay on the dusty sofa, spreadeagled as if she had dropped off to sleep after a Sunday dinner.

Lazar ran to her side to feel her face, look into eyes that stared back at him as he raised the lids. He listened for her breathing, but could detect none. Her neck was bruised and had shed blood which ran in a line down to her right shoulder. He desperately felt for her pulse as his mother had shown him.

Fingers over the vein with his thumb at the back of the wrist. Nothing. He pulled at the legs until Anna's head was level with her body on the sofa and her arms by her side. There was no resistance.

How had his mother taught him life saving at the local swimming baths? What did you do first? Punch the chest or breath in the mouth? The cruel marks on her neck told him that she had been strangled, but was she dead? Her colour had not changed. She was not stiff as his mother explained to him about dead corpses. He talked to her incessantly as he alternatively pushed her chest and opened her mouth to blow three or four times. He felt the chest expand and contract as he combined the efforts of his little fists and his lungs.

He watched her face the whole time for signs of movement. Nothing happened. Again he lifted the lids and spoke her name. 'Anna. Anna.

Don't die. I need you! Tell me you're not dead.' Lazar babbled on about everything he could remember of their trip, and why they were there. How he planned to take Anna with him to Paris. To anywhere where he could track Carl Weisz. 'I cannot do it alone. I have to have you with me. I love you Anna. Don't die.'

There was a sound. A indiscernible sigh. Was it Anna? Or just the air escaping from the deprived lungs? He pushed again and again the sigh sounded in his ear. A long lonely sigh that epitomised all his feelings since the last time he had seen his mother and he had been unable to express the devastation that was inside him.

'Speak to me Anna,' he screamed. 'Speak to me. I know you are alive!'

He began to thump her with all his might in his frustration. His hands were sore and his arms ached and his cheeks were wet with tears.

Suddenly a cough erupted from the depths of Anna's lungs and blasted his face with spittle. Great gasps struggled to get out from her restricted air passages and her body convulsed in its efforts to accommodate the irregular gulps and expirations.

Her eyes opened and searched to focus on anything within reach. Her ears were assaulted by the joyous shouting of Lazar. He threw himself on her and hugged her until she found it difficult to breath again. With her weak arms she gently removed him from her and saw for the first time the little boy that she knew he was. Helpless and dependent. The small being who had run to her on their summer holidays to frolic and gamble on the fields that were their treasure. Susan's son, but Anna's protege. A blueprint for the boy that she hoped to have one day. One day...

'Oh Anna, I am so happy. I couldn't think of anything else except that you would come back to me and we could be together again.'

'It takes more than a miserable brute like him to get rid of me. I knew what was in store. I'm just glad he used his hands and not a rope to strangle me. I just held my breath for a time and then relaxed when I thought it time to "die" – he obviously thought the same.' She rubbed her neck tenderly and tested her head movement. 'There doesn't seem to be much damage – apart from my scratches. Thank goodness you followed me. I don't think I should have recovered if you hadn't come along.'

Lazar cuddled her to him in his best adult way. 'Do you think you can walk?'

'Of course I can.' Anna demonstrated her resolve and stood gingerly on her shaky legs. 'After a fashion,' she grinned.

'We ought to return to the house and collect our things and move quickly in case Carl returns,' Lazar said.

Anna nodded and took him by the hand; he did not resist; and led him out of the front door. She was thinking of Lieutenant Domanski. How could she let him know where and why they had gone?

Carl Weisz sat before the two Russian generals. He was impressed that they had singled him out for their cause. Whatever their reasons and preference, it bothered him not one iota. If they could assist him to reach his dream then all to the good. He would play their tune as long as it suited him. When it didn't, he would play the finale and they could whistle for his services.

The tall, dark, mustachioed general stood by the window. A trick he had employed himself to prevent his features being discernable. The other, smaller, seedier one, sat at his desk and rolled his pen smoothly in his palms, as if warming to his next question.

That this exercise was something special, Carl had no doubt.

It was no ordinary run of the mill employment, as he had enjoyed both during and after the war. No minor favour for the Russian agent working within the Nazi ranks. No favour for the Gestapo Oberbefehishaber, for which he was allowed unrestricted access to multiple supply lines and lucrative contact with the concentration camps. No, this was something deeper and far reaching. The Soviet authorities did not let one of their top men travel hundreds of kilometres for a social meeting. Carl knew the small one as the head of the Russian MVD. He had worked for its parent, the NKVD many times before it split. The other was probably the equivalent in the sister half of the organisation, the MGB. Useful men to know. But then, wasn't he useful to them?

'Did you solve your little problem with the couple who were occupying your house?' The little mousy one's ingratiating smile altered his face to resemble a smooth marble. Carl turned to face him. He was aware that his companion on the car trip was also watching closely. 'There will be no trouble from that quarter. Both have been dealt with.'

Leonid saw the inner satisfaction on Carl's face as he confronted his inquisitors. He knew also that a certain Lieutenant Joe Domanski had been found dead beside his Jeep the day before. 'An unfortunate accident on the treacherous roads into Berlin,' he had heard. Leonid knew better.

'We do have some other candidates to interview on various matters, but you can be assured that we shall have some appropriate enterprise for your special talents in due course.'

Stanislav dismissed him with a wave of his pen and made a final note on the pad in front of him. It had been a long but useful talk. Most of the information divulged by Carl Weisz had checked with the MVD's version, if only that this pompous braggart's account was always in his own favour. His was the truthful version despite indications otherwise. And he was convincing, Stanislav had to concede that. But . . . But there were too many insolubles, too many intricacies of the mind that worried him. He was used to dealing with dedicated fanatics, with unswerving loyalty to the Soviet, willing to die if necessary. And had done many times through Stanislav's direction.

Stanislav favoured the second candidate. Utterly communistic and ruthless. A brilliant brain that could adapt to other cultures and societies. Ideal for the job. Trained in political manoeuvres and the financial nuances of a capitalistic philosophy. Fluent in four languages and knowledgeable in every media, Stanislav could not see how he could be bettered. If his name was to be appended to the records of the project in the matter of the choice of man, then a good loyal party member, utterly devoted to his masters would receive favourable approbation from his Directorate. He could tell that Leonid favoured the alternative. An unstable, brash, demonic tyrant, who had only his own welfare in mind and would stoop to any level to achieve his ambition. Why did Leonid favour this one? Had he seen something that was not apparent in his bulky file? Should he have spent as much time as Leonid with Carl Weisz? What had he learned?

The questions buzzed around in Stanislav's head until he began to see traits in his own choice that perhaps were not the best recommendation for the job. The seeds of doubt were nurtured by Leonid's complete acceptance of the second man's qualities. Stanislav searched his brain for any remark that Leonid had made to the detriment of his choice. He could recall none. Did Leonid know of something that he didn't?

There was only one way to resolve the problem. Ask Leonid outright to name his choice now. And the reason for turning down the second candidate.

'It is time, is it not comrade? We both have had long enough to deliberate on the selection. Time is of an essence in this matter and I am anxious to report to my Directorate of the success of our proposed venture.' Stanislav's smile appeared over the tumbler of vodka to reverse its curve as he threw the draught at the back of his throat.

Leonid noticed the "our" pronoun and smiled to himself at the affrontery of this little man whose quest for glory almost matched that of Carl Weisz. 'Of course comrade,' said Leonid returning the party form of address. 'I have made up my mind as to the best man for the job.'

Stanislav's eyes narrowed as he tried to weigh up his adversary. How could he arrange it so that the choice could be allotted to himself? That would then ensure that as the plan developed and the scheme began to work, the plaudits would sit on his shoulders and not Leonid's.

That the plan would work he had no doubts. Leonid had explained in great detail how the gradual dismemberment of the British democracy could be achieved. They had no watchdogs or secret police to stamp out the slightest sign of deviation from the accepted tenets of the British way of life. It would be almost too easy. Especially for someone as talented as his choice. And he would be under the control of his section of the MVD, the 14th Directorate. 'Who is your choice?'

It was Leonid's turn to smile. 'Not so fast my friend, we must do this democratically. It is a long time since we voted for more than one person.' Leonid laughed uproariously at his castigation of the Soviet Regime. 'I am not used to this freedom of choice.'

The fingers of Stanislav's glass hand tightened around the tumbler. He abhorred the denigration of the party system and anyone else treating it in such cavalier fashion would have faced serious consequences for a remark such as Leonid's. But he let it slide. He had other priorities at the moment. 'How do you suggest we arrange the vote then?'

'Let us follow the democratic system of the west. A box with a slot and two pieces of paper, one for each of us. We each make our choice by name and place the paper in the box. That way neither of us will be influenced by the other. Not that you would of course,' Leonid added as deferentially as he could muster.

'And if the choices agree? Do we automatically accept that that is the final decision?'

Leonid warmed inside. Stanislav was hedging. He wanted his choice but he wanted the better choice to be attributed to him. He was not a hundred per cent sure that the party man would be the ideal candidate. Leonid had placed subtle doubts in his mind to allude to an opinion that the Kremlin may think him too 'conservative.' The comparison irked Stanislav. 'Both for the same man will decide the issue. One for each and we have a stand off and will have to state again our reasons for our preference. Or...' Leonid paused deliberately. 'Or... start our search again.'

Stanislav did not want that. The whole programme may be taken away from his domain and he would end up with no part of it. The votes must tally to succeed. But Leonid would not vote for Stanislav's man. He knew that. Or was he playing a deeper game? Hoping that he Stanislav would vote for this Carl Weisz and secure a triumph for Leonid Chukov? No it must appear that the ultimate choice was that of the MVD Directorate head and that he was instrumental in the correct selection. Stanislav decided to vote for Carl Weisz. The votes would agree and Stanislav would have the pleasure of telling his Directorate that he had responsibility for this supreme project and its inception. He carefully folded his small piece of paper with the name written boldly in black ink and placed it into the box.

Leonid did likewise. He seemed to demur an awful long time before bending his head and shielding the paper from Stanislav. A quick movement of his fingers and the paper joined the first piece in the box.

Stanislav licked his lips. He raised his eyebrows in a silent query as to who should examine the result. Leonid nodded.

The first piece of paper to be revealed was his own. Stanislav spread it triumphantly for Leonid to see. There was no expression on the silent man's face.

The second was folded twice. With trembling fingers the creases were smoothed out and the name revealed. Leonid's choice.

Neither man moved for a second. Leonid of course knew what was on the paper. Stanislav thought he knew, but the letters of Hans Kruger screamed their unwelcome message to him. Leonid had opted for the safer party bet, when all along he had been championing the cause of Carl Weisz.

'Well?' said Leonid, as if he were unaware of the result.

'We have a stand off as you put it,' spat out Stanislav. 'We are no further forward than before.'

'Why did you vote for Carl Weisz, an unstable, belligerent and thoroughly untrustworthy choice?'

'Because you intimated in so many ways that his talents far outweighed any small flaws that he had. He would be revered by the British for the omnipotent megalomaniac he was. I sincerely believe that. That is why I voted for him.' Stanislav's pride overrode all other considerations. He knew deep down that Leonid had wanted Carl Weisz. Why had he voted against his own instincts? He was going soft. He wanted someone else to shoulder the responsibility. He was finished. He would be pensioned off when the Politburo learned of his weakness. 'Should we vote again under the rules of the Soviet political system? That way we shall have the candidate we both wish for.'

Leonid emitted a deep sigh as if acknowledging the other's superiority in decisions and nodded reluctantly. His face showed all the signs of having been outwitted and beaten. A triumph of acting if I may say so myself, thought Leonid as he mentally patted himself on the back.

'This time,' said Stanislav. 'We have one candidate – mine – and we vote.'

'Unanimous,' pronounced Stanislav as the two fresh pieces of paper were opened. 'Carl Weisz will be our ambassador in Britain. But the British will not know it.' For the first time Stanislav laughed, but the underlying sneer was apparent to the man who ostensibly admitted his failure by raising his hand in acknowledgement and sadly leaving the room.

Outside on the pavement, Leonid Chukov lit one of his favourite cigars, and breathed a sigh of utter contentment. He had outwitted the pompous ass. The one person who was certain to succeed, but on his own terms and not that of the Soviet Union, had been elected by the most prominent man in the MVD. When heads started to roll, as roll they must when the inner sanctum discovered who had recommended their man, Stanislav's would be the first. Every official paper on the selection process and investigation into the affair would be examined closely and one name would stand out as the prime mover for Carl Weisz. That name was Stanislav Dzerzhinsky. Leonid made a mental note to submit his report to the Office of the First Directorate first thing in the morning. It would show that his first choice had been the party man, but at the insistence of Comrade Dzershinsky, exercising his right as the officer in control of foreign conscripts, he had been overruled. A second report would be submitted some months after the agent was in place. It would detail certain defects that Leonid had detailed in his first report on candidates which should automatically have disqualified him from consideration. The very defects that Stanislav had thought would work to the advantage of the Soviet cause. The plane taking Leonid Chukov back to Moscow was comfortable and accommodating. Cigars and vodka were in abundance and he was left to his own devices as he settled into compiling his report. Every now and then a female dressed in the distinctive Soviet Air Force uniform attended to his needs. 'More vodka? Coffee? Cigars? Anything?'

Leonid grinned under his mustache. What more could anyone want than that? Except perhaps... he cocked his head in admiration at the tight buttocks thrusting their invitation through the close fitting skirt. There was something about a woman in uniform that dried the palate.

He promised himself that he would investigate the phenomenon some time.

CHAPTER IX

1979

The slightly stooped, nondescript cleaning lady carefully replaced the plastic bottle of Izal in her regulation trolley. Cloths and dusters waved in the wake of her procession down the silent corridor. The large, rather ornate, white door at the far end, inlaid with cream whitebeam pattern, opened easily to her passkey. Pulling her trolley noiselessly after her she entered the sumptuous apartment, her eyes sweeping familiarly over the white leather upholstered settees and lounge chairs. The pure Indian carpet under her feet clung fractionally to each footstep as she made her way to an outer room protected by a contrasting black ebony door with a gold handle. Inside she quickly examined various papers on the desk top and in the drawers that were open. Nothing missed her eagle eyes as she memorised the data. Taking a specially made key from her overall pocket, she inserted the male shaft and the two locked drawers slid open to her gentle pull. Foolscap sheets of notes and figures were carefully laid out on the desk and examined for significance. Having satisfied herself that she had the information she sought, everything was returned to the drawers and the desk left in exactly the same state as when she entered the room.

Now she turned her attention to the dictating machine. Black and sombre and a little frightening, she switched the play button and listened intently to the voice that she recognised so well. A voice that stabbed deep within her brain and raked over painful memories that she had embalmed in time. But the voice swept away the cloak of the passing years and raked the embers of her suffering to white hot. This time she carefully transcribed every word into the notebook and replaced it in the breast pocket of her overall. She assiduously reversed the tape to its previous position and wiped the instrument lovingly with her duster.

Only then did she resort to her cleaning duties in the marble bathroom, the fully fitted kitchen, and the enormous bedroom containing a specially constructed bed to accommodate a big man. The cleaning lady smiled secretly to herself. Silk sheets and pyjamas to match. Heavy brocade wallpaper and curtains, with matching Egyptian wall to wall figured carpet. The trappings of megalomania. A desire to demonstrate to the world that the most important being in it was the owner of the rather brash ostentatious luxury that failed to impress the knowledgeable fashion gurus of the city. But that didn't worry Maximillian Alexander Carl Holst. He set his own fashion and the minions at his command hung on every declaration of his "individuality." Thirty minutes later the cleaning lady left the apartment and made her way to the closet on the fourth floor. Inside she neatly parked her trolley beside the others, removed her company overall and protective gloves, smoothed down her neat dress and walked painfully to the service lift at the end of the corridor.

Her eyes burned bright beneath the shock of grey hair that overhung her forehead. Anyone glancing at the face would see only the lines of suffering etched into the once smooth countenance. Lines that had deepened over the years to give her an air of sophistication in the way that they enhanced rather than distorted her underlying beauty. When she held herself upright, which was difficult, she assumed the stature of a refined lady about to open a bazaar or fete with the perfect affectation of royalty.

Susan Mallory made her way home from the Knightsbridge address via the tube and train to her small house in Chiddingfold. She loved the luscious Surrey pastures, spreading like a green blanket over the rolling contours of the downs. Thick woods broke the smooth passage of her gaze as she followed the undulating lines to the horizon. She had never realised until she came to live in those parts, how much she missed the English scene. Her long forgotten Weymouth haunts which returned now to pull at her heart's memories and glisten her eyes in the fading sun. She was home at last, but she had one last act to carry out to right a wrong that the world had almost forgotten.

On the small, elegant table in the hall, stood the cream telephone that she had seen in Harrod's. An expensive luxury but she had nothing else on which to spend her hard earned wages. So why not she had queried?

Beautiful things create a beautiful mind and I need that aura to maintain the happiness of satisfaction; only happy persons can achieve their goal. Sourness affects their actions and their outlook. They destroy themselves if they constantly live in a world of deceit and lies.

'National Bank Inspection Department, how can I help you?'

The chirpy voice trotted out the customary greeting in not quite the genuine fashion that the Public Relations department had intended. It had now become so much of a stereotype banality that its effect had been nullified to the impatient public.

'May I speak to Peter Mallory please?'

'Certainly madam. Whom shall I say is calling?' There was a little more genuineness creeping into the voice.

'Tell him that it is his mother.' Several seconds passed during which the annoying jingle of some unknown musical cacophony echoed in the receiver.

'I am afraid that Mr. Mallory is not available at the moment. Can I give him a message?'

'Yes please. Would you please let him know that I shall expect him at my home tonight at 8pm.'

Susan Mallory replaced the ivory receiver, went into her lounge and began to write down every scrap of information that she had memorised from her morning's activities in the apartment of Maximillian Holst.

The lush furnishings of the executive lift from the front foyer flattened under the concentrated weight of the size twelve shoes supporting the bulk of Maximillian Holst. It rose smoothly to the fifth floor, and directly into his exclusive apartment. Everything in this room has been chosen by him; the decor, the paintings, the sculptures, the ornamentation. His pride swelled within him as his eyes roved over priceless antiques and artifacts. He knew where every piece had been purchased, the cost, and the value. He never paid the full price for anything. That went against the grain and the gratification of the riches around him was accentuated by the knowledge of his dealing. Not he dealing that he had encountered in his father's day, where each knew the other's weakness and limitations. Maximillian's was by sheer pressure and overbearing, almost blackmailing ability to obtain what he wanted. Prospective sellers soon learnt that to accept the first offer was prudent; to demur was to invite the wrath of this huge domineering tyrant who could destroy you if he so felt inclined. And he did quite often when dealings were not to his liking.

Maximillian poured himself a large brandy and soda and lit one of his Russian cigars. This was the time of day to relax and mull over the events which had transpired. The stock exchange deals that he had done. The latest monthly reports and budgets from his multinational companies. His insider information, constantly being fed to him by his contacts within the dealing rooms of most of the leading stockbrokers in the city. He had direct lines to every jobber, so that he was kept aware of shares available to brokers for onward sale to the public. Normally any valuable share coming on to the market was placed with the brokers by the jobbers for public sale. If the share interested Maximillian then the public never had the chance to participate in the offer. The jobbers were paid very handsomely for their trouble. Far more than they could earn from their commission from the brokers.

He sorted out several papers from his briefcase, read the contents and then shredded them into the waste bin in the corner of his office. Maximillian didn't need a filing system for his financial affairs. His mind contained all the necessary data that he needed. Once digested, it very rarely failed to be retained. That is where I have the advantage, he told himself smugly. My world is in my head. Not some computer, or paper record. It is where I need it and where no one else can get at it. He had learnt the trick of a photographic memory very early in his life, when he used to assist his father in the horse dealing trade in Siszet at the foot of the Carpathian mountains bordering Russia. To make money in horses, you needed more than a good eye for horseflesh and breeding. You needed your wits about you to remember the deals done by the other traders over the past months, the horses in which they dealt, who had bought what horse, who was genuine, and who was not. Carl Taba, the name he had been born with in the village, to his mother Hannah, the eleventh in line to his father's business, had the fastest brain and most guile of all of Jacob's sons. While his brothers worked 14 hours daily in the woodcutting industry on the other side of the river Tisza, Carl accompanied his father on wonderful journeys into the strange lands surrounding the Jewish settlement. The thriving Jewish community had established itself following the Turkish invasion of the 16th century, where whole populations of various ethnic groups made their way westwards to settle in borders, neither belonging to, or wanting to attach themselves to their neighbours. Carl's family was one of a hundred or so Maramoras Jews. They were considered conservative with strong physiques and simple viewpoints. They thrived because of their willingness and ability to work. Hard at anything that they were allowed. The mines were banned to Jews and consequently they had to work at the salt mills and flower and lumber mills for a much less return for their labour. But they survived on a diet of potatoes and gefelite fish. The original stock of the Maramoras sect gave way to various Jewish branches and Carl's family adopted the traditions of the Hassidim, ultra conservative orthodox Jews, who stressed intense emotion as part of worship. Carl was immune to this emotion, but pretended to participate – it was profitable and gave him better status with his contemporaries.

How I would like to have those people around me now, he mused, sipping his brandy. To see the son of Jacob in his palace. To see the trappings of wealth and power. To glory in the control that he had over his empire of readers and viewers. They would never believe that a simple horse dealer could exchange his meagre beginnings for the bounty of an emperor. Emperor Maximillian he idly drew in his mind as a headline for one of his national newspapers. Fools, he cursed under his breath, they cannot yet see that he was the most powerful force in the British media. What he decreed, was published in every part of Britain, read by the majority of the gullible public and believed by most. So why was it that he was not accepted in the highest circles? Given the due respect that his position merited? No matter how he assisted charities and good causes, he knew deep down that his benefactors and the upper echelon of English nobility would never admit him to their 'club.' He could walk among them, talk to them, make money for them, but never be one of them. With all his cunning and universal awareness, he failed to see why. He tossed the annoying thoughts out of his head and went through the draft accounts of World Wide Publishing Corporation, making notes in the margin as to the significance to place on particular figures. Any notes from the accountants to the detriment of the company were ruled through and a kinder version attested to the foot to explain the apparent anomaly. Accounts were for accountants, he swore, not for the makers of empires. I am the accountant. I can give the public the figures it wants. The figures to boost confidence, to make people invest, to create wealth. He had carried his practices with him from the fields of Siszet. The value of any article is what you make the customer believe. The article may not even exist, but if it could be passed from one to another, all believing that it had value, then the actual object did not matter. Much like the antique market of today, he smiled. If I had a bag of horse manure and convinced everyone of its worth, then no one would worry as long as all the desirers of wealth kept buying. How often had he done just that with shares which did not even have a company behind them? Only the final purchaser had lost. But how many millionaires had he created on the way?

The remaining papers that he kept were safely stowed in his drawers, locked and the key retained in his Savile Row waistcoat pocket. The slim key was unaware that its sister had occupied the same space barely an hour before.

Despite his overall confidence which oozed out of him wherever he went, Maximillian Host was conscious of a niggling doubt to his prowess. The cold water from his shower pounded huge shoulders with needle like sharpness. He found it increased his ability to think. To recall little details of the day and the days before. To group them together and place them in little compartments. To assess their worth and retain or discard them. Like now. He had a lot of little compartments filled with irritating questions that had been asked of his boasts about his companies' prospects. Always the same disputing of predicted growth which was at odds with the real figures of the balance sheets. None of his aides had been able to track the perpetrator down, or to identify the person responsible. Sometimes it had been a man, sometimes a woman. But each had obviously studied the balance sheets and the related consolidated balance sheets more than an interested shareholder was capable of. The result was that the immediate confidence in his published results, lauded by all his own newspapers and TV channels, was not completely achieved. It was like a brake block catching a slightly buckled rim momentarily as it sped along the road. Not enough to stop the momentum but sufficient to prevent a free uncluttered wheel spin.

The pure white Chanel soap suds covered the black forest of hairs on his chest and shoulders like snow on a coal heap. Rivers of the expensive foam ran freely over the flabby paunch and the surprisingly slim legs. Changing the needle sharp shower to cold again with a twist of his huge hand he gloried in the punishment to his skin. Torrential rain storms on the steppes of Russia and freezing deluges in Ruthenia constantly reinforced his ego of his invincibility to the elements. It was as if he was challenging god to destroy him with the pestilence and laughing at his puny efforts. As it was now with his self inflicted punishment. His body gloried in it and the warmth surged through his large frame to counteract the biting hailstones of the shower.

Resplendent in his black silk dressing gown, he stepped from his dressing room to replenish his brandy and light another cigar. Time to work.

His beautifully manicured thumb flicked the switch of the Burroughs dictating machine to activate the tape. He began to speak.

"Leo," he said referring to his personal financial assistant Leopold Sochia. "In my top right hand drawer you will find the draft accounts of World Wide Publishing. The notes in the margin are to be conveyed to Price Waterhouse for inclusion in the final audited accounts. The £2.3 million to be received from the sale of publishing rights and warranties to Alexander Associates is to be used to adjust the profit margin for the year. Similarly the amount owed to Alexander Associates is to be discounted for this year and carried forward to next year when I shall deal with the question of re-renting premises held in their name.

The subsidiary accounts can all be dealt with in a similar fashion. Any creditors of less than twelve months are to be deferred to the next fiscal accounting period as is the usual practice. Overall the net profit then showing should be in the region of £2.5 million on World Wide with an overall group profit of £32.7 million. This will be in line with my forecast earlier in the year as you remember and should boost confidence in the obvious profitability that has carried through the core business." Maximillian's face showed not a flicker of subterfuge or deceit. His method of accounting had stood him in good stead for many years and to his mind, it was completely in accordance with his rules for the Companies House regulations regarding compiling a true statement of affairs. He knew every penny that came and went within his companies and the necessity of revealing a set of figures every half year and year was a legal burden that did not sit well on his shoulders.

"Now to the day's market. Bearing in mind the effect that the foregoing will have on related shares in the publishing world, I wish you to buy one hundred thousand ordinary shares in the following companies.

Bristol Post. Carlton Communication. Independent News. News International. Reuters B and United News.

I calculate the cost including commission to be in the region of £.95 million. As tomorrow is the first accounting day the funds will not be due until a fortnight on Monday. Await my instructions for the sale or otherwise of the shares over the intervening period. In the meantime arrange with my brokers to fix a sell limit on all shares 20% above the price paid, but to contact me personally before any action is taken.

The base rate is at present 14%. Far too high a gearing for the group and I wish you to make an appointment with all of the companies' bankers to discuss capping the rates and allowing full set off against the funds accumulating from time to time in subsidiary companies.

Mrs. Thatcher has inherited quite a tidy basket of problems from the socialists. It will take her at least three years to reduce the rates below 10% given favourable circumstances and that will work in our favour. Our overdrafts and loans are at their maximum. The bulk are not due for repayment for some four or five years and if rates drop by the four per cent that I anticipate and inflation remains as high as it is now, it should save the company in excess of £53 million over a five year period. See to it that all Financial Directors have the system in place that no creditors are paid until the debt has been outstanding for twelve months. Their financing of our business should save a further £44 million in interest charges per annum.

I want a detailed projection on the effect of these initiatives on my desk by Monday week. Also a projection of the best stroke worst position on each company given these varying assumed factors.

Finally. The new company Radioflex is struggling to raise capital to finance its operation in the field of network TV. A set up programme of five years is proving too unattractive for the public and investment houses. The projected income from its eventual monopoly of transmission of multiple channels is understated. With the addition of a share in the media satellite now operating on an experimental basis, the income could be quadrupled annually. Get me the names of the satellite entrepreneurs and the Government department that is funding the experiment. There has been union trouble at the print headquarters in the Holborn plant. Issue instructions to the managers that all union members are to be laid off and the business transferred to our printers in Holland. Don't just threaten. Do it. After three months we shall be able to re-open the plant and resume operations on the same wages scale as now."

Maximillian finished abruptly. No personal message or familiarity. Leopold was just an employee who was expected to be grateful for his employment. Like all the others. They only existed to supplement the aspirations of their master in his quest for world domination of others.

Maximillian lit another cigar. The ornate silver and diamond encrusted cigarette lighter nestled in his hand like a good luck token. Something from the old days that had been with him daily as his empire expanded. He fingered the engraving on the side. A large scripted 'A'. On the other 'R'. A for Alix of Hesse. R for Rasputin. He thought of the old manservant serving his time out with a lesser family than illustrious previous employers. Czar Nicholas II and his wife Alix had been served well by their trusted henchman. Until the intervention of Gregory Efimovich Rasputin, the darling of the Romanov court and the supposed curer of the Tsarina's son's haemophilia. He wasn't cured, the old man had told him, but by that time, Rasputin's influence was such that no one in the royal household dare protest at his blatant debauchery and annexation of their rule.

'He was shot and dumped into the river Neva,' the old man remembered. 'Poison had no effect on him and more drastic means were employed.' He reflected as he lit his coarse cigar with the lighter that now nestled in Maximillian's palm. 'Not many were prepared to act against him after the attempts at poisoning failed. They thought he was inhuman. Probably was, but he died that night in 1916 all right. I saw the body when they fished him out. Freezing cold it was, enough to have killed him without the bullets. As we pulled him out, this lighter dropped to the ground and I recovered it without anyone seeing. Once we were satisfied he was dead, we dropped him in the river again.

Maximillian remembered the old man's face, full of pride and triumph, as if he had engineered the whole murder. Perhaps he had, mused Maximillian, he never recovered his position as head of the domestic staff to the Romanovs. 'They were all murdered too, in 1918,' he added sadly. His whole world destroyed by a despot and all he had from his former life was the cigarette lighter which Tsarina Alix of Hesse had given to Rasputin. 'To "R" from "A". That's what the inscription stood for,' he proclaimed as Maximillian studied the precious gift.

'What will you take for the lighter old man?'

'Nothing. It is not for sale. It is the only connection I have with my past. No money can buy that.'

After Maximillian had killed the old man with one thrust of his knife under the ribs, he calmly pocketed the prize and the old man's body joined that of Rasputin in the waters of the Neva.

Many of the artifacts around the room had been obtained by one means or another. Nothing that Maximillian wanted evaded him. His eyes glowed in the semi-darkness relishing the events that had brought him to his present station. Most contrived by his manipulative skills and devised to bring the maximum benefit to one person. Maximillian Holst. Or Boris Vukadovic. Or Werner Kawalek. Or any of the other dozen or so names that he had assumed. But mainly to benefit the little boy who had grown up as Carl Taba until the Russians came and changed the family name to Weisz – White. They were apt to allot common names to all families as they carried out a census of the villages annexed. White – because their family was a shade paler than the normal Jewish gypsies that they had come across.

The brandy mollified the normally sharp edges of his concentration and his mind wandered over his emerging years spent building up the very profitable side line of agent to the horse dealers. He had realised from an early age that the quickest way to make money was to be involved in every horse deal there was. Not to spend time seeking out suitable steeds and bringing them to presentable condition and selling them to the highest bidder. He could find the seller and the buyer and take his cut from each. Mostly neither knew of his connection with the other. Soon he had amassed far more than his father ever had, but his horizons were now stretching into the big outside world where even richer pickings were attainable.

'You say you have three thousand cans of paint available when I want it?' The Lagarhaus Befehelshaber looked at him quizzically. If what this dark brooding Russo/German said was true, then he stood to make quite a tidy profit on the paint required for the barracks. Instead of instituting a request to the central stores at standard price, he was being offered a chance to acquire it at two thirds the price. 'Whenever you want it, I will arrange for it to be delivered to your store. And I will supply the necessary invoices, adjusted of course,' Maximillian laughed as he produced official German army documents from his briefcase, 'to show that it was obtained from the usual source.'

What Maximillian did not tell him was that the payment was in Reichmarks at 84 to the American dollar and that this could be exchanged at a special rate negotiated with the PRISC at 52 per dollar. In addition to the enormous profit on the paint, a further 38% or so was to be gained on the exchange. Several deals on those lines gave him a considerable nest egg to stow away in the various secret addresses in Berlin.

The years flooded back as Maximillian indulged in a very seldom nostalgia for the past. But this was a nostalgia that belonged to him. To continually convince him that he was invulnerable, unbeatable, invincible. To wield that much power was to assume a mantle of godliness; only in the human form that the peasants of today understood and revered. Except for a niggling annoyance that someone somewhere was stalking him, shadowing his every move. He took out his private ledger of investment holdings. Some of his ventures dated back to shortly after he came to England in 1947. Small companies which had trundled along quite happily until he had taken an interest in their assets and injected his own special brand of dynamism and short cuts to profitability. Shares in major publishing companies were littered throughout the summary – shares gradually acquired in nominee names until he had majority control in most of the publishing houses in Britain. And some in Europe. But. He took another list supplied to him by his financial adviser and compiled by an investigator over the past three years. Again there was a list of investments by other nominee companies mainly in the same companies as on the previous list.

It was as if someone was copying his every carefully considered move. Uncannily the dates of the purchase of the various shares invariably matched his own or very shortly after. Some even pre-empted his own audacious dash into the market. "Niemand Nominees" figured prominently in the purchasers of the stocks. His agent had been unable to discover the person or persons behind the trust that had set up the nominee company. Again in Liechtenstein – after his own fashion. Someone was playing him at his own game! But who? And why?

He had made plenty of enemies, he had no one he could honestly call his friend. He was aware that the so called 'friends' were only there because of the pickings from his agile ability to make money for them. To date they had prospered along with him on the roller coaster ride of deceit and lies and blatant misuse of the accountants' terminology to hide the true position of his enormous conglomerate empire.

But it was beginning to crack. He was being forced to take more and more desperate measures to sheer up his crumbling consortium. Every day, doubts and aspersions were raised about one or other of his companies. Speculation, he told the reporters. Pure speculation of jealous competitors. He would not even comment on the specific details that were recorded in his rivals newsprint – they didn't warrant his valuable time. But the vendetta continued and gained pace as previously supportive financial columnists joined the mounting campaign against the Holst empire. Maximillian ground the half smoked cigar into the vast ashtray emblazoned with his personal crest – a gold 'M' stamped on a stylised globe, set into the fine crystal of the glass salver. I will grind another cigar into the face of the person responsible when I have him, he swore. He had been so close to realising his dream of global domination and popularity. A man of the people, he had ordered his editorial staff to impress on every report and every public appearance that he attended. A man of the people, he thought, but not of the people that mattered. The city, the aristocracy, the power men, the government. The inner circle of society. None had accepted him. They had never rejected him, but the open welcome was never as sincere as it should have been. And finally the letter from his contact in the House of Lords. "Despite my lobbying and persuasion over the past year – I have several favours due to me by my colleagues – I regret that it has proved impossible to place your name on the list for consideration for a knighthood. The present PM, whilst sympathetic to your obvious qualification for this honour, has found it unpolitic to forward your name at this time."

The short note still rankled in his memory. 'Favours due to him! What about the favours that were due from him to me?' The muttered words disappeared into the lead glass goblet of brandy with equal venom to the harsh spirit burning his throat. He reached for the telephone.

'Send them round now,' he ordered.

His dark, fathomless eyes, beneath the heavy black eyebrows, dulled to the tenor of uncut coal as his mind sank into a mire of moves and counter moves that were possible against this unseen enemy. Not for a minute did Maximillian ever consider that this 'enemy' would defeat him. He was just an annoyance, a niggling irritant to be got rid of. Like all his adversaries before him. Either submit and join the Maximillian clan or be disposed of in the same way that he had disposed of most of his competitors – permanently. There was always confusion and desperation in most public companies when the main architect of their business mysteriously disappeared. Most boards tended to panic and welcomed the saviour who, although "he had far too many businesses to run", would help them out of their difficulties. And that meant another company would join the mushrooming assemblage of Holst controlled enterprises.

The inter communication buzzer sounded on the wall beside the lift door. Maximillian lifted his special receiver beside him on the table and listened. 'Come up.'

He heard the private lift hum deep below him as it started its journey to his apartment. The hum stopped; the doors slid smoothly open; and into his lounge strode two women. One a tall, moorish looking female; the other smaller, although she was five feet ten inches, with long blonde hair and smoky blue eyes. The former was dressed in a Versace wrap-around sleek satin evening dress, split to the thigh on both sides. As white as her thighs were brown, the contrast was stunning. The second girl wore a similar evening dress in black, enhancing the pure white tone of her visible skin above the low vee cut daringly to her waist. They are perfect, reflected Maximillian. No in betweens. Either black or white. He had no time for waverers – the shadowy no decision makers. The wafflers and the uncertain. Most problems in this world were either black or white. Progress was made more definite by a viewpoint that could not see any middle ground. The middle grounders were always defeated anyway – so why mess about delaying matters when one thrust of his decisive persona could settle any argument instantly. It was expected of him now and he found no resistance. Those who did found to their cost that it did not pay in terms of wealth and stature to oppose him.

Maximillian did not speak. He watched as the girls helped themselves to a drink of champagne from his cooler, refusing the offer to join them. Following the champagne, each female sought the inlaid silver cigarette box by the sofa. Small sachets of cocaine were laid out neatly inside with fine ivory straws in a separate compartment. The fine powder spilled on the black marble topped table as the girls eagerly tipped the contents from the packets. Taking the straws they each snorted a measure in both nostrils leaving the table as shiny as it had been before.

The atmosphere changed. The dark woman pushed a button on the stereo system and music filled the room. The quadraphonic sound swelled over the cloistered walls of the richly decorated room and seeped into the fabric of the furnishings, until it enveloped the three people within.

Moussorgsky's 'Pictures at an Exhibition' slowly unfolded its dark, shattering, fragmented introduction on the moving figures within its midst. Maximillian lay on the floor, stark naked with the two girls gyrating over him as the tempo beat their rhythmical Russian overtones to their dance. High on the cocaine, their senses enlivened and stirred by the drug and the angry violins that stridently berated their antics, they moved their buttocks in ever more thrusting jerks of their pelvises. Each shed the fine gossamer-like gowns in a flood of tumbling silk, like melted milk chocolate spilling its waves into a pool at their feet. Neither wore a brasseiere.

Their peach shaped breasts rose and fell with the music, the hardened nipples jutting outwards for satisfaction. Soon the skimpy nylon panties joined their dresses on the thick carpet and they turned their attention to the bulky figure laid out before them.

Maximillian lay prone with his eyes closed. His enormous girth flattened out around him like a pudding emptied onto the table. Surprisingly he had very little pubic hair. What little there was, was evident by its very blackness. Most was on the shoulders and above his buttocks as the girls heaved him on to his front. Each then sat astride the white whale like creature and began to massage, one from his feet and the other from his shoulders. Slowly the remorseless music floated over them, dictating the fervour and urgency of their manipulative hands.

Violins screeched in protest at the sombre undertones of the tubas, culminating in a clash of cymbals as the girls found the vertebrae at the base of his spine.

Pipes chorused a procession of rapid dance steps as eager hands pummelled every muscle hidden beneath the rolls of fat. The music swelled and fell epitomising the vast steppes of Russia stretching endlessly before Maximillian's unseeing eyes.

The horns joined in and the steady beat of gypsy music intertwined with the loping melody of horses being ridden in the cossack way. With abandon and expert horsemanship. Various sections of the orchestra took up the signal to play their own unique strain representing various tribes within the whole of the gypsy nation. Gradually the tribes were brought together into one triumphant cacophony of mellifluous harmony of intent. To conquer the world. As Genghis Khan had done. As Alexander the Great had done. As the great Roman Empire had done. As Maximillian Alexander Carl Holst would do.

The music became more discordant, demanding that the participants in the game raise their tempo to match. Taking the submissive body in their hands the naked women rolled him over and repeated their massage. His skin shone and rippled as fat was dispersed and re-arranged by the probing fingers. As the four hands converged on the centre of the prone hulk, the body stiffened slightly as the expectancy heightened and the fingers crept ever closer to his growing erection. Not large for such a large man, but thick and straining at the taut skin in anticipation of its desire.

Liberal handfuls of cream eased the tight skin as gentle hands brought it to full elevation. Tonight was the turn of the dark girl to be first. The erotic beat of the orchestrations had brought her to the point where her gyrating limbs produced the wetness that now ran down her thighs as she lowered herself gradually onto the manhood that lay beneath her. The second girl sat astride Maximillian's chest facing her partner and stimulating her nipples with deft caresses of her lips as the dark skinned body arched backwards in supreme ecstasy. Maximillian felt only the drumming on his stomach as her buttocks rammed rhythmically to the music and brought him to a climax as the cymbals clashed their command to conquer, to succeed, to overpower, to reach the heights in his soporific mind that he dreamed about in the outside world beyond the walls of his private chamber.

The girl shuddered uncontrollably as she was clasped by her female friend in a final buttock hugging grasp that tightened her hold on the member inside her. She screamed out loud and suddenly was all spent. Her head lolled and her muscles dissolved into limp sinews, unable to function even to remove herself from her position. She slumped into the white girl's arms and was helped on to the pure white carpet, panting like a puppy.

It was now the turn of the blonde. Everything was meticulously wiped and cleaned with the tissues available as she set to work to coax the organ into a second erection. Again Maximillian did not move his body. The only sign of life was the hesitant quivering from his nether regions when light fingers and a succulent tongue began their work to achieve the impossible. Her cheek was as soft as rose petals against the rough contours of his penis and brought the glimmering of a response from the glistening mens. She moulded her movements to the melodic tones of the 'Ballet of the chicks in their shells' as excited dance chords dictated the expert manipulation of the rising sex within them both. At the moment of discord and raucous brass dominance of the piece, her soft blonde opening took him in one swift plunge and she rode him like the cossacks he used to watch as a boy.

Thighs held tight against the steaming horses's flanks, bouncing on the fur saddles and jarring the fervour inside their groins. At the moment of triumph of rider over horse, the first sign that the body beneath her had life signalled its acceptance of the female's expertise. Maximillian's carcass twitched and shed its final effusion into the ecstatic body holding his manhood. These two girls were the only persons on earth who had a close bodily contact with the man who would be emperor. No other person touched him, or was allowed to, save for the proffered hand if he felt so inclined.

The girls bathed and left as serenely as they had arrived. Impeccable once again in their black and white ensemble, heads tossing glorious tresses as their equilibrium returned from its sexual and cocained stimulation.

Before they departed they had washed and bathed Maximillian's body as carefully and as dedicated as any staff nurse at the Great Ormond Street Hospital in the city.

'Get me Sochia,' Maximillian barked into his portable telephone.

His secretary, a twenty four hours a day job, rubbed her dusty eyes and patched in the call to Leopold Sochia's private line at home. Maximillian had the annoying habit of using her to get various contacts because he hated to he the person making the call. An order of precedence was being maintained to remind all servants and employees that they should show deference to him by speaking first. Except when he had a particularly nasty job to perform, and then surprise and vitriolic abuse were the order of the day.

'Sochia here. What can I do for you Mr. Holst?' Although it was 1.30 in the morning he knew better than to query the time.

'OPEC raised the price of oil this evening by 16%. That makes it a 50% increase in the past year. What do we hold?'

'Approximately $2.7 million at the last valuation three days ago.'

'Buy a further $2.3 million spread around the major oil producing companies in this country and the US.' Anticipating Leopold's next question, he continued. 'Sell sufficient shares from each of the top five publishing companies held in my name. They should be Aegis Group, EMAP, Independent News, Reeds, and Thompsons.'

Leopold did not bother to check the state of the companies mentioned. He had no doubt that the man at the other end of the telephone was more au fait with the current market trends than the up to date report given to him at 4.45pm that afternoon. The information supplied by one of his close contacts on the floor of the London Stock Exchange would be amazed that any other person could be privy to more recent knowledge of the world swings than he. But he did not have the advantage of Maximillian's network system of prices and movements patched into every major stock market in the world.

What London knew at 4pm Maximillian knew at 3.50pm. And that was valuable and very profitable information.

'But that will reduce your holdings to below the level at which you maintain outright control.'

'It is only a temporary measure. The shares will be re-purchased as soon as the oil price peaks – in about 6 months. Libya will follow the example of the other four major oil producers and hike the price by a hefty margin – I would guess at $4 a barrel making $30 overall. Saudi Arabia, Venezuela, United Arab Emirates, and Qatar have all set the precedent for an 85% rise and I see no reason why it will not continue after this year.'

'That will mean a related rise in inflation – higher interest rates.'

'Exactly. With most of our borrowings at their maximum and locked into fixed rates, the real rate of borrowing will decrease as inflation increases. Borrow to the limit on all fixed rate overdrafts and loans and invest in high interest bonds. The rate of income from these should more than cover the interest due. There is nothing I like better than investing in the Banks' bond market with their money, paying their lending costs with it, and still coming out with a profit.' Maximillian's laugh rattled in the receiver as Leopold jerked away from the instrument in admiration and envy. He had worked for Maximillian Holst for eight years and still could not follow the devious machinations of this mogul's computerised brain.

He acknowledged the instructions, faxed the group's private stockbroker to implement the orders five minutes before the exchange opened for business. No point in letting everyone else jump on the bandwagon before the price rose dramatically on the news of the huge purchases and the expected further rise in oil prices. The last thought that Leopold had before he settled beside his snoring and oblivious wife was that Maximillian would probably have connections with the presidents of the cartel of oil producing countries. His influence in the political corridors of power would be guaranteed to them for advance warning of future movements in their prized commodity.

It did not go unnoticed that the holdings of the Holst empire in the major publishers had dramatically reduced. He no longer had the power to outvote other shareholders and bludgeon his way through the annual general meetings to satisfy his own ego – and pocket. But the meetings were scheduled for the following January, by which time the shares would once again be registered in the tycoon's name. Or so he thought.

Peter Mallory noted the information, handed to him that morning by a jobber friend in the media section of the Stock Exchange. Maximillian's holdings were now only a fraction over the holdings of Niemand Nominees in each company. The time to strike had arrived.

'Purchase the entire stock of shares that are being sold today in the following companies.' He listed the same five companies nominated on the sheet before him. 'The funds for the settlement day will be in your hands in the usual manner. A direct transfer from liechtenstein into your partners' business account by Telegraphic Transfer.'

The jobber confirmed the order, working out in his mind the commission accruing from the deal and congratulating himself on the perception of teaming up with this mysterious, lucrative client. For over seven years the procedure had been the same. A telephone call with precise instructions – usually substantial commitments – and the deal was done. The payment instructions were impeccable. If the client was selling then the funds were immediately despatched by the same method to a numbered account in Liechtenstein in the name of Niemand Nominees. The jobber was never advised of the nature of the business of the trust and did not enquire. The funds were guaranteed by an indemnity from the Liechtenstein bank on behalf of the trust. That E type Jaguar I have been promising myself looks as good as mine, the jobber murmured as he signed the order for his associates.

Peter looked at the picture of Wendy framed against the white lace pillows in their little house in Witley. Her dark hair wound around her ears and on to her smooth shoulders to caress the contours of her arms as she stirred slightly in the heat of the night. 'Thank you god for bringing this angel to me,' whispered Peter. 'There can be no better gift that a man can receive than the love of a beautiful woman.' Peter was speaking of a love which had been born out of the most barbarous and depraved circumstances that man could conceive. Perhaps that is why our love is so intense. We have experienced the depths of hopelessness. To reach the heights that our love has attained could only have been engineered by a sense of not ever being able to love again. It is like all enjoyments in life, he argued to himself, – the sweet can only be distinguished by tasting the sour. Restricted margins of exposure to life's depredation and ecstasy lulled the brain into thinking that those mediocre limits were all that one could endure. Give a man a dying thirst and water will be as nectar. A starving man will treat plain bread as caviar. The analogies continued in Peter's brain as he stared at the ceiling. Blank now, but soon the grid would appear. The grid he knew so well that he could name the hut numbers. The gate near where he had hid in the little shed. The perimeter fence, the roads leading to the stark brick bath houses. The tall furnace chimneys, puncturing the pretty ceiling paper with their dark symmetry. He turned and slipped one arm tenderly over the slim waist of Wendy, cupping her left breast in his palm and sealing himself closely to the curve of her buttocks. They were as one. Born to merge their love in the crusade for peace of mind from their unremitting past.

Very soon, Peter promised himself, that crusade will be recompensed. In full. Just as he had felt the supreme emotions of a pure love, born of a corrupt and loathsome imposition by inhuman beings, then his adversary would feel the reverse. The despair and loneliness of a world where he had nothing and no one. Utter and complete destruction of all that he held dear. Just as he had destroyed the lives of his victims and their families forever. Forgiveness did not enter his mind. That word had been obliterated from his thought processes before he could comprehend what the word meant.

In his super size bed, Maximillian also stared at the ceiling. He saw only figures and wealth and the spider's web of impenetrable weaving of his gigantic empire. The threads so numerous and inter-connected that only he could unravel the multi-billion pound worth of it all. No matter that it had been built on a bed of guile, deceit and opportunism. Long ago Maximillian realised that these attributes were necessary in an imperfect world. A world where he could dominate and control. He had perfected the art of maintaining a public appearance of virtue while practising whatever it took to achieve his goal. Machiavelli would have been proud of me, he preened. The star pupil from the backwoods of nowhere. What were the odds against that? But the world did not reckon on a boy called Carl Taba, who progressed through his various stations to become Maximillian Alexander Carl Holst. Even the 'Mach' fits the image, he gratuitously congratulated himself on his choice of names.

As he fell asleep a frown crossed his brow. For the first time in fifty years, his father's face appeared before him. He saw the high Hassidim profile of a long beard, frock coat, large round shtrelimel hat edged with fur. He seemed to be pointing his spindly finger at a host of familiar Jewish faces that stared rapier like at the dreamer until they evaporated into the mists of a swirling black smoke being sucked up by the grey ceiling above.

CHAPTER X

1961

Susan looked out of the shuttered window of her apartment in East Berlin, hardly able to believe that summer was at its highest. In the cloistered atmosphere of the tiny flat, the air was as still as the August moths now that daylight was picking out the startling shadows of the harsh concrete abominations that had been thrown up after the war. Ugly and uncompromising. Suitable for the Soviet regime, she thought. Nothing showed here of the great Russian love of arts and music, of ballet and opera, of everything that people in the world knew of the 'old' Romanov empire.

Now the orders came from faceless men to other faceless men as the Stalinesque propaganda was promulgated relentlessly to the occupied East Germany. Relations with the west had deteriorated, deliberately Susan guessed, so that the Eastern block could take over the majority of the eastern states including what had been a united Germany. No more. Susan had witnessed daily the hard separation that was being more defined and feared for the future of her adopted homeland.

She looked at the calendar on the wall. 13th August 1961. Where had all the years gone? The endless days following the war when she had been shunted from place to place, never being able to put down roots. Until she had been re-united with Sergei and he had brought her some semblance of stability and a happiness that could be enjoyed by the two of them in their own company. Outside the world was as bleak as ever. She was alone. No family. Even her parents in England had died and she hadn't been informed for some months after, via the British Embassy in West Berlin. The last of her known relatives, except perhaps Lazar... But she dare not think about the possibility any more. The years had widened the gulf between her own indomitable belief and the probability that he had never survived the initial escape in 1941. It had taken Sergei many years of patient counselling to get her to come to terms with the fact that she had to start to live her own life. To put to the back of her mind the bitter recriminations and the hate that had almost driven her insane. Life was for living. Not for hating. Those responsible had been punished. Almost all of them. But who could add up the individual contributions to the greatest crime in history? Her lone battle to bring to account her personal adversary would not altar the world one iota. Better let it be and prove to those who had escaped the wrath of their victims, that to be happy and to generate a love of your fellow man was the ultimate triumph of good over evil. She had let go and had blossomed into the 'perfect English rose' again, as Sergei had lovingly christened her.

Thirteen years. Eleven with Sergei. Eleven beautiful years when her thoughts had indeed cherished all that was good about the world. The summers, the winters, the leaves in Autumn. But most of all the Spring. The birth of everything in life that she held dear. The trees pushing green shoots through tough bark. The crocus and daffodil bursting with delight at the success of thrusting their heads to the sun. Birds and animals regenerating their kind as they had done since the dawn of time. All having offspring and prodigy. Hers were gone, but the memory of Lazar and Taghi burned as brightly in her brain as the sun on this hot August midsummer's day.

'They have blocked the passage to West Berlin with barbed wire and guards. A great wall is being built across the city.'

Sergei's words greeted her as she turned from the window, bringing her back to the present. 'Pardon?' she said, not quite attuned to his sudden words.

'I said that the Soviets,' funny how he addresses them as the Soviets Susan thought, 'the Soviets have constructed a barrier between the East and West. No one is allowed across from either side. This is what we have all been fearing. Germany has been split permanently. The East and West have been split permanently. It is what the Socialist Republic has wanted all along. They have won. They will now dominate Europe and pose a threat to the peace that we have all fought so long to attain.'

'They just can't divide a city or a country like that. It's monstrous. It is against all the rights of the citizens of both sides.'

'Since when have you heard of the secretariat of the Russian Republic ever considering citizen's rights? You will now have a taste of what we have had to endure since the rise of Stalin and his henchmen.' Sergei thought for a moment, his brain working overtime to assess the situation. As if there was not a moment to lose. 'Yes!' he exclaimed. 'That is what we must do!'

'What Sergei?' Susan panicked at his urgent manner as he made for the bedroom with the purposeful stride that she knew so well. 'What is it that we must do?'

'We must leave as soon as possible. That's what we must do.'

There was no demurring in his decision. Once made, Susan knew that he would carry it through no matter what. That was one of the traits which had inured her to him when she had found him again in Berlin. And Katrina. Stronger and healthier for the love and care that Susan had bestowed on her from the moment her poor mother had died... Despite her overwhelming desire to search for Lazar and the man who was uppermost in her thoughts, Susan's first duty was to the little girl who had been thrust upon her. A stripling of child, barely able to walk or talk or understand the world around her. Thank God, murmured Susan. She will never know of the dreadful beginnings of her life. At least she will not remember, but she will be told when the time is appropriate.

Sergei had provided the answer to Susan's dilemma. Stay in Germany with him and bring up the child as their own. Susan could not return to England. The papers necessary were too complicated and the prospect of travelling there with a small child with no one to help them was not one that she greeted with her old determination and resolve. Besides, Sergei pointed out, there was the question of her entitlement in Germany. Her husband's business, his property. She could not abandon them. They were rightfully hers. Then perhaps when she had established some financial stability, she could think about a visit to England. And then there was Katrina. She needed to be mothered full time, to be schooled, to be brought up in a loving home, to appreciate the beautiful things in life, not the memories of a hell that should never have directed her future to the care of two perfect strangers.

Susan eventually saw the sense in Sergei's reasoning. A period of consolidation, to reflect and to pick up the threads of her life again. To enjoy for a change, the normal everyday experiences that she longed for each night in bed when she thought of Lazar skipping home from school, Taghi playing in the garden. The excitement of birthdays, Christmas, and a thousand and one other precious snippets that made up the joy of a family. She put all other thoughts out of her head and she blossomed into the quiet country, apple bright girl that she once had been. Before... before... But there was not to be any more before, she rebuked herself. That had gone and had been buried permanently. But in her heart of hearts she knew that nothing as deeply depraving as that episode could ever be wiped from the horror permanently etched into the cells locked away in that part of her brain which had apparently been closed forever. Katrina had emerged as bright as the shine in her eyes. She excelled at everything. It seemed as if she was in a dreadful hurry to assimilate the knowledge that was bursting forth in the new world. Susan and Sergei searched for books of every subject under the sun. They sent her to a private school which had had the sense to see the opportunity of teaching the growing children the old values, the basics of learning, the way that the future could be faced with knowledge. And knowledge was the key to a successful existence. Katrina soaked up the education as if she had only been conceived for the purpose of digesting all that the world of books had to offer. 'She does not go out to play with the other boys and girls. She must learn to mix. It is part of growing up,' she remembered him complaining one day.

'She is content to meet them at her school and to attend the birthday parties that are given. If she wishes to have more of an outside life then she can. She's only eleven, there's plenty of time for her to make special friends.' Susan dismissed Sergei's concern. She remembered her own childhood and her errant ways in the fields of Dorset. But this was different. This was a strange regime. One had to be careful... not to speak out of turn. Most parents guarded their children protectively for their own good, and for the safety of themselves against the ever present watchful party members. No, Katrina was a perfectly balanced child, well mannered – as taught by her mother – and viewed the world through a grown up's perspective.

'Perhaps a little too much of an adult,' admitted Susan, as she watched her studying her latest technology textbook.

'Right!' nodded Sergei. 'She needs to get away from the confines of this awful city. Some country air. A holiday. Don't all children need holidays? And what about us? Stuck here with all the reminders of what we both hate. We need a change of scene, some time to relax, and to … well you know what I mean,' he finished lamely, the question hanging in the air.

'Of course you are right. We live as a family, but we are not as a family should be. Katrina is well cared for and wants for nothing, but we… we … I'm sorry Sergei, but I cannot be the wife that I want to be.' Susan's eyes pleaded with Sergei to understand. The tension that always returned when the subject was raised, stiffened her back and she almost resented his intrusion into her private shield that even after all these years formed an invisible barrier to her inner wanting self.

They had started to live together as soon as the final division of Berlin had been decided by the allied powers. The over officious administration and the necessary bureaucratic paraphernalia were part of the Russian subterfuge to impress upon their previous partners in war, that the Soviet were in charge of the East and would remain so for the foreseeable future. The division had begun. As the months passed it became apparent that unison was out of the question and any attempt to mediate was met with a definite 'niet!'

Sergei had been seconded to supervise the military presence in Berlin and had carried out his orders meticulously according to the diktats of his superiors. But when the American and British protested against the closing of entry to Berlin from the west, he had every sympathy for them. The final part of that once great city would become communist if the two powers buckled under the dominant fist of Stalin. But it did not happen. The attempt to prevent the allies from unifying the western part of Germany was defeated by the inspirational air lift to West Berlin to maintain supplies and keep open communication with their fellow countrymen. Not only did it succeed, but it was the first riposte to the threat of the spreading blanket of Stalin's powers. The blockade was lifted in May 1949. But this only precipitated the further hardening of the division of the German people. East and West had arrived.

Susan and Katrina joined Sergei soon afterwards and set up home in his flat in the suburbs of Friedrichsfeld where some semblance of countryside still survived the scorching advance of the Russian army in 1945. The few remaining trees gave Susan hope for the return of the natural elements in life. The birds and insects and small mammals that no power on earth could influence as this vile political scourge was now doing to her adopted country. No one could altar the sky, the clouds, the dramatic storms that freshened the gasping shoots after the harsh dry summers. They would continue to grow and to multiply long after the fall of this dreaded regime.

Sergei had told her that. He had assured her that the system could only last for so long. It could not sustain the underlying false premise that all men should be equal. It flew in the face of nature itself. No man on earth wanted to be equal to another. For infinite equality only bred boredom and apathy. The challenge of the world was there for those who so chose to take it on. Sergei was so passionate about his beliefs that Susan feared that he would betray himself to his fellow officers. But he assured her that he only discussed his feelings with her and with those he knew to be similarly inclined. But Susan still worried.

Katrina grew into the beautiful, dark, image of what her mother must have been. Susan was able to put form and body onto the remembered face of Rosa and picture her as she was before the holocaust. The mother of this sweepingly handsome, lissome young girl who had survived the trauma of her wretched birth, must have been the main provider of the genes that shaped this outstanding example of Teutonic elegance.

But this country was no place for a growing girl. She was not able to enjoy the freedom that gave an individual the zest for life. Restrictions were severe and luxuries non-existent. Susan harried Sergei to arrange a passage to the west. Anywhere away from this interminable, grinding, and oppressive restriction of people's liberty. Katrina needed to expand on her studies, where she was showing a brilliant aptitude to the new technology in computers. But here was not the place to pursue those aims. The west was moving far ahead of the Soviet Union and the Eastern bloc. The stimulation to her agile brain would soon dissipate and her capabilities confined to the limits of the mundane knowledge of the local college. But there was no way out. Susan did not have official papers. Katrina's papers were only the certification of her mother and the adoption by Susan. They were useless.

The many enquiries they had made of Werner Kawalek's properties and business had proved fruitless. The house where so many happy memories were embedded was no longer in her husband's name. Neither was the warehouse, where so many valuable text books and journals once proudly adorned the multiple shelves and storage cupboards. The building was demolished along with the empty rooms – ransacked or plundered by the hands of the starving inhabitants of Berlin. Or so the official had told them when they finally convinced him that Susan had an interest in the property. Susan knew otherwise. The name appearing on the last register to the title to the land was Boris Vukadovic. He had taken everything. Her husband, her son, her daughter, and now all connections with her past. It was as if her very soul had been assaulted. Defiled. Raped. This monster who had destroyed her family and her reason for being alive. This evil manifestation of the devil who cared for no one. And now she was prevented from seeking him out, if he still lived, by the forces that had aided and abetted his escape.

An aura of acceptance descended on Susan following the discovery of the plunder of her identity. Who was she? You are what you have made yourself. By your possessions, your association with others. Their knowledge of you. She had none of those things. She was a different person. Susan Mallory was no more. She was dead. As dead as Werner, Taghi and Lazar. Lazar, who thankfully had not died in the gas chambers. At least he had had a fighting chance. She liked to think of him now and again, enjoying the boyish things that all youngsters revel in. The games, the fights, the delights of a first kiss, the growing through puberty with all the confusing but wonderful signals to his developing body. But all those things must be put aside. There was no Lazar any more. There was no Taghi or Werner. She was alone in her former life. It had to be forgotten or she would die of remorse. And that was not Susan's way. Sergei cajoled her, berated her, loved her, and cherished her back to some semblance of normality. Katrina helped. She was the new beginning; the hope for a future. She must survive this second holocaust of communistic incarceration. One day Katrina would be free. She would be in England. Susan made that promise to herself in the confines of the dark, comforting cloak of her lonely bedroom.

"As soon as possible." Sergei's words rang in her revitalised brain as she tried to contemplate the significance of his statement. How? When? Where to?

Sergei laughed at her barrage of questions. 'Not so fast my love. There are many details to sort out. But one thing I do know is that it must be soon. The wall will gather strength and security. No longer will men try to escape by the official method of application through the impossible channels. They will ignore the dangers and jump. Freedom is just a few yards away but the wall against success is higher than ever and is now real.' Three have been shot already trying to climb that symbol of all that communism represents.'

Susan was devastated. To think that innocent people, whose only wish in life was to live in freedom had been shot without trial or without any compassion reminded her of a similar regime in the 1930s... and similar men who controlled the destiny of other innocents. 'Will we all go?'

Sergei considered Susan's query carefully. 'No. Three would be too many. Two might manage to time their escape at the point I have in mind, but it will need a third to arrange the diversion for the two minutes that it will take to climb the wall.'

That night in bed Sergei explained his emerging plan to Susan. There was a spot where the barbed wire was not quite complete. He had seen it on his patrol that morning as the workmen toiled frantically to complete the bulwark between the two communities. An abomination forced on people of a like mind by a power that cared little for the national pride of a defeated people. A deliberate imposition of a barrier to enforce the doctrine on to a captive, subdued and lost generation. Their conversion would ensure that generations to come would know no other ideology than the totalitarianism of Lenin.

'I have already said that only two would be able to scale the wall. We shall need help from the other side. I will attend to that . . . '

'But how . . . ?'

'Leave that to me my leibchen,' Sergei said lapsing into German as he knew that Susan loved the word. Literally a bodice – he found that he too appreciated the closeness of their relationship within the word. Far better and more expressive than the word 'love' in English, which they spoke most of the time. 'First we shall have to decide on the date. That will be synchronised with the change of the guard. I can orchestrate that so that the particular guard on that part of the wall is slightly late. The existing guard will be eager to return to his barracks and hopefully will not be as astute as he should be.'

'How will we climb the wall?'

'That is the difficult part. You will have to be pulled from the other side, and of course you will have to climb part of the way yourselves.'

'You say yourselves. Does that mean Katrina and me?'

'Yes. You are fairly light so the men on the other side will be able to hoist you to the top. The only difficulty is if the rope will stand the strain of scraping over the top of the wall. I will have to see if some sort of grease of oil can be spread. But that will mean that the second person will have to cope with a slippy rope. It will already have been pulled through the lubricant once. Perhaps a harness is the answer. There are so many imponderables and we do not have much time. The nights are short and the full moon is due the day after tomorrow. We must catch the darkest night. There can be no practising. It must happen on the first go.' Sergei's thoughts poured out of him as if he was reluctant to think of the consequence of failure. The consequence of success. He would be losing the two persons he loved most in this world. Susan had not considered the outcome, he could tell by the light that had appeared in her eyes. She could only think of England and Dorset . . . and freedom. What freedom remained for him if and when they were successful? A return to the lonely life of before. Married to the Army. To Stalin's inexorable destruction of all that men believed in. A destroyer of initiative, of art, of love, but most of all, a destroyer of souls.

He held Susan in his arms, gently cradling her mass of auburn hair in the crook of his shoulder. She was still awake, as she always was when they had their 'loving.' He didn't know why they had christened it that. Theirs was not loving in the physical sense. Just a state of being together. To hold each other from head to toe in an embrace that gave them the satisfaction which they craved. Susan had never been capable of the act of love since her release from Monowitz Buna and Sergei had accepted the fact that intercourse was impossible. There was a rejection that he knew lay in the depths of her mind. The bestiality of the camp and the savage wrenching of her family from her breast had damaged her libido in some way as to make it abhorrent to her. Her body told her that it needed the stimulation of a loving man, but her psyche dictated otherwise. A barrier as cloistered as the Berlin wall shuttered out the inner feelings that longed to be freed. Perhaps when she was free...? Sergei put it out of his mind. When she was free she would no longer be with him. He fought the instinct to accompany her. Anywhere away from this place. This place that reminded him of all that his country was inflicting on his people. But he could not desert them. One day it would be different. Susan would be with her people and he would be with his. One day she would return to a free country to live together in a free world. To enjoy love. To rejoice in the state of being able to love unreservedly. He knew that day would come. Pray God that it would not be too long.

'What are you thinking about Sergei?'

'You. And Katrina. And me.'

'We are a family aren't we.'

'Yes. We are a family. But you realise that the family has to split to survive.'

'Come with us Sergei. There must be a way. There has to be.' Susan pleading almost broke his heart. She was right. There had to be way for them to be together. But not now. The important thing was to secure their freedom. To give Susan a chance to assuage the hate that festered in her heart.

Until that had been accomplished, he knew that neither of them would ever be free. It had shown in Susan's attitude when even she was unaware of her reaction to little snippets of information that filtered through the restricted press of East Berlin. The luxuries on the other side of the division. The way of life that had once been hers. He caught in her eyes as she lovingly patted children on the street and cuddled babies to her as if she were back in her nursery. The longing, the yearning for the past. She never said anything but Sergei knew it was there. All that she had ever built in this world could never be obliterated from her mind. It lay there waiting to be resurrected. And when that day came, she would be free once again.

'I cannot come. You know that. I am needed this side. To curse your betrayal of me. To denounce you to the party for your treachery. But one day my leibchen, you will return to me and we shall live as husband and wife. No matter how long it takes. Promise?'

'I promise.' There is nothing in this world that will prevent me keeping that promise… one day. She looked at him and saw deep into his dark grey eyes. She saw the love and the understanding and also the torment of losing her. The torment of the years when he could not consummate their love. But they did consummate it in their inner selves. In their dreams and they were complete.

He held her to him, feeling the warmth and closeness of her. Her sweet body smell and the softness of her cheek against his arm. It had been like this always. The tension of his unrequited love had been controlled by an ethereal love that transcended all other. Perhaps he loved her more for their innocence than he would have done if relations had been normal. His early years with his own family had governed the extent of his physical contact with others and heightened it to a higher plane. Because of his non-contact within the family, the slightest caress from Susan had sent shock waves through his body, a succession of convulsions that filled his being with unimagined bolts of lightning, dragging the pit of his stomach up to the back of his brain, to cascade down throughout his body again ready for the next surge. She caressed him now. Tingling the fine hairs at the base of his spine. Stroking and teasing each vertebrae as his mind wandered through the heavens, seeking the ultimate star on which to hang his angel's wings. For that was how she made him feel. An innocent angel, inspired by a love so deep that it need not enter the physical aspects of procreation. It was as pure as the children's love for one another. As innocent as a baby's love for its mother. It was enough. It was a promise of a greater love yet to be.

His toes clenched under hers as his body enclosed the being in his arms. Every inch of her dovetailed into him. Her pert breasts still had the elasticity to snuggle themselves under his strong pectoral muscles, her stomach flattening out on his. Her thighs enclosed his tremoring manhood in the soft dark gentleness of her pubic hair. Neither moved or needed to. She gripped him with a love that told him that she was utterly his. Her body would not allow penetration but her soul would. She did this for him. For the man that she had lived for and loved since that day she had joined him. His whole being cried out to her silently for the gift that god had given him and he held the crescendo of his emotions until his passion demanded satisfaction and he spent himself on this loving object that lay as one with him. Susan felt the involuntary shudder and clung to him until his breathing eased and the tremors in his body abated and he became still. She was fulfilled herself in her mind. She had given sustenance to her man and that was the sum total of all that she was capable of. She could do no more.

'Yes,' she murmured to the sleeping Sergei. 'I will come back to you. I will not grow old, neither will our love grow old. To be together again. To love one another as we deserve to be loved. I promise you that my leibchen.' She smiled and stroked the greying locks from his forehead. His boyishness shone through even now with the deep lines of responsibility and concern etching his handsome face. To make a man happy must be the ultimate satisfaction of all females, she thought. To attain that familiar closeness that no others hold over you. Your mother, father, brothers or sisters. A unique love that grows with the years. His for you and yours for him. She did not love Werner any the less. His memory carried that same unique love in the private moments of her life. But they were like a book to be read again and again. To be enjoyed and put aside. Another life, another time. This man was the moment. Now. Her reason for being. Her salvation from the morass that she so nearly slipped into. Susan slept at last. Dreaming of the green fields of England. The sweeping hills of Dorset. The childhood fantasies in the dappled woods. The faces of her schoolfriends. Her teacher. He mother and father. Her little Taghi ... The last time she had seen her as she screamed for her mother to fetch her from the soldier who was roughly bundling her after her father...

Susan awoke with a scream as her nightmare eclipsed itself into the grey image of a sneering face. A face bloated with disdain at the thousand pleading arms sinking into the fiery abyss... The heavily hooded eyes and bushy eyebrows laughed at her helplessness as the long dormant seed of hate exploded within her.

There were two walls to negotiate Sergei had said. The inner wall where the eight foot high monstrosity of prefabricated blocks of concrete had been surmounted by a course of tubular pipes to make a handhold impossible. On the western side was a smaller more accessible wall topped with roof tiles. Between the two was a six-foot 'moat.'

'The barbed wire is the problem,' Sergei said. 'I have examined the wall from end to end and at only one place can I see a definite division in the wire. It is just opposite the Potsdamer Platz – you remember that?' He paused, seeing the picture of the old Berlin resurrect itself in Susan's mind. 'About 30 metres from there is a church which stands within 10 metres of the wall. To one side there is a warehouse forming a small L shape lit by three street lamps. Those will have to be dealt with when the time comes. In addition the warehouse is occupied by guards who control the section to their left within 200 metres. Frequent foot patrols also pass along the wall which is further protected by 'tank trap' mounds in the road to prevent traffic.'

'It is impossible isn't it?'

'No. It is not impossible. Nothing is impossible. You escaped from the gas chamber. That was impossible, but you did it. Believe my leibchen; and it will happen. I promise you.'

'I don't know if I have the courage to carry it through. I have discussed it with Katrina and she has no doubt that it is the only way out.'

'She will have the courage for both of you. You have shown her a love which she cannot repay. A sacrifice over and above your own inclinations. She will keep you safe and ensure that at last you will be free.' Sergei kissed her on her forehead, hiding the smarting in his eyes as he became more aware of the destruction of his life that losing this woman would cause.

'Tonight we must sit down and discuss in every detail the timing and the route that we must take. Tomorrow we will have a little rehearsal to gain access to the hiding place where you will stay until I have dealt with the lights and the guards. Now – prepare a very tasty supper for us. I won't call it the last supper, that would be too ominous. Let us call it a celebration supper. The celebration of our success on Thursday, we dare not wait any longer. We must strike when they least expect it.'

For some reason Susan could not quite come to terms with the sudden expectation of the freedom for which she had yearned for so long. There was an excitement within her that raised her adrenalin until she thought that she would burst. There was also the utter feeling of despair at being parted from Sergei. The two emotions fought each other constantly, arguing for and against the plan. Where would she be happier? Surely that was the ultimate question. With whom did she want to share the rest of her life. With Sergei? What about her determination to return to England. To recapture the sentiment of her youth. Her childhood. Her teenage years when none of what happened since could ever have been imagined. Could she wipe away the hurt and the hate? The degradation that she still felt for having to undergo the loathsome and foul acts of inhumanity. Her privacy had been invaded and raped. Her self respect had been torn from her. From thousands of others. They had almost been reduced to sub-humans by the vile and obscene attack on the whole nation of Jews. The 'Endlosung der Judenfrage'. How many times had she heard and read that sickening phrase? It echoed in every gas chamber, in every oven, in every empty block of every concentration camp. As empty as the souls of those who had survived. Why should she have been spared? Because she had fought to do so? Because she had been smiled upon by some greater force than fortune? There had to be a reason. And if there was a reason, wasn't it her duty to carry it through?

Susan's mind was racked with self torture as she fought her deepest desires to return to the land of her birth. She did not belong there any more. She was German. Her place was with the man she now loved. With the people who would need every scrap of encouragement to one day free themselves legally. To live in a free country with their own countrymen the other side of the wall. The wall. Everything came back to the wall. It was the barrier that was stopping her from her prime objective. The nazis still existed while the wall stood between her and her goal. It was as if they had built a permanent reminder that what they had failed to achieve in the death camps would be slowly but surely completed in the obscurity of a walled city. A limbo from which there was only one escape. Over the wall.

'Katrina, I want you to help your mother when the time comes to grasp the rope and wrap it around her waist. When she is at the top, the rope will be passed down to you. You will both be wearing gloves, I have them here,' Sergei said producing two pairs of kid leather gloves Susan would have been proud to wear in Bond Street. 'Once at the top you will have to reach over the rounded part and get a grip before releasing your other hand hold. Be careful not to get your hands trapped between the wall the rope.' Sergei demonstrated with a short piece of rope that as they neared the top of the wall their hands would be forced nearer and nearer the wall. 'It will mean that you will have to heave your body upwards at the last moment with one hand free.'

Katrina nodded, her eyes shining and her faintly amber hued skin became alive like a racehorse before the off. She was as ready as a heron poised for the catch. Sergei was spending most of his time explaining to Susan the intricacies of the operation. 'Timing is all important. You must not move from your hiding place until you see the street lamps go out. If they do not go out – do not move. I will fetch you and we shall have to try again another day.'

Susan's face fell. She had a feeling in the pit of her stomach as if she were about to be sick. Perhaps she would be on the night. The thought shocked her. It was a feeling of apprehension she recalled from her childhood and adolescence. An uncomfortable mixture of excitement, fear, and foreboding. She was angry with herself. Here was a man patiently explaining how she and her daughter could obtain freedom and she was full of doubts about her own ability. Or was it doubt about her willingness to go? To leave him. To leave the comparative safety of her home life – albeit a mundane and useless existence.

Sergei filled their cups with the steaming coffee that Susan had made after the rather simple, but tasty – as Sergei had complimented her – boiled beef. 'So we will go over it once more. The date of the escape,' he referred to it always as "the escape" to dispel any notion that it would fail, 'is the day after tomorrow, Thursday. The forecast for the evening is overcast with a little rain expected. That will help us. You, Susan,' he said looking into her tawny eyes framed with the prettiest crows feet that he had ever seen, she remembered him saying, 'you will prepare your clothes. Strong trousers and a thick jumper. Woollen balaclavas from the old jumpers in your drawers. I do not want any part of your skin showing. Any light, no matter how dim, will pick up the lightness in an instant. I need hardly add that strong shoes also are a must. That takes care of the dress. Any questions?'

Katrina looked at him. 'Can we take anything with us?'

'Absolutely not. Just you and your clothing. Nothing else. Only your papers, the ones that you possess. No other personal belongings. And I mean that,' he added as Katrina showed her annoyance. She doesn't really appreciate the situation she is in, Sergei thought. So young. So beautiful. His love for her was as strong as that for Susan. And he was about to lose them both. He hardened his face and turned to the next item.

'You will be taken by me in the staff car at 6.15pm to the rear of the church. A small door will be open at the southern end. You will hide under blankets in the boot of my car until you feel it stop and the engine switch off. Do not move until then.' His finger moved down the list he had prepared. 'It will take approximately seven minutes for me to reach the fourth floor of the warehouse where the main guard overlooking the wall is situated. Seven minutes after the engine stops, you will open the boot, – I have fixed the catch – and you will slip into the church door. On your left there is a further door which leads down into the crypt. The church has not been used for years but the doors are moveable. Stay in the crypt at the front end. That is the end which faces the wall. High on the church wall there is a small grid through which you will be able to see the square made by the church and the warehouse. When the lights go out, make your way back to the main door on the Western side and position yourselves in the porch. The actual point at which you will scale the wall will be roughly thirty metres to your left. On the other side of the wall is an apartment block. Three windows from the right on the top floor a light will be put on and then the curtains drawn. Watch for the light and move as the curtains close. The rope will be waiting for you.'

Susan marvelled at the way in which Sergei calmly dealt out his orders as if it were a game of chess. 'When did you arrange all this Sergei?'

'A long time ago. The system had been set up for some time. It is only now that it is being put into practice. I knew that it would become more and more difficult for us to move to the west. There are now only seven official crossings remaining of the eighty set up when the city first became divided. But very few can escape legally. Now they are becoming desperate to stop the exodus. It betrays the very system that they wish to portray to the world. So I contacted friends on the other side and set up this arrangement. It has not been tested yet. You will be the first to celebrate its inauguration.' He laughed so uproariously that the worried frowns on even Katrina's face melted into smiles of acknowledgement for his resourcefulness. But Susan still had a stomach that was not convinced. The same feeling as when Carl Weisz burst through the door of their home in 1941 …

'That is the easy bit. For my part, I will interrupt the changing of the guard by a diversion. There will be another attempted escape on the far side of the church, away from you. Guards will be sent to investigate just at the turnover. They will assume that their counterparts are already in place in the warehouse. In their turn, their relief will assume that someone else is dealing with the fracas on the northern wall. The lights can only be turned off after the guards have left and I will have to accompany them. Hopefully I shall be able to double back and throw the switch and rejoin them before they realise that I am missing. That will be my alibi. No one will be exempt from suspicion. But if I am with the detail that nearly catches would be emigrants, then I cannot fall under suspicion.' He smiled and drained the last dregs of the strong coffee that had gone cold on the bare table in front of him.

Susan had also gone cold. A cold sweat that crept up from the soles of her feet and engulfed her body like a damp blanket. Sergei was running the risk of being shot for aiding and abetting. His whole life for nothing. The supreme sacrifice for someone who had failed to return his love in the way that her conscience screamed for her to do. Tears fell from her unashamed eyes as she took his hands in hers and kissed the palms as they caught her drops. Katrina softly left the room, her tears brimming on her lashes for her mother and this man, this one man whom she was proud to call her father.

'What if anything goes wrong? How will we contact you? How shall we know? Will you . . . '

'. . . I shall be fine,' he reassured her. 'I have been over the plan a thousand times. Nothing will go wrong. Whatever happens, once you make your move, do not turn back. The guards will be forced to shoot you and I can do nothing about that.' Sergei took her face in his hands and kissed her forehead, her nose, and her mouth in gentle caressing movements that imparted all the love that his body had been crying out for since his childhood. The touch of another.

The feel of another's skin. It's texture. It's warmth. It's security. Like a balm to his uninitiated boyhood, he captured the closeness of his mother, the gruff acquiescence of his father, the innocent contact of his brothers and sisters. She had given him all these things. And now he was letting her go . . .

They wept together into the night.

The catholic priest stood, still as telegraph post. And almost as straight. His back had bent under the years caring for his community. A community torn apart by the devil and the devil's work. Once a god fearing, god loving devotee to his calling, he now stood in doubt and confusion. Since the utter destruction of Berlin in the final assault, he had ceased to believe in his god. There was only the mighty and the vanquished. If the mighty had the conscience of the Lord's teachings then it was fortunate for them to be in command. If they proved not to be so mighty as they needed to be, then the evil encapsulated in Naziism would prevail. That the allies had won he did not attribute to god. It was the way of things. How life transpired. There was no pre-ordained path for mankind. Just a series of chance happenings, helped somewhere along the way by right thinking men. God never had a hand in any of the happenings. How could he? How could he have let a man like Adolph Hitler come to power, usurp the people, twist their minds, and convince them that they would have a better life under his rule? Perhaps in the final analysis, he thought, people are selfish. They want the best for themselves and even at the expense of others, they will take it from whomever is offering the best chance.

Father Luke stood now, looking emotionless at the bare altar. The figure of Our Lady, dusty and careworn. 'Even the Virgin Mary cannot maintain her aura of detachment and superiority,' he intoned to himself, much as he did in his sermons. 'She is the same as all the rest. Her light has gone out, just as it has been extinguished in all who used to worship at her feet.'

He did not hear the quiet footsteps behind him or the wheeze of tightened breathing fighting for some sort of regularity. Because of his stillness, the intruders into his private meditation did not see him at first. Then the younger of the two let out a stifled gasp as she saw him facing the edifice of Our Lady. She saw only the lips moving, distracting the light from his dusty surrounds to fasten on to the whiteness of his teeth as he spoke. Everything else in the church absorbed the light in its dust and debris. Even the light has gone out here, he reflected sadly, musing over his selected theme.

The gasp made him turn. Not in fear; he no longer had extreme emotions; but in curiosity. No one ever entered this empty house, not even god. Who could be creeping about at this hour? He saw the two women, frozen in apprehension. Unable to distinguish who the tall, black figure at the altar was.

'Have you come to pray?' He was surprised by his own voice, still retaining the resonance that inspired his sermons.

'No,... we, er... we did not expect to find anyone here.'

The youthfulness of the young girl's voice stirred something within him. The remembrance of his youth, when the world was good. When people lived life as it should be lived. When he had the kingdom of god in his heart and his hopes reached out to heaven and the humanity in man.

'If you have come to pray, I must leave, for it has little meaning to me any more.' He did not know why he was confessing to these strangers. It just seemed appropriate if they still believed.

The older woman spoke. 'Are you the priest of this parish?'

'Was,' the old man said. 'There is no parish here now.'

'What is your name?'

The father did not mind being questioned. He had been interrogated too many times before. It was routine now. 'Fath.. Luke Streicher.' He paused. 'You recognise the name?'

'No,' said the woman slowly.

'Julius Streicher. He was my son. He is no longer my son. he is dead.' The words were delivered impassively as if memorised from a school primer.

Susan went to the priest and put her arm around his shoulder and led him to a pew. 'Perhaps you should sit down. We have a little time.' The fear of being discovered had departed and the girls relaxed with their companion.

'You say your son is Julius Streicher. I do not know the name.' Susan's puzzled response brought no reaction from the man. 'Was he a priest too?'

Father Luke laughed. 'Perhaps he was in a way. Perhaps he had his own god. Perhaps his was the right way… I do not know any more.'

Suddenly Susan remembered. The Nuremberg war trials. 21 of Hitler's henchmen, plastered across every newspaper for weeks.

Among them she recalled a name "Streicher." Was this his son?

'How can so much evil emanate from a house that teaches the good in people? How can a complete stranger have so much influence over a son who was loved more than life itself?'

Susan could tell that the questions now posed had been invoked many times before in the stillness of what was once this man's spiritual house. He looked at them. At Katrina and her bright expectant face. 'You have the world before you my child,' he surprised himself again by speaking as he used to. 'Use it wisely, for good. And for fighting evil.' His eyes dwelt on the clothes which they wore and the gloves and strong shoes. 'You are escaping aren't you?' he said simply.

'Yes,' said Susan, the honesty of his gaze bringing confidence to her admission. 'We are going to the west.' She saw his eyelids lower as if picturing a world where men were unfettered and worshipped honestly. Where smiles and laughter were natural and spontaneous. Where young girls such as this beautiful, dark haired adolescent, could wander, free as a bird, to pursue the normal ambitions of a teenager with all the zest and vigour that god had given them. She read his thoughts and knew that his inner struggle was destroying him.

'You must pray for us,' she said.

'Pray?' Father Luke raised his eyebrows at the alien word. 'I have forgotten how,' he excused himself.

'You never forget, not if you really want to remember.'

'Please pray for us,' asked Katrina. 'We shall need someone other than our friends tonight.'

Susan clasped his hand in hers and nodded slowly as he sought their faith in his prayers. 'Do you think god will listen after all this time? He is no longer with me. I rejected him a long time ago. He will not hear me.'

'He heard me a long time ago when I thought that he had deserted me. I know now that he is always there… if you want him.'

Father Luke knelt at the altar and began to pray. Stumbling at first, but as his confidence returned his mind fastened on to the litany that was part of his being. As familiar as the names of his family. He prayed for Julius, as he had prayed for him after his defection from the church. He prayed for all the souls who would never worship again. He prayed for the two women who were about to set out on a journey that he would have taken in their place. The film of dust on the Virgin's head did not lay so heavily as before and the shadow of a smile seemed to beam down on to the bowed head of her disciple, as he craved her forgiveness.

Susan and Katrina crouched in the musty confines of the crypt, sustained by the hot coffee and biscuits that Susan had thoughtfully packed. Hours seemed to pass as they waited, dozing fitfully, not daring to sleep for fear of missing the signal. For fear of someone discovering them. Father Luke would have long gone, leaving his presence in the sepulchral atmosphere of the nave.

"Watch for the lights" Sergei had said. They looked toward the small grill on the western side of the cellar through which spindly beams of light found their way through the gathered cobwebs and grime. When they could no longer see the beams, that would be the signal to move. Faint shouts a long distance on their right disturbed the silence of their personal tomb. Shouts that echoed the sounds that she heard nightly on her rough bunk in Monowitz-Buna. Cries of hopelessness. Cries for mothers and fathers, sisters and brothers. Anyone who could comfort their poor demented minds. But no one came. Relief was obtained only when they could cry no more and they were silenced forever.

The cries and the shouting grew louder. The tone of military commands intersected the 'panic' calls. Short, curt, guttural words of command, accompanied by the crunch of heavy boots. Who invented heavy boots, Susan wondered? Surely the architect of all despots in the world. Heavy boots that kicked a man into submission. That ruptured spleens and destroyed kidneys. That spat teeth and eyeballs onto the unsympathetic dust. Every prisoner feared the boot. The boot of the nazi thugs. The boots were running now, away from the church. Away from where they hid. The lights went out!

'Quickly Katrina, we must go.' Susan grabbed Katrina's hand and hustled her out of the cellar, scooping up her bag of belongings and slinging it over her shoulder.

The wall was dark and ominous across the small square in front of the church. The steel barbs on the wire glinted dully in the half light of a star in the southern sky to their left. Sirius. The brightest star in the heavens. It had to choose tonight to peep its fluorescence under the cloud blanket. Susan swore.

Stumbling and running, the two women traversed the open area in record time. The brick furrows, built like a ploughed field, jarred every bone in their legs and they fell gratefully to the ground at the foot of the black barrier between them and freedom.

Where was the gap? Sergei said there would be a breach in the wire big enough for a body. Where the two rolls of wire met. Susan was grateful for the star as she ran her eyes skywards along the glistening spikes. Thirty metres further on the glint disappeared. She had found the gap. Panic struck her.

She had forgotten to wait in the porch as Sergei had instructed. To wait for the light in the window opposite to go on and the curtains to be drawn. They were out now and must remain so. They dare not return to the church. 'I must go back to the other side of the street,' Susan whispered to Katrina. 'I cannot see the window from under this wall. I will wait there and come to you as soon as the light goes on. The rope will follow shortly.' She put a restraining hand on Katrina's mouth as she rose to protest. 'Trust me. We are almost there.'

Katrina crouched even lower beside the wall. She could not see Susan in the dim light. Good, she thought. If I cannot see her it is unlikely that anyone else will. The sounds from further down the wall had subsided into an unintelligible babble. Like the muttering undertones of a crowd awaiting direction.

Susan was back beside her. 'The light has just gone on. Watch for the rope.'

Nothing happened.

Their hearts thumped against their rib cages, forcing heavy pants of breath into the sultry night air.

Something whistled over their heads and slapped against the stones. It lay there like a snake coiled to strike. Susan picked it up and gave two sharp tugs. She felt the resistance the other end. 'Stand up Katrina,' she said.

Before Katrina could protest the rope was around her waist and doubled in front of her. 'You go first Katrina, I shall only hold you up.'

The rope tightened and Katrina scrabbled her legs against the bricks hauling herself bodily to the top and grabbing the coving in the crook of her arm. Another heave and her left arm swung over the rim and she was up and over the wall. So far so good. Susan heard the grunts of more exertions on the second wall and waited for the rope to be tossed over again.

Suddenly the lights came on!

Susan looked left and right and dropped to her stomach as she was illuminated in the triple beams of the three street lamps. Something had gone wrong! Was Sergei all right? Had he been discovered? No thoughts of her own safety entered Susan's head as she lay, not knowing whether to run or stay.

'Come my child. You must hurry.' Father Luke's compelling voice in her ear forced her to think clearly. There was still time. No one knew there was to be an escape . . . yet.

He took the rope dangling from the wall and wound it around Susan giving her the end to tie in front of her. As she gave two tugs, the rope tightened and Father took Susan's weight on to his shoulders, to quell the tremors in her legs. As she went over the top of the wall, she heard the sound of running boots and commands to 'Halte!'and a flurry of shots. Father Luke crumbled underneath the hail of bullets, sitting like a peon at rest at the foot of the wall. More rifles and sub machine guns opened up somewhere to Susan's left and the gap between the walls was sprayed with bullets. Lights seemed to go on everywhere. There was no longer any need for secrecy. Time was more important. Susan sobbed as she surmounted the second wall and saw a line of limousines aimed at the block from where the shots were coming. Every car switched on its lights full beam to dazzle the would be assassin. The shots continued spasmodically but no longer on target. A shout came from the east side of the wall. 'God bless you my children. Live long and happy.'

The priest's last words rang out in the dark night as Susan and Katrina dropped thankfully into the arms of the waiting rescuers. As they poured out their story, Father Luke was making his peace with god. The evil had taken his son but at least two would bear witness to the compassion that was god's and through him, Father Luke's. He was dead before the soldiers reached him. Major Sergei Brovnik reverently closed the old man's eyes before they took him away.

CHAPTER XI

September 1980

Peter was engrossed in the spare room studying the latest share prices and the financial news for any lead on the way that the market had interpreted his unprecedented move in selling the majority of holdings in media companies. Over the past two years he had played cat and mouse with the shares in Maximillian Holst's companies. Selling and buying, creating havoc and concern by all the major banks who held the mogul's shareholdings as security against massive loans. More than once, one of the 'big four' had called him in to demand more of his equity to cover the borrowings. The only way he could supply more shares was by purchase on the open market, by which time the prices had slipped again. Each time he had satisfied the bankers by the skin of his teeth, the shares miraculously recovered sufficiently to hold off the impending threat to call in the receivers. His pride could never stand that. It would be the end of his dreams. The end of all he had fought for. No one could tell Maximillian Holst that he was not worth a penny.

More and more funds were drawn from the secret trusts in Liechtenstein to bolster his flagging companies. Most were trading at a profit – just. But he needed a strong and fully backed share value to justify the banks supporting his further ambitions. He called in favours from all of his colleagues. Strangely they were unavailable or 'tied up' in a new deal. His accountants could not, or would not, juggle with the group's balance sheet any longer. There was no room for manoeuvre. He was caught in a vicious circle. The more shares he lodged as security, the faster the price dropped.

But Peter did not let the media market drop beyond the point where Maximillian Holst was finished. That could be planned for when he was ready. For when the final blow would be struck and he would be avenged for the atrocities and the suffering that this malevolent egotist had spawned. It was time to draw up the final strategy for his downfall.

All the surviving members of the family would be consulted, what was left of them.

'Your tea is ready Peter.' Wendy's welcome interruption to his concentration brightened his attitude from the solemn contemplation of his life's work. He had no doubt in his mind that the course he had taken had been the correct one. As if he had been guided by some higher force since the day when he had slipped into the rear tool box of the lorry about to depart from Auschwitz. He fingered the ring that his mother had given him. Small and bright. Just big enough for his little finger now. At the time his fingers had been too slender to risk wearing it and he had kept it close to his heart on a piece of string from the bag he carried when he escaped. He still had that piece of string. Curled and treasured in his top drawer in an old jewel case. Everything that he had brought with him on that journey to freedom, he had retained. The battered bag, the balaclava and gloves made from the woollen jumper. Not even his adopted mother in Prague had been able to prise any of his former belongings from him. She understood that they were the link to his family. To the past. To his father and mother and sister. The only items that connected that place with where he was now. She had kissed him each night before he went to sleep clutching the pitiful possessions to his body. His love was transmitted to those he remembered by the warmth and the familiarity of his treasures that had been where he had been.

Where he had last seen his family. The parting place . . .

He had never spoken about the ring. It was his private symbol. His mother's love and sacrifice for his life. She had given him that. A chance to survive. A chance to live again. A chance to seek the ultimate retribution for all the wrong in the world that was encapsulated in that unspeakable place. Halina respected his private grief and loved him all the more for it. No man, let alone a child, should have to bear such a terrible burden. But Lazar would see it through to the end, she had no doubt of that.

'When will you move Peter?'

'Soon. There are a lot of details to determine. We have to re-arrange and finalise the holdings so that we are in a position to combat any counter moves that he might make.' Peter was still reluctant to speak Carl Weisz's name in either form. 'But this year will see it through. Christmas would be an apt time, wouldn't you think?' Peter laughed sardonically, enjoying the appositeness of his choice.

'What about the bank?' Wendy asked pensively.

'That is what I want to discuss with you tonight. The operation will have to stop in any case. The new computer complex is due to be installed later this year, you told me. Our perfect system will be scrapped with the rest. Hope whoever buys it is not another bank!'

'No, it is to be scrapped completely. The bank could never risk any part of it being investigated by some prying competitor and learning its secrets... and ours,' she added joining in Peter's laughter.

* * * * *

The cleaning lady clanked her bucket against the steel desk with a resounding clang. George Parker winced as he jolted instinctively at the assault on his senses and settled down to study the printouts foaming like a great wave in front of him.

'Still 'ere then. Aint you got no 'ome to go to?'

'Yes,... and no,' George answered. He looked up at his favourite member of staff ready to bid her goodnight. She did not make for the door as was her usual custom.

'Ere, Mr. Parker, I bin wonderin'. All these 'ere nights what you spend bent over that desk. Must be something important.'

'It is Ethel. Very important.'

She liked how he addressed her by her christian name. Not like some of the stuck up prigs – wouldn't give you so much as a nod... 'Too important to leave with the others at the normal time?'

'There is no normal time in my job Ethel. Crooks don't keep regular hours like you.'

'No, I don't s'pose they do. Come to think of it, the only regular time they get is when they've been put inside.'

George chuckled at her witticism and lit another cigarette, missing the full ashtray with his burnt out match. Ethel deftly picked up the spent match and deposited it with the contents of his ashtray in her bucket.

'They'll be the death of you one day you know.'

'I know. But until then I will enjoy them. Like my food and my wine. I suppose they will kill you in time too.'

'Like as not. But them cigarettes don't do you no good nohow.' Ethel clicked her tongue reprehensively. 'Who are you after?' she said, changing the subject.

'I don't know. Someone, or some persons, who are far cleverer than you or I. I have no proof of what's going on, but I know it is going on. And I don't know how to stop it. Perhaps there is no way stopping it. But I have to try. That's my job.' He shifted his bulk on the well worn chair to ease the strain on his spine. An old injury still pained him from thirty years ago when he had foolishly joined the tug of war team and subjected himself to pressures that he never knew existed.

'Like my job innit? I keep trying to remove stains and marks with different cleaners, but they don't work. Some stains are there to stay. Only thing to do is to change the carpet, or whatever is dirty.'

George was engrossed in his calculations and did not catch the actual words that Ethel was expounding, leaning on her mop. But the gist of her wisdom filtered through his occupied brain cells and implanted themselves on his current theory which was leading him nowhere. 'What did you say Ethel?'

'I said, trying to remove stains is like trying to weed the garden by picking at the weeds. You can't. You either accept the weeds or you dig the whole plot and start again.' Having made her pronouncement, she plonked her mop in the bucket, said goodnight, and made for the door.

'You know something Ethel? You're a treasure. That's what you are.'

'Ere, don't you let my Arnold 'ear you say that. I'm 'is treasure and nobody else's.' She grinned from ear to ear. 'But I won't tell 'im if you don't,' she smirked as she pushed her bottom against the swing door with all the verve of a Pigalle dancer.

She's right, George nodded. You can't get rid of a stain that you cannot "bottom" as his mother used to say. "Chuck it out and buy a new one."

Whatever was going on in the bank's computer system could only be stopped by replacing it. And that was already in hand. Then he would have the proof he had been looking for. The figures would change dramatically and revert to what he had always contended they should be. He started to scrutinise each year's returns of interest and commission, comparing the percentage losses and gains from the overall results. Each branch was instructed to compare their own figures with the general percentage figure supplied by Finance Department as to what they should expect. A variance of each earning factor was allowed to cover the intransigence of fluctuating balances, weekends, uncleared effects, etc. Overall these should still approximate to the parameters given. If not the branch was asked to explain the difference.

The percentages intrigued him. They were, in almost every case, over 3000 branches, well within the margins allowed. Too well within the margins. In fact, he thought, as the figures jumped upwards with every flick of his eyes, you could only obtain that result if you had programmed the computer to produce such figures! Exactly! His excitement grew as he compared figure after figure, column after column. There were practically no abstentions from the reams of results that fell within the criteria required. Impossible!

George had been a great believer in the law of chaos. His own life was a prime example, he admitted. But the law of chaos could never be broken. He had tried it. Ten dice thrown for hours on end and never obtaining ten perfect sixes, or fives, or any number. It never happened and never would happened. The law of chaos determined that in any given situation with a minimum of say ten and upwards, the results would never produce the perfect picture. Drop a pack of playing cards on the floor – never all showing one similar face. Throw a jigsaw into the air – it never fell into a fitted picture. Of course they were all impossible. The greater the number the greater the improbability of any perfect solution occurring. But this one did!

Somehow, the chaos was being controlled from within. Very clever. Perhaps too clever. If he, or they had known of the law of chaos they might have built a contingency instruction to cause the "chaos" intermittently to throw off any suspicion.

But who had been suspicious? Only he. And he wasn't being listened to. Yet.

He started to plot out his conclusions, working through step by step in simple fashion to be able to demonstrate to the woolliest director that something was definitely wrong. Tell them they are losing a lot a money and they will listen. That had always been his method with the overpaid, under qualified, hierarchy, whose only interest in any business was their own gratification of power or financial gain. They would listen to this.

Maximillian Holst was in a cold sweat. The fourth General Manager of one of his banks had called him to come and discuss the future operation of his accounts. The messages on his answering machine and repeated on his fax spelled out the command. Not a request dressed in unctuous and acquiescent terms as he was used to years ago. Those times had gone. The bankers were hard, profit orientated, ambitious businessmen, who would have been thrown out of the old regime. Customers had to pay the going rate and Maximillian Holst was in danger of not being able to meet his dues. The knives were out. How long could he keep them from his door? To keep up the pretence that his empire was solvent? Was omnipotent? That their stake in him was covered many times over by personal wealth?

Bankers are vain, he sneered. They consider themselves above the common business tycoon. They believe that they could run every company better than their customer. How efficiently did they run their business? More and more provision for bad debts were appearing each year, as their previous faith in their managers' ability to judge a good risk was being proved to be just a little optimistic. But there was ample in the pot. Ample funds from the great institutions with which to line their vaults to meet any unforeseen substantial crash. That's why they are anxious to see me, he conjectured. They want to be satisfied that their stake in the Maximillian multinational was covered by the future earning potential of his companies. That would depend on the confidence of the city in his expertise and the worrying influence of the trade unions which were ganging up against him in his war on their outrageous demands. His demands could be just as outrageous. He knew how to use the law and also how to abuse it. He would not hesitate to use either method.

He showered slowly, letting the suds ooze down his immense body. The foam gathering in his loins like scum on a dam.

It was the Annual General Meeting of his new Tele Channel Corporation. A company formed to control the 47 minor transmitting companies both at home and on the continent. Each company purchased for a peppercorn, as the English would have it, he smiled, and moulded into a conglomerate of controlling authorities in the new cable and satellite television of the future. A vast amount of capital had been borrowed to launch the corporation, backed by the projected astronomical returns to be made once the system was in operation. But there were stumbling blocks. His government connections had cooled as his reputation flagged. The necessary licences had not been as forthcoming as he had first envisaged. The banks had put pressure in their own way on certain government departments, but they were not co-operating. It was as if a cancer was slowly moving its insidious tendrils deeper and deeper into his unmanageable network of fabrications and counter fabrications.

He finished dressing and smoothed down the Savile Row double breasted dark blue suit, admiring himself in the mirror. For such a heavy man, the tailors had worked wonders. He appeared like a colossus, but not obese. His Patek Philippe diamond encrusted wrist watch gleamed resplendent beneath his left cuff. Matching diamond cufflinks and tie pin completed the ensemble. He was ready. No one would doubt his affluence. He radiated opulence. His very being represented the dream of every person in England, and probably further, he prided himself. He had beaten them all before, and he would do it again. He put on his Crombie overcoat and black homburg and he was ready for his public.

As he walked out of his private lift to the waiting Rolls Corniche and chauffeur, a small, insignificant cleaning lady slipped between the closing doors. Her bent back hid her bright, eager eyes as a contented smile played around her lips.

Clive Farnworth picked up his brief case, checked the contents, and walked out of his fifth floor work room at the Fraud Office and made for the lift. The official car stood idling at the pavement awaiting his usual sweep across the smooth flags, his brief lowering of his sandy head, and the efficient displacement of his lanky body on the padded leather of the limousine. The driver never stopped to marvel at the meticulous habits of his charges. He could tell by their body movements exactly what state of mind was prevalent. Clive Farnworth was on edge. Despite his apparent calm and usual behaviour, there was an infinitesimal nervousness to his actions. Perhaps he has had a bad night at home with his wife, conjectured the chauffeur. Or an even worse one with a mistress. He chuckled to himself, as he realised that there had never been a commander more suited to the job than this one. Straight as a die and rigidly ethical. The book of moral behaviour could be thrown out of the window. Clive Farnworth practically wrote it.

'The Savoy Hotel.'

'Yes sir.' The instruction was unnecessary, the driver knew that, and probably Commander Farnworth too, but it seemed appropriate to confirm the destination if only to avoid any misunderstanding later.

Clive Farnworth immediately dived into his brief case for a file labelled "Tele Channel Corporation." Inside were bulky reports on all of the major companies under the umbrella of the consortium title. Previously well run small companies who had mysteriously sold out to this leviathan of media conglomerates for next to nothing. The deals had been done before the government and subsequently his department had had notion that the major proportion of people's television viewing would now be joined with the majority of radio and newspaper network ultimately owned by one man. Maximillian Holst. But the publishing business was not as financially sound as Holst's regular bombastic pronouncements made it out to be. The balance sheets and the breakdown of the assets value had been thoroughly investigated by his sister department and the Department of Trade and Industry and the conclusion had been unanimous. Every company with which Holst had an interest had interests in or connections with one of his other companies. The maze of share ownership in each and with each company was virtually impossible to unravel. It amounted to only one conclusion. If the basic value of the major shares in the consortium proved to be of lesser value than that purported, then the whole empire would be in serious danger of collapsing.

That would spell disaster for the country, for the government, and for the future of the confidence in the British reliability in bringing the world to the people. That could not be allowed to happen. Perhaps that was why no one had had the temerity to broach the question of Holst's stranglehold on the media. To rock the boat would have serious repercussions from which the remainder of the publishers and broadcasting agencies would never recover.

Clive scanned the latest proposed draft balance sheet of the Tele Channel Corporation. It looked as good as it was meant to look. More than generous prophecies of future income, linked to a commensurate profit. Of course everyone knew that, provided the capital was available and that Holst captured the market which was admittedly waiting for this giant leap in technology, the bounds of growth were limitless.

But. And Clive and his advisers from the government had registered a unanimous 'but' in their many discussions. The power generated and engendered in this almost global confiscation of control of people's thinking, could not be left in the hands of this one man.

A full dossier on the life and hidden life of Maximillian Holst had been circulated to everyone on the steering committee appointed to investigate, and if necessary, prevent the monopoly coming into being. What they had read only confirmed what most of the knowledgeable financiers in the city had concluded long ago. But no one had bothered to stop the gradual erosion of independent businesses into the multinational that it was about to become. Clive lifted the hand receiver and dialled a number.

'George Parker. Who's calling?'

'It's Clive George. Are you on your way?'

'Not yet. I can make it in half the time that you can. I can walk.'

Clive smiled at his friend's reference to his lack of exercise. 'I'll see you there then.' The phone clicked back into position as George lit another cigarette and pondered his summary of his own problem. Could it be linked to Maximillian Holst? The names were connected. What was the connection in Germany? During the war? Afterwards? His research and Clive's accessibility to a more thorough investigation by the MI5 and its associates in Germany, France, and Poland had brought to light a fascinating co-incidence of movements and crossed paths that surely could not be just 'co-incidence.' Clive would have argued – again – George laughed, at the stupid assertion that if two happenings were similar, it was a 'co-incidence.' Whatever it was called, it certainly had something to do with the disappearance of millions from the bank. Where had it gone? Who had benefited from it? How had it been done? MI5 had been interested of late when their investigations had been assisted by an unusual disclosure from behind the iron curtain that a certain individual had become 'persona non grata.' The description matched that of the media mogul, and their further disclosures tied in with the timings of his arrival in England and MI5's continuing surveillance of him and his activities. Nothing that they could directly attribute to him, but nevertheless the picture had steadily built in their files of a man who sailed close to the wind and had more than the simple background that he claimed. What finally convinced the department of his non-allegiance to the communist block was his total disregard for instructions that had been remitted from time to time to a person MI5 were convinced was Holst. The disclosure could of course be a trap. A double bluff. A ploy to put them off the scent of what Holst was really up to. Each possibility was considered and followed to its logical conclusion. Holst was not a communist. He was a bloated capitalist. More so than the accepted definition of the system. His capitalism eclipsed the known bounds of risk and enterprise. It was an obsession, not only for the riches it brought him, but more importantly for the power and the prestige. He was only happy when he was publicising another of his 'saving' takeovers – the Sir Galahad of failing companies. And of sound businesses that were forced to accept his 'last minute rescues,' engineered by a well trained staff of intermediaries.

Clive hoped that today's meeting would produce some sort of guide as to how to proceed next against this foreboding menace.

George Parker also picked up his rather battered brief case, the bank had offered to replace it as was their custom every three years, but he had declined. The case suited him. It bore the marks of his trade. Every crease and scuff reminded of some triumph; some spark of enlightenment; some sad duty that had fallen to him.

The walk to the Savoy took George exactly nineteen minutes. A normal man would have made it in ten. But George was not normal. He thought as he walked. He worked things out. The balanced rhythm of his legs carrying his bulk along the pavement beat a steady reminder to his brain that an orderly way of thinking always produced results in the end.

During the nineteen minutes he tabulated his findings to date.

Item 1. Funds were being filtered from the system.

Item 2. The bank was not missing any funds.

Item 3. Peter Mallory was connected somehow.

Item 4. Wendy Mallory was Peter Mallory's wife.

Item 5. Wendy Mallory had previously been Katrina Kawalek.

Item 6. Peter Mallory's mother was Susan Kawalek.

Item 7. Maximillian Holst had once used the name of Werner Kawalek.

The doors of the Savoy Hotel swung noiselessly on their well oiled hinges as the liveried doorman ushered him into the opulent reception hall. His thoughts were packed away into a private memory bank as his eyes took over his main preoccupation of seeing and noticing anything and anybody who might add another ingredient to his conundrum. He saw Clive Farnworth. He also saw, to his surprise, Peter Mallory. Peter Mallory did not see him.

'How are you George?'

'Fine thank you. I'd be better if I was not so damned confused.'

'Confused George? You? Tut tut. You're getting old.' Clive's wry grin twisted beneath his twinkling eyes. 'Perhaps we all are,' he sighed, scanning the crowd for familiar faces.

George pointed out Peter Mallory hovering on the edge of the throng. 'What do you think he is doing here?'

'He's your assistant George, why don't you ask him?'

'I will. When the time is appropriate.'

'You don't want him to see you do you?'

'Not if I can help it. If I know he has been here and he doesn't know that I have, it may help me to probe his particular purpose that much better.'

'Well he doesn't know me, so I shall make it my business to sit as close to him as I can. Might learn something.' Clive sidled off talking to every notable financier on his way.

As was the custom, the expectant audience were seated long before the main event. The usual red carpet had been laid down the entire length of the ballroom, expertly converted to a gigantic 'board room' from the revels of the riotous Horseguards Anniversary Dinner the night before. Not a whisp of a streamer nor a biscuit crumb remained. The attendants were impeccable and everyone was seated in super efficient manner – like courtiers awaiting their king.

There was no fanfare of trumpets but if Maximillian Holst thought it would be appreciated, he would have had them. Perhaps when I have the whole of the media in my grip, he preened.

His entrance was nevertheless discreetly 'announced' by the flamboyant throwing open of the huge double doors by two flunkies, who bowed deferentially as he swept in. The ploy worked. The whole of the gathered congregation of devotees, critics, impartial observers, muck rakers, disciples, turned as one. Whatever their particular opinion of this man, they all had one aspect in common. He was a man to be looked at. To be admired. Revered almost not only by those who loved him, but by those who hated him. He was larger than life. The epitome of all that lesser mortals wished to achieve at some time in their mundane lives.

He strode down the carpet dragging the eyes with him. His hair gleamed in soft waves. His Gucci shoes shone with the same intensity, giving the finishing touch to his tailored torso moving determinedly to the podium. His throne. His seat of power. From there he could look each man and woman directly in the eyes from beneath his black bushy brows. He saw everyone; or appeared to. No one held his gaze for long.

'Shall we begin gentlemen?' The smooth charm of his half moon smile was presented in one sweep of his heavy jowls to the semi-circular array of plush chairs. 'At the beginning, I think,' he jokingly added as his beaming face revealed the fine, expertly capped teeth like a jeweller unveiling a string of pearls.

His secretary passed a huge sheaf of papers to his mentor, but he nonchalantly pushed them to one side and began to speak without notes. The Chairman's Statement was his 'piece de resistance'. The time when he was in control. The time when everyone listened to the most powerful man in Britain, expostulating his grandiose plans for his empire. The stuff of dreams, one irreverent reporter had called it, and had suffered the fate of all who spoke publicly about the supremo of the publishing business. The sack.

Although most of what Maximillian Holst had to say had been heard at previous Annual General Meetings of his other corporate enterprises, the dream still persisted and re-kindled the excitement of the mesmerised onlookers. They would go away convinced once again that the future was bright, that their fortunes would improve, would multiply because of this man. A very few were more realistic.

Disturbing, was Clive Farnworth's opinion. Or perhaps that wasn't strong enough he concluded. A deep inbuilt fear of something that he could not quite identify, sat in the pit of his stomach. There was an intense cabbalistic character to this man that lay behind the smooth skinned, black framed mask he displayed to his public.

Clive had always relied on his judgement of a person by the features, especially the area around the eyes. The face could contort to different shades of honesty, guilt, puzzlement, and a thousand other expressions used by thespians. But the eyes were the centre of a man's soul. They betrayed his inner feelings. His face might be saying one thing but his eyes more often than not would betray him. Or confirm his integrity. This man had no integrity. He was a caricature of himself. An image built to fit the ideals of the superior being. But underneath there festered a contrasting persona at variance with his beguiling facade.

What were the secrets he worked so hard to conceal? His real purpose in life? His megalomaniac ambition that drove him to the pinnacle of daring and brinkmanship in business? Plenty of immigrants had similar backgrounds to his. From poor peasant roots and a war torn Europe. But they did not have this man's brutality. Not a physical brutality, but one which could wreak more suffering than the act of beating his opponents with a club. A twisted core of remorseless viciousness that emanated through his eyes as clearly as if he had declared his hatred for mankind. Clive could see it. But then I have had more practice, he shrugged.

The Chairman of the Board was winding up his forecast of the fruits of the future of his corporation, not too subtly admitting that it would all be down to him with his limitless energy and drive. 'And the help of you good people who have had the faith to support me in these troubled times. I shall not forget you and I shall never let you down.' The look of humiliation could have won an award on any other stage but this, and Maximillian resumed his seat to sustained applause.

The routine reports on the various factions within his empire were delivered and received with enthusiasm. There was an aura of contentment among the many shareholders who had had their most optimistic feeling confirmed yet again. Their shareholdings were safe. They were more than that. They were the key to a promised wealth yet to come. The maestro's magic had worked its charm as it was intended to do. Clive grimaced.

'I have a question Mr. Chairman.' The sharp incisive voice rose above the general bonhomie. 'It concerns the Accounts and more particularly the Auditors' Report.'

Maximillian looked up from his discussion with his secretary as to the success of the meeting. 'Who is that?' he whispered, maintaining his fixed grin.

'I don't know. He must be a shareholder, he is sitting in the allotted space for shareholders.'

The Chairman turned to face his questioner. 'What is your question? Please make it brief because I have to leave for Paris in precisely two hours.' Maximillian made even an ordinary query from this insubstantial irritant, a chance to display his worldly interests.

'It concerns the second paragraph of their report,' the voice continued. 'It says, and here I quote, "We conducted our audit in accordance with Auditing Standards issued by the Auditing Practises Board. An audit includes examination on a test basis, of evidence relevant to the amounts and disclosures in the accounts . . . "

Maximillian began to perspire slightly . . .

". . . it also includes an assessment of the significant estimates and judgements made by the Directors in the preparation of the accounts, and whether the accounting policies are appropriate to the Company's circumstances, consistently applied and adequately disclosed . . . "

'Yes, we can all read the notes for ourselves. What is your question?' Maximillian's superbly controlled equanimity was showing just the slightest sign of discord.

'. . . It is the part about the "examination on a test basis of evidence relevant to the accounts" and "the significant estimates and judgements made by the Directors" . . . The speaker paused as all ears took in the breathless silence. No one had had the temerity to delve into the published figures to this extent before. What was the questioner pointing at? The independent reporters in the audience sharpened their pencils.

'. . . My question is, on what basis did the auditors value the main assets in the balance sheet, ie – the stock and debtors?'

Maximillian Holst whispered to his secretary. His smile once again creased his condescending expression as he waved his large hands as if to swat this minor gnat from his vision. 'That is a technical question and one which could take quite a while for the experts,' he laughed and nodded his head in the direction of his auditors, 'to explain fully. That is their job, and we laymen can only rely on their expertise.'

He started to gather his papers together as the voice once again quietened the buzz of apprehension at Maximillian's answer.

'Did the auditors value the stocks and the debtors figure, or did the Directors?'

The question took on a new meaning as its bluntness registered with the assembly. They waited for an answer.

Another whispered confidence with his secretary followed, during which Maximillian's hand could be seen tapping the table in irritation.

'The assets were valued in the usual manner. As they have been for many years. No variance in that practice was deemed necessary and none was asked for by the auditors.' The auditors in question were seen to nod their heads in agreement, but their faces shared the same concern as the remainder of the Board.

'That doesn't answer the question. Who did the valuation?'

'The Directors. That is perfectly acceptable in modern accounting and perfectly legal. To avoid any further lengthy distractions on technicalities we shall now deal with the written questions submitted before the meeting.'

The secretary handed him the first envelope addressed to Maximillian Holst personally. The relief on his face, having circumvented any further delving into his private method of valuation, dissolved instantly as he read the note from the envelope. His face turned ashen as he half rose and stumbled to his feet.

'You will have to excuse me now, but I warned you that I had an urgent appointment. My colleagues will deal with the remainder of your questions in my absence.'

Maximillian rose abruptly and left the podium, weakly raising his hand at the mild applause that accompanied his exit.

The meeting concluded swiftly after the Chairman's departure, but the arguments ranged long and loud about the doubt raised by the questioner as to the efficacy of the figures in the balance sheet. Their previous acceptance of the printed amounts had been part of the general ambience surrounding this demagogue. That ambience was now beginning to look a little tarnished.

'More coffee Mr. Parker?'

George Parker nodded and pushed his cup for a refill. The waiter deftly topped up his cup, added a splash of cream and discreetly disappeared.

Clive absentmindedly stirred his cold coffee. His thoughts were on the meeting at which both had been given more than an inkling of Peter Mallory's interest in Maximillian Holst.

'What do you think George?'

'I think ... ' George paused sipping his coffee noisily... 'I think that my boy has more of a connection with our friend than the similarity of names. Those weren't just questions he posed. There was a deeper, malevolent intent behind them. I could sense it in his tone. So could Holst.'

'I was sitting one row in front of him, about three yards away. You would not have liked the look in his eyes. If those two had been in the room all by themselves, I would not have given you odds for both walking out.'

'Odds Clive? Since when have you considered anything a gamble?'

'I was using the phrase metaphorically, and well you know it. No, there has to be some dark relationship between these two that conjures up the hate that I saw manifest itself today. I have only seen Peter Mallory's virulent stare matched once. By a rattlesnake about to strike.'

'I didn't know you had been to the wild west Clive. Must have been quite a treat for them.' George's subtle leg pull was hidden in the embarrassing gargle of the last dregs of his coffee.

'On business,' Clive replied sharply. 'What, if anything have you been able to find out about your man?'

George thought for minute. 'Not much really. He doesn't open up very easily. Only replies to the general enquiries about his home life. Doesn't say much about his past. I have looked at his personnel file ... not much there either. Born in Berlin before the war ... 1934 I think. Lived there until after the hostilities and came to this country in 1947. Educated at Weymouth Grammar School and joined the bank in 1954 as a late entrant... catching up on his lost schooling I suppose.'

'What about his wife?'

'Rather similar really. Born 1943... place not precise... somewhere in Europe. Came to Britain in 1961, took a computer course at the London School of Economics and joined the bank. Excellent qualifications. Had a natural aptitude for computers. Peter and Wendy were married in 1964. As you say, their backgrounds are so similar that it could not have been chance that brought them together. The common factor is the mother. Peter's blood mother and Wendy's adoptive parent. Was that a coincidence? Sorry, – a concurrence of events, – or is it the answer we are seeking? The reason behind their obvious hatred for this man? What happened to engender this hatred? And when?'

'I think you have the key in your last question. When? The time of whatever transpired will give us the clue to the event that sparked the enmity.' Clive watched George light another cigarette from the stub in his mouth, frowning slightly at his apparent lack of attention. 'You must find out when these two antagonists knew each other.'

'I've been trying to devise a scheme where that can be achieved. I know he won't volunteer the information. I doubt if he would if pushed. But I'll find some common ground between the two to spark off some sort of reaction. If not from him then from his wife.'

'That's it,' exclaimed Clive. 'Invite them to dinner.'

'At my place?' said George incredulously.

'No, that would really put them off – no offence George – but your flat isn't exactly the place to entertain the younger generation is it?' Clive cocked his head waiting for an acknowledgement; none came so he continued. 'Organise a celebration dinner or something. Invite a few guests, others from your department, but arrange it so that you can talk to Peter one to one.'

George was stunned. Never in the 39 years service in the bank had he ever invited any colleagues to dinner with him. Certainly not the crew in the Fraud section of Inspection Department. They never expected it and he never obliged them. They would suspect something. He told Clive so and Clive immediately came up with the answer. 'I'll invite you and a few of your contemporaries to a mutual admiration dinner. It's done all the time.'

'Then you'll pay?'

'Oh no. The evening will be down to you... or rather your expense account. I don't suppose it gets much hammer from entertaining anyway.'

George smiled. 'I can hardly submit expense claims for dinners on my own can I? But you're right. Set it up will you? Somewhere discreet and private, you should know the places which are suitable.'

Albin, the head waiter clucked his tongue reproachfully as the two men left and he surveyed the mountain of ash in the tray and on the white table cloth. His clucking changed to approval when he noticed the size of the tip.

Peter Mallory was highly satisfied with his day off. Another thorn in the thick hide of Carl Weisz. He could say the name now. His day of reckoning was approaching. Everything that he had done over the past nine years was coming to fruition. Just one more decisive step and Carl Weisz would be destroyed. Not only in the eyes of the world's press and the people, but in the eyes of Carl Weisz. That was the part that satisfied Peter the most. The man's realisation that the world's opinion of the great Carl Weisz was nothing. A has-been. A nobody. A thing of the past. An obscure zealot who had returned to the murky oblivion of apathy. His ego would not stand that. His bluster would count no more. No one would jump to his orders or even know that he had ever been obeyed. He would be a 'Niemand'.

From his own bank, the grapevine was already extending its tales from the General Managers' office that the tycoon was held in a taut stricture of financial manoeuvres, dictated by the Senior Lending Manager, over the conduct of his group of accounts with them. Other banks had taken the lead and had applied similar clamps on any further expansion or reckless escapades. The whole network of companies were virtually being run by a team of bank appointees, as near as receivers, as could be created without actually broadcasting to the world that the empire was floating above water – just.

The shares held as security were barely sufficient to cover debts, certainly no margin was enjoyed. And the shares were only supported by the public unawareness of the real situation. The greatest fear of all the concerned banks was that the bubble would eventually burst and the shares plunge to their true asset value. Practically worthless. Several minor banks would sink with the group. The major banks would take on bad debts that would shatter reputations and damage their credibility for the foreseeable future. That could not be allowed to happen. But having dug themselves into the bottomless pit of Maximillian's excesses, there was very little that they could do but keep covering the surface to disguise the facts. They needed a miracle. Peter would give them one.

The telephone buzzed twice before his private jobber spoke.

As soon as he heard Peter's voice he reached for his order pad. Several minutes later and three pages of closely scrawled instructions, he put down his pen, acknowledged the orders and whistled at the enormity of the directives. What was more important to him was the enormity of his commission. He took the brochure out of his top drawer. On the front was a shiny red version of the latest 'E' type Jaguar. Just in time for christmas he murmured as he pictured himself walking into Heron's executive car showroom on the Kensington High Street. His wife would be pleased. So would his girlfriend.

Maximillian Holst seemed to have lost three stones in weight on his journey from the Savoy Hotel. His chauffeur had wisely kept his own council, seeing the traumatic state that enveloped his employer. The doors opened magically to Maximillian's entry to his private lift and he was left alone to brood in a rising panic, matched only by the swift ascendance of his body in the confines of the aluminium shell around him.

Crumpled at his feet was the note from the meeting. "I would like to meet you Carl Weisz. There are a few matters that we have to discuss. Yours Werner Kawalek."

CHAPTER XII

July 1980

Leonid Chukov smiled broadly and clapped loudly at the announcement of the triple jump distance. 17.35 metres. Jaak Uudmae had beaten Victer Saneyev also of the Soviet Republic by 11 centimetres to take the gold medal. The crowd roared their approval. They had been waiting too long for a Russian victory to cheer. Despite the boycott of the games by the USA it had appeared that the Russian athletes were incapable of taking advantage of the reduced competition. Now they were showing their strength in the field events. With the shot put, discus, hammer, and javelin to come, they had high hopes for a further four golds.

Leonid took a sip of vodka from his flask. Life was good. Sitting in the privileged box reserved for the elite of the party, he was a personal guest of the Party Chairman, Leonid Brezhnev. A thank you for the years of faithful service to the communist ideology.

Retirement was all that he had ever hoped. Fifteen years in which he had read, fished, written, enjoyed the ballet and opera. But most of all he had enjoyed the fulfilment of his prophecy. The world was coming to grips with the great, cumbersome machine of Soviet dominance. Slowly but surely the cogs were beginning to grind and falter. This boycott by the USA, West Germany, and Japan was one example of the world's opinion of a system that was abhorrent to all free nations.

The military intervention in Afghanistan was the cue to express that opinion forcibly and discredit the Soviets in front of their own people. These Olympic games would go down in history as the "boycott games."

The applause rose to a crescendo as the official result was announced. The games were in being. Nothing could stop them now. A Britisher had won the 100 metres against all the odds – again possibly because there were no black sprinters from the USA to vie for the title. The British were also expected to win the events that they had dominated for the past four years; the 800 metres and the blue riband of the games; the 1500 metres.

This, Leonid knew, would particularly irk the party members chewing on their cigars in front of him. The one country which should have been brought to its knees was as strong as ever. And to add to the insult, they had elected a woman as premier. No, he chuckled, their man had not delivered. He had engineered the biggest turnabout in Soviet espionage. He had reneged on his sponsors. Not only had he joined the western capitalistic worshippers; he had become one of the most powerful. Every contract that he had signed with the Soviet had been for his own gratification. The Russians had been left with egg on their faces and they had turned on the one whom they considered to be the architect of the fiasco. Namely General Stanislav Dzerzhinsky. Now languishing in a sub-standard apartment in Gorky with a reduced pension, the former head of the MVD was a bitter man. His rival had outwitted him. He, the recognised follower of the most ruthless diktats of the regime, had been summarily retired from the service on 'health grounds.' General Szerzhinnsky, who had never had a day's illness in his life; until he was discharged. He deserved what he got, thought Leonid, without the slightest compassion for his compatriot. The final destruction of the icon of capitalism, so shrewdly chosen by Leonid was imminent. Leonid's former contacts in the U.K. kept him up to date with the position. As he had predicted, Carl Weisz had been unable to resist the opportunity to become the mogul that his character yearned for. Leonid had recognised that. And so, as he had anticipated, had the British public. Eventually. Now he was ripe for the slaughter by the very people he had denigrated and ground in the dust – the journalists, the printers, and the thousands of employees who had felt the wrath of this potentate of publishers.

Leonid watched the women line up for the 100 metres sprint. Every tendon and muscle tensed in anticipation of the instant explosion that would be co-ordinated in one controlled burst of energy from the blocks. Poised like greyhounds in the slips, he smiled, remembering his Shakespeare, ready to dash for their prey. The gold medal hanging on the finishing tape; a blur in the distance. Just under Leonid's nose. He watched intently as the starter raised his gun . . .

The world is dominated by guns, he frowned, remembering his own distaste for any kind of explosive weapon. Swords, knives, ropes, he could cope with. They were part of a man. Part of his armour – a one to one basis for killing an enemy. You had to have courage to kill with a hand weapon at close quarters. He admired those who could and had to, to save their own lives. That was the only criteria for use of any weapon. To defend one's honour or liberty. The Soviet Union was not defending its liberty. It was aggressive in its attack on other cultures which it considered inferior to its own. It could never win. The truer philosophies would not allow it.

His was the only way, to go with the tide, taking care to stay within the parameters, but advocating by devious means, his own true beliefs. He had succeeded in that and was content with his lot. He could not have done more. And he had shown compassion – a rare commodity in one so elevated within the party.

He reflected now on his last years of service. Khrushkev's triumphant tour of Afghanistan in 1960, organised and directed by him. Another medal for meritorious service. The craftily conducted system devised and introduced by one of his departments of 'collectivization' in East Germany. The confiscation of the vast farmlands into government 'co-operatives' had forced thousands to flee to the west. Nearly 6,500 had crossed the border in Easter week – a tremendous upsurge in official refugees. His ploy had worked beautifully. Of the thousands who made the journey, a large part were political refugees who would never have been allowed to leave, but the sheer numbers hid their true identities. Many loyal Germans would return once the barriers were down. Germany would need a reserve of 'old valued citizens' once the communist state crumbled. Leonid congratulated himself on playing a small part in the future.

Among the crowd of farmers applying in 1965 had been one Sergei Brovnik. A former army major. Briefly on his staff, he had recognised in him the same latent dislike of the world he was born into. Nothing on his record showed, but Leonid was too old in the tooth to be fooled by this soldier's outward declaration of loyalty to the party. A kindred spirit, he had breathed, but dare not communicate his empathy to this intelligent individual. He had been surprised when his name had come up on the list for emigration.

Sergei Brovnik – farmer, it said. The same one? Leonid wondered. 'Do we have photographs of those submitting applications for transfer to the west?'

'Yes General, they can be obtained.'

'Do so in the case of this man.'

The clerk hurried away to search the archives. That would take at least a few hours, sighed Leonid. He had despaired of late at the inadequacy of the filing system, which had deteriorated rapidly over the years until only the old and practically infirm clerks could remember under which title any particular subject was likely to be.

It was the same man. The photograph confirmed it. Why would a previously respected former major in the Russian army wish to defect to the west? Money? Ambition? A woman?

The latter was the most likely. That together with the wish to taste the luxury of freedom from a regime that he should never have had to endure. Lucky man if he makes it. I envy him. But it would not be easy with the eagle eyed department of the MVD operating in Stanislav's old constituency in Berlin.

I will help him. The simple resolution came to Leonid without him having to consider all the pitfalls. He is a true Russian in the old sense and we shall need them, or their descendants in the hereafter. I will help him, he reiterated in his mind as if to seal his intent indelibly on his mind.

'Come.'

The door to Leonid's office opened and in strode a tall, proud, grey haired individual. His movements were smooth, but with the cultured training of a military officer. He waited to sit.

'Sit.'

He did so, clasping his hands in his lap.

Why do people do that? Leonid wondered. Like defenders lining up for a free kick. Perhaps he considers this interview could inflict the same damage.

'Your name is Sergei Brovnik?'

'Yes.'

'You are a farmer?'

'Yes.'

'For how long?'

'As long as I can remember.'

'For as long as you have ceased to be a member of the Soviet's armed forces.' Leonid's calm statement was delivered in the same timbre as the former questions and answers. No inference. No retribution. No inkling that it was other than a routine statement.

Sergei blinked. How should he answer this man. This man who he had only known to be his superior when he was attached to his department briefly following the occupation of Berlin. A man whom he knew to be anti MVD – a fair but impassioned ruler of his dominion. How should he answer? There was no other way with this man. The truth.

'Yes. My life is devoted to farming now. I have put my army days behind me. That was another life, another person. I wish to farm and the authorities won't let me.'

Leonid did not miss the implication in his last sentence. Authorities. That meant him and his like. Was he being brave or just too honest? The latter he decided.

'What has happened to your land?'

'It has been confiscated.'

'For the Co-operative?'

'Yes.' Nothing showed in his eyes. Leonid found it a challenge that he rarely encountered. He could assess the true feelings of a man by the movement or otherwise of a gaze, a blink, a contraction. The slightest movement conveyed the passion or deceit, the honesty or the cunning. He had spotted the flaws in Carl Weisz. No one else had. Why did that name spring to mind? One of those thought associations that pop into a head through some unknown influence?

This man was practised in the art of giving nothing away. He would rather die than betray the ideals he believed in. Leonid's admiration was also hidden. Mustn't let him know that I am on the same side. A small giaconda smile smoothed his lips beneath the Stalin mustache.

'And why do you want to go to the west?'

'To rejoin my… wife.'

'She is already there?' Leonid said with some surprise.

'Yes, she.. went in 1961.'

'Why did you not go with her?' A silly question Leonid reflected, but nevertheless waited for his answer.

'Because I was in the armed forces. I had my duty to perform.'

'Admirable I'm sure. If my wife had gone, I would have taken the same view.' Leonid failed to mention that had his wife gone, he would have pressed for the wall to be rebuilt two metres higher to keep her there. 'What is your… wife's name?'

'Susan. She was English before the war.'

'And after?'

'She married a German, a West German. Werner Kawalek.'

Leonid jumped inwardly as his mind started to comb the vast banks of names, recorded in his thirty five years of dealing with the thousand upon thousand individuals that made up his workforce. And those that didn't. Kawalek… his knack for name association went into overdrive as the years rolled back, comparing, matching, looking for some stigmatism to bring up the computer screen in his mind of the significance of this name. Maybe it was the previous flash of Carl Weisz's name that fixed the connection. That day in Berlin. The house. The woman… "I am Werner Kawalek's sister…" and Carl Weisz's instant reaction to the claim. Not this woman… this wasn't major Brovnik's wife was it? How had she introduced herself? Again the cells formed to resuscitate the events of that day… "Anna". Yes that was it. Anna Kawalek.

The touch was still there. The ability to bring to mind every scrap of information he had ever learned. It had kept him in his job and it had designated him as one of the architects of Soviet policy. Or so the Kremlin had always taken for granted.

The competitors were up on their haunches, fingers a hair's breadth from the starting line. The red cinder track, stretching like a rungless ladder before the eight runners, pointed at the symbol of communism in the distance; the gigantic red flag flying over the stadium.

For what seemed an hour the runners hung in immobile suspension. Then the puff of smoke preceded the bang as eight finely tuned athletes rose and launched as one. What was their unified thought Leonid reflected? To beat the other seven? To come first? To achieve greatness? To achieve immortality? For one glorious moment, to escape the mundane existence of a communist state... And the rulers of the Kremlin arrayed before him, knew it. But they would never admit it.

This man is torn between his love for his country and his love for his wife. Or whatever she was. To desert now would mean the betrayal of all that he had lived for. Been brought up to believe in. A whole nation that had failed him. Leonid sympathised with this man's steadfast creed that would not let him accept the present communist doctrine even though it had been forged before his birth. Somewhere in his childhood he had been taught the old values. The old standards. The old religions. They were all still there under the surface. Waiting for the day when they could be released and celebrated as in the old days. 'And if you are granted an exit visa, what will you do in your chosen country?'

'I shall try to farm.. a smallholding... anything to be close to the land. That never changes. The land remains the same no matter what those who walk upon it decree. It gives life. Nourishment. Beauty. Stability. People have forgotten that it controls our lives. And nurtures it too. Without the land we are nothing.'

Leonid had never thought of it in quite the way that Sergei illustrated the simple truth. It was like a new religion. But a religion that had lasted since man first tilled the soil. 'How did your wife get to the west?'

Sergei Brovnik thought for a fraction of a second. 'She went before the wall was completed.'

He's lying. Leonid knew it. Major Brovnik probably knew that he knew it too. But it was as near to the truth as he could get without admitting that she had escaped over the wall.

‘A brave woman. I envy you.’ Sergei could see that Leonid was sincere in his approbation. ‘Why did she leave you?’

‘Because she had a greater cause to pursue in the west.’

‘Another man?’

‘There was another man involved, yes. And her son.’ Sergei didn’t know why he volunteered this additional information. Perhaps it was to divert this general’s attention away from Susan.

‘Her son?’

The probing was gentle and inoffensive. Not like some of his compatriot’s vicious desecration of all the values in a suspect’s mind. To destroy the faith in humanity itself to obtain the answers they were seeking. With this man, the conversation was more like a Sunday afternoon chatting to your favourite uncle. ‘Yes. He escaped to the west during the war.’

‘You say escaped. From whom?’

‘From the nazis. He was interned in a camp. He managed to escape. My… wife never saw him again.’ Sergei’s eyes lost themselves in a yearning for Susan and the dream that they both shared. To be rid of this canker in her heart so that she could open it to him, cleansed and pure. To love him as he knew she hungered to.

‘Was she a Jew?’

‘No. The family’s papers were stolen and they were denounced as Jews by… a friend. Or someone they took to be a friend. Apparently this man made a practice of betraying his friends. And many others too.’ Sergei stopped, uncertain of how much he should tell this benign general. Have I told him too much already? Is he after some excuse to return me to mother Russia to live out my life in misery. In a land where people do not know each other any more. Where love and beliefs and life itself stood in jeopardy from the tyranny ruling the nation.

‘How does she know this man still lives?’

Sergei reflected on Susan’s faith in the almighty. He would never have spared her if Carl Weisz had already met his fate.

But why was this employee of the state interested in Susan’s history? A softening up? A ploy to get him to denounce the Soviet Union? Hadn’t he already shown his love for his country by remaining to serve it after losing Susan?

'He does. I have seen photographs of him in newspapers. He is in England. He is very successful in publishing – my wife's former husband's business. He stole it from her when he took their name.'

Werner Kawalek. Leonid nodded silently as his suspicions were confirmed. His man was indeed the devil that he had always supposed him to be. The description matched that of the numerous reports emanating from England of Carl Weisz's rise to notoriety. If this man's wife – Susan Kawalek as she was, was half as resolute as he, then Mr. Carl Weisz was never going to sleep easy in his bed.

'I wish you luck comrade.' Leonid stretched out his hand in a gesture of understanding. Sergei met it and felt the empathy in the warmth of the clasp. Somehow he also felt a sense of approval and envy in this old campaigner's hand. An opportunity, that given the chance twenty years ago, he would have taken himself. 'You may pick up your visa tomorrow. I will see to it personally.'

'Thank you. I shall not forget you.'

'You had better. As far as I am concerned, we never met.'

The old man turned and left the room by a connecting door. Sergei did not see the look of satisfaction cross his face as he shredded the official notes of the appointment and interview.

The slim, superbly fit figures were up and running, taking four maybe five strides to gain the upright position and then the thoroughbred legs took over and churned the cinders like a treadmill. Nothing showed in the leading four. Neck and neck as if bound by an invisible string. Hands snatching at the air, pulling great lumps toward them, knees bucking and straightening faster than the cossack horses at full gallop.

The finishing line was in sight of the glazed stare of the four contestants. The others were nowhere. Marlies Gohr, Ingrid Auerswald, and Lyudmila Kondratyeva broke the quadruplet band. These were now the medal winners. They knew it and flew like the wind. The tape trailed in the wake of their final lurch across the line and no one could separate the first or second. Except Leonid Chukov from his seat directly opposite the line. His eagle eyes still had the perception of his early teens. He knew. The winner was Lyudmila Kondratyeva – his choice from the beginning. It was in the way she prepared. The way that she settled in her blocks. The way that nothing disturbed her concentration. Not even the two false starts. His assessment of body language and facial character was duly confirmed as the photograph for the first two places showed Kondratyeva had won by one hundredth of a second in 11.06 seconds. A gold medal for the Soviet Union or URS as the gigantic scoreboard proudly announced to the non-Russian speaking world.

The victory was almost as gratifying as the news of Maximillian Holst's brinkmanship in his desperate fight to retain control of his corporate empire. Leonid tucked the pink copy of the Financial Times into his inside pocket as he made his way to the V.I.P. lounge for tea. And his beloved vodka.

CHAPTER XIII

November 1980

There was a definite winter chill in the air as George Parker walked slowly by the ruins of the Norman castle, now created into a peaceful garden for the benefit of the 56,000 inhabitants of Guildford. How uses change, he mused. Constructed as a bastion against the aggression of invading armies, its use now was as a haven for pensioners, young mothers, and off duty students from the Surrey University. The modern square cut cathedral dominated the city giving a misconception as to its true identity by the unimaginative red brick, angular tower sitting atop an equally unattractive red brick base. Architects and planners have no soul, George concluded as he admired the 15th century church at the foot of the main hill of the shopping centre. The visual beauty in this one street should have told them that the contrast between the present and the ethereal efforts of real builders of bygone times would not work. It was as if someone had decided to insult the brilliance of the masters of long ago with the square block monstrosity that dared to be challenged by the 'uninitiated' public, as ugly.

But there was a more important matter on his mind than criticism of this beautiful part of England. The meeting with Peter Mallory and his wife. His senses were alive to the chance of delving a little deeper into the past of this enigma who called himself Peter Mallory. He wet his tongue as he savoured the opportunity in front of him. He also savoured the chance to dine at one of his favourite restaurants out of London. The Toc Blanche. Opened only a few months ago, it had already earned itself a reputation with the connoisseurs of the food trade. Not that that influenced George. If he liked it, then that was good enough. And he knew what he liked. The Maitre D' had been most charming on his first visit, attending to George's particular tastes, as opposed to providing only what was on the menu. He like that. It showed a willingness to please, and to be pleased.

He turned right from the steep gradient, breathing heavily, and made his way through a narrow street to where the welcoming door of the restaurant presented itself unobtrusively to his eager gaze. He noted with satisfaction that Clive was already there, his grey jaguar sitting comfortably half on, half off, the double yellow lined pavement. In the windscreen was an official pass or warrant, George supposed, to excuse this blatant contradiction of the parking laws.

The door opened easily to his touch and he was immediately met by a waiter who took his hat and coat and ushered him to the small bar on the left. There sat Clive with a single malt whisky cradled in his slender fingers.

'Good evening George. Glad you could make it.'

'Otherwise you would have to pay the bill, right?'

Clive laughed. 'No, the cost of this has been designated for your employers. I only organised the party, not the food. Or the wine,' he added significantly. He passed the wine list to George to run his approving eye down the many excellent clarets and burgundies denoted in expertly scripted writing on the vellum. 'The Bordeaux selection is particularly good on the second page, George. That is if you are having meat.'

George read the list quickly, looking for his favourite Chateau and vintages. None as good as the bottle that Monsieur Bertand is storing for me for that special occasion. That might not be too long now, smiled George, in anticipation of his putting together the final pieces of the jigsaw of this case. He no longer regarded it as fraud. It was bigger than that. No doubt the figures were way above anything that he had ever tackled before, but the figures were not the important factor in this. There was something far deeper and ominous surrounding the whole picture. That was why he had tipped off Clive to invite not only his own personal computer expert but two assistants from the bank's fraud office, a couple who may or may not be having an affair. That didn't worry George. They were both quite sharp and responsive to the signals of others. Their corroboration of George's and Clive's impression could be invaluable. Clive had framed the invitation to Peter and Wendy in such a way that it was quite normal for George's assistant to accompany him on this occasion to cement the cohesion between the bank and the Fraud Squad. As Clive was a bachelor, he had also asked Peter if he would be good enough to bring his mother along. 'Too many males can make a boring dinner table, and George and I are too old in the tooth to engage young people like Melissa and Myra, in interesting conversation.'

The final party had been confirmed as George and Clive. David and Melissa from the bank's fraud office. Peter and Wendy. Peter's mother Susan and Myra, Clive's whizz kid computer brain from the bowels of Scotland Yard. Eight in all, making the large round table in the private corner of the restaurant ideal for the purpose. The seating plan had been carefully worked out by Clive and George to give maximum opportunity for obtaining information from each of the three 'Kawalek' family members.

George would sit opposite Clive. That way they could communicate by word of mouth or subtle signs that something of importance was in the air. Wendy would be seated next to Clive's computer girl. Their mutual interest could spark some slight indication of how or where the programme had been manipulated. On George's left would be Susan, Peter's mother. He was quite certain that she had the key to the whole puzzle. He would see. Peter would be on Clive's left . . . that way it would appear that George had no interest in his former life, whereas Clive would naturally ask questions. David and Melissa would fill the gap and make mental notes.

Pierre Gascoigne attended to the seating of the guests as unobtrusively as George had requested. His fussy affectation of a typical French restaurateur added the perfect touch to the magic of the mouthwatering cuisine that appeared, as if by magic, at the snap of his fingers.

George and Clive were in charge of the wines and everyone agreed that their choice would be the perfect match for the five courses. A thin consomme to start with and a delicious terrine of smoked salmon to follow. Filet d'Agneau au Romarin with haricot beans and Jersey new potatoes. The rosemary compressed into the lamb making it especially piquant with the tomatoes and sliced onions. The remainder of the meal was to be left to the choice of the ladies. Susan was enchanted with the two elderly gentlemen. Although a well preserved sixty seven herself, she regarded her two older companions as her peers and anyone entering the restaurant might have taken either of the two for her husband. The excellent choice of wine by George for the first course of a 1971 Puligny Montrachet had everyone talking at once. Just what the two protagonists wanted. It is amazing how the wine of the grape makes people so amenable, marvelled George. I wonder if I am that amenable to the others? He laughed out loud at his thoughts and caught the look of appreciation in the eyes of this glowingly beautiful woman on his left. Someone who has been unused to laughter for many years, he surmised.

'Tell me Susan. May I call you Susan?' Seeing her nod graciously he continued. 'Where were you in 1971? I always play this little game with myself whenever I drink a bottle of vintage wine. I look at the date and I try and remember where and what I was doing in that particular year.'

'1971? I was here in London. In the house I am in now. Nothing particularly exciting happened as I can recall.'

'But it was the year of the great decimalisation. Surely you were as confused as all the rest of the population. The end of Britain's currency as we knew it. Hundreds of years of tradition gone at a stroke. A catastrophe that no one realised was happening. And they all, well most people, accepted the change without so much as a whimper. Little did they realise that within a few years it would herald the biggest hike in inflation that has ever hit this country. And no one took the blame.'

Susan looked at this genial, round, hulk of a man and warmed to his condemnation of the general apathy of a public, uneducated in the ways of finance. She remembered only too well, Peter explaining to her the intricacies of his plan to bring about the downfall of Carl Weisz. But what would this man want to know about that? She giggled more than she wanted as she replied that as far as she was concerned, she had never understood the pounds shillings and pence system anyway.

'It must have presented Peter with quite a problem at that time surely?' George muzzled into his wine to cover his probing question.

'No more than he was used to. He had tested the changeover in a mock exercise many times, including the resultant computer programming that would be necessary to effect the change.'

'Ah, the great god – the computer. One touch of a button and all is right with the world. Ha!'

'I take it you don't like computers. But you must admit that it would be impossible to live without them.' Susan refilled his glass with the remains of the bottle of Pomerol ordered by Clive.

'I loathe computers. But I must use them because the art of manual calculations and brain logic have been lost, or subjugated by a stronger power, but not necessarily a more intelligent power.'

'My daughter, Katrina, has spent her whole life with computers. Ever since she was about seven years of age.'

'Where was that?'

'In Berlin. We were trapped there after the war. East Berlin I mean. Due to the circumstances at that time we could not leave. The wall was already in place long before that ugly stone monstrosity thrust its division between us. My... friend tried to help me and Katrina leave, but it was impossible. In the end we had to literally jump over the wall.' Susan sat and remembered the priest as he shoved at her legs and received the bullets meant for her...

'You have painful memories of those times. I'm sorry to have brought them back. It must have been difficult to come to terms with your old life when you did get back to this country.' George glanced at Clive deep in conversation with Peter. I wonder if he is on the same wavelength as I am? he thought.

'It is quite all right. I can talk about it now. There was a time after... after Auschwitz that I could not. The memory was too horrible. It still is if I dwell on it, but I am able to talk about it if I do not think about it. Do you understand?'

George nodded. He pushed the dish of cheeses towards Susan who selected a French Brie to eat with her claret. George stuck to the Cheddar, his favourite.

'Has Peter told you that we were in Auschwitz, or Birkinau and later Monovitz Buna? No, probably he hasn't. He doesn't like to talk about it either. Who can blame him. His father and sister never escaped the terror of that place.' Susan fell silent and George put his hand on hers and nodded his acquiescence of her mood. He noticed Wendy in quite a different mood to her mother. She was talking agitatedly to her counterpart in the computer fraud section of Clive's office. Now there is a conversation that I would like to be privy to, murmured the happy, slightly tipsy, rotund figure of the bank's Fraud office.

'Where did you have your basic computer education Wendy?'

Wendy had taken to the woman as soon as they were introduced. About the same age, unmarried. Why? she thought, and dismissed it as none of her business. Attractive, obviously on a high salary by the clothes she wore, but not over ostentatious like so many of the single 'liberated' females that were constantly forcing their independence on their workmates. She had class. That certain style. A standard that she aspired to herself, but had never had the temerity to bridge the gap between her average level of income, although higher than many in her age group, and the level where the expensive becomes commonplace.

'In Berlin. We were there after the war. It was difficult, but the East Germans were in the forefront of computer technology and advancement and I suppose I wanted to be part of that scene myself. I soon discovered that I had an aptitude for it and one thing led to another.'

'When did you come to this country?

'In 1961. It seems a lifetime now. I suppose it is a lifetime if you think of what went before it. I try not to.'

'Susan is not your real mother is she? I don't mean to pry but it seems a chance in a thousand that you should meet and marry her son.'

'Not really. When we landed in England the first place we made for was Susan's parents' home in Dorset. They had been dead for some time but the house was held in trust and we discovered that it was held for Lazar, that's Peter's true christian name, and the solicitors gave us his address.'

Myra saw the flash of remembrance sweep across Wendy's eyes as the moment when Susan saw Lazar returned.

'It must have been very emotional.' Myra reached out to touch

Wendy's hand.

'It was the most beautiful moment of my life. More beautiful than the day I married Peter. Each thought the other dead, in that awful place, and suddenly there they were face to face again. After 20 years. No person on earth could have broken the spell between them. Each knew that the other had triumphed over incalculable odds. It was meant to be... that's what they both said... it was ordained.'

Myra sensed that the purpose for which she had been invited was on the tip of Wendy's tongue but was held there by a solemn family trust, too personal to divulge to others.

'I suppose all such deliverances are deemed to be for a purpose. A purpose that grows more strongly after the event. I remember when I was a teenager, I escaped a car accident by declining to go to a local dance with my friends. The car crashed and all were killed. That sort of experience makes you appreciate that somewhere there is a divine providence which decides whether you live or die.' Myra saw Wendy nod slowly as if recalling her own deliverance from a fate that was too awful to contemplate.

'I often think of my mother. What she had to endure. Susan talked to me about her many times. She was very brave. She starved herself so that I could live. I shall never forgive those responsible for that. Or those who profited from the holocaust.' A look of sheer hatred flashed across Wendy's dark eyes and was gone in an instant. Myra shivered. There was a density of enmity in that gaze that transcended all other feelings which this girl had shown. She had met other survivors of the death camps and had marvelled at the equanimity of those who could talk about their captors rationally. The hatred was there, but had been mellowed over the years. They had learned to accept that there was little that could be done and their anger had subsided. They remembered, but they put it out of their minds to enable them to live what was left of a normal life.

'My life feels very humble compared to the sufferings of your family and the thousand of families who must have suffered with you. Were there many of your neighbours in the camps?'

'Every neighbour that was Jewish was taken. Even those who had given up the Jewish practices and could not be distinguished from other non-Jews. But they were betrayed and taken nevertheless. I feel more hatred for the betrayers than for those who were acting under orders, inhuman as they were. For one of your own people to turn against you – that is unforgivable.' Again the pupils dilated into a fixed stare as the object of her hatred replaced the vista of the congenial dinner table.

'I am sorry to have roused so many terrible memories. I had no idea.' Myra changed the subject and chatted about babies and shopping and the latest fashions. Wendy was soon laughing and giggling at her own thoughts on motherhood... still not out of the question, she argued.

Clive had been watching out of the corner of his eye as his assistant was obviously forming a friendly relationship with one of George's suspects. Very ordinary people do not do the things that George insisted they were doing. But then how do you define a very ordinary person? Certainly from what he had heard, these people had the right to hang, draw, and quarter those who had been responsible for their incarceration. But that is the justice of the majority of the population. It was only the law which dictated that you could not do such things. Why was the law so out of touch with the populace? Because it was not made by common consent, but by lawyers; the bane of all police forces, he concluded.

'Your wife is very attractive Peter. She is obviously not English. A mid-European I would say, but then I am always making observations for no reason at all. Habit I suppose.'

'Your habit is correct. She is German. She came to England with my mother. Her own mother was killed... or she died in a concentration camp. She was only two. I was lucky; my mother escaped. I was only eight – but I thought that my mother had died with the rest of my family.' Peter's hands made a gesture of appeal. 'You would think that there can be no other purpose in life after discovering your mother again after 20 years. But we had a common undertaking that was strengthened by our reunion. Wendy and I are the same. We are kindred spirits, almost telepathic. The influence of our common mother might have something to do with it.'

Clive looked at this slim, brooding young man, trying to picture the family before the war came. 'What did your father do in Germany Peter?'

'He was in the publishing trade. Journals, magazines, scientific gazettes. Kawalek Verlag. The name is still respected in publishing circles.'

'Kawalek – was that your name?'

'Yes. Werner was my father. The founder of the firm. It was meant to be my ultimate career, when … when … I grew up.' Peter looked at Clive, embarrassed at his emotion.

'A lot of things changed in the war Peter. My father too was killed. Who knows what I would have become? A city broker, or an Insurance agent. It is in the lap of the gods.'

'Sometimes God needs a little help. When the situation is such that no one cares any more, a nudge in the right direction can help.'

'How do you know that God is not helping you give that little nudge.' Clive's gentle interjection raised Peter's head from the contemplative stare at his glass of Chablis.

'You may very well be right. I hope so.' The final assertion had a ring of conviction that Clive himself had adopted on many a difficult case.

'I come across injustices all the time in my job. I suppose you know that. But it doesn't help when you have done all the spade work and proved to your own satisfaction that someone is a criminal, for the law or the DPP to rule that you have insufficient evidence. I know when someone is guilty. I think we all do to some degree. Wouldn't you say so?'

'Those who have been involved certainly do. They do not need any other witnesses. But who believes them? Sometimes it is better to deal with it yourself.'

Now we are coming to the crux of what the evening is about, breathed Clive. Gently. I don't want him to back off now.

'Take a case I have at the moment.' Clive saw Peter's interested gaze meet his. 'You must be aware that the most difficult case to prove is that of fraud. Several instances over the past ten years have come to the public notice. And there have been some prosecutions. That insurance fellow, friend of Harold Wilson, you remember? Damned difficult to bring to court, but we did it. Set against that are the dozens of cases where the evidence would be insufficient to convict. In court, that is. But we keep our eyes on those who escape and wait for an opportunity. We get them one way or the other. Doesn't sound ethical does it? But if justice is done, then you can ignore the muckraking of your ethics in the Sunday broadsheets. They are always good for a completely distorted view of the facts.'

'You said you were on a case at the moment,' said Peter, bringing Clive back to the original preamble. 'Anyone in public life?'

Did he have a special reason for the last question? wondered Clive. Was he fishing for information that he needed to justify his campaign against the press lord? He had seen the same intense look on his face at the meeting at the Savoy as he saw every time that their conversation alluded to "the nameless magnate." Perhaps I should come right out and denounce Holst and watch for the reaction, pondered Clive. Or should I let Peter name his adversary?

'Yes. It is one of the most baffling that I have ever encountered. There is nothing that we can put our finger on, but the blatant fraud is there. I know it. Under the blanket of accountants, auditors, solicitors, and crooked financial advisers, is the bare bones of a gigantic confidence trick. Another problem is that if it were indeed to be exposed, then it would have repercussions in the city and every banking institution throughout Europe. The question is, do we go in and expose it for what it is, or do we go along with it and hope that it is never discovered by the public?' Clive waited for Peter's answer.

The young man seemed to be struggling with his wish to confide in this genial man sitting on his right, but the years of patience and dedication must not be ruined by letting down his guard so near to the moment of triumph. But he was still curious as to Clive's assessment of the object of his hate.

'I suppose it depends on who it is. Anyone who has committed a crime must be punished. No matter what the consequences. But how you punish him, that is the conundrum. No one in this world has the right to claim immunity because of his position.'

'Then you would have punished those who were given amnesty after the war because they had a contribution to make to the world?'

'Yes. Whatever the contribution, someone, somewhere would have eventually supplied the same thing. Slowing down the process does no harm to anyone in the long run. We move too fast anyway. The world will survive however these motivators of growth and progress try to push the boundaries of natural development. The Greeks have a word for it – "Seegar." It means slowly; take your time; don't rush.'

'And what would you do to those who committed the vilest crimes against humanity in the last war?' Clive decided it was time to test the water. To see if what he suspected lay at the bottom of Peter's train of thoughts.

'They can probably never be prosecuted. It would be a shambles, no evidence that could be believed by people 45 years on. Identification – uncertain. The time element alone would make it nigh impossible to convince a jury of how heinous the crimes were.' Peter reflected for a moment. 'No, the only way is direct justice by those involved. It is the simplest and the best way.' He stared straight at Clive with eyes that held all the suffering of every Jew who had ever died in that holocaust. 'I am not a Jew, but at this moment, I wish that I were.'

Because of his hatred for this particular man? wondered Clive. This man, who himself was a Jew. Did that make it all the more terrible? His thoughts went back to a Jew 2000 years ago who was also betrayed. By a friend. Clive shuddered. He agreed with every word this likeable man said. He could achieve in his own way, what successive police actions could never even approach. But he had to know if the one Peter was thinking of was the man whose name appeared on the front of his current file at the office.

'Many war criminals have been traced and punished. The Simon Wiesenthal Institute has been very active, but its sources are receding and the time factor is against it. Young people like yourself; you would be very young when you were taken to the camp wouldn't you?; are the only ones who can bring the eyewitness evidence to the public.' Clive watched Peter's reaction again, but the eyes remained calm and almost mocking. As if he knew that Clive was pushing for an admission. 'What do you remember of your arrest, if I may use that term?'

Clive was surprised by the frankness of Peter's answer. 'I remember every detail as if it were yesterday. I shall never forget. It was the last time that my family were whole. And one man destroyed all of that in twenty seconds of depraved treachery.' Peter turned his accusing eyes to Clive. 'Tell me. Who will account to the hundreds of Jews for the unspeakable crime committed by this man?'

'I have no answer to that. As you say, those who were not involved cannot judge the actions of those who seek justice in their own way. It is a better justice than the legal system I'm afraid, although as a policeman, I am bound to abide by the law, inadequate as it is.' Just one question and I will have what George is looking for – confirmation of the reason why the Kawalek family hated this man, Maximillian Holst.

'And does this man still live?'

'Yes. He lives. He has changed his name, as he did so many times in the past. But he cannot hide from those of us who knew him. As those with the placards pronounce, the day of reckoning is nigh.'

'But if you know him, why wait for so long before denouncing him?'

Peter smiled. 'How long does it take for your system to bring to justice those whom you know are guilty? And did you not say yourself that it could not always be proved? No; there has to be a satisfaction in justice. No frills. No appeals.' The smile vanished. 'No mercy.' He stood. 'Why so long you ask? As the Greeks say, "Seegar, Mr. Farnworth, Seegar."'

The family rose at Peter's bidding, thanking their hosts for a very pleasant evening. Susan had particularly enjoyed the company, arguing with her son that his boss was not the grumpy ogre that he had made him out to be. George laughed and Peter was embarrassed. Wendy promised to contact Myra for an evening on their own to further discuss the intricacies of the latest computer technology.

George raised his eyebrows in Clive's direction and the tall sandy haired man nodded slowly over the empty table. The signal indicated that they were very near to the solution which they sought.

'I think we have to talk. While it is fresh in my mind.' Clive beckoned for George to get into the rear of the Jaguar through the open door. As the car moved smoothly away, the chauffeur closed the dividing window and started the wipers to clear the light snowflakes that began to smatter the windscreen.

They drove in silence for twenty minutes, carefully sorting the vital pieces of information which each had gathered. Clive spoke first.

'Peter is definitely your man. He has the motive, the opportunity, and the means. What about his mother?'

'She is a very deep, strong woman, with a controlled hate that can only have been preserved for so long by a desire that is yet to be satisfied. The object of her hate lives. As does her resolve to focus that hate on the one man who can release her from her vow. Her story of life in the concentration camp and after was not very pleasant to hear. But the unsaid portions were as plain as if she had written an account of her suffering because of this man. She said I wouldn't know him, a nobody called Carl Weisz, or Boris Vukadovic. And even Werner Kawalek – her husband's name, taken by this monster. Not content with taking their lives, he took everything they owned. For so beautiful a woman to conceal that sort of hatred, it takes a strength very few of us have.'

'I gather you admire her very much.'

'Yes.'

'And you condone what she and her family are doing?'

'What are they doing? We are more than certain that they have raised a very large sum from the bank – to help them – I am not as yet quite sure how, and that they intend revenge of some sort. But what?'

Clive remembered Peter's "day of reckoning is nigh" and told George that whatever was planned was imminent.

'Whatever is planned I am fairly certain that Peter does not intend to eliminate our subject. Myra told me in a quiet moment that Wendy had never advocated assassination as a solution. "Too quick" she said.' Clive looked out at the snow clinging to the frame of the window. 'I tend to agree with her.'

George laughed. 'You always were a pushover for a pretty face. Stick to the facts. What have we?'

The long slender fingers scratched the thinning mop of ginger on the back of Clive's head. He spoke slowly.

'All three of the family were in concentration camps.

All three were betrayed by the same man. Susan and Peter survived the camp; separately; and made their way to England.

Peter married Wendy…'

George interrupted. 'But where does our man come in?'

'Patience George. You remember the names I gave you of Maximillian Holst, those he used before he came to England? Werner Kawalek, Carl Weisz…'

'… of course I do. He is obviously the same man who was operating at the time of the rounding up of the Jews in Berlin. The same man who now calls himself Maximillian Holst. But why haven't they exposed him? What are they planning? And when?'

'What can you do against a man in his position? We cannot even prosecute him, he's too clever. He has built a protective army around him which no lawyer can penetrate without getting his fingers severely burnt. And there is no one willing to have a try.'

'Then how would a person like Peter punish a man like that?'

George's question hung in the silence of the velvet padded interior of the sealed compartment of the swiftly moving car. 'I don't know,' said Clive, 'but I believe he is intelligent enough to make him suffer in a way that will inflict the severest jolt to this man's ego. That is the key. His ego. No one in the higher echelons of society has a greater opinion of himself than Maximillian Holst. To degrade him and expose him would be the logical method of exacting the greatest anguish and mental torture for someone of his genre. He could not stand it. I would say that it would almost send him insane. He was never meant to be less than a megalomaniac.'

George's eyebrows knitted together in concentration. 'I think you may have something there Clive. For once,' he joked. 'Cast you mind back a few meals. Didn't you show me a list of investments that almost tallied. As if someone was copying or anticipating what this Holst was doing?…

'… yes, that's it. That is where the funds are going. Somehow, someone, and we have a good idea who that someone is, has steadily controlled the progress of his adversary, never letting him get too for along the road of success, but giving him enough to whet his appetite. Every now and then he has been balked at some deal or other. We saw evidence of that at the last shareholders' meeting. Awkward questions that Holst had difficulty in answering. Questions that had more than a ring of truth about them. I think we are beginning to get the picture. But how will the final enactment of revenge be augmented?' Not waiting for an answer he continued.

'You've seen it all before with other captains of industry. They go too far and overstretch their resources, and the big bang comes and sweeps everything they had ever owned or enjoyed, out of the window. They are very rarely seen again. Humiliated and ground into the financial dust to spend the rest of their life in miserable exile. With Holst that would mean the end of his life as he wants it. He may even be driven to suicide.'

'You're theorising a bit there aren't you Clive? I know the apparent facts fit, but we have no real proof that your theory is apposite to these circumstances. In any case, we have not been able to connect Peter Mallory or any of his family to the purchasers of the stocks in Holst's companies. If I remember rightly, most of the shares were purchased under the name of a trust. You have the name. What was it?'

'It was foreign. German I think. Newmann or Nieman … no it was Niemand. Every trust involved in the purchase had that name as part of the trust. That doesn't prove anything.'

Clive sat puzzling as to his next train of thought. George redirected it for him.

'Niemand is German for "nobody" isn't it? If you remember your schooldays lessons. A series of trusts all with the pseudonym of "nobody." What does that tell you Clive?' George's triumphant tone told Clive that he already had the answer.

Clive slapped his thigh in excitement. 'Of course! Nobody. No particular person. A group. The Jews that he betrayed. And the Kawaleks. All we have to do now is connect them with the trusts. We know they are registered in Liechtenstein and there's the problem. It will be almost impossible to obtain the names of the trustees, but it's worth a try.'

The car rolled smoothly to a halt outside George's house. The trip up the A3 as far as the M25 and back had been very fruitful, and pleasant, thought George. Ensconced in the luxury of Clive's Jaguar, and fortified by a the odd brandy or two from the inbuilt bar, both were at peace with the world. It had been a good night's work. George laughed. 'And to think that the bank is picking up the tab for this. Can I charge them for the brandies as well Clive?'

'Certainly not. That's my treat. Or Scotland Yard's.' He laughed with George. 'Do you know George. I've just remembered something. Something so insignificant that it almost escaped my notice.'

'What's that Clive?' George prepared himself for another gem of inspiration from his friend. Why did he almost invariably come up with a "coup de grace" on a particular problem? 'OK Clive. I submit to your superior intellect and promise to shower you with praise.'

'Do you know what Peter said to me at one point tonight?' He watched George slowly shake his head. 'It was when he asked me who would account to the hundreds of Jews betrayed by this man. I could not answer him so I put it to him. "Who would?" Do you know what he said?

Again George waited expectantly.

'He said. "Nobody, Mr. Farnworth. Nobody."'

George didn't sleep that night. The phrase that held the clue to his biggest case refused to let his tired mind rest as it continually alternated with his interpretation of the words. "Niemand, Mr. Farnworth. Niemand."

CHAPTER XIV

December 1980

Maximillian Alexander Carl Holst was under pressure. There were no further avenues to be explored to bolster his empire. His credit notes with all of his admirers and supporters had turned sour. Even his stock of gold reserves had been sacrificed to quell the ever increasing demand to supply substantial security to satisfy the banks' auditors. His rage mounted as he noted that the price of gold had gone through the roof. Up $159 in a week to $802 an ounce. He had sold at $543 an ounce only three weeks ago. He had sustained a considerable loss. If only the banks had been more patient as he had demanded that they should be. He had never let them down before had he? He had always provided the margins that they required. Albeit in the form of more shares in his ailing companies that never ceased to sink lower and lower in the equity market. Why? He had had these crises before and had always survived them. Just. But this time, no matter what he did the downward trend continued without any good reason. Public opinion had been swayed. The city had been swayed. And now the Department of Industry were getting too nosey. Before when they threatened to become too involved in what he considered 'his business' he had had the clout and the power to call their bluff and dare them to denounce him. Now that power was waning and the wolves were gathering...

He stared at the note on his desk. A further note, similar to the one he had received at the shareholders' meeting, lay couched in its folds, laughing up at him as if the top and bottom folds were reaching for his face. He could still read the message written precisely in the middle of the cream vellum. "It would be in your interests to meet me. We have a mutual problem to discuss. I suggest 10am on the 18th December. A taxi will pick you up outside your apartment at exactly 9.50am. He has instructions not to bring you to me if he is followed. I have a plan to save your business – be there." Maximillian pulled down the lower half of the one page letter. At the bottom was repeated the name on the original correspondence; "Werner Kawalek."

Was he still alive? After all these years? He had been assured that the whole family had been 'eliminated' as his friend Overgruppenfuhrer Haupman had put it. 'You need have no fear that any of the families whom you "introduced" to us will escape the final solution. The Overgruppenfuhrer had been extremely pleased with the case of American Rye whisky dropped on his desk.

Then who was this imposter who demanded that he meet him? Could he really save his 'business' as he had put it? Or was it blackmail? A chance to cash in on some supposedly ancient story of his participation in the Jewish problem. That had been tried before. But who would believe anyone who contended that he, a Jew himself would perpetrate such a heinous crime?

But all the same the signature worried him. A jolt from the past that he did not need at this moment.

He looked past the signature to the footnote. "If you choose not to come, then I shall have no alternative but to finish your corporative interests immediately. I have the power and the means. Examine your stockholders' register for majority interests. I think you will find that I, and not you, have the controlling rights in ordinary shares. Look for the name – Niemand Nominees. That is who I am."

His huge body gave an involuntary shiver. As his empire crumbled about him he had indulged more and more in satisfying his bodily needs. It was as if he were trying to grow bigger than the threat from the financial centres of the world. To create a fleshy barrier between him and his adversaries. He strode to the table beneath the fifth floor window. Sheets and sheets of computer printouts, delivered by his trusted employee Leopold Sochia. It was there on the blue lined paper in the impersonal letters and figures of an inanimate object that spelled his doom. 58 companies and associated subsidiaries all detailed the truth of the statement in the communication from the grave. Each denoted that his shareholding, held by the banks in support of his borrowings, was overshadowed by a greater holding by nominee companies, headed by the name of 'Niemand.' How had that been allowed to happen? he cursed. Leo had never advised him. He should have done immediately any threat to his control was even marginally posed. Maximillian conveniently forgot the numerous times Leopold had warned him not to sell any shares in any of the companies before consulting him. But cash was needed more urgently over the past year. His creditors had refused to accept his promises of future payment. They wanted hard currency now. Cash or gold. Or negotiable securities. They were not interested in his shares. As his own stake in the various companies decreased, so the holdings of Niemand Nominees took on a more menacing level. And who was buying the discarded shares? More Niemand Nominee companies. Leopold Sochia had been dismissed out of hand immediately. One less employee to pay. But Leopold had taken his redundancy money for himself. He had seen the constant swing in the price of the conglomerate's shares and had played the market to amass more than enough to say goodbye to his employer without a tinge of regret. He was going to get what he deserved, why shouldn't I? he had argued. He had not been a good practising Jew for nothing. The grapevine around the city of London was awash with the imminent collapse of the greatest publishing empire ever built. His Jewish fraternity had put him wise to the fact that Maximillian Holst was not all that he made himself out to be. He was not Kosher. Too many tales were circulating of his past. His day of destiny was due.

Maximillian dressed hurriedly in his usual dark blue double breasted suit. With it he chose a guards' tie, the subject of many a disdainful look by true members in the past, who did not have the courage to tell him to remove it. His black patent shoes reflected the heavy hooded eyes as he inspected them for scuffs. His exquisitely manicured nails swiftly adjusted the shirt cuffs to a Savile Row margin below his sleeves. No one could ever accuse Maximillian Holst of anything but perfection in his dress. It was an image that had earned him more admiration than any other. "Dress like you are somebody and everyone will believe that you are somebody." An old adage which had been handed down to him by his grandfather, a connoisseur of men and their greed. "Supply what they think they are going to get, and charge them for the privilege." He had been carrying out his grandfather's philosophy ever since and it had worked. So what was wrong now? His razor sharp brain could no longer cope with the complexities of the commercial world. It was moving faster than any one man could envisage. Perhaps that was the answer. While he was trying to bring about the biggest revolution in technology through satellite information to the people, his own unchallenged ability to function as a computer was now far too dilatory and retarded. His advantage had vanished. Like the dreams of his younger years. By the meteoric capacity of computers to outthink him.

The Universal lift hummed its way to the ground floor. As swiftly as his rise to fame had been in the early years. His charisma had enchanted financiers, bankers, entrepreneurs, shady dealers; anyone who thought they could make a killing with the help of this colossus of the business world. No one ever asked him for his credentials. He needed none. His ability to act as the go between in million pound contracts was renowned. And he took his commission from all parties involved without any risk on his part. Another of his grandfather's axioms.

The taxi was waiting as predicted. A Jewish driver glanced at the resplendent figure as it slumped into the passenger seat. No instruction was given. None asked. It sped off at the maximum speed possible among the thriving thoroughfare of a Thursday morning in Knightsbridge. Harrods flashed by, soon to be followed by the open spaces of Hyde Park. A suicidal circumvention of the Marble Arch ensued, followed by a regal drive down Park Lane. The Hilton? Maximillian guessed. The taxi sped on. Back to the further side of Hyde Park and onto Knightsbridge again. Weaving in and out of the unending traffic of South Kensington, the taxi finally stopped at an imposing building dominating the white stuccoed, porticoed terraced houses of embassies, solicitors, dentists, and other wealthy inhabitants of that part of Cromwell Road. The tall St. Paul's like tower overshadowed the four smaller towers, spread along the frontage of the world's greatest museum of decorative arts. The Victoria and Albert Museum.

So this is the meeting place. Maximillian shifted his weight onto his strong oak like legs and skipped up the steps to the entrance. He had an addictive habit of trying to portray himself as still young and athletic. The result was comical, although again nobody would dare to tell him the truth.

Other visitors fell aside under his sustained assault on the entrance. A few recognised him and deferred to his precedence.

He approached the desk and gave the name of his contact. A portly attendant pointed out the whereabouts of room 46b, Plaster Casts, fakes and forgeries. 'Straight ahead toward Medieval Treasury, turn right through the corridors of Chinese and Korean artifacts. On your left will be the corridor at right angles to Cromwell Road. First on your right is the room you require.'

It was exactly as he had said. The door admitting him to the Plaster Cast room was a replica of his body. Large enough to admit two or three persons side by side and tall enough to cater for bodily giants as well as 'giants of industry' as he still regarded himself.

The room was empty. Or so he thought. In the far corner was a tall, dark, easily moving man of about 45 years. His hair was black with a faint tint of grey showing at the temples. Slightly wavy, giving his face an angelic look that belied his years. Maximillian glanced at the eyes and knew that this was the man who had written the letter. He was not Werner Kawalek. He was far too young... and yet... 'Good morning.' Always one for a disarming greeting, Maximillian decided to take the initiative.

'I don't think that you will be of that opinion later this morning Mr. Weisz. Take a seat.' The tall man indicated a wooden bench to the side of a cabinet of white alabaster heads of the Caesars of Rome.

'I don't think I know you do I? And you certainly don't know me. My name is not Weisz...'

'...Carl Weisz, formerly Boris Vukadovic, formerly Werner Kawalek, formerly... need I go on?'

The aggressive ebullience disappeared as if it had been drawn from his body by a gigantic pump. His face paled and he searched the eyes of his accuser for an answer; a recognition; a memory from the past. Who was he?

‘Who are you?’ he at last managed to mouth as his breath undulated through his windpipe in irregular bursts.

‘Lazar Kawalek. You remember? I had a mother and a sister. And a father – Werner Kawalek. We were all interned in Auschwitz in 1941 for extermination. But we didn’t die. Not all of us. We had a mission to perform, so two of us were spared. I am now here to complete that mission.’

‘Lazar? Little Lazar? And ... Ta ... Taghi, your sister. Who escaped with you? Not your father?’

‘It is of no consequence to you who escaped and who didn’t. What does matter is the hundreds who did not escape the gas chambers and the furnaces. You are solely responsible for them being there and for the unending torment of the few relatives who did not succumb to the terror.’ Peter Mallory stared at this cringing unbeliever – reduced literally to the size of normality by the ghosts from the past.

‘But how...?’ Maximillian saw that his question was not to be answered. ‘It was not my fault. I was made to do it. I was threatened with death if I did not obey...’

‘I seem to remember that argument at the Nuremberg trials. The argument of a coward and a liar.’ The desultory note in Peter’s voice warned Carl to be cautious. His natural instincts for survival were still functioning. While this apparently convivial meeting was taking place his mind was working overtime to evolve some sort of defence and counter attack. Before he could formulate any sort of plan Peter spoke again.

‘I do not wish to discuss the past with you. I am here to put a proposition to you. It is not exactly a proposition, but an ultimatum. A course of action that I believe you have perfected over the years. It is briefly this ... ’

Maximillian was listening with one ear. His senses were a thousand light years away. In a world that no longer seemed real. A room where he had chatted so many times to the German command. Where Hauptgenerals had curried his favours and many a worthwhile contract had been struck. The room was cheerless. A blank office with two chairs and a desk. He on one side and the Hauptgeneral on the other.

'We have known each other a long time Herr Vukadovic. And you have made a lot of money in one way or the other. It is good that we have a . . . mitarbeiter, if I may use the term. I do not subscribe to the view that all collaborators are traitors. Some, such as yourself, use the function to further their own ends . . .' He paused to watch the reaction from the other side of the desk . . . 'as do we all.'

Maximillian saw himself nod, swiftly considering the Hauptgeneral's motives for this examination. Was he going to be dumped? Had his usefulness lapsed? He saw his own lips part to allow his tongue to slightly wet the cruel line of lighter pink. 'I am asking you now to assist the Third Reich in a far more positive manner than you have ever done before.'

Now it comes. The impossible request which would signal the end of a very lucrative period. 1941, and he had nowhere near enough cash stowed away to set him up after the war. He was tired of working for others. He knew that he was destined for greater power. He could feel it in his gut. It had been planted there by his grandfather and his father. He had seen the way they operated and he soon realised that he could operate on a much grander scale. To reach heights that they could never even imagine. The war had been the beginning. Vast profits which he was still on the threshold of obtaining. And now this. He decided to take the initiative.

'The war is good to many. It is up to each to take advantage of whatever crops up. You yourself have said that many times.' Maximillian was rather pleased that he had been able to quote the Hauptgeneral's own words to him.

'True, true. But we have been dabbling in the peripheries of the spoils of war. Illicit whisky, cigarettes, supplies, medicines. These, while being comparatively lucrative, do not bring the kind of rewards for real enterprise.'

'What are you alluding to Herr General. I sense that you have something in mind that will interest me greatly.' Show enthusiasm, and flatter if you can. His grandfather's teachings were never far from his active mind.

'As you know, we, that is the Reich, are carrying out a programme of purifying the German race in preparation for creating the master race of the world. To achieve this aim it is necessary to remove,' he paused as he emphasised the word, 'certain undesirables. The mentally ill, the infirm, the physically incurable … and of course the Jews.' The Hauptgeneral's eyes flicked momentarily over the features of the man sitting opposite. He saw no sign of disapproval or emotion of any kind.

'What has this to do with me? I am a German citizen and as such follow the doctrine of the Third Reich. The Jews deserve what they get. They owe no allegiance to anyone except themselves and their religion. Pah! I spit on their race.'

The Hauptgeneral smiled. 'Then what I am about to put to you should not cause you any concern.' Maximillian remembered the matter of fact way in which the general described that which would cause no "concern." He had been asked to prepare a list of all known Jewish families in the southern sector of Berlin. To visit them and gain their confidence and to find out the names of other Jews within the catchment area. 'You should have no difficulty in passing as a Jew yourself Boris. You have the aptitude to take on that role. If I did not know better, then I would almost take you for a Jew myself.'

He had laughed a loud raucous laugh which rattled the cheap window frames of the room little more than a hut. He had continued. 'The real profit from this exercise is not the honour that you and I will receive for our dutiful efforts but the value of the possessions of those … deported. Think of how much each family could be worth. Jews do not believe in banks, only possessions. Expensive chattels, jewellery, gold. But most of all their property. What use will the family have for their house when they have been … relocated?' Again the laugh rang out and Maximillian saw himself joining in and shaking hands with this homogeneous partner in the seeking of wealth.

'Do not worry Herr Klaus,' Maximillian assured him, using the Hauptgeneral's first name to signify complete acquiescence to his scheme. 'I already have a large list of families known to me – I have used them for some of my other deals;' the Hauptgeneral nodded; 'and I have no doubt that they will let me have the names of every family known within their circle.' Maximillian paused. 'How will we divide the er... proceeds?'

'I shall take the moveable goods, they will bring a fair return. Anything larger – say heavy items of furniture – can be left to your discretion. Dispose of them how you will. As for the property... let us say that we divide that equally. All properties in the eastern side of Berlin, you will take, you have the greater knowledge of that territory as you originate from there; I will take the west side.' He took out a vast street plan and drew a straight black line from north to south, bisecting the city into the two halves of their future fortune. 'I will supply the necessary transport for the families and of course their goods, while you use your contacts to transfer the houses, and places of business into other names. I will give you a list of the new title holders under whose names the properties are to be registered.'

Maximillian had no need to think any further than the Kawalek house. That had been the first. And their business. The number that followed had added enormously to the estate that he and his Hauptgeneral rapidly established. But the Kawalek's had paid the richest dividends. Not only had he been able to take over their business, but to continue it after the war and expand it beyond any other business that he had taken as his own.

And now the ghost of that first lucrative betrayal was here, telling him how to run his business.

'... You no doubt have noticed over the past nine years, that your success with your companies has not always run smoothly. Opportune purchases of small companies have not always been successful. Your plans for vast expansion have met from time to time with awkward problems and the proposed mergers, takeovers have fallen through. You have not always have had the financial backing from the public to achieve the heights to which you aspire.' Peter spoke quietly and quickly, quoting the various figures and times. The details of which he had spent the last nine years analysing and absorbing to make himself equal to this master of subterfuge. He stared at the fake bust of Caesar across the empty room and spoke to it as if seeking reassurance from it instead of this hulk of a man by his side. He did not want to look at him. The idea sickened him. He must not let his emotions interfere with what he had to do. He continued, knowing that the ears of the man slumped on the bench were listening.

'... Your companies have no substance. I know that, and so do you. They are supported by fictitious stocks, licences, warranties, and copyrights. I have invested in your companies from time to time to create false share values, to protect the investors who have had faith in a sham. And now I have the majority shareholding in all of your main companies and I can control their destiny.' Peter turned to face this evil from the past. 'You are finished Weisz. You have no companies. You have no more reserve funds. You have no power. And I am here to see to it that you never have power again.'

Carl Weisz's face was ashen and drawn. He had foreseen this coming but had ignored the obvious signs, as he always did. His ego was so great that he had assumed that he could rise above the mere facts and bluster his way in his usual fashion, to the top again. He was cornered with nowhere to go. He would be exposed, shamed, humiliated. No one could do that! Not to Maximillian Holst! He had not finished with the world yet! He turned in his seething rage to this impudent clerk on his right.

'I wouldn't do anything foolish Weisz. I have a number of colleagues, Jewish I might add, outside this room who would like nothing better than to restrain you, forcibly,' Peter emphasised, 'should you choose not to cooperate.'

Carl looked at the doorway and saw a black beard and a large shtrelimel hat pass the opening. His frantic eyes sought the other door and shrank from a similar vision of the reminder of his own origins. He licked his dry lips and muttered hoarsely through his tightened throat. 'What do you want me to do?'

'You have no choice Weisz. You will renounce all directorships, chairmanships, and all connections with your corporative businesses. You will sign a transfer deed to the ownership of your private shares and an authority to each bank to sell should they so wish. I have the papers here for your signature.' Peter took his slim briefcase and removed a sheaf of closely typed pages from the leather container. 'I have placed a cross in every space where you are required to sign. Do so.'

Maximillian scrawled his name to each piece of paper as it was handed to him. All were signed in the name of Maximillian Holst. Even the authority to his last private funds in the Trust funds in Liechtenstein. He had never risked any of his former names being recognised and coming back to accuse him. His former proud stance was gone. Even his great form seemed to have shrunk into the voluminous topcoat that he wore against the winter chill. He walked slowly to the door without a backward glance and made his way to the exit. No one recognised him. His military bearing was gone. His ebullient extrovert image no longer existed. To those around him, he was a face in a crowd. As uniform as one ant among others.

No taxi waited for him. No Rolls pulled smoothly to the pavement. He did not carry any money so could not use a bus, even if he knew how. He had to walk. Even as he walked his over active mind sought a solution to this outrage. The banks would not help. His accountants and lawyers could not help. His friends... suddenly he realised that he had no friends. All had deserted him the moment that his demise was made public. As soon as the gravy train stopped, all the passengers had alighted. He was alone, and for the first time in his life he was lonely. What could this imposter from the past prove against him? Nothing. Who would stand up in court, if it came to that, and testify against the great Maximillian Holst? Very few war criminals had been prosecuted, certainly none as obscure as he had been. No, it was all a confidence trick, a device to rob him of his rightful place in the world. He would call an extraordinary meeting of the board of his controlling company, the Global Publishing Company. He would set the record straight, as he always did. His word was absolute, no matter what the rules of Company Law said. He would remain Chairman of his companies; the bits of paper extracted from him by force would not stand against his continued control of his empire.

His walk quickened and he almost felt alive again. He was back in business. Back into his fighting mood, using all necessary ploys to counter this attack on his integrity. Not for one minute did he consider that he was other than a benefactor to the thousands of investors, providers of finance, employees, accountants, lawyers, and any of the incalculable number of people hanging on his every word. The door to the lobby leading to his apartment stood ajar. Men were jostling each other and talking excitedly. The doorman was hopelessly outnumbered as he tried in vain to push them back on to the pavement.

Suddenly they saw him and rushed as one to surround his impressive figure. That was how it should be, he nodded, smiling his ingratiating smile for their benefit. What did they want? These hangers on of the gutter press. He always had a few words for them to lift his profile even further. They lapped it up. And so did the public.

'Is it true Mr. Holst?'

'What will you do now?'

'Why have you reneged on your readers by selling your shares?'

'What will you do now Holst?'

The questions were flung at him before he had a chance to launch into his well known oratory. The last question bit into his pride the most. Being addressed as "Holst" pierced his thick skinned protective barrier, developed over the years to deal with journalistic scum like these. But hadn't he employed the same strata of degenerates to fabricate stories for his newspapers? 'All reports, from whatever source, can be treated with the disdain they deserve. They are so factually untrue they are beneath comment.' Not a flicker of embarrassment touched his florid face. Only his blue-black eyes held the anger and the fear raging throughout his body. The events of the last few days had moved too swiftly for him to counteract the hundreds of rumours circulating in the media. His media! Even his editors were joining the jackals, eager to see him discredited and humiliated. They had the facts now. Solid facts about his shady deals and the fabrication of the balance sheets. No one had the precise details of the true position – that would come in time when independent auditors were appointed to tear his figures apart and reveal to the world that the solid foundation of his conglomerates was mostly paper. Paper which he had made to look infallible. He pushed through the arms and bodies blocking his way, never necessary before, and entered his private lift, sweating at his exertions. The first item he noticed in his mail box was a letter from the landlord of the block which he leased. He recognised the envelope and the significant registered letter stamp in the left hand corner. So what if his rental had not been paid for twelve months? He had left it for that long before hadn't he? But then, he was all powerful, and had funds at his disposal, even if he was reluctant to pay his dues. His debts were considered sound weren't they? Until now.

The disease is spreading. Like a cancer. Each cell is collecting and infecting other cells along the way, charging like a stampede of buffalo, with nothing to stop the inevitable crash at the end. Maximillian poured himself a very large brandy. His mind refused to accept that inevitability as he slowly drank himself into a drunken stupor.

Peter Mallory clutched the briefcase to his chest as he climbed into the taxi at the front of the Victoria and Albert Museum. His life's work had been completed and he felt strangely unemotional. He expected to feel triumphant, overjoyed, ecstatic. Only a sense of emptiness filled him as the taxi wound its way along the Cromwell Road and on past Hyde Park to the small restaurant in Regent Street, where he was to meet Wendy. And his mother.

'It is finished.' he said, so simply that his wife and mother reached out to him over the coffee table and joined him in his silent prayer for the father and sister who could not be there to share their thanks to God.

The tears of joy and sadness rolled down Wendy's face as she remembered Peter's words on that first night in their little cottage in Stretton nine years ago. "And now it begins." It had started to snow again as the three left the restaurant and said their goodbyes. Susan to return to her house in Chiddingfold, Wendy to the National Bank Head Office in Bishopsgate, and Peter to his mundane job at the Bank's Inspection Department. 'We shall celebrate tonight,' he said as they kissed twice on each cheek.

'It is Thursday,' said his mother. 'Why not wait until Saturday night. I feel much more relaxed at weekends. And we can invite some friends.'

Peter and Wendy both agreed that Susan's idea was common sense.

Susan watched as Peter and Wendy disappeared down the Marble Arch Underground steps. Her expression changed to one of concentration as she studied the shopping list she took from her handbag. Nodding to herself she set off in search of the items listed in her neat handwriting. The same grim determination of purpose that Sergei had been unable to expunge, fixed its inexorable grip on her mind. It is not finished, she murmured softly to herself.

CHAPTER XV

Friday 19th December 1980

Clive Farnworth studied the report from his special assistant, not too neatly typed by the two index fingers of the short, insignificant, mousy individual who had worked for him for as long as he could remember. It was wise to have a personal aide who knew his ways and methods and who would report only to him. Hence the self typed, double spaced, junior school spelled contribution before him.

It was headed "Report on Peter Mallory and his movements on Thursday 18th December 1980."

Clive smiled. The heading could not be more descriptive. No subterfuge or dressing up of the words. Just the plain statement of facts. That was why he warmed to this man so much. He had obtained permission from Scotland Yard to include him on the payroll, but further than that, no one really knew what he did. Except for Clive.

The three page report provided some very interesting observations of Peter Mallory's day. The writer was not in the least concerned with the whys and wherefores of what happened, commenting only on the actualities that he had witnessed. These had been faithfully recorded in every detail and submitted to his chief, as he called him, for his assessment.

Clive reached for the telephone and pushed the single button that would automatically connect him with George Parker at the Inspection Department of the National Bank.

'George Parker. What can I do for you?'

'It's not what you can do for me George, but rather what I can do for you.'

'Oh it's you Clive. I thought you had fallen out with me. Or you had given up on the case.' George's sarcasm, beautifully toned to induce a quiet laugh from the other end of the telephone, settled the couple into their conspirational mood immediately.

'I have something which may interest you George. The final pieces that you have been looking for in the Mallory case. You remember the one do you?' he queried, returning the sarcasm.

'OK Clive. So you think you have the answer do you? Well I think I have the answer too. As a matter of fact, that is why I am working late today. What is your excuse?'

Clive looked at his Seiko wristwatch. It showed 6.15pm. Goodness he thought, I had no idea it was that late. 'I never regard time as a barrier to a true investigation George. Crooks work unsociable hours, so why should we be exempt? If you want to catch them, you have to work the same hours, right?'

'My sentiments exactly Clive. Now that we have established the demarcation lines of our individual employment, can we get on to the vital information that you rang me about in the first place?'

'When would you like to see the report on Peter Mallory which my man has just delivered to my office?'

'Why not now? I have some news for you also. We just might be able to help each other.' It was George's turn to laugh and enjoy immensely the gentle banter between them that made their working relationship so much a pleasure. That and the satisfaction of bringing to a conclusion the few really puzzling frauds that cropped up from time to time. This one was the daddy of them all, he could sense that, and his adrenalin had never been higher in the overweight, abused lump that he called his body.

He heaved himself out of the chair and nodded to the cleaning lady. He waited for the usual caustic comment as she assiduously mopped the shining passageway leading to his office.

'You still 'ere sir? Ain't you got no 'ome to go to?'

'Yes. And no.' George paused and the cleaner looked up expectantly, sensing something different about the usual chat. 'How long have we known each other Ethel?'

Ethel Simpson glowed when George Parker used her christian name. He said it in such a way that she felt equal and not the skivvy as most regarded her. 'About eleven years sir. Give or take the odd week or two.'

'Eleven years eh Ethel?' She preened again as her name resounded in the empty office. 'That's a long time, but then in a lifetime, it can be oh so short. I feel I've known you all my life, but I suppose when we retire it will be like the passing of the number nine bus that takes me home from time to time.'

Ethel could not exactly follow George's philosophy or where it was leading but dutifully waited, leaning on her mop for the next words.

'It's like the bank Ethel. You work for an organisation for all your life and you think you know it. But every now and then, it clobbers you with impersonal decisions that have obviously come from individuals who have as much knowledge about the banking system as the cleaners do. Sorry, no insult intended but you know what I mean don't you?'

'I do sir. I can't say that I understand anything about your side of this business, but my side is my realm. I know what materials I need for cleaning – them that decides otherwise don't have to use the blasted stuff they force on me. "All in the cause of uniformity" they say. Well they can keep their uniformity. That doesn't bottom the muck as my cleaners do. I shall carry on using what I like for as long as I'm employed, so there.'

George admired this resolute lady. A gem in all the humdrum administration that was slowly taking all the enjoyment out of working with colleagues from the old days. Where values mattered and not profits. Results in job satisfaction, and not results in the FT Index. The impersonalisation of banking was slowly eroding the relationship between banker and customer, and employee and employer. He shook his head sadly.

'You and I are alike Ethel. We know our job and we just want to be left alone to do it. It's as simple as that.'

'I'm with you there sir. Leave me to mine, and they can 'ave theirs. Goodnight sir, sleep tight.'

George watched as she swept her bucket under her forearm and marched as straight as any Grenadier Guard to her cubby hole at the end of the corridor. Nothing would ever daunt that spirit smiled George – I must remember to get her a nice box of chocolates for christmas.

The French restaurant hastily arranged a table for two in the corner as Clive and George made their apologies for not making a reservation. 'It is quite OK,' lisped Bertand, 'we 'ave just the last table available for you.'

The two men nodded their appreciation and settled themselves in the quiet corner, refreshed by the two Kir Royales that appeared as if by magic in front of them.

'So what's your news Clive?' said George as he studied the stiff vellum handwritten menu that he knew by heart.

'Don't disturb a fellow when he is at important business.'

George looked up to see Clive heavily engaged in reading the wine list, having dispensed with the menu already.

The important matters of food and drink were duly dealt with by the Maitre D' and the cards returned to the hovering waiter. 'Now,' said George. 'What was so special about the report from your man? Has he found where all the missing money is? Why it was stolen? And who actually took it?'

'More or less, yes to all three questions. At least the information gives us plenty to speculate about on those issues. When you have heard the report, then I will be surprised if you do not come to the same conclusion as I have.'

George took the three folded pages, adjusted his reading spectacles, stubbed out his pre-dinner cigarette and lapsed into a concentrated silence. Clive sipped his second Kir Royale and eyed the bottle of Meursault in the ice bucket. He remembered with a certain dreaminess his trip to the Cote de Beaune, down through Alexe Corton land, home of the best burgundies, past the communes of Pommard and Volnay to Meursault, stopping just short of the supreme Puligny and Chassagne Montrachets, the finest vineyards of them all. 'Penny for your thoughts Clive. Or are they private?'

'Sorry George. I was back in the land of Burgundy, anticipating the bottle, I suppose.' He brought his attention back to the matter in hand. 'What do you make of it?'

'I think it is the moment we have been waiting for Clive. Your chap certainly connects Peter Mallory with Holst. And the mother and wife. Also conclusive is the presence of the Jewish fraternity. From the description of their movements, I don't think they were there to give their blessing to Holst do you?'

'No. From the moment that Holst left his apartment to the time he returned to it, my man was with him. Another agent followed Peter once the connection had been made. I might add that my man has inside information from one of the Hassidim Jews that Holst is one of them, but has been ostracised from the religion because of his wartime activities. They have supported Peter Mallory in all that he has done over the past nine years. Today's meeting was the culmination of those years and certain papers were extracted from him. Peter Mallory had those in his possession. I'd love to see the contents, wouldn't you?'

'Perhaps you will have the chance Clive. Now for my bit of news. Peter came to me today and requested a meeting with the board of the bank. Just like that! I told him that it was not quite as easy as that. Most live out of London, some do not even attend all of the meetings, let alone the unofficial ones. He requested that he meet them tomorrow, Saturday.'

'He what?!'

'Tomorrow. Said it was in the interest of this bank and the consortium of bankers supporting Maximillian Holst. Could I get them together for a morning meeting?' George took a breath as if reliving his reaction to Peter's request.

'Well did you?'

'Did I what?'

'Convene a meeting?'

'Of a sort – yes. When I mentioned the matter to the Chief General Manager he got very excited, especially as I also told him that I had news of the biggest fraud against the bank that he could ever envisage. "This is no time to prevaricate on what day the meeting takes place," I told him. The quicker we act the sooner we can take action to prevent any further leakage of funds. I didn't tell him that the leakage had dried up in any case after the installation of the new main frame computer. That shook him and he sent urgent telephone calls and personal messengers to all the directors and General Managers to drop whatever they had planned for the weekend and attend the meeting. No excuse would be tolerated.'

‘Calm down George, you sound as if you had run after them all yourself. Enjoy your meal – slowly – and talk me through your estimation of the situation vis a vis Peter Mallory and Maximillian Holst. If you think you know that is,’ he added, spooning the last piece of scampi into his wryly grinning mouth.

Over the next hour and a half, George went through his theory with Clive, comparing notes on their separate investigations into the nefarious activities of Holst and Peter Mallory. Most of it coincided, they were glad to learn and the whole picture took on a logical sequence as they pieced together the information. At the end, both had enough evidence to put to their respective employers to convince them that all was not as rosy as they were determined to believe.

‘By the way Clive. You are invited. I specially requested your presence as the matter concerns the Serious Fraud Office. The directors all objected strongly, maintaining that they could deal with an internal matter themselves and that to broadcast it to the public would not, as they put it, be in the public’s interest. Ironical isn’t it. When they are to be revealed as the victim of a gigantic fraud, they don’t want anyone, especially the police to know about it. I pointed out that they could not, and should not, hide it under the table. You already knew of the possible extent of the fraud and the connection with your man, so they had no alternative but to allow you to be there. But on one condition. You can only act on what you hear with the express permission of the board, as anything revealed will not be allowed as evidence in any case. I told them that this would be in order. You agree?’

Clive took a deep breath. ‘Do you think that Peter Mallory is going to confess? For what reason. He must know that you have no definite proof that he has done anything. What is his motive?’

‘That, my dear friend, we shall find out tomorrow. Now eat your Dover sole and tell me some of your less salubrious tales of the shadier side of Scotland Yard.’

‘I can do that or I can tell you of a breakthrough in our investigations into the banking system in Liechtenstein.’

‘That would be impossible, they keep their business as tight as our staff expenses purse.' George saw Clive's innocent expression beneath the raised eyebrows, denoting that he had scored once again over his bosom friend. 'You haven't traced the trustees of Niemand Nominees have you?'

A Cheshire cat smile spread across Clive's face as he slowly nodded before he finished the last dregs of his burgundy. He knew he was irritating George by prolonging the agony in wiping each side of his mouth with a napkin and delicately folding it onto his lap again.

'Well? What have you found out?'

'Patience George. The news will be all the better for hearing it over your brandy. That is if you are having one.'

'Bertand! Two brandies please – the usual.'

Bertand hurried to the drinks cupboard and produced their special bottle of Reme Martin. The measures were precisely poured to accommodate the crystal tumblers waiting on the table. 'Leave the bottle Bertand. I've a feeling that we shall need it.' George's request was hardly necessary as he downed the first brandy and replenished his glass before Bertand had a chance to remove the bottle.

'Through various connections and favours owed to me by my correspondents in the finance industry, I do so like to call it that don't you?, I have been able to put together quite a file on our two friends regarding the ownership of the bulk of the shares in Holst's companies. As you know the D.T.I. have been investigating him for some years, but have not been able to gather sufficient evidence that will stand up in court to bring any charges. He has been very clever in that his name is very rarely linked to the share deals, the bogus sale and purchase of the same stocks from one company to another, or the moving of those stocks to support auditors' certificates as to their existence. The only time that he admits to having the controlling interest is through his trust holdings. As he must be the main trustee, if not the sole trustee, then he can dictate to that trust what he requires it to do. All instructions are routed through the international telephone system on private lines, but as you know George, nothing is private if you know how to crack the code.' Clive sat back and watched with satisfaction, the expression on

George's face as he waited for the inevitable.

'We, George, that is my team and I . . . '

'Yes yes Clive, dispense with the salad dressing and get to the meat.'

'As I said George, patience brings its own reward. As I was saying, my team and I have had access to certain calls from this country to Liechtenstein, from which we have been able to discover that Maximillian Holst has bought and sold shares in his own companies, through the trust, to bolster the prices from time to time, or to obtain an unfair advantage over his competitors by falsely boosting his sales figures.'

'But how does that help us in our particular quandary?' George was getting more impatient as Clive seemed utterly detached from the urgency of the situation. Tomorrow was the day when George had to have the vital information to put before the board, notwithstanding anything that Peter Mallory may or may not say. 'Explain yourself Clive and stop playing Sherlock Holmes.'

'Certainly my dear Watson. The crucial point I am coming to George, is that during our . . . er, observations, it became apparent that Holst was not the only one engaged in financial jiggery pokery. A certain other person, with a name familiar to both of us was issuing similar instructions on behalf of another trust maintained in that haven of tax evaders. I don't have to give you his name surely?'

'It certainly wasn't Peter Mallory I know that. Even he would not be silly enough to connect himself with an alien trust. It would be too dangerous, especially over a period of nine years.'

'Exactly George. But who would suspect that he used his real name to set up a trust? The trust that we all know has been matching Holst's for control of his companies. I am talking of course, about Niemand Nominees, the present majority shareholder of Holst's publishing empire.'

'But who is the trustee then? You admit that it isn't Peter Mallory. Is it his mother? His wife? Who?'

Clive was enjoying himself enormously. It was a long time since he had been able to hold forth for so long against his friend's growing agitation.

He savoured the moment, drank his second brandy, and frowned as George lit yet another cigarette.

'The name, George of the trustee which we seek is Lazar Kawalek. Otherwise known as Lazar Peter Kawalek, alias Peter Mallory, presently employed by the National Bank in your own department.'

'I knew it!' exclaimed George, almost spilling his drink but managing somehow to dowse his cigarette with the dribbles from his mouth. 'Niemand Mr. Farnworth, Niemand. That's what he said. Nobody Mr. Farnworth, nobody. Of course he was saying that Niemand will account for the hundreds of Jews betrayed. He meant that the Niemand Trust would take on the task of atoning for the unforgivable sin that had been perpetrated against the Jewish community. They have waited all these years to seek their revenge. And that revenge has been orchestrated by Peter Mallory, an innocent victim with his family of the atrocity committed by Maximillian Holst.'

'I think you have got it in one George. No doubt tomorrow, you will have the missing pieces to your jigsaw given to you by Peter Mallory. Or maybe that he will simply tell the board that he has taken the money and they can whistle for it.'

George pondered over his third brandy. His eyes bore the look of inebriation, but he was as sober as the teetotallers sitting on the next table. They had drunk only iced mineral water all evening and George wished that he had too.

'I am fairly happy with Peter and Wendy. It is the mother, Susan that I have a funny feeling about. She doesn't seem the type to accept that destroying Holst is the epitome of justice. It isn't in her character. She loves, and possibly hates, too much.'

'You worry too much George. You are getting morbid. And you smoke too much. Why don't you stop. It'll kill you you know.'

'So will breathing in these fumes from the street, but nobody can stop that can they? Besides I enjoy smoking. Why live the rest of my life in misery?'

Clive sighed. He had heard it all before and admitted that he could do little about it. Anyway George without a cigarette wouldn't be George, and he loved him for what he was didn't he? 'There is one other thing that you have reminded me of George. Susan, the mother. She left the family group after the meeting with Holst and went shopping on her own.'

'So?'

'She purchased a reel of cotton amongst other things and one other peculiar item for a woman of sixty seven.'

'What was that?'

'It was in one of those memorabilia shops that seemed to have sprung up in the Oxford Road. You know they sell everything from Uncle Sam's hat to the purple heart, and armour and medals and every contraption connected with warfare.'

'Don't tell me she bought a gun!'

'No George. Quite different to that. When my man enquired of the proprietor he produced the same article that she had bought. No doubt you had one when you were small George, and carried it to school with your satchel. It was in a brown cardboard box with a string to put over your shoulder.'

'A gas mask?'

'Yes George, a gas mask. A world war II gas mask. Now why, do you think, does she want one of those?'

CHAPTER XVI

Saturday 20th December 1980

It wasn't a particularly cold December, not like the one of 1941 in Berlin when the bitter air froze the fear in the hearts of the Jewish inhabitants being taken away in ice cold trucks. Blood, nerves, souls froze. The whole population froze at the thought of their destination. Even their words were uttered with the same cold snap as icicles plunging into the snow below from white cluttered gutters. The whole world was frozen in disbelief. And ignorance.

Susan put the pictures out of her mind as the 9.10am train to London pulled into the tiny Witley station. The usual batch of passengers were ensconced in their favourite seats, contemplating the day ahead. Several acknowledged good mornings were exchanged and the engine changed its note to a high whir and moved into the countryside. Just like always, nodded Susan. Everything must be like always. They to their business or shopping in the city, me to my cleaning duties.

She wore the dark green overall of the professional 'Inner Cleaning Company' under her thick brown herring bone coat. A matching fawn hat with a small brim pulled over one eye was enough to give the impression of someone of the lower class going about her business also. She smiled as she clutched the large handbag cum shopping bag on her lap. The final journey. The last time that she would work for the 'Inner Cleaning Company' – her resignation would be posted early next morning and she would have finished her five year stint as the executive cleaner to special clients on the company's books.

She thought of Sergei and the devotion and understanding he had shown over the years. She was glad that it would be over at last. The releasing of the soul, the freeing of her spirit, the final cleansing of the canker that she had inherited from that same day in 1941 when the shattering of her front door heralded the start of a nightmare...

George Parker rose early for a Saturday morning. His usual cup of tea and an hour's read of the Daily Express was forsaken for once. He had to put the finishing touches to his presentation to the National Bank Board of Directors. He also had to assess how he would react to whatever Peter Mallory had to say. A confession? A statement of his involvement in the fraud? Or was he just being clever and announcing that he had information as to who and how the fraud had been committed? The thought stopped George in his tracks. Had he been wrong all along? Was somebody else responsible for the missing funds? What missing funds? He had still to convince the board that funds were missing. No deficit showed in the bank's books. No imbalance of the balance sheet showed that there was any defalcation to be traced. George grimaced. If his memory of the members of the board was accurate, it was going to be a masterful piece of oratory to even get them to accept that someone, somewhere, had slowly filtered the bank's money to some source other than to the bank's coffers.

A quick telephone call to Clive confirmed that he too had prepared his side of the equation as regards the involvement of Maximillian Holst. How or why was again the most difficult hypothesis to justify to the woolly intellect of the majority of the board. 'We'll just have to take it as it comes, George. Be prepared for any eventuality.'

George settled down to study for the last time, the printouts gathered in a great mass on his dining table. If his theory didn't impress them, his intimate knowledge of the source and product of the bank's trading, translated into sterling profits, would. They would always listen to any argument that concerned profits. Or the lack of them.

He heard Susan's train pass within a quarter mile of his place as it wound its way through the suburbs of Haslemere and on to Godalming and the stockbroker belt where most of the directors dwelt. They were going to get a nasty surprise, smiled George.

Peter dressed in his best city suit with the faint pin stripe and a bank tie. Shiny black plain fronted shoes; he never could bother with shoe laces; completed the ensemble. Wendy had laundered and pressed his crisp white shirt and impeccable collar. He too packed his bulky papers into the black leather briefcase, purchased for him as a leaving gift from his colleagues in Manchester. The meeting was due to start at 11am. Lunch had been arranged, as Peter had intimated to George that no one should expect to leave much before 5pm. He looked at his watch. 9.20am. The next train into King's Cross was in five minutes. The walk from the house took only three minutes. He boarded the train precisely at 9.25am and settled in his seat to read the morning's news.

"Crisis at magnate's news corporation HQ. Serious doubts are being aired about the viability of several of Maximillian Holst's companies." The city has taken the stand of at least supporting the current share prices at the last dealings on Friday afternoon. Even so the market took the largest tumble for seven years as a result of the rumours. "It is understood that a statement will be made early next week to 'clear the position' as Holst put it. Can the miracle worker perform the impossible once again?"

Peter let the semblance of a smile pass his lips. If I were a gambler, he reflected, I could make quite a killing over the next week... if I were a gambler.

Lord Quarnley climbed into his company Jaguar holding a slim briefcase in which were several closely typed papers and a breakdown of the last year's profits of the National Bank. As chairman it was his duty to attend all meetings and unofficial meetings. The Chief General Manager usually briefed him on the content of each meeting and they colluded in the presentation of the annual results as far as the press announcement was concerned. Dress it up a little, but be as honest as the results dictate. That had been his motto and no one in Fleet Street could accuse him of deliberately misleading the public. Indeed he went out of his way to point out the extreme steps that had been taken by the bank to keep the public and his customers informed. This in its turn was a good ploy to attract more customers and boost the share value even further. Although he was not unduly worried by today's meeting, it was some time since the bank had convened to discuss "matters which could have a grave impact on the future profits of the bank and its standing in the market place of one of 'highest integrity."' The subject disturbed him. He had every confidence in his team of professional bankers, but when it came to carrying the can, he was the one in the firing line. Thank goodness I have my rolling contract all sewn up, he assured himself. He sank into the comfort of the rear seat of his customised Jaguar with an equal comfort of mind as he thought of his eventual pay off. If and when that day arrived.

Several of the other members of the board had uneasy doubts after the brief details of the meeting had been explained to them by the secretary, Sir John Beenham, who in turn had been briefed by George Parker. Every member but one had been contacted to attend and had agreed in view of the urgency of their secretary's summons.

At precisely 10.59am Lord Quarnley tapped the oak plate stand with his small hand carved gavel to indicate that the meeting was under way. Eighteen faces turned as one to meet the gaze of one of the most influential men in finance. He had been confidently tipped to take over as Governor of the Bank of England within the next five years. Or sooner he thought to himself, if this meeting should dictate a swift resignation and acceptance of the position secretly being held for him.

'Gentlemen. Let me begin by apologising for this very extra-ordinary meeting, convened at such short notice, and to thank you all for attending what will, I sincerely hope, be worthy of the effort and sacrifice that all of you have undoubtedly made today.'

George Parker swore under his breath and grimaced at Clive. Clive returned the opinion by a slight lift of his ginger eyebrows. Both had the satisfaction that whatever the content of Peter Mallory's speech, George would have them reaching for their valium long before the five o'clock deadline.

Susan Mallory alighted from the banging door arrival of her local train to the disembodied echoing of the station's announcements rushing around the glass roof to lose themselves in the muffled tones of metal fatigue of the loudspeakers. No one listened. No one could understand. She wondered idly how many people actually tried to decipher the hollow voices competing with the multifarious sounds of a railway station.

Waterloo was not the best of stations to exit from. She walked steadily through the great doors set under the Anderson shelter like roof and on to the main road to the Thames. As always she walked with her head held high, although in pain, with a strong, steady, almost marching step that had never left her since her days in the girl guides. Gone was the stoop and the frail appearance of a London 'char.' She was Susan Mallory and she had a job to do and she was proud. The last job. The day she had waited for, for thirty nine years. The resolute front that had been so much a barrier to Sergei was visible in full force. All the ghosts of all the captive Jews returned to sustain her as she walked the footbridge over the Thames and made her way towards the West. It was only a short walk from the southern aspects of Hyde Park to Knightsbridge and her job for that day. Her pass key let her into the fifth floor apartment, but she did not take with her the usual trolley or cleaning utensils. Today's job was different. She set about arranging the pure white leather chairs and sofas into a position where all faced inwards. A visit to the kitchen ensured that her preparation would not be impaired. She noted with satisfaction that the Russian lighter stood on the occasional table beside the cigar box. One final check. The brass scales, purloined from a reluctant banker, stood on the desk under the window. The weights, polished to a golden sheen by herself, diverted the morning sun's bright rays into the unblinking eyes of the calmest woman in London. The occupant would be back at about noon; it said so in his diary. She took a small notebook out of her bag and waited.

'Let me introduce you first of all to our... visitors.' Lord Quarnley paused while he consulted his notes. 'Firstly, in the unlikely event that you do not know our Chief Fraud Officer, may I present Mr. George Parker...' George half rose, nodded and sat down. 'On his left, is the Head of the Scotland Yard Serious Fraud Squad Clive Farnworth...' Clive did as George had done. 'Sounds ominous doesn't it?' Lord Quarnley attempted a laugh but swallowed it. 'And finally, at the head of the table is Peter Mallory, a manager attached to our Fraud Office, who I understand originally asked for this meeting.' Peter did not rise. The others looked at him curiously. They were not used to dealing with anyone less than General Manager status and his presence somewhat undermined their collusive harmony.

'Before I ask our visitors to explain what we are gathered here for, I would ask you to consult the folders in front of you to refresh your memory of the results of the bank over the past nine years. The figures have been specially requested by Mr. Parker as they relate to his presentation later this morning. Is that correct Mr. Parker?' George nodded his agreement and the Chairman continued. 'To sum up the gist of what we are about to hear, I will read the note that Mr. Parker had delivered to me. It says . . . bluntly . . . that over the past nine years this bank has suffered a loss of income from its various activities, far in excess of any sums ever recorded in the history of British banking. Rather a bold statement to make, wouldn't you think? But having dealt with Mr. George Parker before, I do not think that he would presume to make such a statement unless there was infallible evidence to support such an assertion.' Every face again turned to the walrus mustachioed visage of the solemn George Parker, shuffling his papers impatiently and wishing that the Chairman would get on with it. 'I therefore would like to hand you over in the first instance to our Fraud Officer to open the debate. You will note that it is to be called a debate for the time being as the minutes are to be regarded as highly secret and not for anyone's ears outside of this room.' The secretary nodded and pursed his lips as he poised over the blank pad in front of him.

'Mr. George Parker.'

George rose and adjusted his stance, looked at the Chairmen and said. 'Do you mind if I sit down for this Mr. Chairman? it could be a long session. Oh . . . and do you mind if I smoke?'

With a chorus of relieved sighs agreeing with him, he lit up and joined the half dozen or so cigarette smokers of the board.

'You have heard the Chairman's statement. Or rather my statement of the possible misappropriation of funds from the bank. I say possible because although I am convinced of the efficacy of my investigations, there could be a simple explanation for the apparent loss of funds through the computer system ...' George glanced at Peter and was pleased to see a thankful acknowledgement from him that he was not being accused before he had said what he had come here to say.

'As I was saying. For the past two years, it has become more and more evident that returns from our commissions and interest charges, while keeping pace with inflation and the various exigencies of charging systems, have produced the expected returns. You will note that I say that we have received the "expected" returns. That in itself is what made me suspicious in the first place.' George bent and selected a printout from his pile. 'Without going into too much detail, I can tell you that the margins that are allowed from each branch bank of the total sums expected from their lending interest and account commission have come up to the required percentage.' He paused. 'Exactly within the parameters given to each branch.' He paused again. Every eye was on his. 'That cannot happen in a non-uniform world. No set of figures agree quarter after quarter, year after year, to such a degree. There has to be a wider variance ...' George saw that he was losing some of the group ... 'To give a simple example. Averages are obtained by adding together all the figures and dividing by the number of figures, right?' They nodded. 'But what if all of the figure from which the average is to be calculated are the same, or almost the same?' They were with him ... 'the answer agrees exactly with that expected, but the first set of figures represents a normal spread from highest to lowest. That is always in the nature of things in any aspect of accounting.' George saw the look of quiet admiration on Peter's face. I'm on to him and he knows it breathed George while he dragged on his almost spent cigarette. He slowly lit another while the gist of what he had said sank in. 'From this printout and the following printouts, one for every quarter since 1971, the returns on commission and interest have been within the band of 1.1% to 2.7% of the overall bank lending figures and between 1.4% and 2.9% of the interest earning deposit account figures.' George looked at each director in turn, seeing more than a curious acceptance of his diatribe from the 'working' members of the board; the General Managers, who dealt with details such as these day after day. 'Nothing unusual about that, you might say. But if I tell you that of the 3,000 odd branches submitting their returns for the nine years detailed here on the desk, some 2,958 quoted a figure of 1.3% for lending and 1.8% for deposits, you will draw your own conclusions. Like the average example I gave you a moment ago, the odds against that must be incalculable. i.e. somewhere the income to the bank is being syphoned off. How, I do not pretend to know. Perhaps, you might think, one of our computer programmers could have enlightened me. No they couldn't. I have asked them and they say it is impossible. But the impossible is happening gentlemen and I have the relevant figures to prove it.' From the sheaf of papers in his briefcase, George distributed copies of each quarter's figures together with the expected returns and the sums which, in his opinion, had been gleaned from the annual harvest. He watched their reaction with growing confidence as they finally realised the enormous implication of what he was saying.

Clive encouraged him with a nod and actually lit the virgin cigarette dangling from his mouth. 'Thanks Clive,' he whispered, 'do you think I have them?'

'If you haven't then I wouldn't bother any further. If they haven't seen the argument then they shouldn't be sitting here earning their appearance money.'

The Chairman rose. 'These are very grave accusations against our computer staff, and indeed against the banking system, if what you say is correct. How can we possibly prove your... theory. There are no ostensible funds missing. How can you prove a fraud if there is no shortfall?'

'If I may have one more minute, Mr. Chairman. I am hoping that the conundrum can be solved by our other guest. It is my submission that his presence here today has a great deal to do with the subject which is before you. Am I right Peter?'

The young man who had been virtually ignored during the previous discussion and discourse by the rumbustious George Parker, was now the centre of attention.

'Thank you Mr. Parker. Your... theory, as the Chairman put it, is perfectly correct. I am here to tell you how for the past nine years I have... borrowed... removed... diverted, call it what you like, a sum of money from the National Bank. That sum gentlemen, is in the region of £270 million pounds. I have the exact figures here and now I propose to tell you how, and why, it was done.'

Not a sound came from any member sat at the gargantuan walnut table on the sixth floor of the National Bank's headquarters in Bishopsgate. Too stunned to even gasp, they sat open mouthed as Peter began his story.

It was one minute past noon when Maximillian Holst walked into his apartment. As he closed the smooth expertly carved door behind him he stopped, observing the rearranged furniture. He was not afraid. He seldom was. The neat construction of a circle puzzled him rather than made him suspect an intruder. He crossed quickly to his wall safe behind the Lowry picture and checked the dial. No interference there. He swung the picture back over the safe, hardly noticing the Salford workers milling around their factory in rags. Paying homage to the owner who provided their means of staying alive. Just. Maximillian had purchased the work of art precisely for that reason. His public, relying on him, their mentor and saviour. That is what life is like and what life should always be like, he had scoffed as he saw the masterpiece hung on his wall.

Everything else seemed to be in its usual place. He hesitated... was there anyone in the apartment? He called out as he strode to the telephone to report... what? Nothing missing. Only chairs and sofas in their wrong place. He turned as he heard the change of air of an opening door.

'What are you doing here at this hour?'

The green overall clad figure walked into the room, maintaining eye contact with the uncertain gaze of her questioner. She deliberately sat in the white leather armchair facing inward from the picture window running the whole length of the flat. 'Sit down Carl.'

'How dare you address me like that! How dare you presume . . . '

'I said sit down Carl. I shall not ask you again.'

The resonance of her voice rang around the depths of Maximillian's brain cells, trying to find some semblance of recorded memory lost in the dark passages of time. Before he could identify the feeling of deja vu, he was interrupted by the voice again. Without realising it, he had sat down.

'You do not remember me do you Carl? Let me introduce myself. I am Susan Kawalek, wife of Werner Kawalek, mother of Lazar and Taghi . . . you remember now?'

A strangled gurgle escaped from the twitching mouth as Maximillian clutched at his throat. It could not be possible. They had all died. He had been assured that they had. This was all a dream. A result of the last few weeks of strain and the struggle to fend off the sharks of Fleet Street . . . and his creditors. 'I . . . I . . . '

'You thought we were dead, is that what you are trying to say? As you can see, I am very much alive.' Susan's eyes burned into his, conveying all the hatred that she had conserved for so long. 'And so is my son Lazar. But you already know that don't you?'

Maximillian's great capacity for adapting to a situation came to his rescue as he regained some of his equilibrium and bluster. 'What are you here for? What can you hope to achieve? Telling the newspapers won't altar things. They'll never believe you. A cleaning woman's word against the most important man in London? Ha!' His mind was working rapidly as he considered his options. She was in his flat. A cleaning lady. He could get rid of her as easily as throwing out the rubbish. But what of her son? Perhaps the best ploy would be to play it her way until he was sure of his ground.

Susan rose, crossed to the door and locked it with the key that Maximillian had carelessly thrown on the side table.

Her hand delved into her overall pocket and stayed there.

'That won't do you any good. I can easily overpower you and call for help.' He picked up the telephone and started to dial.

'It's dead Carl. Finished. Just like you. My son has done a good job over the years. He has taken everything you owned. You have nothing. No assets. No money. No one. Your life is finished. You have nowhere to run…'

'Why you…' Maximillian rose in his rage at the taunt of being a nobody. Reduced to the serf like Jew of his beginnings.

Before he could cross to Susan, she removed her hand from the pocket on her right thigh. 'I wouldn't do that if I were you Carl.' She stepped back and raised her right hand to show a dull metal object clenched in her fist, looking ridiculously like a small pineapple.

Maximillian's charge halted as if he had hit a brick wall.

'Yes, you recognise this don't you Carl? Not one of your playthings now is it? But you have had dealings with it in the past. A lot of money can be made out of armaments can't they Carl? especially if they have cost you nothing in the first place.' Susan walked steadily around the chair and sat in her original place. 'Sit down Carl, we have a lot of talking to do.'

This time, the large man did not hesitate. He knew that the object in her hand held him captive… for the moment.

'This Carl, is a hand grenade. It works on the principle of a chemically controlled fuse that will detonate its explosive TNT in four seconds. The outer iron shell will fragment and impact in all directions. Anyone standing within five yards of the explosion will be killed instantly.' The icy eyes never left his as she unfurled her fingers to reveal the deadly squared pattern beneath. 'You will note that the pin has been removed.' She showed him the small spindle concealed in her left pocket. 'Pulling the pin allows the lever at the top to spring up and start the time scale. My thumb is at present holding down the lever. As long as I maintain pressure on the lever we are safe.' Maximillian's face had gone from one of wild fury to a pasty grey. His eyes sunk even further beneath the thick black bushy brows as his tongue sought to moisten his parched dry lips. He was incapable of making any kind of sound as his throat constricted to force more oxygen to his heaving lungs.

'I have no fear of dying Carl. I have died once haven't I? A death that you could never even start to imagine. The cold of the washhouse floor.

The bare pipes and grey walls. The hiss as the first gas is released through the shower heads... but you know of these things don't you Carl? You have witnessed the killing of hundreds of Jews in this way haven't you? Haven't you!?' she screamed.

The drained hulk opposite barely managed to nod his answer as Susan continued. She told him of the families who had suffered. The deprivation and the hopelessness of those who were spared for a few more days. The children clinging to their gaunt parents, like starving dogs. She told him of the destruction of people's minds, their faith, their conception of reality. In the end, most were like zombies, wandering, lost in a world that was not real, waiting to die. The release they all craved for. The only inevitable conclusion to their existence on earth.

'Do you remember the families whom you betrayed Carl? The love that you destroyed? The future that you so callously tossed aside for your own gratification? Not just my family, but a hundred others. I have a list of names here Carl, would you like to read it? Perhaps you will remember the people who trusted you, who treated you as one of them. They have all gone now Carl. To a place that you can never hope to meet them again. But you will meet them here Carl. For I will bring them back to you... Raphael and Lucie Levy and their children, Paul and Suzanne Grinberg and their three children, Victor Weissman, his parents and brother, Elisha and Rosa Bernheim,... ' Susan deliberately read out the names of every family on the list. Sometimes stopping to describe in detail the family's circumstances before they were taken away. The list was endless. A chronicle of a whole community, taken from this earth by an evil force, countenanced by inhuman souls and ignored by governments. '... and finally the Rosenbergs. I never knew the father, but the mother was everything a mother could be.' She told him of Rosa Rosenberg and her little daughter on the brink of starvation. She told him of Rosa's death and of Katrina's re-birth. 'That small bundle of bones is now my adopted daughter. She has not replaced Taghi, no one could do that. But she has brought some sort of sanity back into my life.' Not a glint of a tear had moistened the steadfast eyes as she closed the notebook and replaced it in her handbag.

Maximillian showed no remorse or recognition of the names. Only the flickering fear in his dull stare gave an indication that he had heard the indictment against him.

Susan rose and crossed to the fireplace. 'Do you feel the cold Carl? I do. I have always felt the cold. It reminds me of the days in the camp when cold was as common as food was scarce. Thin emaciated bodies feel the cold Carl. Not like yours. Warmed by the cold inflicted on the poor wretches, as you stole their goods and their land. Did that keep you warm Carl. The knowledge that they could never return to claim their family possessions? Never return to avenge themselves for the bestial greed of scum like you?'

Susan stopped herself. Calmly she cautioned, it could not be done if her emotions took control of her actions. He had to suffer. Unemotionally as those in the death camps had had to suffer.

'We shall have a little warmth Carl. To keep away the winter chill.' The artificial coal fire, built into the wall, burst into life as she pushed the automatic lighting mechanism and turned the fire effect on full. The gas ignited and cast a rosy glow on the white pile carpet. 'Quite reminiscent of the bitter winters of Auschwitz isn't it Carl?'

Maximillian watched from his stance on the sofa, never letting his gaze wander from the right hand of Susan. For once in his life he was helpless. Any move and the lever would be sprung and they both would die. A sudden movement from Susan puzzled him. She had reached under the artificial coals and placed a small piece of metal, rather like a lamplighter's dowser over each gas jet in turn. The flickering fire stopped as each jet was smothered with the device. But the gas continued to hiss out of the small orifices.

Susan then went to the door and taking a reel of adhesive tape from her bag began to seal the gap between the left hand edge, continuing over the top along the lintel and down the other side. When she had finished she treated the window lights in the same way.

'What are you doing?...' Maximillian at last managed to gasp. But he knew the answer the minute she had put out the burning flames.

'I am creating a gas house Carl. These are far better surroundings than those Jewish families had to say their last goodbyes but it will have to do.'

'You can't! You can't just kill me like that! You'll never get away with it.' His bluster returned for a fraction as he half rose to rush to the door. Panicking he made for the kitchen, but was blocked by Susan brandishing the grenade in his face. 'Sit down Carl. We have a long wait.'

Maximillian was blubbering now, his legs unable to support him any more, tears rolling down his jowly cheeks, his hands beseeching the woman who sat opposite.

'What do you want me to do?' he implored.

'Do Carl? I want you to die. Slowly.'

A light lunch had been delivered to the bank's boardroom by impeccably dressed messengers, who departed as silently as they had arrived. The proceedings were interrupted for the briefest of moments while those who felt like eating, nibbled at the exquisite sandwiches and petit fours provided. Very few felt like eating.

Peter had been talking for almost an hour and the interest had not lagged for one second. This was the man who proclaimed to have committed the biggest fraud in history. And here he was calmly describing his childhood and the years following. They had heard of his German roots and the night when his family had been snatched, literally, on the 20th December 1941, for the death camps. The significance of the date did not escape George Parker's or Clive Farnworth's notice.

'I don't suppose that any of you here today have had the experience of ending your life as you know it within the space of twenty seconds. Everything that you have ever believed in, have ever enjoyed, have ever loved, destroyed by a force that you are unable to fight.' The gathered quorum fidgeted uneasily at how their own cocooned lives had protected them from such barbarity. Those who had fought in the war appreciated the degradation of the Jewish inhabitants of those countries who saw fit not to interfere with the genocide.

'After I escaped from the camp I made my way to England and found my grandparents in Weymouth. They educated me and cared for me. But my one ruling passion was to fulfil the promise that I gave to my mother. Even at the age of innocence, the thought never left my mind. To eventually account to the population who had been destroyed by one man above all others. That man's name was Carl Weisz. You know him better by the name he now uses. Maximillian Alexander Carl Holst.'

The intense attention to Peter's recount of his early years was broken by several gasps of astonishment as the directors stared in disbelief at Peter's assertion.

'Should any of you doubt my word, I would ask our other guest, Inspector Clive Farnworth to verify my statement.'

All eyes turned to Clive, some daring him to accuse such a captain of industry of such vile crimes. Clive opened his blue folder and read out the aliases of Carl Weisz and the data which had been gathered through his European network. 'And finally, this man took the name of Maximillian Holst shortly after landing in England.'

There were no questions.

'So gentlemen, at the tender age of sixteen, I formulated my plan to seek the justice that was ours. Mine, my family's and the hundreds of Jewish families who could not act. The question was: how do you defeat a man who has everything? A millionaire. The head of a publishing company that rightfully belongs to you? There is only one way. Beat him at his own game. For that I would have to have funds. The Jewish families living in England and those I still knew in Germany, hadn't the resources necessary to combat this bastion of the art of fraud. So, I joined the bank. Where else is there a ready source of funds of the size that I required?'

Despite the shocked faces of the directors, George could not help an involuntary chuckle, but managed to suppress it with a cough and a smothering handkerchief.

'I don't mean that I joined the bank with the express intention of stealing money from them. It seemed a good place and career to learn about making money through investments and discovering the world of business and how the entrepreneurs made their money. I soon realised that to amass the amount I would need to fight Holst would take more than shrewd investment. I am firmly of the belief that no one who makes millions, makes it completely honestly.' He looked at each in turn around the table as he placed his hand in his pocket and produced a small black box and placed it in front of him.

'This gentlemen, is the means by which I acquired the fortune that I mentioned earlier.' Opening the lid he took out a small white square of what looked like plastic. A flattened cube, no bigger than an Oxo. 'This is a microchip. The phenomenon of the twentieth century. It can control so many functions that the mind cannot conceive its capacity. But you probably know all about that.' Peter glanced in the direction of the Head of Computer Operations, a General Manager responsible for all accounting procedures. Leonard Crooks nodded, but raised his eyes to ask a question. 'I appreciate what you are saying, but our security is such that no rogue chip, if that is what you are implying, can be so changed and programmed to bypass the rigorous controls which we employ every minute of the day.' Heads nodded and turned once again to Peter.

'Agreed Mr. Crooks. But what if a new chip were introduced, alien to the rest of the microchips and programmed to do just what you have described as impossible?'

'No such chip exists.' The small grey haired man hesitated. 'To my knowledge.'

'If I may be permitted to fill in the gap between joining the bank and the start of my... operation. In 1961 my mother and her adopted daughter escaped from East Berlin. Naturally they came looking for me. You will remember that I thought my mother was dead. They contacted my grandparents to learn that they had died and left the property in trust for my mother and me. Even they had the faith to still believe that their daughter would return one day. I will not relate the eventual meeting as it is immaterial to this discourse, only to tell you that Katrina, my mother's adopted daughter eventually became my wife. There was the missing key. She had studied computers in East Berlin where the advancement in technology was far in excess of ours. She could programme computers to carry out any process, whatever the system was employed. She also agreed with Mr. Crooks that she could not amend a chip's instructions without it being spotted immediately. This is where her contacts in East Berlin provided the tool that I had been looking for. Her old teacher was a genius. Even at that stage in the late fifties and early sixties he had communication with his contemporaries in the USA who were experimenting with integrated circuits, so minute that this chip here,' the small white silicon square was held aloft as Peter showed its size, 'can hold 50,000 circuits, all programmed to act with or in isolation from their counterparts.' George was enjoying himself. He was enthralled at the revelations that Peter was making, ticking off in his own mind, the similarities to his own theories. But how did he amend the bank's computer system? Guaranteed foolproof by the makers and original programmers. George shrugged. There is no such thing as foolproof. Clive had told him that years ago. 'Always work on the premise that someone, somewhere, has the guile to go one step further than the protectors or guardians of our infallible boundaries.' He was hearing one such destroyer of the bastion of the bank's self satisfied complacency. He sat back to enjoy some more. Completely disloyal, but he surprised himself... he didn't care.

Peter went on to explain the intricacies of the chip he required, and with Katrina's or Wendy's help, the Jewish wizard in East Berlin constructed such a chip and smuggled it out to Susan's sister in Bad Durkheim. From there it was comparatively simple to swap it for the master chip in the central computer base in Cheshire.

The audacity of the scheme was only just having its effect on the older members of the board who were desperately trying to come to terms with the shock to their smug attitude of invulnerability. One had a question – Sir Michael Manders.

'How is it that you have managed, as you say you have, to... er... steal so many millions from the bank, if those in charge,' and he looked reprovingly at the General Managers, 'have not reported any loss?'

'You have heard Mr. Parker's earlier comments on the funds which never appear in our system. These funds are the dross, or fractions, that never get accounted for. Excesses that are less than the rounded off portions of interest application or commission amounts. Small sums of one or two, or sometimes more pence, which are dispensed with to save insignificant sums being applied to accounts. The easiest example to illustrate this is your foreign travel money. It never translates into exact exchange. There is always a surplus which the bank takes up at regular intervals and 'loses' it in its profits. Instead of the bank 'losing ' it, my chip passes it on with all the other surpluses from a hundred different sources. Think of the vast amounts being dealt with each day by the foreign exchange dealers; the arbitrage department; the transfer to international agents; the thousands of payments to foreign nationals. These are just the tip of the iceberg. Once installed, even I was astounded at the range of services it could affect, and take a percentage. When I tell you that in the last year of operation, and solely from the normal interest income, the chip netted £17.4 million, you will appreciate the scope of the enterprise.'

Shouts of anger greeted Peter's words as he sat and poured himself a glass of water from the carafe glinting on the polished table between him and the Chairman.

'And where is this money?'

'What have you done with it?'

'You are nothing but a common thief.'

Peter took the insults calmly and faced each in turn until the Chairman called for order.

Lord Quarnley cleared his throat. He realised that he was not dealing with an ordinary junior manager, an underling who he could fire or threaten with serious charges. There was a determined and almost proud aura to his confession, as if he was holding something back. He obviously didn't fear for the consequences of his theft. For that was what it was. So what was he doing here, throwing himself to the wolves?

'Supposing what you say is true, and we do not have any proof that you have… taken this money. What did you intend to do with it. Or rather what did you use the funds for?'

'I am coming to that. But to reassure you all that the money is safe, I have here certain documents and certifications of my holdings in various companies and investment houses in the city. The list, you will see, certifies that I hold, or rather my trust holds, the main block of shares in all of Maximillian Holst's companies. The trust in fact, has the power to close, or to save these companies. I believe that in all, the total borrowings of these companies from the consortium of bankers who backed Holst, is in the region of £547 million. The National Bank, I know are committed to £212 million of that sum. Your security is only worth two thirds of that at present on the open market if... and it is a big if. If the present opinion of the assets backing the share value is maintained. If that value is exposed, then the whole corporate business will collapse with vast debts and everyone will lose.'

The enormity of Peter's challenge set the adrenalin racing in George's blood. Not since his exposure of an international ring of Pakistani traders playing the uncleared's system in Manchester, had he felt so excited. He knew there was more to come. He was not disappointed.

'Look at your papers, gentlemen. The total value of the trust, the Niemand Nominees Trust, is £341 million. Slightly in excess of the amount that I have... purloined, shall we say.' George almost forgot to light his cigarette from the one in his mouth. His choking was a delight to Clive, who reminded him that it would kill him one day.

'Not before I've heard this out. I couldn't bear to miss it.'

'The main item that should interest you all is the heading at the top of your sheet that details the trustees of Niemand Nominees Trust.'

Scanning down the list of names unfamiliar to anyone in the room, George saw that most were of Jewish origin except the final entry. "NATIONAL BANK PLC" was there in bold letters.

'So you see gentlemen, the funds have always been in the bank's name from the moment that they left its premises.'

Peter rose and excused himself 'to stretch the legs and allow the board to assimilate the facts in front of them.'

The Chairman nodded weakly.

'I shall return in twenty minutes, at say 3.30pm to conclude my business and to put to you my proposition for saving the situation vis a vis Holst and his bankers.'

George watched in admiration and delight as the victor strode from the hallowed panelling of the boardroom, leaving in his wake the most stunned audience that had ever sat at an extraordinary meeting. And it was uniquely extraordinary, smiled George as he rose to follow Peter.

* * * * *

The incessant hiss of the gas jets contrasted sharply with the laboured breathing of Maximillian Holst. It was as if his body were trying to dispense with the necessity of sucking in the polluted air. But his lung muscles continued to jerk his body in great reluctant gasps, reminiscent of the last heaving shudders of a giant beached whale.

Susan's eyes were resolute. Her steady shallow breathing belying the torture inside her. 'We are dying Carl. Saying goodbye to the life we knew. You, of course, have nothing to leave. It has all gone. Like the homes and the memories of those Jews whose history is no more. Lifelines from before Christ, snuffed out as surely as I snuffed out those burners. I think they are a little fierce don't you? Let's turn them down a little. You are dying too quickly Carl. I want you to suffer. To remember all those who suffered because of you. All those poor souls who trusted you.' She moved to the fire and slowly decreased the burner level.

Susan returned to her handbag and took out a black rubberised object with a thick cellophane visor. A world war gas mask. She quickly donned the smelly mask and gratefully breathed the filtered air provided by the baffle. How long does this work for, she wondered?

Maximillian Holst's eyes were closed. His great body unable to face death or the woman who sat opposite. Each screaming gulp brought with it the face of one of the Jewish families of Berlin. Each had an accusing finger pointing at him. Long, spindly fingers, shorn of all rings and jewellery. Fingers with no nails, faces with no features, bare shaven heads and naked bodies, all burning, burning, and causing this foul, retching agony in his lungs. He wanted to die. But he didn't. The breathing continued and eased slightly. Was he going to be saved? Was it all a dream? Leo would save him. But Leo had been sacked. Someone, somewhere would save him, wouldn't they?

Susan's muffled voice came to him through the red haze in front of his eyes. He opened them and saw something from the depths of hell. A black headed monster with one large gleaming eye and protruding snout, moving ever closer to devour him. His scream rent the soundproof room and finding no exit, shot through his body to grind itself against the silent scream of his lungs.

'I calculate that it will take another hour and a half for you to take your last breath Carl. Or sooner should you care to strike a match. But that is not your way is it Carl? A coward to the end. Count the seconds, the minutes. Each one is a betrayed soul. A little girl. A young boy. A grandfather, an uncle. A whole family. They need to rest Carl. To sit with God and know that the cause of them being there is no more...'

It was difficult to talk now, as Susan rose and went into the kitchen. Her thumb was white from the pressure that she had exerted on the small metal grenade in her hand. She slowly opened her fingers and read the words stamped on the bottom. "Dummy. For training purposes only." Her aching thumb released the spring lever and the deadly looking but innocent device was replaced in her pocket. Suppressing a wry smile she took the small reel of cotton out of her bag and climbed on the stool. Above the tiled floor of the kitchen hung an antique lantern. Placing the lantern on the Egyptian mosaic working surface, she carefully tied the thin cotton thread to the hook. About five feet should be enough. That would give approximately two minutes of time for the thread to snap. The careful calculations filled Susan's head as she fetched the diamond studded lighter from the desk in the lounge. She had tried the ornate lever twice before Holst's arrival and was satisfied that it would work. Next she fetched the £5 of silver weight from the collection in front of the Victorian brass scales. Feeling the heaviness in her hand, she was confident that her timing was correct. She returned to the lounge. And to the motionless lump of flesh that was just recognisable as Maximillian Holst.

The eyes were open. Unable to close as his heart pounded against his bursting ribs. Hands and feet were splayed from the body like a giant blow up balloon of the seaside sailor advertisement. It was nearly time.

Susan checked her watch. 4.22pm. A few more minutes and it would all be over. She sat and waited.

The eighteen men assembled quickly after the short break, glancing silently at each other in contrast to the initial burst of confused argument as Peter had left the room.

'You had guessed had you Mr. Parker?'

'More or less. I didn't have the fine details, but my thesis was being constructed on the right lines. Of course I had no proof, but . . . '

'But you gathered from the evening dinner exercise, enough information to prepare your case against me.'

George laughed. 'So you knew?' He lit a cigarette. 'Do you know Peter, I don't think I could have proved a thing if you hadn't convened this meeting.'

'That was the idea. I didn't want you involved in this. You are too good a fraud officer to have to admit defeat. I still believe that there are some in there who will not admit that a fraud has taken place.' Peter walked toward the polished marbled entrance to the executive wash room. 'I think the final part will please them. It should do, they have no alternative.'

Lord Quarnley's gavel hit the oak saucer and the meeting was under way.

The sun had set an hour ago, but no one had noticed. The grey sky darkened, enclosing the coterie of bankers in the stark glare of the diffused florescence from above.

'Finally gentlemen, I have to explain how the funds helped me to discharge the responsibility which had been placed on me from that day in 1941.' Peter spoke with a quiet conviction in every word he uttered. His dark hair, so like his father's, was neatly parted and groomed, as if he were best man at a friend's wedding. Only there was no atmosphere of revelry, only a sombre concentration of eighteen men's minds on a situation that spelt disaster for the bank.

'I tracked Holst's progress from the moment I landed in England. I studied his methods, his successes and his failures. His constant boasts to the city and finance houses. His growing reputation as god's gift to ailing companies. Very few, including this bank, doubted for one minute that he was anything but a true entrepreneur of unusual talents. Most bent over backwards to accommodate his excesses. Greed, I would call it gentlemen. This bank wasn't the only institution to fall for his guile. Profit was the name of the game and where there was profit, and this was obscene profit bordering on the immoral, there is always someone willing to participate. And this bank participated more than any other.'

Guilty shadows of half recalled meetings crossed the lowered eyes of those who had sanctioned the enormous demands of Maximillian Holst and his corporate empire.

George waited. This is getting better and better, he chortled. Nothing more gratifying than seeing the overbearing members of the board squirming at the truth.

'I matched Holst, month after month in his quest for power. Never letting him have absolute power, or losing the degree of power that he needed. He had to have it all, before I could destroy him once and for all. As the funds began to increase from the bank, I was able to interfere with more authority in his affairs. If he had continued unchecked, he could have bankrupted the City of London. A sobering thought gentlemen. One person was able to achieve that, without any voice raised in opposition. In fact, most were jumping at the chance of taking their cut of the colossal profits that his scheming projected.' Peter watched as George lit yet another cigarette and made a note. 'Paper profits. Just like the security you hold at present. Worthless paper.' As Peter picked up a sheet from the desk, the overhead lights caught the small gold ring on his little finger. He twirled it once round his finger and continued.

The following hour was filled with details of the deals which he had instigated, and the multifarious activities that had to be researched by his band of Jewish helpers. If anything happened in the city, one or other would have a nose to the scent of Holst's objective.

'Finally gentlemen, I have a proposition to put to you. One which I am sure will appeal to those of you who wish to salvage the good name of

British banking and particularly the good name of this bank.' Each board member immediately sat up straighter in their leather chairs, easing the damp loins that sweated under the weight of their bodies and the central heating.

'As I have said, I, or our trust, holds the bulk of the shares in Holst's companies, as well as several million in separate investments that were made to maintain the value of the overall portfolio. The financial newspapers on Friday forecast a bombshell in the Holst empire. Let us give them one shall we? They have been getting more and more adventurous in their opinion of their champion, far too late I may add, and suspicion has risen almost to panic proportions. If no announcement is made by Monday then the stock market will crash, thousands of subsidiary businesses will be unable to continue, our credit with our European and American partners will plummet, ... I think you have the picture gentlemen. We need a miracle. Or rather a simple solution. I can give you one.'

The congealed sweat had gone cold under the thighs of the ageing circle of financiers. They feared for their jobs, or their names, or their reputations. All they could see was disaster.

The Chairman spoke. A long forgotten childhood ailment resurrected itself as his vocal chords were stricken with a nervous laryngitis. The hoarseness manifested itself in every board member's throats as he croaked. 'We do not appear to have any alternative young man. Let us have your proposition.'

Maximillian Alexander Carl Holst was dead.

Carl Weisz was dead. The man who had adopted every name which would give him a hold or an advantage over others, was dead.

He had drawn his last whisper of a breath at 4.34pm. The last words that he discerned through his exploding eardrums were Susan's. "Die Carl, I will see to it that you have an apt funeral service."

She turned her attention to the kitchen. Her fingers were sensitive to the thread as she deftly fashioned a slip knot on the end of the hanging line. The milk churn shaped weight slipped easily through the noose, to be tightened up around the bottle like neck. Carefully now, she cautioned, as she gently lowered the weight until it took the strain of the fine cotton. With infinite patience she eased her hands away until it hung suspended at an angle like a drunken acrobat.

Nothing happened. Then it began to turn on its axis. Slowly at first, gathering speed as the spun cotton thread strained to unwind from the coil that gave it its strength. Soon it was spinning steadily as the threads parted and forced the separation upwards. Exactly under the weight was the Russian lighter, the lever poised over the wheel touching the flint.

Susan's exit from the apartment was swift and sure. Out of the door, leaving the key on the inside, down one flight to the store cupboard. The overall was deposited on its usual peg and replaced with her herring bone coat and hat. On the second floor she met a party of late office workers and joined them on their way down the workers' stairway. Slightly surprised at her bonhomie and apparent familiarity of their group, they left chatting through the lobby, bidding goodnight to the doorman, and out to mingle with the dwindling Saturday afternoon shoppers.

Fifteen seconds later, a large explosion shook Knightsbridge, emanating from a fifth floor penthouse. As Susan had calculated, the damage was contained within that level and with a minimal impact to surrounding buildings.

The slim insignificant cleaning lady with the old fashioned felt hat hurried across the Meccano like bridge over the dark waters of the Thames. Stopping to admire the view of the south bank, a small weighted bag found its way from beneath her coat and into the murky waters below to join a thousand other unwanted cast offs lying quietly in their muddy bed. Waterloo was abuzz with travellers as she purchased her ticket for Chiddingfold at the usual machine and made her way to the 5.20pm train on platform 2.

'Good evening ma'am,' smiled the Station Master.

'Oh it will be,' the lady beamed.

CHAPTER XVII

Christmas Eve 1980

'PUBLISHING MAGNATE DIES! ACCIDENT? SUICIDE? MURDER? IRA?' Every Sunday newspaper carried the headlines of the "tragic" death of Maximillian Holst. The Sunday Times correspondent summed up the feelings of the public when he wrote, "The greatest tycoon ever to hold the fortunes of the City of London in his grasp, lost his final gamble last night. At 4.37pm yesterday afternoon, a tremendous explosion shook the area around Knightsbridge. The source was later confirmed as the fifth floor penthouse of Maximillian Holst. No exterior damage was sustained. It was thought at first that the IRA were involved, but lack of the usual warnings led the police to believe that a gas leak was the cause of the tragedy. Maximillian Holst's remains were found in the apartment which was completely gutted. 'It must have been like a gigantic oven,' one fireman observed. The coroner has expressed the opinion that Mr. Holst died from the inhalation of gas before the explosion took place. Among the debris, an antique cigar lighter, believed to have belonged to the Russian Royal household, was found and is a probable cause of the accident."

Leonid Chukov sat in his dacha thirteen kilometres from the Black Sea. The enormous snow drifts of the great steppes of Russia a million miles from his haven. The giant firs in front of the large picture window framed the contours of the rolling countryside stretched as far as the eye could see. Very much like an English winter in Surrey was the thought that struck him. He had been there once before the war. It had impressed him enormously. It was probably the very beginning of his deep hatred of the society in which he was forced to live, he admitted. Doesn't matter now. I have everything I want. His protege had performed true to his prediction and another nail had been hammered into the red communist regime that was slowly but inexorably crumbling about the inhabitants of the Kremlin. Sakhorov had been exiled to Gorki. Several other dissidents had been expelled. Alexei Nicolaievich Kosygin, former Premier of the Soviet Union had resigned in October, or had been forced to resign, and had died just a few days ago. The great impenetrable fabric of Marxism was showing the first cracks of dissatisfaction from within. The rigid dominance of Stalinism had been broken. The economy was bankrupt, but no one would admit it.

Leonid smiled to himself. Everything that I prophesied would happen, is taking place. Not all at once, but if the inherent longevity of my family runs true to form, I shall see it in another ten years or so. He topped up his tumbler of Vodka. Life was good without the constrictions of power, without the attentions of his wife, no longer a discordant rasp to his sense of equanimity. She had died shortly after Stanilav Dzerzhinsky, alone and unremembered for their part in the Soviet machine.

'Here's to the future.' Leonid mouthed aloud his toast to better things to come. 'I wonder if that Major Brovnik ever found his Shangri-la as I have done? He deserved to. He was very much like me.' The old general's words were lost in the rafters of his comfortable mausoleum as he settled down to finish the bottle that would ease him into his nightly, untroubled, unrepentant slumber.

George Parker took the glass of vintage port from the handsome woman in front of him. By her side was an equally handsome, vibrantly striking, grey haired man. His eyes shone with pride as his arm rested lightly on the shoulders of the woman he loved. She was ten years younger and no longer walked with a stoop. Her pain had gone, and with it the savage ache that had plagued her for nearly forty years. Sergei and she were one now and were as young in their hearts and their lovemaking as they had wanted to be when first they met.

'Thank you Mrs. Mallory... or Mrs... Susan. I appreciate your kind thought in inviting me here today. There was no necessity you know. I have spent other Christmas Eves alone...'

'Nonsense. When Peter told me, I was very pleased that we could include you in our party. After all, you have been part of us for a long time now haven't you?' she teased.

The twinkling eyes turned to her husband and her laughter brought a response from George that he thought he was incapable of. 'If I had ever wanted to marry, you are exactly the type of woman I would have chosen. But then,' he shrugged, 'there can never be another like you.'

Sergei clapped him on his back, refilled his glass, and thanked George for his gracious compliment. Susan blushed and kissed George lightly on the cheek. 'Thank you George. You make me feel very much alive.'

After a superb dinner that night, everyone had more than a festival happiness about them. It was if their childhood had returned and they were enjoying the simple pleasures of just being in each other's company.

'Tell me Peter. How did the board decide on your proposition?'

Peter turned from a glowing Wendy, busy serving an excellent after dinner brandy. 'They saw the logic in what I told them. They could forestall the stock market crash on the Monday if they made a prompt announcement that Holst no longer held any control or interest in the vast empire that he had controlled. His papers signed to that effect were secure in the bank's vaults until they could be dealt with and representatives from the Venture Capital arm appointed to key positions in the 59 companies involved. The most important point to get across to the nervous financial writers of Fleet Street, was that ample funds were available to meet all liabilities and that outstanding debts of more than three months would be settled immediately. You remember that I told you that there was a considerable portfolio of non-Holst related shares – well those could be realised and utilised to discharge the outstanding creditors. This, together with the consortium of banks' assertion that they were more than happy to continue support of the greatly reduced borrowings, would keep the city happy. Following the news, of course, you will be aware that the shares held as security automatically rose sharply, bringing the banks a handsome margin over their lending position to keep everyone happy.'

'And was the bank happy with the total sum that you handed back to them?' said George as he shook his head in wonder at the simplicity of it all.

'Yes. Every penny from every source of the bank's income over the nine years, has been accounted for and tallies with the notes that I have been making in my ledger.'

'And what a ledger!' laughed the rotund man through the haze of cigarette smoke forming a blanket around him.

'Destroyed and burnt, like the evil that spawned it,' observed Peter. But the bonhomie of their talk was not affected by the comparison that reminded them all of less happier days.

'What will you do Peter?'

Wendy's husband glanced mischievously at his mother. 'The bank have accepted my resignation,' he said in mock solemnity, 'and they have offered Wendy a post where she can supervise and check every programme designed for the new generation of "on line" computers which are on the horizon. The management were happy to have her expertise and co-operation,' laughed Peter. 'As for me. I am in the process of taking over my father's old business. Kawalek Verlag, you remember? The business is still registered under the name of Werner Kawalek my father. Despite Holst's attempts to transfer the warehouse in Berlin to himself as Boris Vukadovic, I have learnt from our old solicitors in Germany, that they have confirmed that the transfer was illegal. The business and the assets are mine. I am looking forward to the challenge.' His eyes brightened as Wendy kissed him.

'Don't forget we have a holiday in Prague first. You promised to take me to see your "second mother." And Lisa and Georg and Staszek and ... I forget the others ... and Anna!'

'I will my love. You will meet them all.' Peter held her hand as he turned once again to George. 'And what will you do George? – I can call you that now I am no longer in your employ can't I?'

'I can tell you what I am going to do right now, if I may. I am going to fetch the sack from my car like a good Santa Claus. You all deserve a present for the pleasure you have given me, not just tonight, but for the past nine years.' He paused, trying to express his thoughts for the terrible events of their past. He couldn't. He only knew that he felt part of the lovely family and half turned in embarrassment. 'I am glad it's over,' he said at last.

Every member of the family knew just what he meant.

'Thank you Lazar,' Susan choked through her tears. 'It is the most beautiful present I have ever received in my life.'

In her hand she held the gold ring which had maintained the bond between them throughout the years of their separation. 'I knew that if I found you, it would be through the ring that bound us together. Thank you my son.'

'And thank you mother. For remembering.' Peter held up a dark blue, exquisitely tailored overcoat with velvet trimmings.

'For the coat which you never had chance to wear, my son.'

CHAPTER XVIII

2 January 1981

Bertand fussed around his two favourite customers as they relaxed with their coffee and brandy. The table had been swept clean and straightened as officiously as a nurse tucks up her charges.

'Thank you Bertand. That was an excellent meal. Not too heavy and not too rich. Perfection in other words. As always.' Bertand beamed at George's compliments like a child conquering a ladder for the first time.

'Steady George, 'said Clive, 'you'll be encouraging him to up the prices next. Always leave a little room for doubt. That way he will try all the harder next time.'

The excellent Montrachet bottle was dead in its bucket. Only the green round bottom showing above the stiff white napkin. George turned his attention to the sloping shoulders of the Bordeaux bottle resting on the snowy softness of the table cloth. Inside the bottle nestled the last glassful of the Chateau Haut Batailley that he had promised himself when he had something to celebrate. Clive had chosen a burgundy, a Corton Charlemagne, both vintages were 1961, the superb year when every vintner in France gave thanks to god for the once in a lifetime harvest of luscious grapes.

'We have pushed the boat out a little tonight old friend.' The words were expressed more to the ceiling than to Clive.

'We had a boat worth pushing out old boy.' Clive returned the observation as blandly as George's had been delivered.

The two men sat in silence for several minutes, contemplating their joint participation in the saving of the British economy. That is how they had both described it, in their semi-inebriated euphoria. The fog above George's head cleared for a second, allowing him to see a thread of cotton hanging from the overhead lampshade. The image jerked some unsatisfied detail in his mind. He forced himself to think hard. To think hard of a niggling detail which would not let his enjoyment of the moment be complete.

'Clive.' said George.

'You have a question. I can tell.'

'Yes Clive.' George stubbed out his cigarette and concentrated on a whirl of words running around his brain.

'You remember when you gave me a list of the articles purchased by Mrs. Mallory on that shopping trip on ... on ... whenever it was?'

'Yes George.'

'Well, I think we both agree that we have a good idea what most of the objects were for, don't we?'

'Yes George.'

'The flame dowser; the sealing tape; the gas mask, and the dummy grenade.'

'Yes George,' Clive said with a resignation born of long practised tolerance of his friend's attention to detail.

'Well. It still beats me what on earth she would want with a reel of cotton.'

'Probably tying up a few loose ends,' said a straightfaced Clive.

George looked deeply into his claret glass and smiled. 'Yes Clive, I believe you're right.'